Finalist, Ned Kelly Awards for Best Novel by the Crime Writers Association of Australia

"With intelligence and wry humour, David A. Rollins crafts an all-too-believable story about power, corruption, and cover-up that has shocking international consequences.... Strong characters, nonstop action, and superb suspense... Vin Cooper has a **powerful, true voice that never wavers.**" —Nelson DeMille

"Sucked me right in...punchy, Chandleresque wit... **take this one to the beach and you'll leave with sunburn.**" —*Sydney Morning Herald*

"Conspiracy aficionados are going to love Australian author Rollins's thriller.... **A real page-turner** ... Sure, the book is a **white-knuckle read on a par with anything that James Patterson or Nelson DeMille might offer,** but the insights into what drives world politics (for example, the war in Iraq) are so plausible and well thought out that the reader may come away with a feeling that it's all real—only the names have been changed to protect the guilty. Highly recommended."
—*Library Journal* (starred review)

"A slick military thriller... **Fast and frightening.**"
—*Kirkus Reviews*

THE DEATH TRUST

DAVID ROLLINS

BANTAM BOOKS

THE DEATH TRUST
A Bantam Book

PUBLISHING HISTORY
Bantam hardcover edition published October 2007
Bantam mass market edition / February 2009

Published by Bantam Dell
A Division of Random House, Inc.
New York, New York

Library of Congress Catalog Card Number: 2007010271

ISBN 978-0-553-59000-5

Printed in the United States of America
Published simultaneously in Canada

www.bantamdell.com

OPM   10 9 8 7 6 5 4 3

In the councils of government, we must guard against the acquisition of unwarranted influence, whether sought or unsought, by the military-industrial complex. The potential for the disastrous rise of misplaced power exists and will persist.

—Dwight D. Eisenhower, Farewell Address,
   January 17, 1961

I would remind you that extremism in the defense of liberty is no vice. And let me remind you also that moderation in the pursuit of justice is no virtue.

—Barry Goldwater, American Republican

The sleep of reason brings forth monsters.

—Goya

The meek don't want it.

—Anon.

THE DEATH TRUST

Twelve months ago

Corporal Dante P. Ambrose climbed into the front seat of the Humvee beside the driver, relieved to be out of the sun. His black skin glistened in places where the sweat from his pores had sluiced away the fine, light brown sand that coated everything in Iraq. A single river of sweat had cut a valley through the layers of grit down his forehead, like the Tigris through the desert.

Behind him, Sergeant Peyton Scott grunted as he tried to get comfortable in the rear seat. His shirt and pants had stuck to his skin, and the ceramic plate in his vest pushed up against his chin when he sat, limiting mobility. He felt trussed like a pig. *All I need is a goddamn apple in my mouth,* he thought. "How's that coffee coming along?" he said.

"We ain't having coffee. We're having tea," replied Corporal Ambrose.

"What?" said someone.

"What kind of a faggot drink is tea?" said someone else.

"Fuckin' *tea*?" said another.

Ambrose shrugged. "Don't have it, then. I'll drink it all myself."

"What's wrong with coffee?" Peyton asked.

"Nothin'," Ambrose replied. "But . . . they drink tea in India. Y'know, that country is damn hot, and they've had thousands of years of continuous civilization. What they learned is that tea keeps you cool, man. You know what I'm sayin'?"

"You been into those *Reader's Digest*s again, ain't choo?" said one of the men. "Learnin' a bunch of useless shit."

A voice in the back called out, "If they's so goddamn smart, Corporal, how come they didn't invent the A-bomb?"

"You think inventing the A-bomb was smart?" said another.

The driver weighed in. "Whatever, dey's smart enough not to be in Eye-rak."

"Okay, okay," said Peyton, capitulating. "I'll give tea a try."

"Comin' right up, boss." Ambrose picked up the tin pot from a bracket mounted behind the window and burned his fingertips. "Freakin' motherfucker!" he hissed, putting his fingers in his mouth for a couple of seconds. Several of the men laughed. Ambrose swore again and then spat out the door to get rid of the grit deposited by his fingers. He was more careful with the pot the second time, gripping the rim with a piece of rag. The soldiers used the Humvee's windshield to focus and intensify the sun's heat, but it was hardly necessary. The air itself was hot enough to blister paint.

The sun that scorched Baghdad in May was a pitiless and implacable enemy, and the marine combat uniform—combat boots, webbing, flaks, and Kevlar helmet—was utterly defeated by it. And it'd get worse as the months rolled on. The only defense was to keep drinking water, keep swallowing salt pills, keep sweating, and keep swabbing antiseptic cream on the dry, chapped skin behind their testicles. The men grumbled and bitched about the conditions, as was a grunt's right.

The rest of the men had by now squeezed into the

Humvee and were tossing their cups into the front seat for Corporal Ambrose to fill. He poured out the heavily sugared brew and handed back the cups. The men threw it down quickly, scalding their tongues, swearing.

Alpha company hadn't lost a man—not even a scratch—since their deployment to Iraq over a year ago. Not many units could say that. The United Nations force, to which the marine brigade was attached, was taking a pounding from the insurgents, but Alpha company had been careful. And they'd been lucky. So far. The patrol about to be concluded was not unlike so many others. Uneventful. They'd been given several blocks of poor residential area to scour, tasked to search for and confiscate weapons. None had been seized, but everyone knew the place was still awash with them— old AK-47s, pistols, rocket-propelled grenades, even MP-5s and American M16s—because, every time there was a wedding or a national soccer victory or a massive bomb blast somewhere, the guns came out and began banging away at the sky in support. The slugs always came back to earth and, when they did, they were every bit as lethal as aimed rounds fired from the shoulder. Baghdad was like an insane spaghetti western. Sergeant Scott called it "a couscous western on crack."

"Okay, let's head on back to the ranch," said Scott. The driver didn't need to be told twice, and he eased some boot pressure onto the accelerator pedal. The Humvee moved off, its tires crunching over a road surface littered with pulverized concrete, gravel, and bits of bomb casing, this having been the scene of a recent minor skirmish. Scott watched the road pass by through a hole in the door, one of many drilled by shrapnel fragments collected on previous patrols when the vehicle had been in use with another unit. The motion and the heat were vaguely hypnotizing, and Scott's thoughts drifted to the prospect of a shower when they reached the relative safety of the compound. Occasional mortars and homemade rockets were routinely lobbed in over the walls, but they only rarely claimed lives. These were just something to put up with, something you were aware of, like the flies and the heat. But having a shower, letting the cool waters wash away the sweat and the grime and the goddamn sand, that was something to look forward to.

The four-vehicle convoy snaked through the tan dwellings so compressed together that the air itself seemed to have been squeezed from the narrow road. Scott heard Ambrose say, "What the fuck?" and the words snapped him out of the daydream. "Choo take a wrong turn, Marine?" Ambrose asked the driver. The Humvee was forced to stop because the blackened carcass of a vehicle ahead blocked the way.

"No, Corporal. I'm just retracing our steps on the GPS, unless the fuckin' gadget's lyin'. This is the way we come in for sure."

The lane was narrow and there was not enough room in which to turn around. The four Humvees reversed back down the street into an intersection and moved off in the one remaining direction available. Moments later, the marine patrol burst into the open space beside the wide gray river. Free from the shadows, the sun's heat radiated off the walls of the buildings and into the cabin.

Corporal Ambrose looked past the driver, out his window, and scoped the Tigris beyond. It was nothing like the Mississippi that rolled majestically past his town back home, through lush green countryside. He was about to comment on this when the front of the vehicle suddenly imploded. In fact, the Humvee stopped as if KO'd by a massive punch. Steam and smoke billowed from under the buckled hood, while on the road a pool of oil spread rapidly beneath the engine like blood pumping from an arterial wound. The soldier behind the wheel began screaming when he realized his legs were smoldering and bleeding profusely, the alloy firewall being about as effective as tissue paper against shrapnel.

"Jesus fuck!"

"Shit!"

"Hey, what—"

"Out. Get out. Clear the vehicle," snapped Scott.

The men evacuated fast and headed for cover behind the crippled Humvee, half carrying, half dragging the wounded driver. What had knocked out their vehicle? Was it a land mine, or something else?

The three remaining Humvees pulled up behind in a staggered line. The mounted machine guns were manned and the men swept them through the arcs, but there wasn't anything to shoot at. The rest of Scott's patrol took up positions on the ground and against an adjacent wall, looking for movement, for something to target. The road was eerily quiet but for the rough idling engines of the remaining Humvees and the groans from the wounded man. Scott felt uneasy. He was unsure how to read the situation. Damn it, he wasn't even sure there *was* a situation.

Ambrose made his way to the sergeant, staying low. The patrol had stopped in an area protected by a high wall on one side and the wide-open expanse of the Tigris River on the other. "What do you reckon took us out, boss?" he asked.

"Beats the fuck out of me," said Scott. The area they were in was actually quite peaceful. He glanced at their Humvee. If they had set off a mine, the pattern of damage would have been quite different. It was more likely that a projectile of some kind had hit them. That raised another question: Where had it come from? Tense and not a little baffled, Scott stood and looked around for movement. They'd have to leave the Humvee behind, push it to the side of the road, destroy it, and cram into the remaining vehicles. The wreck would be stripped clean by the locals before it could be recovered the following day. "Okay, let's get the hell out of here and push on. We've got—" But, as Sergeant Scott spoke, Ambrose saw his sergeant's head turn inside out beneath his helmet and dissolve in a puff of red atomized droplets that sprayed onto him, spattering his face and neck. Ambrose blinked while his mind struggled to process the image burned onto his retinas and the reason for the sudden cool sensation on his skin.

Sergeant Scott's body continued to stand for several long seconds, M-4 at the ready, seemingly unaware that its head had been completely removed. And then, like some kind of incomplete monster of Frankenstein, the grotesque figure took two faltering steps toward Ambrose. The rifle clattered to the ground, and what was left of Sergeant Scott reached out as if searching for support. But then the corpse collapsed to the earth and quivered where it lay. Thick crimson blood oozed from the shredded neck.

The men, having snapped out of the shock of what they'd just witnessed, began spraying the road ahead with full metal jackets. But there was nothing to target and certainly no one to shoot at. Eventually they ran out of ammunition. Bewildered, Alpha company stood and looked around, the barrels of their weapons smoking. The only sound that remained was the uneven thump of a faraway gunship and the lumpy, irregular hum of their transports' idling engines.

A week ago

General Abraham Scott felt the shudder through the airframe, but attached no significance to it. He banked the sailplane into the area beneath the fluffy cumulus cloud and sensed the lift of the thermal in the seat of his pants and in his inner ear. When he positioned the aircraft properly and the shaft of rising warm air caressed the long and slender wings, the current acted like an invisible elevator. The needle on the altimeter moved steadily around the face of the instrument and the pressure within his ears built. He swallowed, releasing that pressure, and his hearing returned to normal. The glider shot out of the thermal beneath the cloud and Scott followed another aircraft riding the warm air rising off a wide expanse of plowed field far below.

The general looked about and took in the unobstructed view of the Rhineland as the glider climbed higher. The sky was an iridescent blue on this unseasonably warm day early in May. Winter would undoubtedly return before spring took serious hold. Beneath, Germany was a patchwork of dark forest and green fields dissected by roadways.

With the radio turned off, it was blissfully quiet within the bubble formed by the Plexiglas dome around him. When Scott pushed it, barrel rolling and looping through the perfection of the mid-morning, there was the rush of air, a whistling over the glider's surfaces, but within the thermal, the aircraft almost seemed to waft silently like a feather, apparently lighter than the air itself. The sun warmed his face, and General Scott allowed himself a moment of peace. And, yes, happiness.

Away to the east lay the broad expanse of Ramstein Air Base, a huge NATO facility, the U.S.'s statement about its commitment to the defense of Europe in the face of an invasion from the Soviets. That threat had passed and now a new foe had stepped forward to fill the gap, but perhaps not the one everyone thought of. The sight of the base, a vast beige and black scar surrounded by greenery, brought the anguish back. Scott frowned and then closed his eyes. He didn't want to think about Ramstein, nor of what he'd discovered. He didn't even want to think about his son, his beautiful boy, Peyton, a marine sergeant, killed on the streets of Baghdad. He didn't want to think about the C-130s returning from the Middle East with their cargo of American boys wrapped sightless in black zippered bags, basting in their own fluids, the bags sloshing as they were lifted off the transport plane's ramp. Those thoughts seemed to desecrate the pristine cleanliness of a world populated by clouds and air currents.

Scott wrenched his mind free of the thoughts and realizations that had changed his politics, his relationship with his wife, his country—everything, in fact—and tried to concentrate on the moment. He scanned the sky above his head. Around five hundred feet above, the other sailplane was circling like a white bird of prey in the invisible thermal. Flying was the solitary corner of his life left untouched by the sickness that had invaded the very core of his being. Here, in this environment with a control stick between his knees, he felt free, unchained, the lead sheath peeled back from his heart. Here, nothing could touch him.

The needle on the altimeter nudged twelve thousand feet. Scott retrimmed the glider for aerobatics as he left the thermal. Away to his right, the other glider circled gracefully. He knew the pilot, Captain Aleveldt, a member of the Royal Netherlands Air Force and fellow soaring enthusiast.

Scott's sailplane shuddered again, and he blamed the vibration on rough air. The glider climbed and Scott watched the needle on the airspeed indicator drop. When it touched the correct number, he pulled back hard on the stick and then pushed the left rudder pedal to the floor. The glider responded instantly, rolling inverted through a tight barrel before settling into a controlled corkscrewlike descent. Scott's stomach bounced into his throat briefly as the world went haywire, the blue of the sky and the green of the ground tumbling and rolling together. In the spin, the horizon settled down and rushed from left to right across the Perspex canopy. Scott calmly watched the needle on the altimeter unwind around the dial. The ground was eleven thousand feet away but it was approaching fast. And then the unthinkable happened. The right wing collapsed, folding vertically beside his shoulder. The glider toppled sideways, like a swing with the chain cut on one side, and accelerated. It spun faster to the right. The nose dropped and the cockpit filled with the increasing roar of rushing air as the glider plunged downward. General Scott knew instantly that he was a dead man. The glider spun faster with the uneven forces acting on it. Scott's head was jammed to one side and he felt his neck would break with the strain. The violence of the airflow suddenly ripped the wing clean away, like an arm wrenched from its socket. The thirty feet of wing began a slow spiral away on a divergent course. With its departure went much of the wind noise inside the cockpit.

General Scott was a religious man. Soon, he knew, he would be joining his son. The thought resigned him to his fate and he took his hands off the control stick. He placed them on his knees, closed his eyes, and waited.

With the departure of the wing, the glider's wild rotation slowed and its vertical speed increased. It also began to tumble. The massive forces built, and ripped the other wing off. The fuselage of the glider, released from this air brake, accelerated once more. Scott opened his eyes. Only the greenery of the earth now filled the canopy on this endless ride. The vibration made it impossible to focus on the useless instrument panel in front of him. The general's weight in the nose of what was now a fiberglass missile caused it to roll inverted.

Scott remembered the day his son returned from Iraq in a C-130. At first, he had not the nerve to unzip the bag. If he looked upon the face of his boy in death, would he ever sleep again? But he needed to be sure. The autopsy. He had to look inside that black plastic cocoon. They had given him no choice. The stench of death hung over the bags laid out on the concrete. Scott remembered the sound the zipper made as he pulled it down, like bullets fired from a silenced machine gun. What he saw when he looked within filled him with a pain like none he'd ever known and he howled there as he knelt, bent over the one thing in his life that he truly loved unselfishly.

The missile was now nudging over two hundred and forty miles per hour. The tailplane was next to go. The airflow snapped it, and the missile, now shaped and weighted like a bullet, shot downward at over two hundred and eighty miles per hour.

The vibration smashed Scott's jaws together and shattered several of his teeth. Blood filled his mouth as the lacerated stumps sliced up his gums. The final memory to flash into his mind with searing clarity was the moment when it had all been made plain to him. The Establishment, its cynical First Convention. Tears streamed from his clenched eyelids. How many sons and daughters, brothers and sisters had been killed because of it? And yet here he was, a four-star general, an overseer for the voracious machine.

General Scott hit the base of a towering pine tree at two hundred and ninety-one miles per hour. There was no pain. He could no longer feel a thing.

ONE

Today

I had no idea what woke me up early, until I caught a whiff of my own breath. Then my tooth began to ache and I thought it could be that. But it could also have been a premonition of *sleepus interruptus*, because no sooner did my eyes overcome the crust gluing them together than the doorbell chimed, and then chimed again. I got to it on the fourth intonation, when whoever was on the other side of the door decided a bar of "Greensleeves" didn't perhaps convey the proper desired authority and began underlining the urgency with their fist.

"Vin, c'mon, man. I know you're in there," said Major Arlen Wayne, solving the day's first mystery—namely, who was making all the goddamn noise assaulting my alcohol-poisoned gray matter. Arlen was practically my only friend left on the planet—when my ex-wife moved out, she took most of them with her. Arlen and I had been out on the town drinking, celebrating my divorce coming through as well as the conviction for murder handed down on a case I'd been working on. Arlen knew I was "in there" on account of him being the person who brought me home the previous night. I think.

I opened the door to a sliver of light and he pushed his way in. "Go away," I said as Arlen threw back the curtains and let in the day. I'm not a morning person. I've been known to punch people for waking me before a reasonable hour, which varies according to the time I went to sleep the night before and the condition I was in when my head hit the pillow.

My name is Vincent Cooper, Major Vin Cooper, Special Agent in the United States Air Force Office of Special Investigations—the OSI. I work major crime. Homicides, mainly. I'm thirty-four, look twenty-eight, so I tell myself, and occasionally act eighteen, so my ex says.

I shuffled past Arlen, keeping to the protection of the shadows, and lay down on my bed, burying my head under the pillow.

"C'mon, Vin," he said.

"You already said that," I told him, my voice muffled by the pillow.

"The big cheese wants you in her office. ASAP. So get your shit together. And I'd bring my passport if I were you."

"Am I going somewhere?"

"Germany, I think."

I groaned.

The big cheese is the OSI's second-in-command. She's one tough old boot, a brigadier general. Her name is Winifred Gruyere, which explains why we call her the big cheese. But not, of course, to her face. She's probably the most terrifying person I've ever met: short, built like a Buick, eyes that don't blink, and large pores that remind me of the way a pancake looks when it's cooking. She's fifty-five, I think (it's hard to tell—she could be a hundred and fifty), and is the new power running OSI, replacing the previous general who spent most of his time on the golf course getting his handicap below embarrassing. "What's it about?" I asked, taking the pillow off my head.

"When you turn on your cell phone, you're going to

hear a few heated messages. You know it's against the rules to turn it off."

I shrugged. "Battery ran low." That wasn't true. The real reason was that I hate the damn things.

"What about your pager?"

"It got wet."

Arlen shook his head and changed the subject. "You heard of a General Scott?"

"No. Should I have?"

"He was the CO of Ramstein Air Base. A four-star heavy hitter, married to the daughter of the Vice President of our fair land."

Like most people, I'm a bit slow on the uptake after a night on the suds, but I'm not stupid. "I'm assuming the past tense you're using is significant."

"Yeah. Did you get who he was married to?"

"I got it." Ramstein AB is a vast NATO facility in Germany, shared by a bunch of other air forces. But U.S. forces have by far the biggest presence there. Pretty much everything going to Europe and to the Middle East transits through Ramstein. It's a giant military hub. "Do you know how he was killed?" I asked as I shuffled into the bathroom for a shower.

"The wings fell off his glider."

A shiver ran the full length of my spine and into my legs. I am not good with flying.

I had moved here to the town of Brandywine, Maryland, when Brenda and I decided life would be better all round if we no longer shared each other's. We'd hit the wall. My issues revolved around the fact that I didn't see the wall coming. And just maybe that was a big part of our problem: Even when I was home,

I wasn't. The reality of our marriage was staring me in the face, only I never took the time to open my eyes.

Anyway, where was I? Yeah, Brandywine, somewhere south of D.C. It sounded like my kind of town before I moved here, given my situation, and indeed they do have one or two good bars. The reality is that it's more of a family town stuck in the middle of five-acre lots with developers licking their chops at the prospect of making the place completely faceless. A lot of air force people live here, renting. On the weekends, dads throw balls to their kids in the parks while moms lay out blankets, setting up picnics. I felt like the place was rubbing my marital failure in my face and I was thinking I might have to move.

Those Disney scenes were in full swing as Arlen and I drove past, this being a Saturday morning. Winter was fast becoming a memory. It was mid-May, and warm. The sun was out and the sky was a pale blue, softened by haze floating down from D.C. But I wasn't really there, "in the moment," as my ex-wife would have said. My brain was trying to pick through the information passed on by Arlen, though not with much success. It's hard to concentrate when you have a headache that'd knock down a buffalo fighting it out with a toothache for supremacy.

Arlen piloted the Chrysler onto Route 5 and accelerated into the traffic heading generally north toward Andrews Air Force Base, where OSI is headquartered. We drove through the rural landscape. People used to grow tobacco here until the government persuaded them it would be far better if they just accepted a handout. These days a lot of folks still left on the land farm old car wrecks and broken-down washing machines, herds of which collect in their front yards. I was thinking about this as I either dozed off or suffered a mild brain seizure, because the fifteen miles to the base seemed to pass in a matter of seconds. The brief sleep did me some good, though, and the handful of Tylenols I had swallowed before leaving home were well and truly on top of things at last, having corralled the buffalo and knocked the barbs off the toothache. I was almost feeling positive, "seizing the day," as my ex would have said. A meaty case would be good for me, take my mind off said ex, and I silently thanked General Scott for going and getting himself killed.

OSI, or AFOSI if you want to be anal about it, has a command structure which sits outside the usual operational framework of the USAF. That is to say, we're autonomous. Our buck stops at the desk of the Inspector General, Office of the Secretary of the Air Force, rather than the commanding officer of a particular base or region, or even the Secretary of Defense. The OSI exists because, like any large organization, the USAF has its share of rotten apples, people who murder, rape, embezzle, rob, traffic in drugs and/or sex, commit fraud or arson, and so on. To say OSI is a busy little outfit is an understatement. And, just like any internal-affairs unit operating within an organization, we're not particularly popular with the arms we oversee. We're a negative force, as Brenda used to tell me, always looking for the bad in people rather than the good. Well, *duh* is just about all you can say to that pearl of wisdom. We don't exist to hand out gold stars to hall monitors. According to Brenda, the OSI is high on destructive energy. Or something. Brenda went off the deep end, lost her marbles, call it what you will, the minute she began to walk down the endless path of personal development. I wouldn't have been surprised if she believed any and all evil could be expunged if it could just be seated in a room with an aromatherapy burner heating up the right combination of oils.

Okay, I'm getting myself worked up again. The truth is, I'm not sure whether it was entirely thoughts of my former spouse that were to blame for my foul mood, or the toothache that had managed to find a way back through the Tylenol barrier.

Arlen stopped at the guard post at the southern entrance to the base as a pair of F-16s in close formation ripped past low overhead. He got our credentials inspected by a bored noncom armed with a loaded M16, while I tried to get in touch with Mr. Happy hiding somewhere deep within. *You're a single guy again,* I said to myself. *That's got to be worth a smile, don't it?*

TWO

Come in," said Brigadier General Winifred Gruyere when I appeared in the doorway. I did as I was asked. I stood at attention in front of her desk for some time, waiting for a further sign that she acknowledged my presence. In fairness, I don't think this was some kind of tactic. She was sifting through files on her desk, like a seagull pecking among food scraps it suddenly realizes are cigarette butts—with initial interest followed by distaste.

I saw my name and number on one of those cigarette butts. Eventually the general picked it out and opened it. I gathered she had been going over the service records of a number of fellow special agents. Without looking up, she ran through a summary. "Special Agent Vin Cooper, rank of major. You studied history at NYU, graduated, and entered the service as a second lieutenant. You put in for the CCTs, the combat air-controller squadron, where you trained with SEALs, Marine Force Recon, et cetera. You saw action in Kosovo and received the Purple Heart."

At this point, and for the first time, Gruyere lifted her eyes above the half-moons of her spectacles and locked them on to mine. She was trying to imagine whether the soldier standing in front of her was the same person she was reading about.

"I've read the citation your CO put in," she said. "You should have received the Bronze Star."

I felt like saying thank you, but didn't, and continued to keep my eyes leveled on the bookshelf behind her.

"You then transferred to OSI. In Afghanistan you took down a drug gang. A local senior politician had been killed by a car bomb and it looked like a strike by the Taliban. You proved otherwise, that it was an operation mounted by a group of U.S. soldiers set on eliminating the competition. You were shot and wounded and received a second Purple Heart. I see you also survived a helo crash on that one. Seems you're a hard man to kill, Cooper."

"Yes, ma'am," I said, giving her the response I thought she was looking for.

"Next came the episode of the brigadier general." Gruyere shook her head. "Now, that was a sorry shit piece of business."

I agreed. The asshole beat his gay lover's head to jam because he caught him in an embrace with someone who turned out to be the young man's half brother.

"So what the fuck's gone wrong, Special Agent? Seems to me you're not the man you were."

Swearing just sounds plain odd when it comes from the mouth of a woman old enough to be your grandma. "I don't know, ma'am," I said.

"That much is obvious, Cooper."

The general was possibly referring to the charge of assault against me. The man on whose face my knuckles played the anvil chorus happened to be a full bird colonel, which never goes down well on one's record, even if the charges are eventually dropped because there are, as they say, extenuating circumstances. I'd caught the colonel in question in fellatio delicto with my wife, and I'm sorry, but rank does not extend to those privileges.

"Separation and divorce are never easy burdens," Gruyere remarked, breaking in on my trip down memory lane. She shook her head and continued. "Aside from the assault, says here you've been arrested three times in the past year for drunk and disorderly behavior."

I'd forgotten about those items, possibly because, as the record said, I was drunk at the time. And I was sure it was only twice, but I kept that to myself.

"I'll let you in on my problem, Cooper. I need an investigator, a very good investigator. A year ago I'd have said you were that man, but, going through this," she motioned at the file on the desk in front of her as if it were kitchen trash, "I've got serious doubts. The trouble is, someone upstairs likes you. But I've got a feeling that, with you, we're scraping the bottom of the barrel." She glared at me over her glasses. "Yeah, that's what it feels like to me."

I continued to study the bookshelf behind her. What friends upstairs? I wondered. As far as I knew, Arlen was it in the friends department, and he wasn't so much upstairs as sideways in the room down the hall.

"At ease, Special Agent, and take a seat. Give me a reason to believe. Talk to me."

I did as I was told and sat in the chair beside me. "General, I'll be straight with you. I've had a hell of a year. Sounds like you've got the broad sweep of it there in front of you, but maybe not the details. My divorce came through yesterday and that closes the book on a few chapters I'd like to forget were ever written."

"Major, cut the folksy shit and just reassure me you're the man for the job."

General officers, it seems to me, can occasionally be capricious, uncaring of the fates of mere mortals, and, although I knew why I'd been summoned, I thought it best to play dumb. I can be good at that. "What job, ma'am?" I asked innocently.

"If you don't know why you're here, Cooper, then you're not half the investigator your record says you are. Or were." The general tilted her head and looked at me as if I were a puzzle with several pieces squeezed into the wrong holes. "Dismissed."

Gruyere then began shuffling papers. I'd played it badly. If getting me on the case was Plan A, I'd just managed to convince her to go with Plan B.

I cleared my throat. "Ma'am, General Abraham Scott, a seriously connected four-star, commanding U.S. forces in Europe, stationed at Ramstein Air Base, has been killed in a glider crash."

"Well, so much for security," Gruyere muttered to herself. "Who brought you in?"

"Major Arlen Wayne, General."

"Did he tell you about Scott?"

"No, ma'am. Caught it on CNN." That was a lie, of course, but an easy one for her to swallow.

"CNN! I might have known they'd get onto it eventually."

Gruyere pursed her lips. She went back to shuffling her files, then said, "Well, Major, you seem to have been given the overview. There are additional details from the crash investigation team's preliminary findings, as well as a summary report from OSI there on the ground. I don't have to tell you what a shit storm this has caused in the Pentagon, General Scott's connections by marriage notwithstanding. COMAIRNORTH— General Scott's command—is a vital cog in the defense of the United States, as well as Europe. I don't care what else you've got on your plate. Consider yourself reassigned."

"Yes, ma'am."

"You will be the SAC on this one."

"Yes, ma'am."

"There's a C-21 departing for Ramstein in eighty-six minutes. You'll be on it. And, Special Agent, you'll report directly and *only* to me. Is that clear?"

"Yes, ma'am."

Gruyere leaned forward. "You'll be liaising with the author of the preliminary investigation, Special Agent Anna Masters. Dismissed."

I didn't move as I was expected to.

Gruyere sighed. "Something on your mind, Cooper?"

"Ma'am, I was hoping to see a dentist this morning." The Tylenol had worn off completely and I was chewing razor blades.

"They've got dentists in Germany, too. Can't it wait till then?" Gruyere was getting impatient.

I shoved the tip of my tongue into the hole once filled with amalgam. It was huge and bottomless, like you could drop a stone into it and not hear it strike the floor. But the pressure applied by my tongue helped. Maybe I could get by with a double dose of those painkillers. "Yes, ma'am."

Gruyere's body language told me I'd answered correctly. "Don't blow this one, Vin. It's either the biggest case of your career, or the last."

"Yes, ma'am."

"Oh, and Special Agent?"

"Yes, ma'am?"

"For the third and final time, dismissed."

I walked back into the sunshine. So I was to be SAC, special agent in charge. If someone was needed to take the fall, it'd be me who'd get the push. I should've been an acrobat.

THREE

As I said, I'm not good with flying. Not anymore. Not since Afghanistan. But they're into it with a passion in the USAF, as you might expect. The C-21 waiting on the apron at Andrews AFB was a small austere aircraft full of naked aluminum, basically a Learjet without the executive leather. It was like riding inside an empty high-speed can of Coca-Cola. Thoughts of plowing into the Atlantic halfway to Europe took my mind off the tooth. While the plane was being fueled, I read through the reports handed over by General Gruyere. They were dry reading, especially the chief crash-investigator's assessment on the remains of the weapon that killed the general—Scott's privately owned sailplane. Dry it may have been, but it still caused me to break a sweat.

I wondered what Special Agent Masters was like. If her debrief was anything to go by, she was the unemotional, unimaginative type. I was struck by the feeling that no one seemed to *know* General Scott. But then, general officers are, as a rule, remote characters to those below them in rank—the burden of command and so on.

The C-21's pilot, a lieutenant colonel, told me it was time to board and my stomach did a purl and dropped a stitch. I took a sleeping pill, downing it with some water from the cooler. With luck I'd be asleep before he punched the starter button. I walked to the plane and was shown a seat. To take my mind off the impending takeoff, I read through General Abraham Scott's record. It was impressive. There was lots to read about flying. Skyraider pilot in Vietnam—two tours. A stint in the Pentagon. Back to flying duties after converting to fast jets. Grenada followed. He then took command of a wing of F-4 Phantoms. Next was a tour of the U.S. Embassy in Moscow just before the fall of communism. Scott assisted in the development of fighter tactics for the USAF's new fighter, the F-16 Falcon. It went on like this, each step a few more rungs up the ladder. Back to the Pentagon. Brussels came afterwards—his first NATO gig. He put in some time as Deputy Chief of Staff of the Air Force, then it was off to Ramstein. The guy was being seriously groomed. I wondered whether his marriage to the VP's daughter had anything to do with this confident rise through the ranks.

I glanced out the small porthole window. We were still on the ground, delayed.

Scott was fifty-five years of age, or would have been. Pretty young to be where he was. He had one child—a sergeant in the marines, deceased. I rummaged through the folder until I found the general's photograph. He was wearing his dress blues, cap off. The left side of his jacket held so many different colored ribbons it looked like a painter's drop sheet. The photo made Scott appear like a waxwork in Madame Tussaud's, but then, don't all these publicity shots? The smile on his face was forced, like it was going to evaporate an instant after the flash went off. A crease between his dark eyebrows suggested his more natural expression was a frown. He looked somewhat like Gregory Peck's not-so-good-looking brother—the tanned skin with salt-and-pepper hair. Photos of people who've died violently always creep me out a little. Maybe it's the smile. You know they've got nothing to smile about now.

I returned the photo to the folder and slotted it back into my bag. Or at least I think that's what I did because, almost immediately after, I must have fallen asleep. I dreamed about Special Agent Anna Masters for some reason. I pictured her as looking a lot like Gruyere, although not as attractive. Brenda was in there, too, I think, although how exactly I fail to recall. As the aircraft slipped into its descent, the change in motion, engine pitch, and so on jolted me awake. I was gripping the seat with my fingernails digging into the upholstery. I'm well aware this seems like odd behavior for an air force officer.

We taxied to a refueling point on the ground at some Royal Air Force base in England, and deplaned while the C-21 was juiced for the final leg. It turned into a four-hour layover while the pilots waited for another passenger, an RAF squadron leader returning to Ramstein. It was dark, cold, and wet, wind blowing the rain horizontal under the tarmac lights. I hoped Germany was more welcoming. I'd never been there, but my grandfather had. I remembered him saying that it was not a very friendly place, and that people had shot at him and his tank often. But that was a long time ago.

The run to Ramstein, which is apparently situated in the heart of the Rhineland, wherever that is, took another few hours. I slept—this time dreamlessly—and woke with the copilot, a young lieutenant, giving my shoulder a shake.

"Sir . . . sir, we're here."

"Wha . . . ?"

* * *

Relieved to be alive after so long in the air, I ducked to fit through the C-21's door and took in my new surroundings. It was early morning. The sun was up. It was cold, around forty-five degrees. The place smelled of rain and burnt JP-8 jet fuel. Even at this hour there was a lot of jet noise: planes starting up and shutting down, planes taxiing, planes taking off and landing. The vast apron was a parking lot of USAF C-130 transport planes, more than thirty in all, some painted low-vis gray, others in dark green or desert camouflage. There was a row of Polish F-16 Falcons, as well as a flight of four Vietnam War–vintage F-4 Phantoms operated by the Turkish Air Force. With the exception of these old clunkers, I could have been scoping any air force base anywhere in the world. There was nothing in the least unique about it, nothing particularly "German" about the place, and certainly there were no cheery "Welcome to Deutschland!" banners strung up anywhere. And, thankfully, there didn't appear to be any tanks running around getting shot at or otherwise.

Suspended in the air over the control tower were the arches of two enormous, crisply defined rainbows, glowing in the morning light. They served as the welcoming committee until a Humvee squealed to a stop nearby. The driver's door swung open and a woman pushed herself out from behind the steering wheel. "Special Agent Cooper? Special Agent Masters," she said over the ambient jet noise. Masters saluted and I returned it. "How was your flight?"

"Great," I said.

"Great," she replied. I had the impression I could have said, "Like sticking my head in a bucket of octopus shit" and she still would've said great.

"I'll take you to your quarters. I tried to find you accommodation on the base but couldn't. It's all booked solid. I thought it would be best if you were in the thick of things." She shrugged. "You got luggage?"

I reached back into the C-21 and pulled out my bag. It wasn't a big bag and there wasn't much in it.

"I hope you've got thermals in there," Masters observed. "It gets pretty cold around here."

So, I'd just met the woman and already she was thinking about my underwear. Once upon a time I would have grabbed that thought and run with it, but my ego had taken a pounding during the separation and divorce, and so I let it go without comment. Masters was nothing like I imagined her, at least to look at. That she wasn't a clone of Gruyere was a relief, given we'd be spending a fair bit of time together on this investigation. She was tall, around five eleven, with chocolate-colored hair pulled back in a regulation bun. With heels, we'd be eyeball to eyeball. Hers, by the way, were unusual—a smoky green at the outer edges and a gold-flecked blue that deepened in color around the pupil. They were extraordinary eyes, the kind you see in mascara ads in women's magazines. And no doubt Masters knew it. Being a cop, I'm pretty good at guessing, but I had no idea what her weight was because she was wearing a loose-fitting, Airman Battle Uniform with a bulky Goretex jacket over the top that was maybe a size or two too big. She had good cheekbones, and a few small freckles scattered across the bridge of her small nose. The freckles together with her accent pegged her as Californian. She had an attractive face, except that it was completely devoid of pleasure or happiness. At least, to be seeing me. And if I was imagining the bored hostility aimed right at me, then maybe, in words Brenda might have used, I really did need to do something about reempowering my self-esteem.

"Lieutenant General Wolfgang von Koeppen is a neat freak. You might like to take a shower and use a razor before you meet with him," she said bluntly.

"Yeah, thanks." While I didn't know Masters, I'd seen the disapproval on her face plenty of times before. It was the "you look like shit" expression. I tried not to let it affect our relationship right off the bat.

"Your meeting has been rescheduled for oh-nine-fifteen. Once I take you to your quarters, you'll have half an hour to freshen up. The general is anxious to meet with you."

Masters maneuvered the Humvee through a set of low office buildings and turned toward a nest of houses that could have been designed by an unimaginative child—a door with a window on either side, and a simple gable roof over the top. The color scheme was uniformly gray. The Ritz-Carlton it wasn't.

"That's the on-base accommodation I couldn't get you into," she said.

"My luck's improving, then," I replied.

We reached an intersection and Masters turned left, into a large parking lot. "We have to change vehicles," she said.

That made sense. Being so wide, the Humvee was not road-friendly, especially if the road narrowed and meandered through a town.

Masters pulled up beside a purple midsized Mercedes-Benz. "That's mine," she said, with a vague hint of pride, gesturing at the vehicle. "You can pick a Mercedes up here for a song."

We got out of the Humvee and into the Merc. It was a nice car inside—smelled of leather and wood. "It looks new," I said.

"Actually, it's fifteen years old," she replied. "It was

a promotional car for a local printer. The color made it hard to sell. I got it cheap."

I can do small talk with the best of them, but, for molar reasons, my heart wasn't in it. "Before we go much further, do I have time to see a dentist?"

"No," said Masters without missing a beat, pulling out of the parking lot and joining the queue exiting the base via the security gate. "Why?"

"Toothache."

"Aside from the fact that we've got to get you cleaned up before you meet with the general, it's oh-seven-thirty. Dentistry's a nine-to-five gig. I've got some Tylenols in the glove compartment if you need them."

"No, thanks," I said. Given the number I'd eaten over the past twenty-four hours, I was vaguely concerned about my liver. I folded my arms and buried my tongue in the hole. The cold was finding its way through my cheek and into the root. The pain was making me short-tempered, and I'm usually such a lovely, placid soul.

"I've got you a room in K-town. It's small, but it's clean."

"K-town?"

"Kaiserslautern. Everyone calls it K-town. Back in '55, it was the biggest community of U.S. citizens outside of America. At the moment, there are around forty-five thousand of us living there. We've got American football, American hot dogs, American cinemas, American shopping malls—"

"America," I said. "Don't leave home without it."

Masters responded with cool silence.

My new, temporary partner was young and possessed a perfect set of teeth. Her bio, thoughtfully included in my briefing notes, said she was twenty-six and held the rank of major. Twenty-six was too young to be a major. Masters was either very good at her job, or very good *on* the job. She came across as efficient, officious, and no doubt had several volumes of air force articles surgically inserted up her ass for round-the-clock reference.

I turned my attention to the world zipping by. The countryside was flat and rural, a bit like the area around Brandywine, only the German landscape was neater, more orderly, almost manicured. The small, immaculate farms were separated by stands of towering pines. Intermittent showers sprinkled from fluffy, toy-like clouds pasted against a pale blue watercolor sky, and I counted one, two, three, four rainbows this time. The street signs we passed bore long, unpronounceable names for towns and cities up ahead, and any moment I expected to see a gingerbread house and maybe a witch chasing two kids around it on her broom. But then I saw a sign with the familiar golden butt that told me I was only four kilometers away from the world's favorite hamburger, and I felt less like I'd been hijacked by a Grimm's fairy tale.

K-town—Kaiserslautern—seemed to appear out of nowhere. The outskirts of the town were devoid of the usual three-mile strip of auto-body repairers and retailers and fast-food restaurants selling more or less the same stack of pancakes. This was America done the way the U.S. military likes it, probably not that far from how Germany likes it: anal.

We drove through the town, past American-style malls. There were joggers everywhere wearing Nike, Russell Athletic, and Everlast. All the street signs were in English. The only clue that I wasn't in some U.S.

town, maybe somewhere north on the east coast, were all the Mercedes running around—even Mercedes cabs. K-town was bigger than I expected, not that I had spent much time speculating on its dimensions.

We skirted the city center, which had the usual collection of midsized glass office towers, and drove through an area populated by huge U.S.-military warehouses. I tried to think about where to get this investigation started but couldn't. Eventually, Masters slowed. We turned into a tree-lined street and began looking for a place to park. "This is it," she said, pulling against the curb.

I got out and grabbed my bag from the backseat. Masters crossed the road and walked up to a sign that said, *Pensione Freedom. U.S. Servicemen Serviced with a Smile.* I wondered how many U.S. servicemen had been amused by the quaint, unintentional turn of phrase. I followed the major and took the flight of four stairs up into the foyer. The place smelled of disinfectant and sausage, a not entirely unpleasant combination. A tall square-shaped frau with blond hair turning to gray at the roots came through a door behind the counter. Her shoulders were broad and barely cleared the doorjamb. She was not particularly pleased to see us, or even displeased. Indifferent, I'd say, nailed her attitude. If she were ever asked to describe me, I don't think she'd be able to. That suited me fine. If I were anonymous, I could come and go as I pleased, unobserved, no questions asked.

"*Morgen,*" said Masters. "There should be a booking under the name of Cooper."

The frau consulted her PC screen and said, "*Ja.*" She slid a card across the counter with all my details already filled in. "Sign, *bitte,*" she said. I did as asked and received a key in return, along with half a dozen of the pensione's business cards.

"No smoking in zer rooms. Vee haff detectors. Room zree-oh-zree, level zree, turn right," the frau said with sausage breath, nodding at the narrow fifties-style elevator opposite the counter.

"I'm going to get a cup of coffee down the road," said Masters. "Oh, before I forget, you'll need these." She handed me a large envelope. "Your common access card—your CAC—will get you in and out of Ramstein. You'll find a cell phone and pager in there, too, as well as a swipe card to get you into OSI on the base. See you in, say, twenty."

She turned and walked out before I could offer an alternate plan. The receptionist had slipped away too, gone back to her bratwurst. I was alone in the foyer with a bag that contained four pairs of underwear and socks, a spare shirt, and a toothbrush I was too afraid to use. To be honest, I don't like being told what to do, which might be an odd thing for someone in the military to say. But I especially don't like it when I'm being ordered around by an officer of the same rank. So I walked out.

Okay, I needed a shower, but what I needed more than anything else was that dentist, or at least some serious painkillers. Deodorant would've been good, too, and some mouthwash. I was thinking that maybe I could rinse my teeth clean. I also needed a car. It occurred to me that General Scott's second-in-command wasn't the person I should interview first. That honor went to the chief crash investigator. And I also wanted to talk to the person everyone seemed most concerned about, not, it seemed, because her husband had been killed, but because of who her father was.

I found a tourist office and took a map of K-town. I

asked the woman behind the counter for the nearest tooth doctor and was told that he didn't open till 0900, confirming what Masters had said. That was still half an hour away. I found a pharmacy and bought the strongest analgesic available without a prescription.

Next stop, Hertz. I rented a Mercedes—what else?— and a map of the Rhineland-Palatinate, the province I found myself in. By the time I got back behind the wheel, the painkillers were working—mercifully—and I found myself able to at last concentrate on the job.

I drove back down the highway, retracing my steps to Ramstein, fumbling with Masters's report, holding it against the steering wheel as I read. Two miles beyond the Kaiserslautern city limit, the pager beeped. WHERE ARE YOU? it said. I turned it off. A handful of seconds later, the cell began ringing. I was about to turn that off, too, but decided to see what was up.

"Major, what are you doing?" said the voice on the other end.

"Driving. Do they do it on the left side of the road here, or the right?"

"What?"

"I'm on the road to Ramstein, which I know sounds like a song title or an old Bob Hope movie, but—"

"Special Agent Cooper, we agreed that you were going to meet me in the foyer."

"No, *you* agreed on that, but I'm not sure who with. Hey, I hired a Mercedes, like yours only newer. I think I prefer Chevrolet." I can be infuriating, especially when I want to be, and this was one of those times. It was obvious that Masters didn't want me here, probably because she thought she was more than capable. She was treating me like I was a pain in the ass, and I objected to that because she didn't even know me. And, apart from these interpersonal observations, as far as I could see from her report, her investigation had gotten precisely nowhere. It was all typed out neat and tidy and all her verbs were conjugated correctly, but the whole was utterly devoid of any imagination or intuition. She didn't get it. Scott had been killed, but the big question on everyone's lips was whether someone had helped him along, even though no one was prepared to even voice that option, except for Gruyere, and her only admission on that point was the fact that she'd sent me here. Masters had asked questions and people had answered them, but she didn't appear to have questioned the answers.

"You've got a meeting with Lieutenant General von Koeppen in fifteen minutes," Masters said.

"But I haven't had a shower or a shave and I'm still wearing yesterday's nonthermal underwear."

Silence.

I wondered whether she was the type who uses silence as a weapon to keep her partner in line. Not my kind of woman. "Okay, then," I said, keeping it light and cheery. "I'll catch up with you later." I didn't wait for an answer. I ended the call and turned off the cell. That was against the rules, of course. In this business, people get nervous if they can't contact you 24/7. I opened the glove compartment and threw the phone in, closing the hatch after it.

A short time later, I turned off the highway and into the security post. The guard scanned my CAC card with a portable gizmo and checked that I looked as handsome in real life as I did in the photo. Satisfied, he then said, "Thank you, sir," and waved me through. Before moving off, I asked for directions to Hangar B3. Ramstein, as I said, is a huge facility, and the soldier had to go back inside and consult a map. He returned moments later with a photocopy of the base layout. A line drawn in blue ink meandered across the page to the hangar.

Ten minutes later, I pulled up outside my destination. B3 was at least the size of two, possibly three, football fields. It was *so* big, it was impossible to tell how big. I walked to a side door feeling dwarfed by the structure. Huge overhead lights illuminated the interior. There were several C-5 Galaxies parked inside—transport planes roughly the size of 747s. I stopped an airman and asked for further directions. He pointed down the far corner of the hangar.

I eventually found what I was looking for, an area sealed off by walls of plastic and tape. Signs warned that this was a restricted area and that access was for authorized personnel only. I did what any investigator worth his pay would do and figured the signs weren't talking to me. I parted the plastic and looked inside. On the floor were the remains of what I assumed was General Scott's glider—pretty much every little piece—laid out for examination. The plane had hit the ground with such force that it appeared to have literally exploded. At least a dozen personnel were picking through these remains, cataloguing them. It was a mammoth task. There weren't many whole sections left intact.

I made my way to what would have been the cockpit. There was a lot of dried blood on the pieces. That figured. The human body is really just a big bag of water. When it hits the ground at over one hundred and fifty miles per hour, it bursts.

"You right there, mate?" said a voice behind me. The man wore the uniform of a Royal Air Force squadron leader, except his accent was about as English as mine. Australian. I'd come to recognize the accent after a stint in Afghanistan, where Australia's Special Forces, the

Special Air Service, were deployed. Those boys were smart and very tough. I owed my life to half a dozen of them.

"Special Agent Vin Cooper," I said, flashing him my OSI creds.

"Wayne Roach."

I recognized the name. Roach was heading the crash team investigating the wreckage. He was looking for cause. His was the signature on the report I'd read.

"OSI. Not the local branch, I take it?" he asked.

"Flew in this morning."

"You working with that Masters chick on this?"

"Yeah."

"Lucky man. She's a spunkrat. Young to be a major, too. Rumor has it she can suck-start an F-16."

That gave me an interesting perspective on Masters. She had a reputation. Also, this guy thought her meteoric rise through the ranks had something to do with qualities other than those for which officers usually received promotion. I didn't add to the conversation, which might have made the squadron leader nervous. Parts of the services are, in some ways, even more PC than private enterprises.

He cleared his throat and said, "You read the preliminary?"

I nodded. "You've had a couple more days with this since you and your team did the initial write-up. Got anything to add?"

"Yeah, as a matter of fact."

I followed the squadron leader to a bench covered with various items of metal and fiberglass. Roach was short and bald, and the crotch of his pants appeared to get sucked up his butt as he walked, springing off his toes with each step. His uniform was a size too small for his frame, which didn't help. Maybe he was getting fat and didn't realize it. Or couldn't accept it.

Hanging on the wall behind the bench was a large photograph of the smiling, relaxed General Scott standing next to his sailplane. The aircraft's wingspan was a tad under sixty feet. The nose where the pilot sat was small and bulbous, with a large Perspex bubble canopy. Now, only shards of the glider remained—slightly more than what remained of the general, according to Masters's report. I ran my eyes over the individual pieces spread out across the floor and found it difficult to imagine that this was the aircraft in the picture. Roach picked up an aluminum bracket.

"I can tell you now that General Scott's plane was sabotaged." He held up a piece of metal. "Check this out."

Sabotage meant murder. I didn't bat an eyelid at the news, though once the folks Stateside heard it, the shit would definitely fly. "What is it?" I asked.

"The wings of the glider slide off and on to make transporting it from field to field possible. That makes this piece crucial. It's the bracket that clamps the main wing spar to the fuselage." Roach pulled the clamp apart and the top section split into two separate pieces across a fine, ragged crack. "That's not supposed to happen, by the way," he said. "This is seven-oh-seven-five—aircraft-grade aluminum alloy. It's light and, as you might expect, extremely strong. At least, it's supposed to be."

He passed me a black-and-white photo. "What's this?" I asked.

"A photo," he said, being a wiseass. "Well, actually, it's called a macrograph—makes it easy to see the metal's crystal structure. This is what seven-oh-seven-five should look like." He passed me another black-and-white print. "Compare them."

I put the two prints side by side. On one, the crystals were big; on the other, they were small. Easy to see the difference, sure, but I still didn't know squat.

"Basic metallurgy lesson number one: When the crystals are small, the metal is good and strong," Roach said. "The bigger those crystals get, the weaker the metal becomes. Milled nonferrous metals like aluminum don't take kindly to stress. They have almost zero elasticity. Put too much stress on them and they don't bend or deform, they just crack. *Pah-ting*," he said, musically.

"Do you mind putting it together for me like I was a five-year-old, Squadron Leader?"

Roach swapped the photos for a couple of bits of aluminum he'd recovered from his bench. "We've duplicated what we believe happened to the failed clamp that held on the general's wings. We heated and cooled it rapidly a couple of dozen times. Doing that to a metal—just about any metal—changes its crystal structure, making it weaker. The seven-oh-seven-five in your left hand failed at one-tenth the load of the seven-oh-seven-five in your right. Take a closer look."

I did as I was asked and examined the metals. On the outside, they appeared identical. In cross-section where they'd cracked, though, one piece had broken clean while the other had a porous honeycomb appearance.

"Nothing like this could happen by accident?" I asked. I knew the answer to that before I asked the question, but I've found it sometimes pays to ask the obvious.

"No bloody way," the squadron leader said, shaking

his head. "Someone got to the general's plane, removed the clamp, and then went to work on it, or exchanged it for this one, knowing full well what the consequences of that would be."

"Don't stop now, Squadron Leader. You've got a captive audience here. What happened when that clamp failed?"

"You read about it in the report," he said.

"I've read an eyewitness account. Tell me in your own words what you think happened."

He shrugged. "On the morning of the crash, the general and another pilot were chasing thermals, maybe ten miles from the base. The weather was good and the conditions were ideal for soaring. The general, like the pilot in the other plane, was climbing to around twelve thousand feet and then doing aerobatics—loops, rolls, and spins—down to around five thousand feet. They'd apparently done that twice—gone up and then come down—before the general's day flew into the crapper. When he reached altitude for the third time, he put the glider into a flat spin. I reckon the clamp was probably already broken by then, but it's impossible to say. According to the witness, the right-hand wing on the general's plane appeared to fold. The airflow ripped it clean away a second or two later as what was left of the aircraft began a spiral dive.

"It dove like that, spinning, for several thousand feet before the g-forces tore the other wing off. Within moments, gravity accelerated the wreckage to around two hundred and fifty miles per hour. General Scott would've had plenty of time to contemplate his end before it came. From the clamp letting go to impact took around thirty seconds. That's a lot of time for your life to flash before your eyes." Roach paused. Maybe he was picturing the man trapped inside his fiberglass coffin heading for the ground. I certainly could. Roach snapped out of it and cleared his throat. "The tail broke off at about two thousand feet of altitude. The nose of the aircraft hit a tree, which is why so little of it was left intact. Not much of the tree left, either. The general's remains—what they could find, at any rate—were scooped into buckets with a ladle. Shooting the bugger with a twelve-gauge at close range wouldn't have been nearly as effective, or messy. Not a great way to get your card punched." Roach paused for another moment of consideration before asking, "Anything else, Special Agent?"

"Yes," I managed to say. The saliva glands in my mouth were working overtime and my skin was clammy. I knew what was coming. I made it to a basin against the wall before my stomach let go. I'd be lying if I said my reaction to Roach's re-creation had nothing to do with my own experiences in the air. The Australian had just brought it all back—the fear, the helplessness, the feeling in your guts when the hard floor beneath drops away revealing an abyss. And you just . . . fall . . . My stomach heaved again.

"You okay, mate?"

"Yeah, I'm on one of those weird fad diets," I said. I cupped my hands under the water and splashed my face.

Roach continued, "I didn't know him—the general—but, for what it's worth, those who did, say he was a pretty cool CO. A workaholic, apparently. First in, last out." That phrase struck a chord with me. *First in, last out*—the motto of the combat air controllers, the lunatic squadron of which I was once a member.

"How long would it have taken the clamp to fail?" I asked, wiping my face on a hand towel.

"Yeah, well, I guess that's the problem—from your

point of view, anyway," Roach observed. "Pinpointing when the clamp was tampered with would be a guess. Could've been a couple of days ago; could've been months."

Given the number of people at Ramstein and the fact that anyone could have had access to the glider, that gave me roughly forty thousand suspects. In other words, I had a trail to the murderer that was as dead as the victim. "Doesn't anyone kill with a nine-millimeter anymore, preferably with their prints all over it?"

"Pardon?"

"Never mind. Just thinking aloud." I didn't bother asking him if he knew why Scott had been killed, or by whom. Coming up with answers to those questions was why OSI paid me so much money. Yeah, right. I cleared my throat and asked the tough question. "What about the people who maintained the plane? You got a signed maintenance schedule anywhere?"

Roach smiled and snorted at the same time. "Take your pick from over two thousand engineering personnel—Americans, Dutch, English, German, French. The general didn't have a crew chief on his plane. If he needed something done, he'd just ask someone to do it. The reality is that just about everyone and anyone on this base had access. And, as for a maintenance schedule, this was a glider, not a military aircraft—or even a powered private plane. It's really no more than a snag sheet and there are no signatures."

"Great."

"Yeah, well..." said the Australian, fiddling with the clamp.

Okay, so my list of suspects had shrunk from forty thousand to two thousand, but it might as well have been a million. I had one dead general, one sabotaged plane, no maintenance schedule, and no leads. I comforted myself with the knowledge that killing a general is a big deal. Someone on this base had to know *something*. I just had to find that person. "So, the glider pilot who witnessed the crash—" I glanced at my notebook. His name was Captain Reinoud Aleveldt, Royal Netherlands Air Force. "You got anything more from him?"

"No," said Roach.

"How about a number for him here on the base?"

Roach nodded and walked over to the phone on the wall. On a bench beside it was a base directory, a book the size and thickness of the average novel. Another reminder of the size of Ramstein. "How long have you been here, Squadron Leader?"

"Coming up for six weeks now. Why do you ask?"

"Because if there was someone wandering around here, someone who wasn't NATO, you haven't been here long enough to know whether they were out of place."

"Yeah, but bases like this..." he shook his head, "...with people coming and going all the time, wearing different uniforms, speaking different languages, you've got Buckley's chance of keeping tabs on people. You just assume if they've got through the front gate, or come in on an aircraft, they're okay. If you didn't operate on that assumption, you'd never get your job done."

I wondered who "Buckley" was and assumed he was probably one very unlucky guy. I also thought about the security check I'd experienced at the front gate. It was pretty thorough, though hardly a retina scan. I had to show my CAC card, the identity card issued to every serving member of U.S. forces, and my name was probably also on some kind of database. As far as the CAC card went, an intruder would need to steal one and have a vague similarity to the photo on it. The reality was that, for a determined adversary, it wouldn't have been impossible to slip through the net, certainly not for one with a premeditated plan to kill the base's commander.

"Anything else, Special Agent?" asked the Australian, butting in on my speculation.

"Yeah, can you recommend a good dentist?"

"Wouldn't get anything done here, mate. These blokes are butchers. You need an Aussie dentist—best in the world."

Australia was a long way to go to get a tooth filled. I was hoping I'd find one a bit closer, but I wasn't having much luck on that front. "Thanks for your time," I said.

"The full revised report is in the process of being written up. Should have it done by this evening."

"Send a copy to me care of OSI here. We're in the phone book." At least, I assumed OSI was in it.

"No worries, mate," he said as I turned and walked out. So, Scott had been murdered. This had suddenly become a very serious deal, no matter who his old lady's daddy was. Generals generally do not get murdered for the reasons the rest of us do. In fact, when you're a general and you get killed violently by persons unknown, the motive that leads to that kind of demise could possibly have implications for national security. That's what I was thinking as I walked toward the hangar's exit, a rectangle of bright light in the dark corrugated wall.

Outside, I noted it was still cold, although the sun was doing its best to rectify that situation. The clouds and rainbows had gone, chased away by a breeze that went straight through my ABU as if I wasn't wearing one. Three C-130s taxied past, making a hell of a racket. Beyond was the distant roar of a fast jet accelerating down one of the runways in full afterburner. I flipped open my pad and checked the copious notes I'd made interviewing Squadron Leader Roach. They amounted to one solitary line on the page, the name and phone number of the Dutch air force captain, Aleveldt. I wondered if he'd be able to make things any clearer for me, but I could definitely pass on a repeat of the account of Scott plunging to his death from twelve thousand feet.

The screech of tires caught my attention and lifted my eyes from the notebook. It was a purple Mercedes. Little puffs of dust and burnt rubber boiled around the tires as they shuddered, locked up solid. The door flew open. "What the hell do you think you're doing?" Masters demanded to know as she stomped toward me, hands jammed deep in her jacket pockets.

"Investigating an assassination," I said, which had the gratifying effect of stopping her dead in her tracks.

FOUR

Special Agent Masters drove. She ground her jaw, the small pencil-like muscles flexing. "I'd appreciate it if you wouldn't just disappear off on your own. I don't know whether you realize this, Special Agent, but we are not fucking playacting around here. People like General von Koeppen have things to do. You see them when *they're* ready, not when it fits into *your* schedule."

I listened to this lecture and wondered whether I should bite. She was reminding me of my ex—not the words so much as the moral certainty that she was right and that I was a moron. "Stop the car."

"What?"

"I said stop the goddamn car." I reached across her and pulled on the hand brake. The Mercedes skidded sideways to a stop.

"Let's get a couple of ground rules straight," I said as the car rocked on its suspension. "I don't know what organization you belong to, but I'm basically a cop. I don't give a damn about rank or privilege when I'm on a case. Also, I don't answer to you or the CO here. I promise you, my boss back home is a lot scarier than both of you combined."

Masters folded her arms and shot a glance of pure poison at me.

"Before I saw von Koeppen," I continued, "I wanted to know what kind of investigation I was running—"

"*You're* running?"

"That's what the SAC usually does."

"Who said you were the special agent in charge here?"

Gruyere hadn't brought Masters up to speed. What did the big cheese expect us to do? Duke it out over who was boss?

"You were sent to *assist* me," she said.

"Whatever," I said. If you need to tell people you're running the show, then you probably aren't. If Masters wanted the poison chalice of SAC, she could have it. I changed the subject. "Squadron Leader Roach's findings are critical. Now we can go and see your CO and tell him what's up."

"What makes you think Ramstein OSI can't handle this on our own?" she said, holding me with those eyes.

Oh, right. Insecurity. I said, "What *I* think is neither here nor there, Special Agent. It's what Washington thinks." As I said this, I wondered whether I should come clean and tell Masters exactly what Washington thought of *me*, but I didn't want to spoil my little speech with reality and reinforce her already negative view.

"Are you that good an investigator, Cooper, that you can just waltz in here and show us yokels how to do it right?"

Perhaps Masters felt she had me on the run. "I'll let you in on a secret, Special Agent. I don't want to be here any more than you don't want me to be here," I informed her. "I was doing perfectly well back in Maryland, ending my marriage and screwing things up in my own life. Now I have to put all that on pause to hold your hand here—figuratively, of course." My patience had pretty much run out. And my toothache was back. I was hungry. I also had absolutely no idea how a NATO command, let alone one as seriously big as Ramstein, worked. Masters was right. I was way out of my depth. And, on top of that, I stank. I really should have taken that shower when I could have.

The look on Masters's face was the same one I had seen on Gruyere's—the puzzle-with-the-missing-pieces one. "Are you usually so . . . ?"

"Lovable?"

"Sarcastic, negative, contrary."

"It's the toothache talking. I'll be much better when I have something to distract me from the pain. Like, if you could just shoot me in the leg or something."

"Can we go now?" she said. "It's nine ten. We're late."

I shrugged. She eased the Merc out from the curb.

The administration building was a long way from Roach's hangar, so the drive was a good opportunity to take in the base.

Something from Masters's direction landed in my lap. It was a bag of what looked like dried apple stems.

"What're these?" I asked.

"Cloves," said Masters. "I bought them back in K-town."

"For me?"

I picked up the bag and took a closer look at the contents.

"My grandma's recipe for toothache. Hold one against the tooth with your tongue and the clove will numb the nerve. They're good for the breath, too. You should take half a dozen."

"Thanks," I said, "I think." I suddenly felt bad about being so pushy.

Masters's cell saved me from apologizing. It began playing an old KC and the Sunshine Band number, which transported me to my high-school prom, the backseat of my parents' car, and a pro-wrestling bout with the catch on my date's bra.

"Yes, sir," she said, then "yes, sir," followed by another, "yes, sir." Masters managed to pull the fang out of the record groove and said, "We're at the building now, sir."

"Let me guess: Colonel Klink?" I asked.

"General von Koeppen," she corrected as the front wheels of her Merc hit the driveway a little too fast and the oil pan clanged on the road.

"Yeah, that's what I said—Colonel Klink. Can you ring him back and tell him I know *nuh-sink, nuh-sink...*"

Masters and I stood at attention. Wolfgang von Koeppen looked nothing like the buffoon in *Hogan's Heroes*, which was disappointing. Instead, he was tall, lean, and tanned, with blond hair and blue eyes. He wouldn't have been out of place in a Ralph Lauren ad, standing behind the spoked wheel of an old sloop, sweater tied around his shoulders, a pretty young thing behind him laughing in the breeze. Or perhaps sitting in the backseat of a black Mercedes wearing the uniform of the Gestapo Reichsführer, directing a somber queue of women and children toward a railway car.

"That will be all, Anna," he said to Masters in an accent that was vaguely English. Something in the way she turned and walked out told me that Masters didn't appreciate being dismissed. We were, after all, conducting this investigation together. I was at a loss as to why she didn't stand her ground. She would have been within her rights to do so. "At ease, Major," he said, giving me the once-over.

"Special Agent," I said, getting up the German's nose from the starting gate.

"Yes, of course. Special Agent."

Ordinarily, I'd have been in civilian clothes while on the job: a suit, or maybe pants and a blazer for that relaxed, hard-ass look. It's easier to interview an officer, especially one higher up the ladder than you, when he or she has no idea what your rank is. Back at Brandywine, when Arlen had grouped "your passport" and "Ramstein" in the same sentence, I'd decided to put on an ABU. If I was headed to an air base in Germany, wearing a standard Airman Battle Uniform would make moving around the place a lot easier. In a suit, I'd be stopped every other minute and asked to show ID. But I was now experiencing the downside of that decision. General von Koeppen looked me up and down and I could tell he didn't like what he was seeing: an officer of inferior rank, and a rumpled one at that. Maybe Masters was right about the whole neatness thing. At least the feeling between Himmler and me was mutual from the get-go.

The general motioned for me to sit. He said, "The circumstances that have brought you to Ramstein are indeed unfortunate—" At that moment, one of his phones rang. He apologized and picked up the handset. *"Ja,"* he began. The call immediately consumed his attention. He swiveled in his seat and looked out the window at the C-5s and C-130s parked on the ramp below. I couldn't understand anything he was saying, given that *ja* was the sum total of my grasp of the language. With his back to me, I used the opportunity to scope out his office. The place smelled powerfully of pine and vanilla—an air-freshener, I guessed—and the room was spotless. I wondered if he would have the chair I was sitting in disinfected after I left.

Occupying one complete wall was a bookshelf with glass doors, presumably to keep out the nonexistent dust, which housed a number of rows of red and green leather-bound tomes. Against another wall was a glass cabinet containing a pilot's flight helmet, complete with oxygen mask, as well as a beautifully finished scale model of a Tornado, a fighter, the German air force's equivalent of our F-15 Strike Eagle. Above this cabinet, a number of framed photos, some black-and-white but most in color, were symmetrically arrayed. A few showed the general with his squadron buddies, presumably, at various postings throughout Europe. Others had him riding at show-jumping events or standing beside assorted nags with ribbons around their necks. I recognized a face in one of these photos: Prince Charles, the future King of England. Other faces began to look familiar. One photo featured the general and a former U.S. president laughing together. Others showed him trackside at Formula One motor races with drivers and/or Hollywood stars. This guy was a player.

I turned my attention to the general's desk. It was a vast gray granite number. There was the ubiquitous laptop, another smaller model of the Tornado, and a couple of phones. No in-trays or paper of any kind. I wondered how "hands-on" he was. Roach had commented that Scott was a known workaholic, and I found myself wondering how much of the big picture Scott allowed his German comrade to handle. Zip, most likely. Thanks to the briefing notes provided Stateside, I knew the number-two position at Ramstein had to be filled by a German officer of the rank of lieutenant general. The chief of staff was a British air vice marshal. The French had their finger in the pie, too, along with the Belgians, the Czechs, the Poles, and more than half a dozen other nations. Being a North Atlantic Treaty Organization facility, the makeup of the combined HQ here had been set up to reflect NATO's diversity. How the hell they got anything organized was beyond me.

"It's a good plane, *ja*?"

"Certainly looks the business," I said, caught out. While my eyes had been snooping around, von Koeppen had finished his call.

"Do you fly?"

"As little as possible. I've developed issues with it over time."

"A great shame. Well, an air force needs all types of talents to function properly, doesn't it? And yours must be exceptional for your Pentagon to have sent you all the way to investigate an accident, albeit a tragic one."

He was trying hard, working it.

"A murder investigation, actually. The crash investigation team has concluded that General Scott's plane was sabotaged."

"Sabotage!" he said, jumping up as if his butt had suddenly located a nail in the seat of his leather chair.

He walked around his office a couple of times with one hand on his waist and the other a balled fist against his chin. "General Scott...murdered?" He shook his head. "I don't believe it. God!"

I let von Koeppen have a moment uninterrupted with the brutal reality.

"That poor woman," he said. "Mrs. Scott will be devastated. Have you informed her yet?"

"No, sir."

"When will you do that?"

"After I leave here."

Von Koeppen went to his window and watched a couple of those Turkish F-4s take off. "I don't believe it," he said again, shaking his head.

"If you don't mind, I have to ask you some questions."

"Of course."

"Do you know anyone who may have wanted to kill the general?" Just about every murder investigation has that question asked at some stage. You always hope the answer's yes.

"No," he said, sticking to the usual pattern.

"No enemies?"

"No."

"Did he gamble? Have any bad habits that might have brought him into contact with the wrong crowd?"

"No. General Scott was exactly what he seemed. He was at the top of his game, a fine pilot and an able administrator. He was also my friend. How was it done?"

"A vital part of his glider was tampered with."

"What? How?"

"We don't know yet, sir."

"Who would have wanted him dead?" he asked, directing the question at the mirror shine of his black leather shoes.

And why? I added mentally.

"You will break the news gently to his widow...?"

No, I'll bash her over the head with it. "Of course, General."

"Anything you need to solve this crime, just ask," he said. "It's a terrible business..."

"Maybe one thing, sir."

"Yes?"

Despite what I'd said to Gruyere about hearing the news of Scott's death on CNN, I was reasonably sure that the story had not yet been made public. "I think it would be a good idea to release selective details to the press before they start printing unsubstantiated rumors. I would suggest also that we attribute General

Scott's death to accidental causes. At least for the time being."

"Of course. Good idea."

The phone rang again.

Von Koeppen excused himself and grabbed the handset with annoyance. "*Ja,*" he said. His tone instantly changed to one of deep concern. "*Ja,* of course, of course. *Ja,* I'll tell him."

Whoever was on the other end of the line was upset and giving von Koeppen both barrels. It sounded like a woman. He hung up, his face a mixture of embarrassment and anger. "Did you give orders for the police to seize General Scott's files?"

What?

Before I could answer, he said, "That was Mrs. Harmony Scott. She is *very* distressed. I order you to release her husband's effects back to her."

I assumed this was Masters's doing. If so, General von Koeppen placed me in a pickle. Masters and I weren't much of a team, but she was the only team I had. She hadn't warned me about going straight to Scott's widow's home, which could have been tit for tat with von Koeppen for his offhand dismissal of her. But I hoped it was for some other more substantial reason, because my reply to the acting NATO commander at Ramstein Air Base was, "No, sir. I won't do that."

"I'm giving you a direct order, *Major,*" he said, stressing my rank to remind me who was boss. We were back to that superiority shit again.

I stood and faced him. "I'm sorry, *General,* but I cannot obey that order." I was amazed at how quickly the dynamics in the room had changed. Masters must have left von Koeppen's office, driven like Michael Schumacher over to Scott's house, and sealed the victim's records, ignoring as she did so the widow's attack of apoplexia. I wondered if this was the reason why Masters so readily left von Koeppen's office. Whatever, the woman had balls.

The door opened and a tall blonde with an unbelievably ample chest, wearing the uniform of a sergeant in the USAF, entered the room. She had to be von Koeppen's PA—hand-picked, I had no doubt, because of her efficiency. The sergeant informed her boss that some famous person was on the line and gave the name. The name she dropped was familiar and then it clicked—the President of Germany had called for a chat. Von Koeppen's face had flushed a bright red and his eyes were locked with mine. He was a man unused to having his orders ignored. But he knew, and I knew, and I knew he knew, that I answered to a higher authority—namely the big cheese back at Andrews. The general blinked first. A call from the German president himself could not be ignored. "Dismissed, Special Agent," he said with an imperious wave for the benefit of his PA.

The sergeant held the door open for me. I heard von Koeppen pick up the handset and start talking in a jocular fashion, switching from shitty to happy camper on a dime. The performance reminded me that generals are as much politicians as soldiers. As I passed the noncom, I happened to catch her name tag, and not because it was clinging to possibly the most spectacular hills this side of the Himalayas. It was because I caught the smile, a faint one, one that implied she appreciated seeing von Koeppen with a bug fisted up his colon. Maybe the general wasn't well regarded, and I was suddenly interested to know why.

FIVE

I wanted to have a few words with von Koeppen's PA, but it would have to wait. I bummed a lift back to my rental outside Roach's hangar. At the security gate, I asked for, and was given, the dead general's residential address. Before the airman gave it up he checked my identity again and cleared it with Ramstein's OSI office.

The drive back to Kaiserslautern was uneventful and it gave me time to think. I've been present many times when bad news has been delivered to the friends and relatives of murder victims. Von Koeppen's reaction to the news was a terrific performance. Even though I didn't like the man, I believed his shock was genuine. A high percentage of murders are committed by people close to the victim and that fact was going through my mind when I broke the news to him, my personal radar tuned in. But something didn't feel right. I had expected to be grilled about where the investigation was, what Roach's findings had been, whether Washington had been informed, who I would be interviewing, and so on. But there was none of that. He expressed his sorrow and surprise that Scott's violent end had been the result of persons unknown, and then I was sent on my way. He seemed most concerned about Harmony Scott. Was that because she was a widow left alone by her loving husband, or because her father was America's top head-kicker? Or some other reason? I gave a mental shrug. I still had no suspects. I also still had an exposed nerve in a left lower molar. I drove down the highway with my knees doing the steering while my hands searched for the packet of cloves. The dried herb worked wonders, especially when combined with chemicals from Pfizer. I thanked Masters's granny and popped two of the little black stems into my mouth.

Not surprisingly, General Scott and his wife lived on the opposite side of town from where I was staying. The drive to their home took me past the entrance to the Palatinate Forest, one of the largest remaining contiguous forests in Germany, or so the tourist blurb on my map said.

I pulled up behind three camouflage-painted Land Rovers, each wearing the white star on blue of the NCMP—the NATO Combined Military Police. A purple Mercedes headed the column. It was a sprawling home with exposed wooden beams and red-painted stucco in the local style. Impressive and ugly. I left my vehicle and walked up the path that bisected an immaculate lawn punctuated by gardens full of brightly colored flowers. Beside the house, nestling up against it in taupe-painted board with a curved white stone-chip driveway leading up to it, was a three-car garage. Inside were two white Mercedes and a crystal blue 1968 Mustang coupe. At the halfway point between front gate and front door sat a large fountain with water gushing from the mouths of leaping bronze virgins cavorting with dolphins and heroically muscled Teutons. What else?

The massive oak front door swung open just as I was about to lift the heavy brass door knocker: an eagle hinged at its beak, a small deer skewered in its talons.

Nice. Eight people stumbled out onto the covered porch, Masters among them. Each carried a brown cardboard document storage box. Masters had a laptop under an arm, protecting it like a running back shielding the ball. Everyone appeared to be in retreat, fighting a rearguard action. Snapping at their heels was a small, anorexic woman with perfectly coifed blond hair and makeup to match. She wore a black silk blouse with a tan suede skirt. What with the coloring, bone structure, and attitude I was reminded of a Doberman-whippet cross.

"Who are you?" she demanded when she saw me. Her accent was Boston with a touch of London fog. Before I had a chance to answer, she said, "I know who you are. You're the ringleader of this insult to my husband. I've just spoken to General von Koeppen about you." She read the name on my uniform. "Yes, Cooper, that's right. Now, have my husband's effects returned to his study *immediately.*" She spoke like someone used to being obeyed.

"As I explained to you, Mrs. Scott," said Masters, jumping in, I suspected, more for my benefit than for the widow's, "we are securing General Scott's records as part of our investigation into his murder. Whoever killed your husband tried hard to make it look like an accident, ma'am. When the word gets around that we know what really happened, the killer or killers may get nervous, and bold. If there is any evidence contained in these records that may lead to their identity, and the murderer knows that, then quite possibly you'll be in danger. Removing them to a more secure place puts you out of harm's way."

It was a good speech, but wide of the truth. Security was an issue, sure, but, more accurately, Masters had acted quickly to remove the general's records from his house so that we could pick through them at our leisure, in a place of our choosing, rather than have Mrs. Harmony Scott continually hovering over our shoulders. A couple of seconds with the general's widow told me Masters had done the right thing. And, as Masters said, just maybe we'd find something of interest among these records. I had to admit, it was a good piece of decisive police work.

"I want you to know officially that I object, and that I will do *everything* in my power to have my husband's effects returned. I will also do my best to put a full stop on your impertinent careers."

Mrs. Scott had a whiskey aura. It wasn't quite midday and already she was into the sauce. Despite her unpleasant manner, I felt sorry for her on the one hand and thirsty on the other. Losing someone close was tough, but at least she had single malt to lean on. Whiskey was also my crutch of choice, with bourbon as the footstool. "I'm sorry for your loss, Mrs. Scott," I said, "but I agree with Special Agent Masters. We have no leads on your husband's killer. We don't know who, or why. Removing his records might help remedy that situation. I will also be recommending to General von Koeppen that you receive twenty-four-hour protection."

Harmony Scott stared at me with a cold ferocity in her pale gray eyes and I saw in them her father, the Vice President: Jefferson Cutter, the man often referred to as "Jeff the Cutter," "the Ripper," or "Toe Cutter" by the Washington press corps. At sixty-eight years of age, JC was getting on in life now but he was still supposedly the most powerful man in D.C. In fact, Cutter was also called the Ventriloquist, on account of that's how far his hand went up the President's ass. Harmony Scott's stare was unsettling, the way a viper holds you before it strikes. But only her eyes held anger, danger. The rest of her face was completely devoid of expression, like it belonged to someone else, a mask of porcelain and just as cold. Botox. "You will do no such thing," she said, taking a step toward me, getting inside my personal space—coiling—so that I had to take half a step back. Then she turned and went inside her home, slamming the heavy front door in our faces.

"A pleasure to meet you, ma'am," I said. I had a bunch of questions I wanted to put to the widow, but they would have to wait until she was in a more amenable mood to answer them. "Where's the hired help?" I asked.

"Let go," said Masters as we walked down the stairs. "Fired months ago. She gets a professional cleaning company in once a week."

"The woman's in that big house alone? No friends or relatives?"

Masters nodded.

"What about her mother?" I asked.

"She doesn't have one."

"What, ever?"

"I believe her mother died in childbirth."

"You're starting to scare me," I said.

Masters shrugged. Her cell began playing that KC and the Sunshine Band number. She answered it. "It's for you."

"Me?" I took the phone and stepped off the porch into the garden, and began to walk slowly back to the front gate.

"What in fuck's name is going on there, Cooper?" snarled the voice through the speaker. "You've been there less than a day and already I'm being pressured to have you sent home." It was General Gruyere.

"General, I'm just doing my job."

"That's not what I'm hearing."

I glanced at my Seiko. I figured von Koeppen must have called her as soon as he got off the line with his president, a good forty minutes ago. It was just after 0600 back at Andrews. I sympathized with Gruyere's mood. If someone woke *me* at that ungodly hour, I'd have to shoot them. "Also, I've been trying to ring you on your cell for the last ten minutes."

"It's in my coat in the car, General. The battery might have died."

"Why have you seized General Scott's records?"

Seized was perhaps too strong a word. I explained that we had merely secured them and provided the reasoning for doing that, which Gruyere largely accepted, though she added a warning. "Do try to avoid getting that woman angry, Special Agent. She has powerful allies neither you nor I want to mess with. Now, tell me you've got the paperwork for this in order."

"The paperwork in order?" I repeated, loud enough for Masters to catch.

I already knew the answer to that. Masters shook her head, confirming it. My heart sank. "Yes, General. Of course we have."

"Bullshit, Special Agent," said Gruyere, calling my bluff. The silence was pregnant.

"I will organize things officially from my end, but this is it, Cooper." The general's words were careful and deliberate. She was not impressed. "Remember what I told you before you left here yesterday."

I remembered: *It's either the biggest case of your career, or the last.* "Yes, ma'am." I read her loud and clear.

"Now, tell me what you know," she said.

I filled the general in on Roach's findings.

"Damn it to hell . . ." she said. "And no suspects?"

"No, ma'am."

"No leads?"

"No, ma'am."

"Better get on with it, then, hadn't you?"

"Yes, ma'am," I said as the line went dead.

I took a couple of deep breaths. Out with the bad, in with the good, as a certain colonel used to instruct me and my wife in our relationship counseling sessions before I stopped going—before I caught him in the shower with said wife on her knees giving his erection a good scrub with the back of her throat. The cops were shuttling boxes into the trucks. Masters put General Scott's computer on the front passenger seat of her car and locked the door closed behind her.

"Thanks," she said as she walked over. "You didn't have to do that."

I handed back her cell. "Do what?"

"Cover for me."

I wasn't sure what to say, how to handle this apology. And not because I hadn't received any positive feedback from the female of the species for some time. I was annoyed with Masters for racing off to secure Scott's papers without at least warning me. Doing it without getting the proper clearances and authorizations also rankled. Did she think Scott's widow would just pass his things over happily? It was also probably the sort of thing I'd have done myself had I thought of it. I gave in to my gentler side and said, "Forget it. Let's just try to make this teamwork thing happen as the big cheese intended."

"The big who?"

"Never mind. Where are you taking all this stuff?"

"We've got a spare office at OSI on the base. I'm going to set that up as an operations room. Do you know where OSI is?"

"No, but I'll find it. The guy on the front gate and I are on a first-name basis now."

One of the policemen mumbled something at Masters, saluted, and then headed back to the lead vehicle. The three trucks pulled away.

"I'm going to head back and get Scott's things behind a locked door. You?"

"I want to talk to the captain who watched Scott's plane go down. Then I'm going to talk to General von Koeppen's PA. I'd like to know a bit more about their working relationship."

"Whose? Between von Koeppen and his PA?"

"No, the relationship between Scott and von Koeppen."

"Oh, right."

"Anything more you can tell me about Herr General, other than he dresses in leather chaps and prances around his office with a feather duster?"

"Who said anything about a feather duster?" She laughed, and that surprised me. I'd been thinking that perhaps the scowl on her face was permanent. "Actually, I haven't had much to do with him. He's a bit of a ladies' man, or so I've heard—base gossip. So . . . why don't I catch up with you after you interview von Koeppen's PA? That'll give me enough time to get things organized back at the office."

"Sounds good." I liked this new era of cooperation. I was in a NATO facility, after all. It was a pleasant change to be in someone's good books, even if I had to be chewed out by my boss to get there. Talk of von Koeppen's reputation reminded me of Roach's comments on Masters, but I thought, on the whole, it would be best to keep that knowledge to myself, at least while things were going so well between us.

"Okay, I'll see you later," said Masters, walking back to my rental.

"Where're you going?"

She opened the passenger door, leaned in, and came out with my cell and pager. She thumbed them so that I could hear the "on" beeps, and then dropped them back onto the passenger seat.

"Yeah, I was going to do that," I said.

"Sure you were," Masters replied.

I got behind the wheel and the gadgets immediately started buzzing and ringing with stored messages. I was further distracted by an awful smell inside the car. Maybe Hertz had inadvertently left something decaying under my seat. I groped under it with my hand, which brought my nose closer to the source of the troubling odor. Me. I looked at myself in the mirror behind the sun visor. I hadn't had a shower for close to forty-eight hours and my five-o'clock shadow was putting in overtime. On top of this I'd eaten nothing, unless two blister cards of codeine could be considered food, and my breath smelled of something rotting sprinkled with cloves. I was fast becoming a walking biological weapon.

SIX

The building that housed logistics was a flat brown block with small, mean windows sheathed in silver heat film. I parked the rental in a visitor's spot out front and jogged the stairs to the third landing. It was warm inside.

A passing sergeant gave me the directions to Captain Reinoud Aleveldt's cubicle. I threaded my way through the maze of partitions; most were empty. I glanced at my Seiko: 1315. Lunchtime. After a couple of false turns I arrived at a workspace plastered with photos and torn-out magazine spreads of various gliders. Captain Aleveldt wasn't in his chair.

"Yes? Can I help you?" asked a voice behind me. I turned and saw a man with hair the color of cheddar cheese, ruddy pale skin, and thick fleshy lips that were red-raw dry and wind-chapped. He licked them. He wore running gear ironed with such precision that the knife-edge creases in his shorts were carried on by the creases in his T-shirt. I took a shot. "Captain Reinoud Aleveldt? You got a minute?"

"Actually, I was just on my way out." The guy was itching to get away and he kept shifting his weight from foot to foot. If he'd been two, I'd have taken him to the potty.

Who gives a fuck? As a general rule, I don't prepare people I want to question with a preemptive phone call. I like their answers to be off-the-cuff, especially when I'm not sure how a witness fits into the investigation, as was the case here. "Special Agent Vin Cooper, OSI," I told Aleveldt, flashing my ID to further refine his attention. "Just a few questions, if you don't mind. I'm investigating the assassination of General Scott." Why sugarcoat it?

The news appeared to hit Aleveldt like a punch under the rib cage. His jaw dropped slightly, his eyes went wide. I could read him so clearly I considered asking whether he'd like to play a few hands of canasta. "Assassination? But—"

"Got somewhere we can talk, Captain? Like a room with a door?"

He led the way to a meeting room, no doubt resigned to missing his jog, or whatever they did hereabouts for exercise. On two of the walls were enormous Whiteboards filled with hieroglyphics and scribbles slightly less decipherable than Greek. Or, given Aleveldt's nationality, maybe double Dutch. We both took seats at a cheap black Formica boardroom-style table. "Your English is good," I said.

"We have to learn it in school." He was in a daze, still struggling to come to grips with the revised reality of the general's demise. ". . . Assassinated?" he repeated.

"Murdered, assassinated—take your pick." I reached inside my coat, pulled out the notebook, and flipped it open. I've found that if people think I'm writing things down, it focuses their minds—perhaps because they realize someone further on down the line could well hold them to their answers. "How often did you fly with General Scott?" I asked, getting on with it.

"I'm a soaring enthusiast; so was Scotty."

"Scotty?"

"Away from Ramstein, we were friends."

He licked those red lips and swallowed—that nervous swallow people do. "I saw what happened. One of his wings just . . . broke off. There was nothing he could have done."

Roach's terrifying description came back to me with a rush. My balls felt like they were falling, dragging me down with them. I crossed my legs. "You haven't answered my question."

"Sorry . . . which was?"

"How often did you fly with General Scott?"

"Whenever the conditions were right and he was around—A dozen, fifteen times a year."

"Is that a lot?"

"It is when you consider that we don't fly often in winter. Once the weather breaks, it's almost every weekend."

"Did you talk to him before going up the last time?"

"Yes. We discussed the conditions. We were both keen to get airborne."

"Did the general seem concerned about anything that day—anything other than the flying conditions? Anything about his behavior that struck you as odd?" These are the sorts of questions you ask when straws are all you can see and you start clutching at them.

"No, sir. Scotty usually arrived tense, on edge, but that wouldn't last long. Soaring's a Zen experience. Just you and the elements. I can highly recommend it."

"Gravity and I don't get along," I said. I could tell he was looking at me as if to say, "You could sure use some of that Zen shit, pal." If I were him, I'd be looking at me strangely, too. Again I reminded myself I should have detoured and cleaned myself up when I had the chance.

"How was his plane sabotaged, sir?"

"A clamp that held the wings on failed. It'd been tampered with."

Aleveldt shook his head and frowned. "General Scott was a careful pilot. Always did the walk-around—checked everything, sometimes twice. It's ironic. Is that the right word?"

"Depends what you mean by it."

"He spent several thousand dollars upgrading his sailplane several months ago, over the winter when not much soaring is done—to make it safer."

"Yeah, ironic will do nicely," I said as a tingle went up the back of my neck and shrank the skin on my scalp. This could be a small but important break. Although it was by no means certain, there was a good chance that it was this very upgrade that provided the opportunity for the clamp to be replaced with a faulty unit. "What did he have done?"

"Avionics. A global positioning system for cross-country flying, a better radio set—more powerful, lighter. Had a couple of instruments replaced, too."

"Do you know who did the work?"

"Sorry. Can't help you there. I do a lot of the maintenance on my own plane, but the general was in a different league. Some airframe specialist—whoever was on at the time and depending on what was needed—would do it for him."

I remembered the conversation I had with Roach on this subject and that feeling across the top of my scalp evaporated.

"Do you know why anyone would want to kill the general?" Aleveldt asked.

"That was *my* next question."

"No, no. I don't understand it. The general was liked and respected. He flew in Vietnam. A war hero. He knew how to look after his people. I could see that. Everyone could."

Well, obviously someone couldn't, I thought.

"He wasn't like you'd expect a general officer to be," he insisted.

"You mean like General von Koeppen?" It just slipped out. I couldn't help myself.

Aleveldt bunted it away with a shrug. "Scotty was different."

"So there was nothing about his behavior at all that struck you as odd? He was just the same happy-go-lucky, nice-guy commander of one of the biggest military facilities in the world, who just happened to piss off the wrong mystery people enough for them to kill him in a pretty horrible way." The living General Scott was still a complete mystery to me. I'd read through his career highlights, met his wife, been to his house, spent some time with his second-in-command, interviewed his gliding buddy, seen the movie, bought the T-shirt and I still knew virtually nothing about the man—what made him tick. Aleveldt shifted in his seat. There was something on his mind. "Go on, Captain," I said.

"About a year ago . . ."

"What?"

"He lost a lot of weight, and he wasn't heavy to start with. He lost the *joie de vivre*. His son was killed."

"His boy was a marine, right?" I recalled that Scott's son was a sergeant in a rifle company. The brief didn't cover the details of his death.

"General Scott loved his son. They were very close. He was killed in Baghdad, on patrol. There was a problem with it."

I understood that this would be an issue for any parent, having a son killed, whether it happened on Uncle Sam's watch or not, but I knew that wasn't quite what Aleveldt meant. "How? What kind of problem?"

"There was confusion over his death."

"In what way?"

"The forms that accompanied his son's body said he'd been killed by a land mine."

That didn't sound too confusing to me—tens of thousands of unfortunate people are killed by land mines sitting in the dirt all over the world—and that must have shown on my face.

"Land mines don't take your head off, sir," Aleveldt said.

I knew a bit about land mines. They were planted in areas in Afghanistan defended by the Taliban. We had planted a bunch of them ourselves. There were also land mines in the areas once contested by the Soviets. And there were land mines sewn by the mujahedeen who fought against them. For a while, there were more land mines planted in Afghanistan than poppies, and they plant a lot of poppies in Afghanistan. Land mines come in many varieties, from the homemade types to those manufactured with ingenious Swiss-watch precision. There are land mines that'll remove your foot, land mines to stop tanks, and land mines for just about everything in between. I couldn't, however, think of a single variety that specialized in decapitation. "Then what did?"

"I don't know."

"Did General Scott talk to you about any of this?"

"No."

"Then how do you know so much about it?"

"People talk. A friend of mine was there when General Scott opened his son's body bag."

I tried to imagine what it might be like, peeling down the zipper and taking a peek inside at the corpse of your own boy—or what was left of him. It would be the kind of experience that could break a man's spirit completely. Captain Aleveldt stared at the floor, his shoulders hunched as if he too was imagining it. I mentally gave myself a shake. As a witness, Aleveldt wasn't worth a hell of a lot, hearsay and supposition not given too much credence in a military courtroom. He had, however, provided me with some new questions which required answers. I suddenly felt like I was going somewhere, even if it was in a bunch of divergent directions all at once. "Who's this friend of yours, Captain?"

"A doctor. Captain François Philippe."

"He French? In the Armée de l'Air?"

"No, Belgian. Flemish. He worked in the hospital morgue. François told me that the general asked him to conduct an autopsy on the body."

"Okay, you said 'worked.' Past tense," I said as I jotted this down.

"He was transferred eleven months ago."

"You got contact details for him?"

"Back in my cubicle, Special Agent."

"So, General Scott. You were saying that he was somehow different after the death of his son?"

"Yes."

"How exactly?"

"I don't think he cared whether he lived or died."

That stopped me. I wondered whether Roach had considered the possibility that General Scott had sabotaged his own glider—played a kind of Russian roulette with it. But then why would he go to the trouble of installing all the new avionics? That didn't make much sense. "Are you talking suicide?"

He thought about that, then shook his head. "No, I don't think so, sir. He didn't seem like the type, if you know what I mean."

I nodded. There wasn't much more I could ask the captain about General Scott; at least, not for the moment. "Are you around, Captain, if I need to talk to you some more—not heading out on leave or anything?"

"No, sir."

"Good. Well, if you could give me Captain Philippe's details..."

"Sure."

I followed him back to his cubicle. Aleveldt checked an address book, copied the information to a Post-It note, and handed it to me. I stuck it in my notebook. "I hope you get the bastards, Special Agent," he said.

"We'll do our best, Captain," I said absently as my phone rang. I knew the number on the screen. "Excuse me," I said as I answered it.

"How're you doing?" Masters asked.

"Yeah, my grandmother's suitcase," I said.

"Can't talk?"

"Stuffed racoons. Can you believe that?"

"Okay, well, we're sorting through Scott's papers."

"Find anything interesting?"

"Not yet, we've only just started. Are you coming back here?"

"On the way," I said. I rang off and dropped the phone back in my pocket, but it began to ring again. This time I didn't recognize the number. "Hello..."

"Special Agent Cooper?"

"Yes."

"Sergeant Fischer. You might not remember me, sir, but we met briefly this morning."

I remembered her all right: Sergeant Audrey Fischer, the PA in von Koeppen's office with the unbelievable secretarial skills. "That's right," I said after a moment of respectful silence where I pretended to scan my memory banks for recollection. "How can I help you, Sergeant?"

"It's about General Scott. I have some information that might help you find his killer."

SEVEN

The sun was doing its best, but there was no heat in it, even though it was mid-afternoon. The clouds had moved back after a period of absence, their edges outlined with a brittle golden wire. I pulled in to the visitor's space at the foot of the OSI building, grabbed my bits and pieces from the passenger seat, and went inside.

"Cooper, over here," said Masters, from down the end of a short, brightly lit hallway.

She held the door open for me. The room was a chaos of desks, phones, opened boxes, and Whiteboards. NCMP noncoms were getting it all sorted out. "This is us for the duration," she said. "Your swipe card will get you in. One thing, though—if we're going to work together, you have to take a shower. If I could, I'd make it an order. I can't, so I'll make it a plea. There's one up on the second floor. We've also found you a clean ACU, razor, deodorant. All the things you need—and take it from me, you need them—are all in that bag there on the chair." She motioned at a Nike gym bag. "Out the door, up the stairs on your right. Keep going till you get to the second landing. It's the first door on your right."

I didn't know whether to be grateful or offended. "Thanks," I said, choosing the former.

"When I can get within ten feet of you and still breathe, we'll talk. How'd it go with Captain Aleveldt?"

"Good," I said.

"While you're turning yourself back into a human being, you can consider what this means," she said as she handed me a sheaf of computer printouts.

The cover sheet held four columns of figures. There were no labels on the sheet to indicate what the figures meant, just row after row of numbers.

"There's tons of stuff like this. Scott was researching something in detail, but I have no idea what."

"Okay," I said.

I flicked through the wad of printouts. Each page was like the last: columns of figures. There was no context for the information.

"We've only just started going through this stuff," she said with a wave of her hand, indicating the boxes. "But this looks interesting."

"What?" I asked.

She handed me a small brown tag made from dense, fibrous card. I took a close look at it. It was some kind of certificate, and it looked familiar. I suddenly realized what it was when I saw the handwritten words "Peyton Scott, Sgt., USMC" followed by his serial number and the stamp of the United States 28th Combat Support Hospital, Baghdad. There were several other details on it, including a bar code and medical officer's printed name with his signature above it. "It's a bag tag," I said.

"Yeah," agreed Masters. "What do we know about his son?"

"Not much, except that he's dead." I turned the tag over, but there was nothing on the reverse side. This was the tag affixed to Peyton Scott's body bag so that it could be readily identified coming off the C-17 that brought it from Iraq. Cause of death was loosely described on the tag as "massive trauma." Which, given the extent of Sergeant Scott's injuries, was still an understatement.

"There's a bit of bad news, too," said Masters. "The base dental hospital is overloaded, checking through a bunch of U.S. Army and Air Force people rotating out of the Middle East. The earliest you can get an appointment is in three days. You okay with that?"

The distant throb in my jaw was like a bad storm that, while still visible, had mostly rolled over the horizon. The pills were working. Or maybe the monster chewing through my tooth had devoured so much of what remained that there was nothing left for it to consume. Whatever, the pain was bearable, at least for the moment. "I'll survive. Thanks."

I suddenly realized that I was bone tired. I'd managed to grab a few stressed-out hours of sleep on the red-eye coming over, but that had been more my body's attempt to marshal its waning recovery powers after yet another serious attempt to poison it with alcohol. I'd been going for some time without good sleep or food. If I was going to keep functioning at a level above zombie, I would need both.

"Out the door, up the stairs, first door on the right . . ." she said behind me as I picked up the Nike bag and shuffled out the door.

I found the shower room, closed the door, and stripped. I rummaged through the gear Masters had provided. There was a towel, soap, deodorant, toothpaste, a new toothbrush, a razor—the basics of personal grooming. I was a little disappointed to find there was no Calvin Klein to splash on after shaving but, then again, not really. I looked in the mirror. I looked awful. The lines under my eyes were etched deep and I had bags the size of a Samsonite under each lid. I wondered what effect a subcutaneous injection of botulism would do for me—it worked wonders for Harmony Scott.

The news in the mirror wasn't all bad. The overhead light accentuated the stomach muscles still loitering from my time with Special Forces. By rights I should have added a few layers of macaroni and cheese and maybe a corn dog or two to this six-pack of mine, but I'd always been blessed with a high metabolic rate. The pink divot of scar tissue about two inches above my right nipple was a constant reminder that I had no right to be here. Touching it brought back the memories and the sensation of falling—the fear—and it made me want to grab hold of my testicles, secure them. I lifted my right arm, exposing the ragged scar from my armpit to elbow where a ricochet from a Kalashnikov had dug a channel as it tumbled through skin and muscle. There was also a chunk of muscle—around three and a half ounces' worth, according to the attending surgeon— pared from my left quadricep, courtesy of a fragment of 88mm mortar on its way to somewhere else in a hurry. Apparently, the surgeon said, it was my own damn fault for trying to detain it. Looking on the bright side, the wounds had a certain symmetry about them— neither side of my body had been spared. I turned away from the mirror and turned on the faucets. The bathroom became a steam room within a minute. I climbed under the powerful jet of hot water and let it weave its magic. I closed my eyes and thought about the last twenty-four hours. It felt more like a week had passed since Arlen dragged me out of the sack.

Without a doubt, Special Agent Anna Masters was making a supreme effort to be open and helpful. I decided then and there to reciprocate. Part of me, the damaged, wounded side that could still see his marriage counselor's balls clacking against his wife's chin, warned, "Women—they're not to be trusted," but the professional side of me, the one that said two brains working together on a tough case are better than one, prevailed. I also silently praised Masters again for having the good sense to get the general's records out from under his widow's roof.

I soaped myself down, washed my hair, shaved in the shower, and went back over the interviews with Roach, Himmler, and Aleveldt; the brief moment in the delightful company of the grieving Harmony Scott; and the interview to come with Sergeant Fischer. I must have been thinking about it all too long because there was a knock on the door. "You okay in there?" It was Masters.

"Yeah, fine," I said. "Care to join me?" Silence. That's the trouble with these on-base facilities—the showers never run out of hot water and go cold on you, so how do you know when to get out? I spat out the cloves, cleaned my teeth very carefully, ate two more codeine tablets, and dressed in the borrowed clothes. The new undershorts were briefs rather than boxers, but I could live with it.

I stuffed the Nike bag with my dirty laundry and went downstairs. "Good," said Masters when I made an entrance. "At least now I don't have to stay upwind of you."

I ignored the comment. "Have you got the general's computer booted up yet?"

"Yes, as a matter of fact." She looked over my shoulder and said, "Flight Lieutenant Bishop? You got a second?"

A man of around twenty-five got up from behind a bank of electrical equipment and came over. "Yes, ma'am?"

"RAF Flight Lieutenant Peter Bishop, Special Agent

Vincent Cooper. He's heading up this investigation," she said.

Did Masters just say I was running this show?

"Special Agent," he said, turning toward me.

Yeah, she just did.

"The flight lieutenant here is the nearest thing we've got to Bill Gates, although I don't think he's nearly as rich."

I wondered why Masters had capitulated on the SAC thing. Maybe she realized the special agent in charge was wearing a big red bull's-eye on his or her chest if things turned to crap.

Flight Lieutenant Peter Bishop was a big coffee-colored man with gelled, spiky black hair, black eyes, and big chubby cheeks that reminded me of hamburger buns, but my hunger was starting to affect my brain and they probably didn't look like that at all. I could feel perspiration beading on my skin. It was my tooth again. I ran my hand gently beside my jaw. Was it beginning to swell? "How's it going with the general's computer?" I asked.

"Nice machine, sir." Bishop's accent reminded me of the characters in the movie *Lock, Stock and Two Smoking Barrels.* "It's a superseded Dolch NotePAC. I can start it up but I can't get past the user screen. The general had a pass code. That's going to take time to sidestep."

"How much time, Lieutenant?" I asked.

"Couple of hours, sir. More or less."

"Take less," I said.

"Yes, sir," he said.

"C'mon, leave this for now," I said to Masters, gesturing at the office work around us. I then told her about Sergeant Fischer's claim that she had something that might help us out, without putting it quite as theatrically as the sergeant herself had. And yes, I should admit up front that I'd considered interviewing Sergeant Fischer solo, and yes, not for entirely professional reasons. But I'd never done that kind of thing before and decided not to start now. Besides, that would have gone against the newfound spirit of cooperation growing between Masters and me. What was NATO's motto? I remembered seeing it on some banner somewhere. It was something mindlessly gung ho and nineties like "One mission, one team." Yeah, that was it. I grabbed a spare camouflage jacket and stuffed my cell and beeper in the pocket.

Masters drove; I made notes. Beneath *Captain Reinoud Aleveldt*, I jotted *Captain François Philippe*, the name of the medical officer who'd witnessed Scott's horror at seeing his son's remains. Beneath theirs, I wrote *Fischer, Harmony, Himmler, U.S. Army Hospital—Baghdad, Morgue*. I also doodled a question mark and gave it a drop shadow.

EIGHT

We drove to the Melting Pot, as the base's coffee shop was called, a half-assed attempt at creating a relaxed environment for off-duty servicemen and -women. I say half-assed because putting up photos of planes in this place was akin to hanging lovingly framed posters of skinned beef hindquarters in a butcher's shop. I'd have thought island beaches would have been a more escapist theme here for people far from home and surrounded three hundred and sixty-five days a year with jet whine. The bleached and faded photos looked like they'd been left outside and acid-rained on, and showed the men and the machinery that had been stationed here over the past four and a half decades, daring the Soviet Union to take its best shot. Many photos were signed by famous airmen. I recognized speed-of-sound man Chuck Yeager and his WWII co-ace, Bud Anderson. I also recognized a young von Koeppen leaning out of a cockpit wearing Ray-Ban Aviators and grinning like Goofy at the camera. I felt bad for Chuck and Bud having to share a wall with a known Nazi war criminal.

People drinking lattes and reading various foreign-language newspapers occupied most of the tables. I felt watched as we made our way to an empty table in a corner. The place smelled of coffee and doughnuts and JP-4 convecting off the flight line somewhere beyond the row of uninspiring bunker-like buildings lining the street opposite. The smell of food got my saliva glands going and my stomach contracted. I had to eat *something*, even if it was just deep-fried dough rolled in sugar.

We were a couple of minutes late but then so was Sergeant Fischer. "Okay," I said to Masters as von Koeppen's PA entered the shop. The sergeant and I exchanged quick waves of recognition across the room. She made her way over, threading through the tables, swinging her hips between them with the rhythm of a samba dancer. The newspapers dipped so that their readers could get a better view, and I couldn't blame them.

The sergeant was even more spectacular than I remembered her from the morning. Her tousled fair hair was a halo around a flawless olive complexion. The gathering chill of the late-afternoon air had rouged her full, high cheeks, and her eyes were pale sapphires. She was tall, almost intimidatingly so for any male under six feet. She wore the standard ABU designed to hide any trace of sexuality, only on Fischer it instead revealed a fine figure with breasts that stood out before her like a couple of missile warheads ready for launch. Every guy in the joint, including me, swallowed.

"Can we get you a coffee, Sergeant?" I asked, making a supreme attempt at nonchalance before she took a seat between Masters and me.

"Thank you, no," said Fischer with the soft vowels of the deep South.

"Special Agent?"

"Espresso, thanks," said Masters.

I noticed the two women sizing each other up, much like von Koeppen and I had done. If I was not mistaken, Sergeant Fischer appeared to be vaguely intimidated by Masters, and not because of her job, either. It suddenly dawned on me when I looked at Special Agent Anna Masters that she, like Fischer, was also a serious piece of work, and the way we—or rather she—was gawked at when we came into this place suddenly made sense.

A waiter came over and took the order, which included half a dozen doughnuts. My stomach rumbled with anticipation at the promise of food.

"Before we start, do you mind if we record the interview?" asked Masters.

Fischer eyed the device.

"Don't let it worry you, Sergeant," Masters said. "It's just more reliable than our note-taking."

Fischer relaxed. "Okay."

"Now, I believe you have some information," said Masters. Things had settled down between them while the waiter was distracting me. I got the feeling that their silent bout had resulted in a draw.

"Yes. While I'm General von Koeppen's PA, I also did a little work for General Scott when things got busy. I liked him. He worked hard. At least, he did before his son was KIA in Iraq. He was pretty broken up about it. He went gliding a lot..."

I nodded and was about to say we knew that when the sergeant added, "...and he started seeing another woman."

"He was having an affair?" I blurted. Fischer had caught me completely off guard. General Scott didn't seem the type, but I was rapidly coming to the conclusion that there was no "type" where affairs were concerned.

"Yeah." She was dismissive.

"How do you know that? Did he confide in you?" Masters asked.

She shrugged. "This is Europe; men have mistresses.

He had another cell phone, not a NATO one, a secret phone he used for his private calls."

"How do *you* know about it?" I asked.

"Because I arranged the cell for him—one of those prepaid jobs. No bills, and no list of numbers for the spouse to examine every month. I think he cared about his wife very much."

"Yeah, I'm sure," I said. Given the circumstances of my divorce, I was not quite ready to accept Deception as an emotionally caring institution.

Fischer ignored my sarcasm, as did Masters. Sisters, already.

"Do you have the number?" Masters asked.

"Yes," said Fischer. "General Scott told me I could call him if I ever needed to."

"Did you?"

Masters rephrased my question. "Were you also having an affair with General Scott?"

"No, ma'am," she said, shaking her head.

The way she said it, I believed her. I also believed she'd left a few wrecked marriages in her wake, and none of them hers. "Do you know who the other woman was?" I asked.

"No, sir, he never told me."

Masters again. "Do you know where he kept this other cell?"

"No, ma'am."

Masters and I both let it all sink in. I was now wondering whether General Scott had been killed for the same reasons we mere mortals are, after all. I thought of his official air force photo: sitting straight, eyes bright, smiling at the camera, his four stars the symbols of control over a sizeable chunk of the world's military might—a man, as von Koeppen had said, at the top of his game. An adulterer. I also found myself wondering what Harmony Scott would do if she caught her man up to his nuts in some other woman's guts. "Could you put the number of the general's private cell into mine?" I asked Fischer, passing it across. She took it out of my hand, leaning forward. I caught a glimpse of cleavage. I wondered whether she'd presented it on purpose. And then I wondered hopefully whether she'd do it again. For the past year or so, wallowing in the bunker oil spillage that was my private life, I'd been celibate, hardly noticing the existence of the opposite sex, preferring to lean on my three buddies Arlen Wayne, Jack Daniel's, and Glenkeith. But now, sandwiched between these two women with my divorce behind me, parts that had been asleep for some time were waking up, having a stretch, and inquiring about the chances of some exercise. Fischer keyed in the number, then handed back my cell.

I cleared my throat and asked, "What about you and General von Koeppen?"

"I make it a rule never to sleep with the boss, if that's what you mean," she said. The way she said it, holding my gaze with the barest hint of a smile, indicated that this little rule of hers didn't necessarily include a particular special agent. "And General von Koeppen is not my type," she said.

The question had to be asked, what was her type? But I refrained. Instead, I asked, "What sort of working relationship did Scott and von Koeppen enjoy?"

" 'Enjoy' is hardly the word I'd use. There was a fair bit of tension between them."

"Did this tension have a particular cause?"

"Not as far as I know. The working relationship between the two of them was never great." Fischer gave this some consideration and then added, "Look, I don't want to give you the impression that General Scott and were confidants. We weren't. He was a secretive man. The business with the cell was unusual. Pretty much all of the time our relationship was by the book."

"Can you tell us anything about how his son died?"

"All I can tell you is what the whole base knew— that the poor bastard opened his own son's body bag."

I saw Masters flinch. Yeah, it was a far from pleasant image, one that had stayed with me since the interview with Aleveldt.

Fischer took a deep breath. "The general took some time off after that. Three weeks, according to the records. Managing leave is one of my administration duties."

"Have you heard any scuttlebutt about the way Scott's son was killed in Baghdad?"

Fischer shook her head slowly, considering that. "No, sir."

"Had anything struck you as odd in General Scott's behavior in the weeks prior to his death?" asked Masters.

"No."

"Do you know anyone who'd want to kill him?" I asked.

The PA shook her head again. "No, I don't, but I bet you'll have a better idea yourselves after you find the person he bought that phone to talk to."

I changed tack. "Sergeant, you don't like General von Koeppen. Why?"

"Off the record?" she asked.

"Sure." I cleared this first with a little eye contact with Masters.

"Do you mind turning that off?" Fischer gestured at the recorder.

Masters hit the button.

"So this is totally off the record?" Fischer asked again.

I nodded.

"Well...I think he's a vain, supercilious cock-sucker."

"Could you be more specific, Sergeant?" I said with the straightest face I could muster.

"He couldn't lead a thirsty horse to water, sir. He's a lazy, inconsistent, narcissistic sleazebag."

"Is von Koeppen also having an affair?" asked Masters, rapid fire, beating me to the question.

"He's always sniffing around, ma'am," said Fischer. "Preferably young women. He seems pretty successful with them, too. I don't know where he finds them all."

That nailed my unasked question about von Koeppen's preferred brand of squeeze. Masters cleared her throat. If I didn't know better, I'd have said she was blushing. And something about this rising color forged another question in my head, but not one for Fischer. I had nothing more to ask the PA for the moment and Masters also seemed to have suddenly run dry. The interview was over. Masters picked up her recorder, dropped it in her bag, and rose, apparently keen to send the sergeant on her way. Fischer took the hint and stood. "Thank you for your help, Sergeant," Masters said. "Do you mind if we call you again if we think of anything else?"

"Yes...I mean no, ma'am. Sure," said Fischer.

"Thanks, Sarge, we'll be in touch," I said, forcing my eye line to stay above the PA's neck. It took every ounce of willpower. I could feel Masters watching me. I'm told the Europeans handle this sort of dilemma totally differently from us Americans. They just go ahead and look.

Newspapers and magazines were lowered again as Fischer made her way out.

I sat and reached for a doughnut. At last, food. "What do you make of that?" I said, mouth full.

"That Scott had another woman? Kind of opens up the territory a bit, doesn't it?"

"Yeah. Doughnut?"

Masters declined the offer as I reached for another.

We rehashed what we knew about Peyton Scott, about the state of his corpse, about the autopsy report, and about how the two didn't gel. The death of the son kept cropping up, and I couldn't help feeling it was significant to the killing of General Scott in a way we didn't yet understand. And there was the other question unrelated to father and son that I wanted to ask Masters, but I wasn't sure how she'd take it.

I ate all the doughnuts while we talked. Eventually we came full circle. "So, how do we find this other woman?" asked Masters.

"The missing cell will take us straight to her."

"Yeah, but how do we find that?"

"I have an idea," I said.

NINE

It was dark by the time we left the Melting Pot. The wind was up and the temperature had dropped to the mid-fifties. I wasn't dressed for it and the cold sliced through my clothing. I'd had enough for one day. In the silence, Masters said, "A bit of housekeeping. I've ordered a couple of extra ABUs for you. They should arrive tomorrow. Your rank is lieutenant, right?"

I didn't bite. I was too damn tired to spar. Also, the question I wanted to ask Masters was sucking away much of my attention. My cell rang. "Hello."

"Sir, Flight Lieutenant Bishop here," said the voice.

Bishop . . . Bishop . . .

"I'm working on the general's computer, sir," said the flight lieutenant helpfully.

It came back to me. "Right. Sorry, Peter, it has been a hell of a day."

"That's okay, sir. Just wanted to tell you. I've struck a problem."

"What kind of problem?" I repeated for Masters's sake.

"Managed to get past the general's user code, but he's running a program called Dungeon."

"What's that?"

"Dungeon is what it sounds like—a lockup, only one for your files. It's a tough nut to crack. Four levels, each one trickier than the last to get through. The general has around one meg of files locked away—not a lot, really."

"But he probably wouldn't bother unless those files were important."

"A reasonable assumption, Special Agent."

"You going to be able to break into it?"

"I'm not sure yet. I'll need a couple days for each level, maybe more. I can't even guarantee I'm going to be able to crack the innermost levels."

"Do what you can, Flight Lieutenant."

"Yes, sir," he said, ending the call.

"What's up?" asked Masters.

"The general's computer. All his files are locked in a kind of prison with no visitors allowed. Bishop's starting to tunnel in, but he's going to need time, and a file baked into a cake." I rubbed my face with both hands. It felt good so I did it again.

"A what?" Masters looked confused.

"Never mind," I said. "I'm just tired."

"Yeah, you look dead on your feet, Cooper. Leave your car here and I'll give you a lift back to K-town."

"Sure, thanks." I was hoping she'd offer, but didn't want to ask. "You live in K-town?"

"Out on the edge where you're less likely to get hit by a jogger."

I folded my arms against my body and turned the heater up as we cleared the security post. Warm air funneled from the duct, making me more drowsy.

"So where is it?" she asked.

"Where's what?"

"Scott's cell. We recovered his NATO one in his study. I've already asked to have the last fifteen months of records pulled and sent over."

"Let me have a Columbo moment. We'll both find out tomorrow if I'm right."

"Fair enough."

In truth, I wasn't a hundred percent sure we'd find it, especially if its battery was flat, which could have been the case. The reflective cat's eyes buried in the road zipped past like slow-motion tracers. Eventually Masters said, "She was flirting with you, you know."

"Who? Oh, you mean—"

"Yeah."

"Did I pass the test?"

Masters swung out of the lane and passed a big rig. "Barely."

The silence closed in like the darkness around the Mercedes's headlight beams.

That question I was sitting on, waiting to ask Masters . . . I hoped I was wrong but I already knew the answer. I also hoped it would have no bearing on anything we were working on. I couldn't hold on to it any longer. "So when were you and von Koeppen seeing each other?" I asked as casually as possible.

Silence.

"We stopped well over a year ago."

Silence.

Eventually she asked, "How did you know?"

"Just a guess." Masters was protective about him on the one hand and dismissive on the other. And whenever he came up in conversation, she'd change either color or the subject or both. *Actually, I haven't had much to do with him. He's a bit of a ladies' man, or so I've heard— base gossip.* I couldn't imagine what she saw in him. "It's not going to get in the way, is it?" I asked.

"No."

"Good."

We sat in silence for the rest of the drive. Maybe Masters thought my lack of conversation was some kind of reproach, but I was so tired I was having trouble clearing a path from my brain to my mouth.

We drove like that all the way to the Pensione Freedom. "Oh-eight-hundred in the foyer. Okay?" she said as the Mercedes came to a stop beneath the trees opposite the pensione's steps.

"Oh-eight-hundred," I repeated. I felt like I should say something rousing about the progress we'd made thus far, move the mood on from our first meeting. But I've never been a big fan of locker-room speeches.

I got out of the car and tapped it lightly on the roof. I watched as Masters drove off slowly. Breaking glass distracted me. A couple of backpackers with Canadian flags sewn to their packs were swaying precariously, either because of the weight of the loads that towered over their heads, or because they were rolling drunk. Canadians. Probably both, I decided, as one bent to pick up the broken bottle they'd dropped. He toppled sideways and lay on the ground like a cockroach sprayed with insect killer, legs and arms flailing, unable to right himself. His buddy burst into fits of laughter and collapsed in the gutter, quivering hysterically.

They were having too much fun. I ignored them and walked up the stairs of the pensione. The foyer was empty, a bell provided for tenants requiring assistance after six P.M. The space was lit with brutal fluorescent tubes and the light bounced off the walls and turned the skin on my hands a purple color. My nose told me that bratwurst was no longer on the menu. Tonight, it was either boiled boot or cabbage and potato. Despite this, my stomach growled audibly. Half a dozen doughnuts hadn't filled the hole for long.

I walked the two blocks to a McDonald's I'd seen on the way in. Wary that the truce between my toothache and the drugs might be fragile, I bought a couple of cheeseburgers because they were soft and easy to eat. They tasted of clove.

I'm not sure whether codeine is a hallucinogen but I had some pretty freaky dreams, mostly about people with missing heads.

Then the case kept me awake and I went a few rounds wrestling with the sheets. The sheets won and so I got up and paced in the dark. I told myself that this case was no different from any other I'd worked on. What I needed was some distance. I was too close to the individual details and they were meaningless because of that, like those mounds and scratches on the ground in Mexico that become figures or animals or geometric patterns when they're viewed from altitude. I also wondered how long I, or rather we—OSI—would have on our own before some other agency began sniffing around. Within half an hour I was in a cab to Ramstein. On the way there I left a message on Masters's cell, telling her not to bother picking me up.

Masters had done a good job securing the OSI block at the base. At the entrance stood a massive French MP who looked like a refrigerator with a two-day growth. He smelled of garlic and Gauloises. My swipe card got me in the front door and I walked up to two other NCMP people armed with M16 carbines covering the door to the windowless bunker that contained the general's papers. I swiped the door and went in. Boxes were placed on gray Formica tables and there was a fair bit of paper scattered around, in the process of being catalogued. It appeared that the general had been pretty systematic with his filing, only much of his fastidiousness had been undone by our rush to relocate his records.

I didn't really know where to start, so I just sat down

with one of the boxes and began sifting through the contents at random.

Two hours later, Masters walked in with a cappuccino for us both. "Morning," she said.

"Morgen," I replied.

"How'd you sleep?"

"Like a baby—"

"Good."

"—with colic."

"Oh . . . Tooth still bugging you?"

"Among other things."

The guarded way Masters looked at me when I said that told me she thought one of those other things was her one-time relationship with von Koeppen. Frankly, I hadn't given it any thought. It was a long time in the past and had no bearing on anything. That's if I took Masters at her word, and I had no reason to doubt her.

She came over with the coffee and a newspaper. Without the camouflage jacket on, I could see she had a hell of a figure—athletic, but without the roidal gym-junkie shoulders or thighs that can turn a woman's figure into a parody. She was wearing perfume, too—Issey Miyake, if I was not mistaken. My favorite. Her hair wasn't tied back and it fell around her face and shoulders like ribbons of dark chocolate silk. "And, anyway, I wanted to get an early start—we've got a lot to do," I said to get my mind off what it would be like burying my nose in her hair. I relieved her of one of the coffees.

"The news is out," she said. "Front page."

I turned the newspaper over. It was the *International Herald Tribune.* The world was the usual insane mess with people happily blowing up themselves and each other all across the globe. I recognized a face. It was Scott, and he was smiling. "Accident Kills Top U.S.

General," said the headline. There were a few paragraphs about why he was a top U.S. general, and nothing about him being assassinated. "That was quick," I said. "Von Koeppen must have had the *Tribune* over for tea.

"My turn for show-and-tell," I said as I handed her a small waxy slip of paper.

"What's this?" she asked.

"A receipt." It was difficult to read. The print was fine, and fading. "Aurora Aviation, for three thousand eight hundred and forty euros. We might not be able to find out who did the work on Scott's glider, but at least we know who he bought those new bits and pieces from."

Masters nodded. "Good find."

I exchanged it for a yellowing press clipping, also from Scott's files. "So's this."

She frowned as her eyes flicked over the headline: "Death Row." The picture accompanying it showed a long line of what were either body bags or sleeping sea lions lying on the tarmac behind the ramp of a transport plane. A couple of soldiers were carrying another one between them down the ramp, which narrowed the odds about what they were carrying, given that sea lions weigh half a ton each. I'd read the accompanying article a dozen times and almost knew it by heart. The gist of it was that this row of dead soldiers on the Ramstein tarmac represented one month of our butcher's bill from the war in Iraq. It was also the first time a press photographer had managed to snap such a scene, Washington fearing the effect such a picture would have on the psyche of the folks back home.

I remembered this photo, this story. When it appeared in newspapers across the country, it rekindled the debates about whether the price in blood America was paying in the Middle East was worth it. So perhaps

Washington had been right after all to keep this sort of imagery out of the public domain. But then maybe censoring the reality of the war was worse, denying America the awful truth—of the choices we had made, and the personal consequences that flowed from them. And there was something very real and very brutal about body bags, especially when there were so many of them.

"I remember this," said Masters, echoing my thoughts. "Caused a real flap."

I handed her the letter General Scott had received shortly after the photo had been published. It was a very impressive letter headed with a bald eagle clutching a bunch of arrows in one talon and an olive branch in the other. The top left corner had a staple in it with a small torn section of newsprint. The article Masters was reading had originally been attached to the letter but had separated at some stage. The author had handwritten the note with a fountain pen; the script was elaborate.

Masters read aloud.

"Dear Abraham,
The President and I were dismayed to see that security could be breached at such an important facility as Ramstein. Photos such as this one recently taken at your facility, images we have been at pains to keep out of the public forum, have a disheartening effect that is incalculable. I strongly recommend that this incident be investigated and that the persons involved in the security breach be officially reprimanded. Do your best to see that it doesn't happen again.
Sincerely,
Jefferson Cutter
Vice President of the United States of America."

"Terse," I said.

"Yeah."

"Was any investigation ever carried out?" I asked.

"No, not to my knowledge."

"Don't you think that's odd?"

"What? That Scott was asked to investigate how a photograph like this could be taken, and didn't? I'm sure he had his reasons, but he didn't think to let me in on them."

"No . . . I guess not." I wanted to know why Scott had ignored such a strong recommendation from the VP, his father-in-law.

"Do you think this business with the body bags is important in the scheme of things?" Masters asked.

"You mean in our investigation into Scott's murder?"

"Yeah."

I shrugged. "We don't know what's important and what's not. At least, not yet. By the way, I rang the night desk of *The Washington Post* to see if I could get some contact details for the journalist responsible."

Masters glanced at the clipping. "Alan Cobain."

"Yeah."

"You *have* been busy."

"He's dead. Killed in Iraq covering the war. About a month after this article appeared. He was abducted. They found his body ten days later. Or what was left of it, anyway—looked like he'd been attacked by sharks."

"Oh, that's a shame," said Masters.

"Especially if you were Alan Cobain."

TEN

Masters's NCMP noncoms were continuing their task of archiving Scott's papers.

"Who's this Captain François Philippe?" Masters asked, looking at the Whiteboard where I'd transferred the list of people I'd made in my notebook.

"Medical officer. He's the guy Scott had perform an unofficial autopsy on his son's body here at the base hospital. What's your French like?"

"*Très bien. Pourquoi?*"

"You've got the job. Would you mind giving him a call and asking him about it? He doesn't speak much English, apparently."

"Sure."

"Here's his number." I opened my notebook and gave her the Post-It.

A USAF sergeant seconded to the NCMPs hovered on the edge of our conversation. He was a large man with short orange hair that reminded me of shoe-brush bristles. Politely, he said, "Excuse me. Special Agent Masters? I've got the chief medical officer on the line. He'd like to have a quick word."

Masters took the handset, spoke briefly into it, then hung up. "General Scott's body is being released later this morning."

"How far away is the hospital?" I asked.

"A ten-minute drive, give or take."

"Let's go, then," I said. Instead of calling this

François Philippe, we could pay the guy a visit. Maybe, with all this talk of autopsies, the CMO's ears were burning. We had a full day ahead and the morgue at Landstuhl Medical Center was on my list of places to see anyway. It was a couple of miles south of Ramstein. We took an SUV.

The weather was much like the previous day's, with little cotton-ball clouds, a low mist, a touch of sunshine, and a procession of rainbows. It all reminded me of the lid on a chocolate box. "See anything else interesting in Scott's records?" Masters asked.

"Plenty. He conversed with two previous presidents as if they were best buddies. He had a wide circle of friends in politics, most of them people he flew with who went on to Congress or the Senate after leaving the military. He was a prolific letter-writer—wrote to his son every two weeks. There are citations, awards, requests from charities and associations—he was a meticulous record-keeper. And then it all stopped."

"What did?"

"The letter writing, the keeping of records—it all stops."

"Are you saying you think someone has beaten us to them? Already?"

"What I mean is he suddenly had no time left to write to anyone. He just started producing figures. Numbers. Pages and pages of numbers. He became preoccupied with something—like it was driving him crazy."

Masters pulled over momentarily in order to let a convoy of rigs loaded with tanks pass.

"You familiar with that Spielberg movie—*Close Encounters of the Third Kind*?"

"Sort of," she said.

"Do you remember how the people in it get obsessed

with the flattop mountain the aliens are going to land on? It's all they think about? They dream about it, draw it, become consumed by it?"

"Vaguely."

"Well, that's like our general. Scott was consumed by something. I have no idea what it was, but it was big and it was scaring him."

"You have a good imagination, Special Agent."

"Okay, okay, so the scaring thing I made up."

"Apart from the numbers puzzle, did you find anything else of interest?"

"Yeah, as a matter of fact." I reached into my coat pocket and pulled out several sheets of folded computer printout.

"What's that?"

"Computer printout," I said.

Masters gave me a look of flat boredom. "You know, getting anything out of you is like pulling teeth."

"Would you please? I'd appreciate it."

"The printout?" Masters asked, doing a fair job of keeping her exasperation reined in.

"Oh, right. So ... which airport has the designation RIX—Romeo India X-ray?" I asked, wrestling with the printout.

"I think that's Riga International—Latvia," said Masters, her interest ignited. "Why?"

"This is a printout from Ramstein's air traffic control flight log for a period last year—fourteen months ago, actually. There are several flights marked out in the month of December with green highlight pen. They're all C-130s heading off to Riga—RIX. I found it in one of the boxes with a handful of flight-progress strips—the little strips of paper the air traffic controllers use to help them identify aircraft as they're handed from one flight information sector to another."

"Don't patronize me, Cooper. I'm air force too, remember?" Masters kept her eyes on the road, but I could sense it took a force of effort.

"Sorry. I was just thinking aloud, that's all. Y'know, if you listen hard enough, you can hear the gears whirring." I pointed to my forehead.

"Forget it," she said. "So . . . Riga . . ."

"Riga," I repeated. "I don't know why Scott highlighted these flights, or even if it was him who did the highlighting. It was just in with his papers . . ." I wasn't sure where I was going—round in circles, probably.

Masters turned off the road and into a broad parking lot laid out before a large, utterly charmless four-story block designed by someone who probably should have chosen another career. She pulled into a bay and turned off the ignition. "Look, I was thinking last night after I dropped you off . . . I want to talk to you—about me and General von Koeppen. Sort of clear the air."

"There's no need," I said. "Unless you know something about the guy that's going to help us crack this nut, I don't need to know." I had the feeling Masters was embarrassed about her relationship with von Koeppen. But everyone makes mistakes. Hell, I married mine. "So," I said. "Who are we seeing here?"

Masters took a breath and let it out. "A Royal Canadian Air Force major by the name of Pierre Lamont," she said.

"A Canadian. Great, I love Canadians, especially those wacky French Canadians." Actually, I don't. If there's one thing I dislike more than a Canadian, it's a French Canadian. And even the Canadians agree, which is one of their few redeeming traits. "Have you heard the one about the two young boys playing in the front yard of their Toronto home when the neighbor's

Rottweiler hops the fence and starts attacking one of the boys?"

"No," said Masters. "Do I want to?"

"We're about to visit the morgue. Humor me."

Masters looked at me in a way that said it had better be good.

"So, as I said, the neighbor's Rottweiler hops the fence and attacks one of the boys. The other boy picks up his hockey stick and smacks the dog over the back of the neck, killing it.

"News of all this gets around and soon a reporter from the *Toronto Star* shows up and talks to the young hero. 'I can see the headlines tomorrow,' he says. '"Toronto Maple Leaf Fan Uses Hockey Stick to Deliver Crushing Blow to Attacking Dog."'

"The kid replies, 'But sir, I'm not a Maple Leaf fan.'

"The reporter reconsiders and says, 'Okay, how about—"Blue Jays Fan Uses Stick to Strike Out Attacking Beast?"'

"Again the kid says, 'But I'm not a Blue Jays fan, either.'

"'Then what team *do* you like, for Christ's sake?' says the reporter.

"'I'm a Montreal Canadiens fan, sir!'

"To which the reporter says, 'Shit, well then, how about—"French Bastard Kills Neighbor's Beloved Pet?"'"

"Can we go now?" Masters said, without the hint of a smile.

"I've got others."

"No," she said, getting out of the SUV.

Masters walked briskly to the hospital's main entrance. "I've been here before," she said. "It's in the basement."

"Where else?" I followed Masters.

We took the stairwell. It got cooler as we descended, as we closed in on the Grim Reaper's rumpus room. We came out of the stairwell into a brightly lit hallway built for heavy traffic, and pushed through a set of double swing doors, the sort made from thick, translucent plastic sheeting. The air here was heavily laced with formaldehyde, top notes of human excrement, and various gastric odors. I was thinking death's deodorant.

We saw some movement, a shadow on a wall, and followed it through into a concrete cave lined with stainless-steel doors. Another room split off from this main cavern, where bodies loosely wrapped in plastic were stacked two deep on shelves from floor to ceiling. In another chamber, I could see a naked black man lying on a stainless-steel bed, dark fluids seeping into deep channels. The head and one side of the corpse were crushed flat and resembled a spreading ink stain. A man in a green coat was cutting into the man's thorax with gusto, like he was carving into a tough Thanksgiving turkey.

"Got run over by a tank," said the voice behind us. "Although that's not what killed him. Myocardial infarction. Can I help you?"

"We're looking for Major Pierre Lamont," I said, badging him.

"That'd be me."

Lamont might have had a French-sounding name but he didn't have the accent. He was painfully thin and I wondered if his job had permanently put him off his food. His skin had a yellow tinge, the color a specimen gets when it's been sitting in a jar of preservative. His hair, what remained of it, was black gristle, and his red-rimmed eyes sagged in their sockets. The guy had obviously seen far too much horror for anyone to bear and if his demeanor wasn't aware of it, at least the rest of him was. He'd clearly been down in this place too long and was in serious need of a good piece of steak and a few hours on a beach.

"Do you mind if we take a look at the body?" Masters asked.

Given that he called us, Lamont knew whose body Masters was referring to. "Body? I wouldn't call it that, but you can certainly take a look." We followed him to one of the stainless-steel doors. "Unlike Mr. Flapjack in there," he motioned toward the room where the guy who ended up as chewing gum on the bottom of a tank track was being filleted, "I can't tell you exactly what killed General Scott—put it down to a whole range of failures that happened within the split second of him being liquefied. Think roadkill."

Major Lamont had a loud, deep voice that didn't seem possible coming from a human built like a Slim Jim.

"Did you test for drugs, Major?"

"Yep. Found traces of paracetamol—maybe Scott had had a headache. Nothing else."

Masters was covering off the suicide angle. Did the general take a dose of something before he went up, knowing full well his glider would fail? Make the plunge easier?

Lamont cracked open the fridge and pulled out the tray. Inside were two square stainless-steel tubs of what looked like ruddy omelette mixture, with a few chunky knucklebones thrown in. One of the tubs had hair in it.

"*Voilà,*" Lamont said as if presenting the *plat du jour*.

"Shit," said Masters under her breath.

Lamont pushed the tubs back into the Westinghouse. "They'll need to line his coffin with plastic," he said cheerfully.

I could feel the clammy sweat, that hot and cold feeling of phobia coming over me. *This is what happens when you fly. See?* In my mind I could picture Scott plummeting in his plane, being dragged down by the hand of gravity. Except it wasn't Scott pinned in the Perspex bubble of the glider; it was me. I was "projecting," as my ex would have said—empathizing. The crash had reduced the man to a couple of bowls of pudding and all I could think about was myself, my own fears surfacing and threatening to overwhelm me. I had to get a grip, concentrate, redirect, or lose it completely. "Major," I said, "do you have a Captain François Philippe working here?"

"Did. Nice fella. Shame about what happened to him."

"What happened to him?"

"He transferred out around twelve months ago. Died in a house fire soon after."

"Oh," was all I could manage.

"Mother, father, sister—all killed. Electrical fire in the roof, apparently."

Was it that imagination of mine again or was there a fair bit of nonrandom death going on? "Do you know anything about an autopsy he performed on General Scott's son, a marine combat sergeant KIA in Baghdad?" I asked.

"Yeah, I did hear something about that. We can check the records, if you like."

"Thanks," I said. Masters was looking at me, frowning, but it was more a frown of concern for my well-being than the displeasure I was used to seeing on a woman's face. It made a nice change. I knew I looked green, like one of the many people down here gone well past their bury-by date, but the worst of it had passed. I'd be okay and I conveyed as much with a nod.

Lamont made his way through a series of chambers filled with stainless-steel racks waiting for somebody, or, should I say, some body? "You expecting a few guests?" I asked as we entered the fourth room.

"No. You've gotta remember, this place was built when the folks back home thought the Russkies were going to pour across Germany in their tanks. Turned out the only thing the Russians could pour was vodka, but how were we to know that back then? We've got enough space here for five thousand dead at any one time. These chambers are like the Energizer bunny—they just go on and on."

We passed several men and women wheeling gurneys carrying corpses covered in plastic. Many had suffered massive and obvious trauma—the wheelees, not the wheelers. "We occasionally get a little extra work from Iraq. The overload. We've certainly got the facilities, but a few more hands would be good."

I thought he was going to say he'd prefer those hands to be connected to living arms, given that we'd just passed a gurney carrying a collection of assorted detached limbs, pushed by a woman who was so blasé she could have been cruising an aisle at Wal-Mart, but he refrained. Instead, he opened a door. Warm air and light beckoned from within. We'd crossed back over into the land of the living. I never thought I'd be so pleased to see bored individuals yawning at their computers. The major took a seat behind a PC with a Garfield clinging to the side of the monitor with sucker feet, and an "I ♥ NY" sticker on the plastic frame above the screen. His screensaver was a cocker spaniel whose eyes reminded me of Lamont's—red and sad. "Okay, now, let . . . me . . . see . . ." he said as he clicked through several files and folders till he got the one he was after. His fingers clattered over the keyboard and the screen filled with a table, orange type on a black background.

"Here we go. Captain François Philippe." A list of autopsies completed by the captain during his time at Ramstein filled the screen. Lamont paged down till he came to the end—Philippe's last month at the facility. "Well, that's strange..." he said.

"What is?" said Masters, quicker than me on the draw.

"As I said, yes, I do remember Philippe talking about doing this autopsy—quietly—for General Scott on his son. I would have thought he'd have at least made a record of his findings, but there's nothing here."

"Could the record have been erased if it were on the database?" asked Masters.

"No, Major, not here. And maybe not anywhere. The program gives us some leeway to alter things while the autopsy is underway, but, once the work is done and the pathology is complete, the save button is hit and that's that. We have no access to the main database from our end. Zero. It's all hubbed back at the U.S. Department of Defense. And I doubt even those guys could change or delete things. You don't want to be screwing around with death records, otherwise how will Saint Peter know who's coming to dinner, right?"

"Okay," I said. "Can you call up the original autopsy report?"

"Sure. Let me see...Scott...Scott..."

The screen pulled up a list of Scotts. There were plenty of them who were no more, but only one Peyton.

"Nothing too out of the ordinary here," said Lamont. "Don't know why General Scott would have wanted a second opinion, but..." He shook his head. "According to this, the U.S. Army Hospital at Baghdad did the autopsy as per standard operating procedure, and he was then issued a death certificate so that the IRS could drop off and go find another host to suck on. They bagged and tagged him, put him on a plane, and sent him home."

"Cause of death?" I asked.

"Massive trauma caused by an argument with a land mine. The sergeant seems to have come off second best. Chest wounds, sliced aorta, et cetera."

"You don't know anything about Peyton Scott being decapitated?"

"No. The paperwork doesn't lie."

"Can you tell me who signed off on the autopsy?"

"Sure." He scrolled down. "A Captain Homer Veitch."

"You know him?" I asked.

Lamont glanced sideways at me. "It's a big army."

Okay, dumb question. "You don't see a lot of soldiers here who've been autopsied back in Iraq?"

"No, sir. If they've already had an autopsy performed, they don't make it down here and we don't see any paperwork. If they come to Ramstein, it's mostly because they're in transit."

"What about other autopsies Captain Veitch has performed. Can we look at records of them?"

"Sure." Lamont shrugged. His fingers stroked the keys and the screen refreshed. "Hmmm," he said.

"What?" I asked, leaning forward.

"Nothing: screen's blank. The autopsy Veitch performed on Peyton Scott is the only one he has done. None before, none since."

"What does that tell you?" I asked, needing it spelled out.

"Can't say for sure," said Lamont. "Veitch might have stepped on a land mine himself ten minutes after finishing with young Peyton and ended up under someone else's knife. The circle of life, y'know."

"Is that likely, Captain?" asked Masters.

"Not really, no, ma'am," he said.

I made a note to check on this Captain Homer Veitch, but I had a gut feeling the guy never existed.

"Anything else I can do for you, sir, ma'am?" Lamont said, swiveling in his chair to look at us both.

"You could print me out a copy of the autopsy on Peyton Scott," I said.

"Sure." Lamont called it back up on screen and hit command-print. The HP LaserJet whirred and a yellow sheet slotted into the tray.

"Anything else?" I asked Masters.

"Actually, yeah," she said. "Do you remember the photo of a series of body bags lined up on the apron here appearing in *The Washington Post*?"

"Yes, ma'am."

"Were they on their way down to you here?"

"I can't recall for sure, Special Agent, but we were getting a fair bit of overflow work from Iraq at the time."

Masters took this in.

"You done?" I asked.

"Yes, I think so," said Masters.

"Me, too. Captain, we'd appreciate it if you'd keep all this quiet."

"Keep what quiet, sir?" he replied, blinking, as if I'd just hit him with the *Men in Black* light.

Masters and I took the elevator up in silence. It was big enough to garage an Abrams Main Battle Tank, more evidence that at one time a veritable stampede of dead people was expected to come this way. I was looking forward to seeing the sunshine, but I'd have settled for sleet. It was just good to be away from that place.

I pulled out the cell when we walked into the fresh air and called OSI. I eventually got through to Flight

Lieutenant Bishop. I wanted to know whether he could look up army personnel records, and he told me that his position at air force security gave him a triple-A security rating. Or the equivalent thereof. I guessed that meant he could, so I gave him all Captain Homer Veitch's particulars, which amounted to pretty much just that—the man's name and rank.

"What did you make of all that?" asked Masters when I put the cell away.

I sucked in a lungful of fresh air gratefully, like a smoker having his first morning coffin nail, and said, "General Scott's son died a year ago. But rumor has it the sergeant's wounds didn't match the autopsy report that accompanied the body."

Masters nodded.

"And the forged autopsy signed off by Captain Homer Veitch. Who is he and why would he do that? Then there's the Belgian, Captain Philippe. He supposedly performed a second autopsy, yet there's no record of it. As far as the system's aware, Peyton Scott died of wounds suffered when his vehicle ran over a land mine. Only that doesn't exactly align with the scuttlebutt that the sergeant was decapitated."

"And the only person who can confirm this—Captain Philippe—has conveniently died in a house fire," said Masters.

"Yeah, it's all very neat," I said, "unless you happened to be one of these four dead people."

"Who's the fourth?"

"Alan Cobain. The journalist that took the photo of all the body bags."

"That's right."

Yesterday, we had one dead general. Now we had a pyramid of corpses. My mind was recalling General Scott sloshing around in his stainless-steel tubs. He hadn't died well, and neither had his son. Captain Philippe had also met his maker in a particularly nasty way. Cobain, too, died badly. I was thinking there was a lot to be said for ending it all in your sleep with a spilled tumbler of medicinal brandy and the electric blanket on—much more civilized. I was also thinking that something was rotten in Denmark or wherever things rot down, although it could also have been the formaldehyde clinging to my nasal passages.

ELEVEN

We need to go see Harmony Scott," I said as we turned onto the road. It was after eleven-thirty, and by the time we drove to K-town it would be well after midday.

"Okay," said Masters, stopping and executing a three-point turn in a gap in the traffic, "but shouldn't we at least phone ahead first?"

"What, and spoil the surprise?"

Masters glanced at me, this time without comment. She was getting used to my ways. We changed vehicles at the parking lot and took my rental. I made a protest about minimizing the wear and tear on Masters's purple people-eater, but the real reason was that I like to drive. Being a passenger makes me feel like I've lost control, an admission Brenda's Colonel Squeeze would have had a field day with. We drove through the security checkpoint and turned onto the open road.

"So what was going on with you back there?" said Masters.

"Back where?"

"In the morgue. I really thought you were going to lose it. What's that all about?"

"Nothing."

"Sure looked like something to me."

I glanced at Masters. Was she enjoying herself? Yeah, she damn well was.

"I had oatmeal for breakfast and seeing the general like that, well . . ."

"Bullshit, Cooper. You've got issues with something. Why can't you just give it up?"

Definitely enjoying herself.

Having a phobia about flying is not something an officer in the air force readily admits. I had good reasons for that phobia, too. And I was just starting to feel a little better about getting airborne—the trip across the Atlantic in the C-21 was proof of that. I only needed three sleeping pills to take me out rather than a handful. But then seeing General Scott's glider smashed into fiberglass splinters, and then the general himself—the way he'd ended up—brought it all back, my last tour in Afghanistan. And the feeling was not pleasant. I remembered the ragged fighting on the mountaintop, firing out the back of a CH-47 helo, protecting a bunch of injured U.S. Special Forces pinned down by Taliban fighters high in the mountains, me firing on them as they jumped and slid across the scree toward soldiers cut off from the main body, their knife blades slashing and glinting in the sunlight. And I remembered suddenly being knocked to the checker plate by a hit that felt as if a sledgehammer had driven a railway spike through my chest, and I was being whipped and thrashed around on the end of my lifeline like a trout fly, wheezing bubbles of foaming blood through the sucking hole in my chest, the helo in a vicious spin, going down, falling . . .

"I said are you okay?"

I realized suddenly that we had stopped and that I was sweating, hunched over the steering wheel, gripping it with white-knuckle anxiety. A truck flashed by with its horn blaring, raising in pitch as it swept past, trailing a vortex of air that rattled our windows and rocked the Mercedes. I also noticed that Special Agent Masters wasn't enjoying herself so much anymore. I eased some pressure onto the accelerator pedal and we picked up speed. I checked the rearview mirror. I could easily have caused a pileup. "Yeah, I'm okay," I said.

"No you're not," she said. "Want to talk about it?"

"Not really."

"You sure?"

"Look, maybe some night when we've drunk a bottle of something distilled in Kentucky."

"Okay."

"And we're both naked in the Jacuzzi."

Masters faced me and shook her head. "Don't you *ever* give it a rest, Cooper?"

In this age of sexual harassment, I got away with that caveman comment because I'd just damn near killed both of us, and a little levity, even if sexual in nature, seemed like small beans. But the image of Masters and me naked in the hot tub persisted. In the theater of my mind, she was sitting with her arms tightly folded across her breasts and a frown superglued to her face. Our relationship had thawed but the figurative water was still icy. But I was happy to stay in the tub because it took my mind off that morning in Afghanistan.

"So, the widow Scott," said Masters when we reached the edge of K-town after several miles spent in silence. "What do you want to do?"

"I wouldn't mind taking a snoop around outside. Do you think you can keep her occupied?"

"I'll try. How much time will you need?"

"Five minutes—ten at the most. I want to have a look at General Scott's car, the old Mustang."

"You know, Major, you are incredibly sexist," said Masters smugly.

"Am I? Why's that?"

"Why couldn't the Mustang be Mrs. Scott's car?"

"Well, I guess it could, but I doubt it."

"And why's that?"

"Because its license plate says GLIDER."

TWELVE

I watched from the car as Masters walked up the cinder path and made her way around the fountain. I lost her until she climbed the steps to the porch and stood in front of the door. She rang the bell. Rang it again. Thirty long seconds later, the door opened a fraction. I could see her having to talk her way inside. Eventually the door opened wide and the darkness behind it swallowed her.

I got out of the rental and took the driveway. The cinders crunched underfoot, so I detoured onto the grass. The neighborhood here was quiet and serene, the kind of place where the day's single biggest event was the arrival of the mailman. Off to the south, the Palatinate Forest made the hills look as if they'd been upholstered with dark green fuzz, and the usual riot of rainbows—or whatever the collective noun is for a bunch of the things—hovered overhead. The air was calm and the sun's thin light shining between the purple and gray clouds held a rumor of warmth.

The Scotts' garage was spacious. It was dry inside, and smelled of cold concrete, gasoline, and grease, the old Mustang probably contributing two out of three of those smells. There was a workbench running the full length of the back of the garage, and various woodworking tools spotted with rust and dust lay scattered over it. The skeleton of an old chair was held in the jaws of a bench vise, the job—whatever it was—half finished. Like the tools, the chair was covered with dust, layers of it. The scene reminded me of pictures I'd seen of Pompeii. Some disaster had happened here, something that had forced the carpenter to leave in a hurry and not come back. I half expected to see a plate of food, now petrified, left behind. I knew exactly what that disaster was—the clues were up on the wall: photographs, dozens of them, showing father and son enjoying quality time together. It was almost possible to chart Peyton's life through the photos. There was one of him as a baby in a nurse's arms. There was Peyton the boy, throwing a ball; Peyton, the young teen, sitting in the cockpit of some aircraft; Peyton and father, fishing; Peyton water-skiing. There was also Peyton with various girls; Peyton graduating from college; Peyton in the cockpit of Scott's glider; Peyton in the uniform of a U.S. Marine sergeant; Peyton with his squad on the biscuit-colored streets of Iraq. There was also the clipping of Alan Cobain's article "Death Row," with its sad accompanying picture. Father and son were undoubtedly close. I took the snapshot of Peyton in uniform and pocketed it.

The driver's door of the Mustang was locked, as was the passenger door. I conducted a quick search for the keys and ran my hand over the tires under the wheel arches. Nothing. I looked on the tool board, hoping to find them on a hook. The search there was also fruitless, but I found the next best thing—a thin metal bracket. I removed the chair frame from the vise and used the jaws to curl the end of the bracket into a hook. Then I opened up the space between the Mustang's window and the door panel with a screwdriver, fed the tool down into the guts of the door, and jiggled it around until I snagged what I was looking for. The button popped up and I was in.

I slid behind the Mustang's wheel and had the eerie feeling of being inside General Scott's skin. The smell of grease and vinyl—the smell of old car—was strong. I took the cell from my pocket, called up the number from the memory, and hit the green button. Seconds later, there was a muffled buzz emanating from under the seat, not on the floor, but right up inside the springs. I had to get out of the car and kneel on the floor to get the angle. The cell stopped buzzing so I had to ring again. Eventually, on the third redial, I found it: General Scott's private cell phone. There were one hundred and twenty missed calls indicated on the screen, and only one bar of battery power left. The thing had nearly lost its charge. If it had run out of gas completely, it might not have been found for a considerable time. Scott's gliding and his car were part of his other life—the one outside the base. If the cell was going to be anywhere predictable, it would be somewhere in this car. That was my theory, anyway, and the intuition had paid off. "You've still got it, pal," I said as I checked the cell's received calls.

According to the memory, there'd been only one other caller besides me. A single message had been left in voice mail, if an empty silence punctuated by breathing could be considered a message. Whoever it was on the other end had decided not to say anything and had hung up, but the automatic message service didn't realize that and kept re-calling and re-calling to let the deceased general know that he had a message. Creepy—worse, even, than looking at photos of the dead when they were alive. I checked the cell's phone book. No names or numbers had been stored there. This was like the Bat Phone: It had a single use only, and that was to call one specific person, the person who'd left the message of silence.

THIRTEEN

I followed the voices inside the house. The entry hall behind the front door was lined with polished wood panels the color and texture of desiccated cockroach. Portraits of old men and dreary landscapes painted in oils hung on the walls. If this was how the other half lived, they could have it. My one-room apartment back in Brandywine wasn't much, but at least it had a pulse.

I caught up with the widow and Special Agent Masters in what I took to be General Scott's study. The room was paneled in more dark wood, and books stocked the shelves from chest height to ceiling across three walls. Like most military pilots, General Scott also had mementos of his years flying—the ubiquitous helmet and oxygen mask, and a model of the aircraft in which he'd made his combat reputation, the Douglas Skyraider. His desk was a dark mahogany number, the color of molasses. There were several photos of Peyton, photos I was now familiar with, framed on the desk and on the bookshelves. I ran my eyes across the general's library and noted the consistent theme.

Mrs. Scott wore a black dress shrink-wrapped onto her little chicken bones, and black shoes. Her blond hair had been worked into a tight coif on top of her head, with not a strand loose. The makeup was heavy, with dark liner circling her pale gray eyes, brown lipstick, and she smelled of foundation cream, perfume, whiskey, and stale cigarettes. The overall effect was grim. She appeared to be in a mood. This wasn't something that could be interpreted from her features, for they were as empty and unruffled as a body of water in a vacuum. On the moon, say. But her tone betrayed her. "I was just telling your partner that I don't appreciate the invasion of privacy," she said, the powdered wattle of loose skin under her neck vibrating, reminding me of an aging turkey. "And who said you could just walk into my home?"

"I beg your pardon, ma'am," I said. "The door was ajar and I thought you left it that way for me. I'm sorry."

"Well, I didn't. Now, what do you want? Your partner doesn't seem able to get the hint. I have a funeral to prepare for." She fixed me with those gray lidless eyes of hers: It was vaguely like being struck with an ice pick.

"Yes, Mrs. Scott. This is an awful day for you and I'm sorry we have to intrude on it," I said in full reverse, beeping furiously. "But, as you know, your husband was a very important man. Washington wants to know why he was murdered, in case there are national security issues."

"Don't presume to tell *me* what Washington wants, Major," said Harmony, alluding to her family's position of power. "And my husband wasn't murdered. He killed himself."

"Killed himself? Why wou—"

"There's a lot you don't know about Abraham Scott. Did you know that he was having an affair, Special Agent? A tawdry affair with some slut he kept in a hotel room on the other side of town?"

She knows? "An affair—"

"If you're going to keep repeating everything I say . . ."

My jacket covered my name tag. "Special Agent Vincent Cooper, ma'am."

". . . then this conversation will be even longer and more tedious than it otherwise would be. It's obvious. Abraham killed himself because he couldn't go on without our son, Peyton. The two were very close. We were all close. Until Peyton was killed in Iraq. You do know about that, at least?" she asked with a frigid smile of condescension.

"Yes."

"Your assistant here—or are you *her* assistant . . . ?"

"We're a team."

Masters nodded.

"How nice. Well, your teammate informed me yesterday that Abraham's glider had been sabotaged."

"That's right. We believe—"

"Well, I can't tell you how many times Abraham told me he had no intention of dying of old age pushing around a walker. He wanted to end it in that glider. Said so many times. It's obvious he fixed the plane himself to make that happen."

"Are you sure, ma'am? Suicide?" Masters and I exchanged a glance.

"I knew my husband. That's what happens after twenty-four years of marriage—you get to know someone. How well do *you* know him?"

Having met Harmony Scott twice now, what I couldn't understand was why General Scott hadn't killed himself sooner. "Not very well, ma'am." The lady was a bully, just like her dear old dad, Vice President Toe Cutter. "Did your husband know you knew about his affair?"

"If he did, he never mentioned it," replied Mrs.

Scott. "It's not the sort of thing a husband talks about with his wife. Not among people of my generation, at any rate."

"Then if he didn't tell you, how did you know about it?" asked Masters, tag-teaming.

"Because, as I said, after twenty-four years of marriage, you know."

"And knowing about it, or sensing it—did that change your relationship with the general?" Masters continued fearlessly.

Harmony turned her ice picks on Masters and I could see my partner shift uneasily as they hacked into her. It was a tough question. It contained the hint that we were sniffing around for a motive for murder, and that the dead man's wife might possibly be considered a suspect.

"What in hell's name are you insinuating?" she asked, her voice going up in volume and pitch like a ripsaw biting into a nail hidden in the wood.

"Mrs. Scott, did your husband ever talk to you about a second autopsy performed on your son?" I intervened, changing tack and sparing Masters a mauling.

"What? No," said Harmony, diverted.

"He never mentioned it?"

"Never."

"Well, thank you for your time, Mrs. Scott," I said. "We're sorry to bother you."

Her lips pursed and she walked out of the study and down the hallway toward the front door, which was framed by bloodred light streaming through stained-glass windows. We were expected to follow. Harmony Scott opened the door and became a black silhouette against the daylight pouring in, and, from the set of her body—one hand on the bone of her hip—an impatient one. I made my way quickly down the hall, overtaking

Masters, not because I was keen to comply with Harmony Scott's body language, but because of General Scott's cell in my pocket. It was ringing, vibrating against my leg with an incoming call.

The door banged shut behind us as I fumbled with the phone. The number on its screen I recognized as the one previously captured by the cell, the number for a landline in Kaiserslautern. As I put it to my ear Masters raised her eyebrows at me as if to ask, "Is that Scott's phone?"

I nodded. "Hello? *Morgen? Ja?*" I said, covering all the bases.

Silence.

"Hello?"

More silence.

"Hello!" I took the question out of my voice and replaced it with a demand. The caller was still there, trying to decide whether to hang up or answer. Mine was obviously not the voice the person on the other end of the line expected to hear. I decided to gamble. "This is Special Agent Cooper. Your phone number has been previously logged on this cell and a police car is right now on the way to your front door. It will be there within three minutes."

I hoped the caller had seen enough police television shows to believe this bullshit.

More silence and then, suddenly, "Hello." It was a woman's voice, uncertain, reluctant.

"Who are you? What is your name?" I didn't for a second think these questions would be answered, but then the woman said, "Varvara. My name is Varvara Kadyrov."

FOURTEEN

I was getting to know the stretch of road between Ramstein AB and K-town pretty well, but the town itself was a different matter. Masters took the pilot's seat.

"The address puts her in the historic part—the old town," she told me.

"Who lives there?" I asked.

"In the old town? Locals with money, and staff officers without dependents. Von Koeppen—people like that."

I glanced at her. This was our first break. Not knowing where von Koeppen lived, but finding this woman, the one General Scott was apparently putting a hump into.

"Was the phone where you thought it would be?" asked Masters, overtaking a line of cabs, sitting on the horn as she passed so that they wouldn't pull out in front of us.

"Pretty much," I said. That won a smile from Masters, a genuine one this time.

"You're good at this," she said.

I can deal with abuse; compliments are hard. I ignored it and instead took the photo of Peyton Scott out of my pocket, the one I'd taken from the garage, and propped it on top of the dash. "We need to find out more about this guy."

Masters weaved through the traffic like a fighter

pilot on a bandit's six. "Mrs. Scott was lying when she said she knew nothing about that second autopsy."

"Yeah," I said. I felt that, too.

"And her coming out with the news about her husband having an affair—what did you make of that?"

"I think she said it to throw us. It was almost like she enjoyed telling us. She knows we're going to find out about this other woman. I'd say she was just getting in first, sort of taking the wind from our sails. Question is, why the games?"

Masters nodded. We were making headway, and not just on the case. "What about the suicide thing?" she asked.

"I guess it's possible."

"But do you think it's likely?"

I considered that before answering. It was the question I'd been chewing on myself, and having difficulty swallowing. "Last night I'd have said definitely not, but now?" I shrugged. "I'm not a hundred percent sure either way, but not because of anything the widow has said. We know that Scott was badly broken up about his son's death. It hit him hard." In other words, the palings were up my ass as I sat up there on top of the fence. I remembered the photos of Peyton on the garage wall and on display in the study. The collections were like shrines. But there was something odd about the photos, something niggling at me. I had that feeling. The one where I know the answer will come. It just takes time. Though hopefully not a year's time, when I'm lying on a beach somewhere.

"But there was nearly thirteen months between the death of the son and the death of the father. If General Scott was suicidal over the news of Peyton, why would the old man take so long to end it all?"

"I don't know," I said. That was a good question. "Maybe we can ask Varvara. She might know."

"Did you notice the books in the general's study?" she asked. "War history of the last century—almost every single title."

"The guy was a general. I'd have been surprised if he had a reference library on macramé," I said. I'd noticed his books, too. He was a big fan of WWII, especially of the conflict in the Pacific.

"I took some pics of his study, his books, when Harmony wasn't looking." Masters accelerated into a gap in the traffic and then hit the brakes to avoid crashing into the tail end of a semi.

"Do you always drive like this?" I asked.

"When it's a rental." Masters appeared oblivious to this near-death experience.

"Remind me to insist we take your car next time. Why the sudden rush?"

"You're the one who said we'd be there in three minutes. And what kind of name is Varvara, anyway? Where does a name like that come from?"

We pulled into a parking space outside a newish apartment building that was mostly glass. Actually, it was mostly sky and rainbows if I was to be poetic about it—reflections thereof. Varvara had said she lived on the seventh floor, which Masters confirmed with a simple directory assistance call to the local phone company. Apartment 703. We took the elevator to the seventh floor. The building seemed deserted, although that was probably because most of its residents were at work. Mindless Muzak filtered through hidden speakers and was sucked into the thick carpet underfoot.

Apartment 703 was a short walk from the elevator. I rang the doorbell and waited. Varvara was taking her time. I knocked. I heard a rustle behind the door and a shadow filtered across the spy hole. "Who are you?" came a muffled female voice.

"Varvara Kadyrov? OSI. You're expecting us."

"Show me ID."

Masters and I shared a look. We reached into our coats, pulled our badges, and held them up where they could be seen. The lady was nervous. After a moment or two of hesitation, chains and latches were released and the door opened.

My first impressions of our hostess were colored by the polished nickel-plated Colt 45 that appeared the size of a cannon in her petite hand, which she pointed at my face, chest, groin, and face again as she waved it about. It was a ceremonial pistol, probably the general's, but it could kill just as effectively as any ten-dollar throw-down. "You come alone?" she asked.

"Yes," I said.

Varvara's eyes swept from me to Masters, and then back to me. She was having trouble believing me.

"We're alone. Now put the gun down," said Masters in a soothing voice, trying to hypnotize the woman with calmness. It didn't seem to be working.

"You have come to kill me," she declared, hand flexing on the grip, squeezing it, finger squirming inside the trigger guard. The hammer was cocked and I was starting to sweat. I've been shot a couple of times and I've learned it's not pleasant.

"No, we're here to ask you some questions," I told her. "Nice, *easy* questions."

"Abraham said you would come." Her eyes flicked from me to Masters and back again, not sure who to settle on.

"Put the gun down, Ms. Kadyrov," I said. She didn't hear me. The fear in her eyes told me that. Instead she took a two-handed grip on the weapon waggling inches from my nose and turned her face away, either preparing herself for the crushing explosion to come, or to shield her face from mine as it splattered back at her after being dissolved by the slug. I snatched out with my left hand as she clamped her eyes shut, a reflex grab. I wrapped my fingers around the gun and my pinky slipped between hammer and pistol body. Her muscles contracted and the hammer slammed home, the pain it caused completely out of proportion to the almost inaudible *chick* sound. "Oh, shit!" I shouted. My damn finger might as well have been closed in a car door. "Jesus," I yelled a couple of times as I did a circuit of her room with the Colt dangling from my pinky. I cocked the hammer and released the digit, then seated the hammer back. I held the gun by my side while I shook my hand and completed a second lap of the room. "Fucking, fuck fuck!" I said. I examined my finger—all the skin had been stripped around the second joint and the pad was already blowing up with a blister full of blood. I wriggled it. Nothing broken. I removed the seven-round magazine, pulled back the slider, and ejected the round in the spout. That extra round told me Abraham Scott had loaded it for her.

Masters had Ms. Kadyrov against the wall, her forearm jammed up against her neck and one of her arms twisted behind her back.

"Let her go," I said.

"What?"

"Let her go."

"But she—"

"I don't have any cuffs and neither do you, Special Agent. She's not a suspect. Let her go." It was obvious that Varvara Kadyrov was scared witless of something. Someone. Masters released the woman, who continued to lean against the wall, knocking a Miró print askew. She was crying silently, her back convulsing in short spasms. She turned and sagged against the wall, sobbing, her hand covering her mouth and nose. Masters looked at me, uncertain of what to do. I motioned at her with a waggle of the gun to comfort the woman. She put her arm around Ms. Kadyrov's shoulders, brought her across to a brown leather sofa in the middle of the room, and seated her.

"We are special agents with the air force, Ms. Kadyrov. Police," I said, giving my hand another shake. "We're here to investigate the death of General Scott. It was me who spoke to you on his cell." The day's edition of the *Trib* was on the coffee table; her late lover's photo was on the front page. I walked into the kitchen, filled a glass with water, carried it back, and put it in front of her. The apartment was small but light, the furniture all new. The place could have been a spread in an Ikea catalogue. Everything had probably been bought at the same time, even the Miró prints, when Varvara Kadyrov moved into this place.

Varvara leaned forward and took the glass. I noticed for the first time how strikingly beautiful she was. What is it with this place, I wondered. Do they put down ugly people at birth here, or just refuse them entry? "Ms. Kadyrov, did General Scott tell you people might come to kill you?"

"Yes," she said, sipping the water. I gestured at the newspaper in front of her. "You knew the general was dead, yet you called his cell."

"I wanted to know if it had been found, so that I could be prepared."

My pinkie throbbed, reminding me. Yeah, she'd been prepared to blow my head off. The woman looked at me over the rim of the glass and I was struck almost dumb by the bluest pair of eyes I'd ever seen, a concentrated blue that appeared to project particles of blueness.

I swallowed and tried not to stare. Her hair was thick and so black it even shone blue in places, and fell loose to the small of her back. She wore a thin blue cardigan over a fitted pink T-shirt, faded hipster jeans, and Nikes. "Are you Russian?" I asked. Her accent was unusual—different from German.

"Latvian."

"From Riga?" Masters asked.

Varvara nodded and wiped her eyes with the back of a hand. Masters and I exchanged a glance. *The highlighted flights on the ATC management printout. RIX. Riga.*

"Who would be trying to kill you?"

"People . . . I don't know."

I tried a different approach. "Ms. Kadyrov, were you and General Scott lovers?"

The woman shook her head vehemently. "No."

"What was your relationship with him?"

"He helped me, took me away. I was grateful."

How grateful? I wondered. "What did he take you away from?"

"Riga."

"Is that where you met?"

"Yes."

"How did you meet?" Women who looked like Varvara didn't hang around the PX. Well, not the PX in *my* air force, at any rate.

"At a club. My boss introduced us."

"What kind of club?"

"A table-dancing club. I was a dancer."

I looked at Varvara with fresh eyes. Yeah, a stripper in a titty bar. That fit, possibly one of the few things that did in this case so far. General Abraham Scott—you ol' dog, you . . .

"Are the people he took you away from the same people who killed him?" Masters asked, taking the questioning off in a direction away from lingerie and poles.

"No. Different people, but the same."

I was starting to feel confused. I hoped that English being a second language for Varvara was where the confusion lay, rather than in deliberate obfuscation.

"Abraham gave me the gun. He said they would try to kill him and that they might come for me."

They.

"Abraham was a good man. I loved him as a father," she said, picking up the *Trib*, looking at the photo of the smiling but now very dead Abraham Scott, and then dropping it back on the table. "Will you kill them?" she asked.

"I don't know who *they* are, Ms. Kadyrov. We were hoping you could help us out on that," I said.

"The establishment killed him—the same people also killed his son."

"But he was killed in Baghdad," Masters said.

"Yes. That's where they killed him."

They, again. I asked once more. "Who are *they*, Ms. Kadyrov?"

Varvara shook her head. "I told you, the establishment."

The establishment. The ubiquitous *they*. The *them* to our *us*.

"Did General Scott talk to you about his son's death?" Masters asked.

"Yes. He was very sad, and then, when he found out, he was very angry."

"Found out what?" I asked, playing good cop–dumb-ass cop. No prizes for guessing which one I was.

"That they had him killed. I can't tell you more. You should ask Abraham's wife. Harmony."

This raised Masters's eyebrows. "What does Harmony know?"

"She knows everything. Abraham was in Riga when his wife phoned him with the news. He was very upset. He loved his son very much. He flew home immediately. I saw him again a week later. He was a very different man. Angry, and so very sad."

"Was Abraham a regular visitor to Riga?"

"He came several times."

"Why?"

"I don't know," Varvara said, draining the glass.

Looking at Ms. Kadyrov, I had a pretty good idea why. It was obvious we were spinning our wheels here. I wondered whether it was worth attaching a security detail to the Latvian. Were her fears for her safety just a little paranoia, or did these people, whoever *they* were, want her dead? And why would anyone want to kill her? Unless she knew more than she was prepared to divulge, I couldn't see that she'd be a threat to anyone, with the possible exception of Harmony Scott, who, it seemed, knew exactly in whose sauce her husband was dipping his salami. I didn't buy the whole "we were just friends" routine Varvara Kadyrov put on about her relationship with Scott. It was pretty obvious Abraham was bumping uglies with this Russian doll whenever the opportunity arose, so to speak. Christ, who wouldn't? The woman was about as drop-dead as they came, and, with an accent that made her sound like a Bond girl, she was fantasy on a stick. "Thank you for your time, Ms. Kadyrov," I said. "Oh, and I'll be keeping this." I pulled the big silver Colt out of my pocket, flashing it. "But we'll assign security to guard your apartment."

"Yes, thank you. I do not feel safe," she said.

I put a card from the Pensione Freedom on the table and wrote both Masters's cell number and mine on the reverse side. "If you think of anything that might help this investigation, please call either of us," I said, gesturing at Masters with a tilt of my head. "Also, we might have some more questions at a later time so we'd appreciate it if you'd let us know if you're going somewhere."

"Yes, of course," Varvara said. "I'm sorry about your finger. Is it okay?"

"I'll live," I said. I reached into my pocket and pulled out the general's cell. It had my prints all over it and wouldn't be much use as evidence. More important were the calls he made on it, and we could get a record of those from the phone company. "You might as well have this," I said, handing the cell to her. General Scott certainly had no more use for it.

"Thank you. Good-bye," said Varvara Kadyrov as the door clicked shut. Masters and I walked down the hall to a Muzak version of a Ricky Martin tune, which, come to think of it, didn't make it any worse.

"We should have arrested her," said Masters as we waited for the elevator.

"Why?" I asked. "What for?"

"Assault with a deadly weapon, for one thing. I don't appreciate being threatened with a loaded gun."

"She was terrified," I said. "And I'd say Abraham Scott was the only friend she had in this country. As for the gun, from the way she held it, I don't think she's ever fired one." *And it wasn't you she was pointing it at.* "Also, I think there's more she can tell us. We just need to reassure her we're the good guys, rather than on the side of Doctor No."

"Who?"

"Never mind." My tooth was aching and the cell in my pocket was buzzing. I answered it, listened for a handful of seconds, and then dropped it back in my pocket.

"Who was that?" inquired Masters.

"Bishop. I think it's quite possible people would have noticed Captain Veitch dissecting Peyton Scott," I said.

"Because . . . ?"

"It's not often you see a dead guy performing an autopsy on another dead guy. Something like that would probably draw an audience."

"What?"

"Bishop just told me Captain Homer Veitch had been dead almost a month before he supposedly performed the autopsy on Peyton Scott. He was killed in a car-bomb incident in Fallujah."

FIFTEEN

We set a course to the OSI building. I drove. I was now doubting the breakthrough we really needed on this case would be found at Ramstein. All the roads seemed to lead back to Peyton. The news about Veitch was just more confirmation. Varvara, Fischer, Aleveldt, even Harmony in her way, had said Scott went off the rails when his son was killed.

I checked the time. It was getting late. What was left of General Scott was by now on a plane heading back home for the funeral in a leakproof container. The air force was giving him the big send-off, buried with full military honors. I guessed Harmony Scott would probably be with her husband's remains, accompanying them home. The other feeling I had was that, with the possible exceptions of Varvara and Gruyere, there wasn't a lot of overt enthusiasm to find out what had happened to General Scott, and why. Maybe that was my imagination. I was surprised that his widow and his second-in-command weren't a little more persistent about uncovering the whys and wherefores surrounding the man's death. I could see, though, that Harmony at least had a good reason for happily saying farewell to her husband without shedding a tear: one Varvara Kadyrov. And as for von Koeppen, according to his PA, Sergeant Fischer, he couldn't see much past a mirror, especially if his face was in it. Having an impressive individual like Scott sitting in the corner office would have put a serious damper on his id. But were these respective issues for each party motive enough for murder? And what of Varvara's mysterious "people"?

Masters and I were both mulling events over in our minds, which cut the conversation down to zero. I turned onto the freeway and activated the cruise control.

Masters was the first to break the silence. "So let's go through what we know, putting it in some sort of chronological order."

"Brains before beauty, Special Agent," I said, giving her the floor.

Masters pushed on. "Okay, so General Scott notes some odd flights to Riga and decides to check them out. We don't know what he finds there. Shortly thereafter, Peyton is killed in Iraq. For some reason—another unknown—Scott doesn't believe the autopsy report. He checks his son's body bag and finds that the kid's head is missing, which doesn't match up with the fine print on the official death certificate. He souvenirs the son's toe tag and gets a second opinion from a Captain Philippe—"

"Who's immediately transferred so that he can arrive home in time to be barbequed along with the rest of his family in a house fire," I added.

Masters nodded. "And then Scott disappears for a few weeks. He turns up in Riga at the end of that period to see Varvara, who he then brings back to Ramstein. A few months after that, the photo of the body bags on the Ramstein apron finds its way into the papers under the byline of a journalist who subsequently turns up dead. Somewhere along the way, Harmony Scott finds out about Varvara—"

"So, full of jealousy, she sneaks onto the base and

tampers with her womanizing husband's glider to make its wings fall off," I said as we pulled up at a Ramstein Air Base security post.

I gave the French corporal our CAC cards to scan. He passed them through the machine, handed them back, and then waved us on. "And everyone lives happily ever after, unless you have pretty much anything to do with Peyton, in which case you seem to die in an unfortunate accident." Our hypothesis had more holes in it than a roadside speed sign in Alabama. "Okay, I'd like to chase down several things," I said. "One: What did Scott uncover in Riga, apart from Varvara? Two: Where did he disappear to in the weeks after Peyton was killed? Three: Why didn't Scott believe the autopsy report that accompanied his son's body back from Iraq? Four: How is the U.S. Army managing to get dead guys to perform autopsies? And five: Why are those police putting Scott's records in the back of that Humvee?"

"What?" said Masters, followed by, "Shit!" when she saw that the general's records—the ones we'd secured for our investigation—were indeed being carted out of the OSI offices. I pulled up behind the Humvee in question and we both jumped out. "Airman! Stop there!" Masters snarled at one of the NCMPs coming out the door with a cardboard box in his arms. She positioned herself to block his path. I had to admit, my partner was growing on me. She knew what was going on and stood up to anyone. Even me.

"Keep it moving," said General von Koeppen, striding through the door, herding another airman carrying boxes before him.

Masters stood aside and let von Koeppen and the MP pass. Okay, so she stood up to *almost* everyone.

"Excuse me, General, but these records have been secured as part of the OSI investigation—over which you have no jurisdiction—into the murder of General Scott." I sounded righteous even to me.

"But it seems there was no murder, Special Agent." Von Koeppen pushed past carrying the laptop I recognized as belonging to Scott.

"What?" I said, the best question I could manage in the confusion.

"A suicide note has been found. It seems Mrs. Scott was correct. General Scott killed himself. I have taken it upon myself to ensure that his personal effects are returned to his grieving widow forthwith. I expect your new orders will come through soon enough. In fact, I believe there's a C-5 heading back to Washington, D.C., in a couple of hours. Perhaps it might suit you to be on it."

Von Koeppen seemed keen for me to get lost. I thought he was going to offer to drive me out to the plane then and there. But instead he climbed into the front seat of one of the Humvees and slammed the door.

I admit that this unexpected turn had caused me a mental meltdown. If there were flies about, my mouth would probably have been wide enough to catch them. What goddamn suicide note? Where had it come from? Why were we, the investigating team, apparently the last to know about it? And why would a lieutenant general, a three-star, get so involved with the details of this case that he would actually come down here to supervise the removal of potential evidence? And as for the suicide note? Suicide notes are usually only left behind in movies. In the real world, most people who decide to take their own lives do so because they believe their lives are worthless, or that existence is futile. Either way, they are usually of the view that no one will give a shit if they turn off the lights themselves.

Leaving a "good-bye, cruel world" note usually doesn't fit with this state of mind.

"They just marched in and told us to stop work, sir," said a British voice beside me as I watched the Humvees roll away. It was Peter Bishop. "Just like when you're taking an exam and your time's up. Only these people made their point with M-16s."

"Do we have a copy of this so-called suicide note?" I asked.

"Actually, we have the original," replied Bishop as he handed me a plastic evidence bag containing an envelope and a single sheet of white unlined paper. Several neat lines were handwritten on it, the sort of writing you'd expect a general to have—careful, controlled.

"Do you mind if I have a look?" asked Masters. I passed it to her and she read it aloud.

> *"5/17*
> *Harmony,*
> *I don't want to do this anymore. Things are so*
> *complicated on the one hand, but so simple on the*
> *other. Where did we go wrong? It wasn't just Peyton.*
> *I'm sorry for the pain I've caused you, will cause you*
> *with my selfishness.*
> *Abe"*

Short and sweet, with the whiff of vaudeville about it. And if it was genuine, which I doubted, after what, a quarter-century of marriage, it wasn't exactly a fond farewell. But then, I'd met the addressee.

"General von Koeppen told us Mrs. Scott found it beside his bed, tucked into one of the books he was reading," said Bishop. "She was picking up some things and it fell out."

Suicide. We'd discounted it, and yet here was a note supposedly written in the general's own hand, heavily implying he intended to leave Planet Earth permanently. My cell rang. "Hello," I snapped, annoyed, distracted.

"General Gruyere."

"General," I said, surprised, sounding like she'd just jumped out from behind a door and given me a scare.

"A sad business. Suicide."

"Only just heard about it myself, General." News was sure traveling damn fast between Germany and the U.S. these days.

"You're Johnny-on-the-spot, Special Agent," she said. "What do you think?"

"I wouldn't mind running some tests on the note *allegedly* left by General Scott, ma'am."

"Allegedly? Didn't his wife find it?"

"Yes, ma'am."

"The wife he'd been married to for twenty-four years."

"The same, ma'am."

"Don't you think she'd be able to recognize her own husband's handwriting by now?"

"Yes, ma'am."

"So why the hesitation?"

Good question. Why *was* I quibbling? We had no evidence at all that contradicted the note in my hand—that Scott had taken his own life. It was unlikely, but he *could* have tampered with his own glider. The business with Peyton, the affair with Varvara . . . Was all that enough to make Scott take a high-altitude dive into the earth? I couldn't answer those questions with any satisfaction. And so, packing up and heading home just didn't feel right.

"Special Agent Cooper?"

"I'm not sure, General."

"Do you suspect foul play?"

Well, did I? "Can I speak honestly, ma'am?"

"You may," said Gruyere.

"There's a lot going on here with this case and we, Special Agent Masters and I, we don't know where it's going. I have to tell you, ma'am, before this note turned up, several things were looking pretty iffy."

"Like what?"

I laid it out for her—the autopsy, Peyton, the circle of death that seemed to be closing around General Scott, Captain Veitch, Riga. I also told her about Varvara. When I'd finished, I felt like reminding her that I'd only been on the job here a couple of days. That's because, in the telling, I knew that what we had was thin.

"Well, Vincent," she said, unconvinced, using the name only my mother called me by, "you can leave Special Agent Masters to tie up any loose ends. I think it's fair to say this has stopped being a murder investigation."

I could sense the relief in Gruyere's voice. With the exception of the question of the anomalous autopsy and the mysterious Captain Veitch, Masters and I had turned up little. As she saw it, General Scott had ceased to be a critical cog in the well-oiled and highly lethal U.S. war machine. She believed that he had become—for reasons that had the whiff of sex and betrayal about them—a fallible and frightened man. And he had killed himself. No need for a homicide cop to hang around when no homicide had been committed.

In short, she wanted me home.

"No need to hurry," she added. "Take the evening off and we'll see you back Stateside tomorrow."

Gee, thanks. "Well, that's all, folks," I said to Masters

after the call was terminated. She'd been close by, frowning, listening to my side of the conversation, not needing the blanks filled in. She could guess. Flight Lieutenant Bishop, though, had been standing out of earshot. He wandered over when he saw that I was no longer speaking into my coat sleeve. "Thanks for all your help, Peter," I said, putting out my hand.

"So, we're done, sir?" he said as we shook.

"And dusted," I replied.

We saluted, and that was the end of my investigation into the death of General Abraham Scott. The Brit wandered back inside the OSI building. Masters would see through the remaining details, just as Gruyere had said.

"Can I give you a lift back to K-town, Vin?" Masters was getting all chummy now that it seemed she'd be getting rid of me.

"Thanks, but no thanks. Have to return the rental, anyway."

"Look, I know we started out rough," she said, "but I think I misjudged you."

"I doubt it," I said.

She smiled, and I don't think I ever wanted to kiss a woman as much as I wanted to kiss Anna Masters at that moment, take her in my arms and go into liplock until we both needed a Chap Stick. Perhaps it was the sudden change in my status at Ramstein.

"So, do you believe he killed himself?" she asked.

"Not a chance," I said.

SIXTEEN

It was still light when I arrived at the Pensione Freedom. I'd returned the rental, eaten at a local restaurant that served something vaguely reminiscent of macaroni and cheese, and, by the time I'd finished, I was ready to put the day in the past tense. My tooth was playing up again, probably because there was nothing to distract it, and the codeine-and-clove combo was running out of steam.

The drunken backpackers I'd encountered the day before were giggling and guffawing in the foyer when I went in—stoned, by the look of them. They must have read the sign out front and obviously, although they weren't U.S. servicemen, were hoping to get laid. I considered spoiling their fantasy and explaining that the only thing getting screwed at this hotel was the English language, but thought better of it. They were on life's adventure. Let them discover its idiosyncrasies on their own.

I went up to my room, showered, shaved, popped more painkillers, rolled the toothbrush around two-thirds of my mouth, and crawled into bed. I lay there for a time, staring at the ceiling, considering my last conversation with General Gruyere. She wanted hard facts, evidence—things in short supply. I could tell she wasn't interested in what my gut was telling me. And I had a fair idea why. Harmony Scott's dear old dad lived just up the road from Andrews AFB. There'd be enormous pressure to get the case of Abraham Scott's death resolved, and a suicide verdict was neater than murder. And so it goes. I closed my eyes and for some reason the parade of Peyton Scott photos on the workbench and in Scott's study drifted through my mind.

Many combat vets have a recurring dream that takes them back to events they'd rather forget, only imagination has made the memories even worse, twisting them into a frightening parody of reality. I'm no exception. Mine goes something like this: The sky is dark blue when I look up into it because I'm at altitude, close to space, and the air is as brittle as thin ice. I've come in by CH-47, a massive twin-rotor helo that's about as big as a shipping container and slightly less aerodynamic. I'm perched on a hilltop inside the Pakistan border with half a dozen infantrymen. My mission is to plant a pineapple tree, which our pilots will use to help them line up on so that they can bomb a nest of scorpions. (For the pineapple tree, read radio beacon, and those scorpions are Taliban and al-Qaeda insurgents. I don't know why a pineapple tree, but the scorpions at least make some sense.) I dig the hole required to plant the tree with a pick, breaking through the frozen rocky sand, and the infantry guys are crouched in a ring around me, their weapons pointing out.

The next time I look up, the infantry are being ripped apart by these scorpions, big fuckers, which suddenly morph into ragheads with eight arms and legs wielding steel blades. Heads are parted from shoulders; my men are being quartered by these creatures of subconscious gene-splicing. The helo is circling, trailing a thick gray rope I realize is smoke. It has been hit. I see a man in a hatch firing a machine gun and the glowing red tracers accelerate as they close the distance between us, smashing into these "talibugs." Some are hit and they roll around squeaking while yellow stuff oozes out of them. I lift up my foot and there's one squashed into the tread under my shoe. Don't ask me how this can be, given the man-sized dimensions of the creatures—this is a dream, right?

So anyway, the helo attempts a landing but is driven off by enemy fire. And then suddenly, from a neighboring hillside, a fusillade of incoming lead. I somehow know it's half a dozen Australian Special Air Service soldiers over there, across the valley. Snipers. They've worked their way into a position that gives them a clear line of fire and are picking off the scorpion/Taliban creatures. The helo circles before landing on the hill and the machine-gunner in the hatchway is shot and tumbles, dangling out the back of the aircraft from his safety harness like a tea bag. The CH-47 touches down. The four of us still alive and capable of walking drag our dead and wounded to its ramp, shooting as we go. A head comes off the man beside me and rolls away down the hill, gathering speed as if it's a bowling ball. A scorpion is among us. I turn and empty my clip into the freak show.

I take a bullet in the chest and another under my arm an instant later. The pain burns and I feel like I'm being dismembered alive with a blowtorch. I drag two more bodies up onto the ramp and collapse.

The next thing I know, I'm lying on the open ramp, flying between the hills, but the helo is out of control, bucking and diving. I'm rolling around, close to falling off, out the back. I know I'm going to die, but I always wake up alive.

* * *

I sat up in the dark, sweating and shivering. There was noise from the main street finding its way through the closed window. My conscious mind went over the blanks in the dream, filling them in. Just two of us escaped the scorpions' nest we'd been set down on. But fate hadn't finished with us. Our helo took more hits. The pilot was killed instantly, the copilot was fatally wounded. The CH-47 made a crash landing on the valley floor and somehow managed not to burst into flames. The Aussie SAS guys on the hill sniped at the Taliban and al-Qaeda fighters, picking them off one by one as they tried to reach us, scrabbling across the scree, knives flashing in the sun, bent on separating more heads from their rightful owners. A Cobra gunship arrived after twenty minutes, shot up the remainder of the enemy, and then flew overwatch till another CH-47 came by to pick up the survivors. Or, should I say, survivor. Me.

I needed air. The bedside clock said it was just after ten P.M. I made my way to the window and opened it. It'd been raining. I breathed deeply in the hope of ridding my mind of the scorpions and getting my heart rate back under control. The night smelled of wet road and car exhaust. The street below was a procession of slow lights reflecting on its mirrored surface. I recognized one of the vehicles parked opposite the pensione: a purple Mercedes. I'd seen only one of those in this town. Was Special Agent Masters staking me out? There was a soft tap on the door. I was naked. I threw on a pair of boxers. Who else could it be? I opened the door. "Hey, what are you doing he—" I said. The words caught in my throat.

It took a moment for my brain to adjust and recognize the woman silhouetted in the light of the hallway. Perhaps it was because she was dressed so differently this time, in a fashionable raincoat that ended above the knee and was cinched tight around her waist. The delicate silver high heels on her feet made her taller than I remembered. Her straight black hair was tousled with that postcoital unruliness, and, instead of a gun, this time she pointed a retractable umbrella in my direction.

"So, are you asking me in?"

"Sure," I said, stepping aside. I felt underdressed in my boxers.

Varvara closed the door behind her and removed her coat. It crumpled to the floor. The Latvian woman stood naked in her high heels in front of me, and my concerns about whipping on some extra clothes evaporated.

"It's cold in here," she whispered, stroking an erect nipple with her fingertips.

"Is it?" I said.

She took a step forward and slipped a cold hand inside my shorts, instantly finding what she was looking for. It would have been hard to miss. My endocrine system was going nuts, dumping a pharmacopeia of hormones into my bloodstream, and the ability to think rationally was rapidly going down. A part of my brain said, *Give in to it, pal. It's been a long time and you're in danger of reclaiming your virginity.* Another part said, *No! She's part of an investigation and you don't do that kind of thing, remember?* To which the first part hit back, *The investigation's over, pal.*

Varvara led the way to the bed, in total control. She pushed me down and knelt beside me, her hair tickling the skin of my lower belly. Any resistance I might have had dissolved when I felt the heat of her mouth close around me. The question of why Varvara had decided to come here and fuck the daylights out of me was intriguing, but I was convinced to put it on hold, at least for a little while.

"What happened here?" Varvara asked, her head on my shoulder as her fingers traced the puckered scar of the bullet wound on my chest.

"A birthmark," I said. I was feeling light-headed, filled with a warm, sleepy glow. I sensed her slip out of bed.

A light came on, throwing a wedge of yellow onto the bedroom floor. My mind wandered. Maybe the promise in the Pensione Freedom's slogan was accurate after all. Varvara had just provided me with landmark sex, sex I would happily build a monument on and conduct tourist buses to.

She padded back to the bed. "I like the lights on, don't you?"

"Only when the scenery's spectacular," I said, my eyes watching her. Her body was disturbingly spectacular, almost too good to be real, like that of a life-size Barbie doll.

"Do you like what you see?"

"Yes," I said, calling it as I saw it. Her legs were long and smooth and her breasts were on the large side, although perfectly in proportion to her height. They were firm as only a young woman's can be, the nipples large, pink, and permanently hard, apparently. But it was her waist that was truly extraordinary. It was tiny; my fingertips almost touched when I wrapped my hands around her.

She pulled back the sheets and straddled me. "Did you know that in Riga there are eight women for every man?"

"Sounds like paradise," I said.

She laughed. "Yes, if you are a man. But if you are a woman, you need a . . . a . . . I think it's called a gimmick?"

"What do you mean?"

"There are too many women, many of them beautiful. I am also Russian. My grandparents were resettled in Riga by Stalin after the war. In their day, life was okay. The Russians were the rulers. But today," she shrugged, "it is a different story. The Russians are no longer welcome in Latvia. So, I was a Russian and a woman—I needed a gimmick to survive there. I am luckier than many. I have good genes and men find me attractive. I learned to dance, and then I met a man, a Chechen, called Alu Radakov. They say he is a separatist leader. A powerful man in Riga. He liked the way I danced and promised to make me rich."

"How was he going to do that?"

"He owned clubs where women dance on tables. Alu had me improved so that men would find me more attractive."

"What?" I asked, unable to completely expunge the horror from my voice. "What do you mean by improved?"

"Implants here and here," she said, pointing to her cheeks, chin, and then playfully giving her bare butt a slap, "collagen injections, breast aug . . . aug—"

"Augmentation."

"Yes, that's it—and liposuction. My face is my own, but I have been body-sculpted, an implant here and there. And, of course, I've had ribs removed."

"This Alu guy had your ribs removed?" I said, now fully aghast.

"Yes. Don't you like my waist? See how narrow it is." Varvara tracked the curves of her upper body, moving her hands slowly down and over her breasts, cupping them, and then down her midriff.

My mind was struggling with this. Varvara's body had been scarred, but not in the name or pursuit of some greater cause as mine arguably had been. She'd been surgically remodeled by some monster so that fat businessmen and politicians would slip more dollars in her G-string. That was not all I was struggling with. My problem was that Varvara was completely unperturbed by it. Indeed, she was so unconcerned that she had started to rock gently against me, and, God help me, I was hardening. I watched her breasts move rhythmically to the thrusts of her pelvis as I found my way inside her.

SEVENTEEN

I want to tell you why I came here," Varvara said when our breathing had slowed and the muffled sounds of the traffic in the street below penetrated our consciousness. She lifted her head from the crook of my arm.

"Aside from sampling the delights of the love god," I said.

"Who?"

"Never mind."

"If I tell you, you promise you will not get cross?"

"I swear, I don't have a cross bone in my body," I said. "Or any bones, for that matter. I think they've all turned to Jell-O."

"It was wrong what happened this afternoon in my apartment. I thought you had come to kill me. The gun. I nearly shot you. I wanted to make up for that."

"Make-up sex. A worthy reason."

"Also, I want you to find Abraham's killer. He was murdered. I came here to convince you not to give up."

"Oh," I said. That presented a problem. Varvara obviously didn't know about the suicide note. How could she? Now I wished I'd listened to the "no" vote in my head and kept my pants on. I'd taken advantage of this woman, abused my position of power. Varvara hadn't come here because she was attracted to me, but because she wanted something done, and she'd paid for it in the world's oldest currency. I worked my way out from under her body and sat up in bed, feeling like shit. "Varvara, there's been a development in the case."

"Yes?" Her voice was expectant.

"General Scott left a suicide note," I said. There was no other way to tell her but to give it to her straight.

"No! Abraham did *not* kill himself. Don't you see? She just wants you to believe that!" Varvara sat up beside me, her chest heaving.

"Who? Who wants me to believe that?"

"She! His wife. That Harmony bitch. *She* found this suicide note, didn't she?"

"Well, yes..."

"You see. It's a forgery. Abraham would *never* kill himself. You can't let them win."

Them? "There's nothing I can do, Varvara. The case is closed. I'm going back to America tomorrow."

Varvara leapt out of bed, yelling at me at the top of her voice in a language that was probably Russian. She put her heels on and jammed her arms through the sleeves of her raincoat. Then she turned and shouted something unpleasant, waving a finger at me. She spun around, and I thought she was looking for something to throw at me but, no, she was searching for her umbrella. She scooped it up and stormed out of the room, slamming the door behind her with a bang that echoed in my ears.

I stood, not quite knowing what to do. And then the door flew open. "Show me letter!" she demanded.

I owed her at least that much, but the letter was back at OSI, Ramstein, wasn't it? Maybe not. I picked my jacket up off the chair. It was heavy. I felt the deep pockets and they were stuffed full. "Could you step out of the light so I can take a closer look, please?" I asked nicely. The request calmed Varvara. I emptied the contents of the pockets onto the bed. I had my notebook, a wad of the mysterious printout packed with columns of figures. I also had Peyton Scott's toe tag, the photograph of him from Scott's garage, a copy of the Veitch autopsy performed on the sergeant in Baghdad, the cell phone and pager, the nickel-plated Colt, a bag of cloves, a box of codeine, and a clear plastic evidence bag with General Scott's handwritten note inside. The events at the OSI building had thrown me off my game and I'd forgotten to hand all this to Masters so that she could return it to Harmony Scott. I remembered we'd also intended to put a security detail on Varvara, but that too had fallen by the wayside. I handed the bagged note to Varvara. "Don't open it," I said. "Fingerprints." In fact, I was more interested in whose saliva would be found on the envelope's seal, or whether minute fibers might have been captured. Had the letter even been examined by forensics?

"It is fake," she said after barely a few seconds' examination.

I knew she was going to say that, but I was intrigued nonetheless. "Why?"

"I show you," she said, "but you must come to my apartment."

"Your apartment?" I said.

"Yes, I have other letters from Abraham. You will see the difference. This is not even a good copy. You cannot trust her."

"What kind of relationship did you have with Scott?" I asked, sidestepping another diatribe about Harmony.

"I told you."

"Tell me again."

"He took care of me. He was a good man. Not like others I have met."

"In the dance club."

"Yes."

"Who or what is the establishment?" I asked, taking a stab in the dark.

"Bad people," she said. "You don't believe me about this?"

"Which bad people?"

"People who would kill Abraham."

Round and round we go... "Look, Varvara, no matter what happened between us tonight, I want you to know that I also believe General Scott was murdered. But you and I are the only people I know who do, with the possible exception of Special Agent Masters. But proving he was killed is not going to be easy, even if this note *does* turn out to be a forgery—" I stopped. Scott's death had been executed with precision, and anyone even remotely connected with it seemed to be chewing a dirt sandwich. That thought got me thinking about Harmony Scott. Either she was in real danger and the crone was making it almost impossible for us to protect her, or she was every bit as evil as Varvara believed her to be. I hadn't warmed to her, but that didn't make her a cold-blooded killer. I checked the time. It was getting on to 0200, and my plane back to the States was departing at 0830. If I was going to keep this case alive, I needed to get moving and find something solid I could wave in front of the big cheese to show that a crime had been committed. Proof that the suicide letter was a forgery was a start, but that's all it was, especially if his wife and any handwriting experts she could muster begged to differ. "Okay," I said, throwing on some clothes. "Let's go." I picked up the cell, the cloves, the Colt 45, and the bagged note and threw the covers over the rest of the evidence. I hung the do-not-disturb sign on the door. We took the elevator to the lobby. Out on the strip, I noted that Masters's Mercedes had gone. So had most of the traffic, except for the cabs prowling for late-night fares. We grabbed one and headed across town.

"You have a toothache?" she asked.

"Yeah, how'd you guess?"

"I saw the cloves, and I smelled them on your breath. Much better than dentists. I hate dentists."

Varvara had one of those perfect smiles that were a little too good to be true, and I wondered what the teeth she was born with would have been like.

"You should try Russian tarragon. Good for teeth, and tastes good on meat."

"Okay . . . I'll give it a go next time I'm doing a roast," I said, hoping to close down the subject. I popped a codeine tablet and chewed on a couple of cloves in lieu of Russian tarragon. To take my mind off my mouth, I went back to thinking about Harmony Scott. I wondered what the Toe Cutter would make of his little girl being a person of interest in her husband's murder investigation. As far as I knew, no U.S. Vice President had been placed in a similar position. But I knew enough about this one to know he'd fight hard if cornered, and that I'd be considered the enemy.

And then, as has happened often enough to me in the past, I had a revelation that came out of nowhere and hit me like a phone book, about those photos up in Scott's garage. Perhaps seeing the picture of Peyton again, smiling his soon-to-be-dead smile, prompted me. In all of those photos, Harmony Scott made not a single appearance, not even a cameo. It was as if the woman hadn't existed in the life of the father and son, not even when Peyton was a kid. Was that natural? No.

I considered questioning Varvara about the relationship General Scott had with his wife but decided against it. The answers I'd get were more likely to reflect Varvara's feelings about Harmony than Scott's.

Varvara talked to the cab driver in English, telling him to go left and then right and so on. Before long, we pulled up outside her apartment building. I paid the driver and levered myself out of the car. The recent bedroom Olympics made me feel like I'd ridden bareback cross-country for a week. "Do you think I'm walking funny?" I asked as we arrived at the front security door and Varvara waved her pass card at a sensor buried in the wall.

She shrugged. "How do I know this is not your normal walk?"

"Good point," I said.

The elevator ride was swift, the invisible speakers playing Deep Purple's "Smoke on the Water" Mooged to the point where it had about as much soul as air-conditioning hum.

The kerosene fumes only hit me when the elevator arrived at Varvara's floor and the doors slid open. The place smelled like the ramp at Ramstein Air Base when those ageing Turkish F-4s were running up. A couple of people in their pajamas were milling around the hallway like lobotomy patients, looking dazed and confused. The fumes were telling them something was wrong, but what? Varvara put her key in her door and turned it. "Ah!" she exclaimed when her fingers brushed the metal handle.

I touched the door. It was hot. There was a fire on the other side. And then the alarm went off, a howling screech that turned into a siren and then back to a screech. The sound gave the growing crowd in the hallway something to think about and they bumped into each other as panic took hold. "Get out!" I yelled at them, and swung back toward the door.

I briefly reconsidered the wisdom of opening it. Doing so would feed the fire beyond with oxygen. I decided to wait somewhere safe for the fire brigade, like outside. "We have to leave," I yelled.

Varvara had different ideas. "No!"

"Come on," I insisted.

"My cat," she said. "We must save it."

Risk two lives to save a feline. Yeah, that made sense. But I owed Varvara, didn't I?

"Get down," I told her. With Varvara on her knees behind me, I pushed the door open. The room was ablaze. I heard a roar as a ball of flame rolled across the ceiling and burst through the doorway above our heads. There was a sprinkler system. Why wasn't the damn thing sprinkling? The smell of kerosene was pungent.

I was about to close the door and retreat to the fire escape, along with the residents now heading there at a sprint, when Varvara ran past me into the blazing room. *Shit*. I followed.

"What are you doing?" I yelled over the alarm and the noise the fire was making as it chewed through her belongings. I glanced around, hoping to see her cat. Black and gray smoke boiled off the floor.

"There!" she yelled over the alarm, pointing at a small bookcase happily turning itself into charcoal as the fire ate it.

"I don't see a cat," I said. It was hard to breathe.

"The last one on the end. You must get it," Varvara yelled, coughing, pointing at a large, old book.

Whatever I was going to do, it had to be done quick. There were no fire extinguishers or handy wet blankets lying around, but there were plants. I picked up one and threw it against the wall above the bookshelf. The pot shattered and damp earth showered the flames, giving them something to think about. I picked up the other pot and repeated the throw. The flames retreated some more. I ran forward and plucked the book from the shelf. It was hot, but hadn't begun to burn. The heat and smoke were unbearable and I was starting to feel dizzy. Varvara was on her knees, gagging. Hacking and coughing, I scooped her under my arm and staggered into the hallway, my eyes streaming with tears. "I'm sorry about your cat," I wheezed. "I don't think it made it."

"That's okay," she said, sucking in clean air between gasps. "I don't have one."

A roadblock had been set up by the local police to keep the sightseers clear of the area and give the firefighters unobstructed access. Several fire engines were on the scene with more on the way, their sirens competing with each other to disturb the sleep of as many people as possible. A couple of television helicopters were also hovering, no doubt hoping to get some footage of people leaping to their deaths. But the building had been evacuated in a relatively orderly fashion and everyone seemed to be accounted for. I gave Masters a call. Her phone rang unanswered so I left a brief message.

The two apartments on either side of Varvara's were well alight before the first fire trucks arrived, which meant hers had been consumed by the flames. We stood watching as they fought to get the blaze under control, lashing it with high-pressure water from cannons atop their truck-mounted extending ladders.

Varvara shivered beside me with shock and mild exposure, clutching her book. A woman from a neighboring building draped a blanket over her shoulders and muttered a few words of comfort I didn't catch. The majority of the evacuated residents milled around aimlessly or stood mesmerized by the activity, immobilized by the realization that most of their possessions were being ruined by the deluge of water cascading from the floors above. A small but fast-flowing river passed through the foyer and ended in a waterfall down the front steps. A red sneaker rode the current onto the sidewalk.

A couple of fire investigators arrived on the scene. They quickly ascertained in which apartment the fire had started by asking a knot of residents. Fingers pointed at Varvara. The men made their way over. Both were well over six feet—I'm talking girth—and either close proximity to fire played havoc with the capillaries on their noses or both these guys were on the German drinking team. They spoke in German until Varvara said, *"Ich verstehe nicht. Sprechen Sie Englisch?"* whereupon they switched to an accented English that made me think they were doing Schwarzenegger.

"Vee believf it vass in your apartment zat zee fire started in?"

"Yeah," I said.

They turned to me. "Who are you? Do you liff here?"

I badged Tweedledum and Tweedledee and told them Varvara was a witness in a case I was investigating. I also told them that I believed an accelerant—kerosene—had been used to kick the fire along. That got their interest, arson being the sexiest word in a firefighter's lexicon. That's when Varvara joined the conversation and spoiled the party.

"I had a kerosene heater. I might have left it on," she said between chattering teeth.

"What?" I said, thrown completely.

"You haff a kerosene heater?" repeated one of the investigators.

"I don't like warm wind from air-conditioning. It dries the skin, no? So I turn it off," said Varvara. "I was cold. I put the heater on before I went out. And I left it on so that my apartment would be warm when I came home."

The investigators took this in with a mood shift that included a roll of their eyeballs. A ditzy female who forgot to turn off her heater gave them a professional soft-on. Varvara's admission made me look bad, and I half expected the firemen to tell me to run along. In my own mind I was seeing a couple of guys in black spreading kerosene around the place before flicking a match onto the Axminster, rather than Varvara firing up a heater before she stepped out into the night because she was cold, wearing nothing but a raincoat and a smile. It hadn't occurred to me that the fire might have been a genuine accident. Maybe this case was getting to me. Maybe I was starting to see bad guys where there were only shadows. Next thing, I'd be checking under the bed for monsters before I put out the lights. And yet, the timing of the fire didn't feel right, down in my gut, no matter what Varvara told the locals. House fires were cropping up a little too often to be coincidental, it seemed to me. And in my book, coincidences are on the same page as the Easter Bunny.

"I think the sprinkler system failed," I said when the question-and-answer session with Varvara slowed.

"*Ja*," said the beer barrel taking notes. "Vee know.

Zee system zey haff used in ziss building—vee haff had problems viss it before. *Danke.*"

There were a few more questions about insurance policies and a Smokey-the-Bear lecture about fire-safing appliances before leaving the home, and then they wandered off to talk to other witnesses.

"Did you leave your heater on?" I asked when the investigators were out of earshot.

"No," she said.

"Then why say you did?"

"You don't realize what is going on." Her tears had made her mascara run, giving her raccoon eyes.

"So fill me in."

"She wanted to make sure I wouldn't be able to give you anything Abraham had written."

" 'She' being Harmony Scott?"

"Of course."

"So you make up some fairy tale about your heater. And let's not forget the cat. You know, when they finally go in there and have a look, they'll know you were lying. And then they'll want to know why you were lying."

"Yes."

"So, tell me why?"

"Why what?"

"Why did you lie?"

"I have reasons."

I sucked in the sweet night air. My brain needed oxygen to kick it back into gear after breathing the equivalent of a hundred packs of Marlboros. So Varvara's apartment *had* been torched. That accorded with my worldview that there are no such things as co-incidences, but having my own beliefs reinforced didn't provide much comfort in this instance. A pattern had emerged and the blackened top floor of Varvara's apartment building had cemented it. I was dealing with some kind of conspiracy. That, in policing terms, is a bit like defining a symphony as a tune with lots of notes. I had no idea what kind of conspiracy I was dealing with, or who was involved in it. As far as Varvara was concerned, Harmony Scott was the puppet master, but I wasn't convinced.

"Do you not want to see this book?"

I caught a glimpse of the cover. *Gone with the Wind.* "No, thanks. Caught the movie."

Varvara ignored me and opened it up. It wasn't a book at all, but a compartment for holding valuables disguised as a book. Inside was a German passport.

"Whose is that?" I asked.

"I'm from Deutschland, didn't you know?"

"No, I didn't." If that passport was false, it was reason enough for Varvara to throw the fire investigators off the scent. Setting a person's home on fire was not usually considered a random act. By calling it an accident, she had deftly sidestepped a whole other police investigation that would put her under the magnifying glass. I was about to ask her about that passport when a small folded note fluttered out of it. Varvara caught it mid flight.

"This is enough proof," she said, handing it to me. "You read it."

> *Dear Varvara*
> *I'll meet you at departures at 1730.*
> *A*

"What am I looking at?" I asked.

"Abe wrote this to me when we went on a trip several months ago."

"Yeah, but what am I supposed to be looking *for*?"

"Now look at your letter," she said impatiently.

I pulled the bag from my pocket and walked under a streetlight to compare the two.

"Do you see it?" she asked over my shoulder, excitement in her voice.

"See what?" Aside from the suicide letter being signed "Abe" while this note was signed "A," to this untrained eye—mine—the handwriting appeared identical.

Varvara growled in frustration. She stabbed the note with a red, manicured fingernail. "Can't you *see*?"

" 'I'll meet you at departures at seventeen-thirty.' Yeah, the guy's meeting you at seventeen hundred and thirty hours. Obviously a romantic." Some people just couldn't leave the parade ground.

"*Dubiina! Jebat moi lisiy cherep!*" she said, throwing her hands at the sky.

I could tell that our relationship was in danger of going backward. "What did you call me?"

"I didn't call you anything, I just said, 'Fuck my bald skull'—something we Russians say in Latvia."

"Colorful," I said. "So, now tell me what we risked becoming charbroiled to get?"

"Abraham spent many years in Europe, dealing with Europeans. He picked up European habits."

"Such as?"

"Crossing the number seven."

I looked at the notes again. The seven on Varvara's note was indeed crossed, while the seven in the date at the top of the suicide letter wasn't. "That's all?"

"Writing number sevens this way was Abraham's writing. But this way?" She shook her head adamantly.

As evidence went, it was slim. Was a pen stroke the length of a single piece of fly shit enough to tell General

Gruyere that the suicide letter was a forgery and that therefore General Scott had indeed been murdered?

"Has anyone seen a Special Agent Cooper here?" demanded a familiar voice behind me. The music I knew I would have to face sooner or later was playing. Special Agent Masters had arrived.

EIGHTEEN

esus, are you okay?" she asked when she joined us.
"I'm a bit rare on one side. My butt could probably do with another minute or so," I said.

Masters ignored me and concentrated on Varvara.
"Do you need treatment for burns?"

"No, we're okay," I said.

"I'm asking Varvara."

Masters took a break from attending Varvara and
gave me a cursory inspection. "You've lost an eyebrow.
Singed clean away."

I glanced at my forearms. They were black with soot
and sweat and the hair on them was also gone.

"When you said there'd been a bit of a fire," she said,
gesturing at the fire trucks and emergency vehicles, "I
didn't take your call seriously. I could have got here
quicker."

"Forget it," I said. I wondered how long it would
take Special Agent Masters's concern to be replaced
with the question undoubtedly on her mind: namely,
what I happened to be doing at Varvara's apartment at
three in the morning. And then I remembered seeing
Masters's Mercedes parked outside the Pensione
Freedom just before Varvara made her spectacular entrance there. If she'd seen the Latvian arrive, Masters
probably believed she already had the answer to that
one. I gave a mental shrug. She was a grown-up,
wasn't she? Nevertheless, I made a lame attempt to

throw her off course. "Varvara came by my hotel earlier this evening to let me know that she could prove the letter was a forgery. She brought me back here and we found her apartment on fire. Ms. Kadyrov believes the fire was started to prevent us using other samples of General Scott's handwriting she had to compare them with the suicide note." This, of course, was at odds with what Varvara had told the fireman.

"Then why didn't she just bring some of this evidence to your apartment in the first place?" asked Masters.

There it was. Masters was on the hunt.

"I was not sure I could trust him," Varvara said, apparently playing along.

Masters again. "What changed your mind?"

Why did I feel like a trap had been set and my foot was poised above its steel jaws? I was about to open my mouth and say something defensive—I have no idea what—when Varvara sprang those jaws shut: "Because we fucked and a woman knows afterwards if she can trust a man, no?"

Thanks a bunch, Varvara.

Special Agent Masters fixed me with a look of pure ice and said, "Yes, trust *is* in short supply these days. Almost as much as professionalism."

"We managed to save an example of the general's handwriting," I said, pushing on. Were Masters and I married? No. Was the case officially closed? Yes. Did I feel like I'd let Masters down? Yes. Did I have to be tucked up in bed by eight P.M. with a Dr. Seuss? No. A score of justifications ran through my head, but, the fact was, I felt guilty. "Varvara, you want to show the Special Agent?"

She nodded and led Masters under the streetlight.

The major's reaction was swift, if not a little more animated than my own. "Are you fucking kidding me, Cooper?" she said, looking up.

"Can I speak with you a moment, Special Agent?" I said, walking into the shadows.

Masters followed. "What?" she asked. "And it had better be good."

"Whether you or I think that note helps build a case for murder, the fact is *someone* thought the apartment was worthwhile torching. And what if Ms. Kadyrov had been home when whoever turned up with a can of kerosene and a Zippo? The *timing* of this is what's so wrong."

"Get to the point," she said.

"You know Scott was murdered and so do I. And it's not just murder: There's something going on here, something very big—Peyton, the two autopsies, Philippe, Veitch, the journalist . . . Either we can work together and get to the bottom of it, or you can let the people who did it walk. And, if you do, it's because the scale of it has you scared. Or maybe you're just jealous that I got laid."

"What?" Masters's hands went to her hips and a sardonic smile twisted her lips. A storm was building, the proverbial quiet before all hell breaks loose. And then it burst. "I have *never* met anyone as arrogant as you in my life. You are *so* sure of your own righteousness it makes me sick! I thought I could work with you. I really tried, but I can't. You are not a team player. And now *this*!" she jabbed a finger in the direction of Varvara.

"So it's jealousy, then," I said.

"You are so out on your own on this, Cooper," Masters said, shaking her head.

"I mean it, the green-eyed monster has you."

"Get over yourself, Cooper."

"Then tell me what you were doing outside my apartment earlier this evening. Were you spying on me—waiting to see whether I went out for a cheeseburger, or something equally heinous?"

Masters's arms were folded tight, protecting her. "What makes you think I was there?" she demanded.

"Because that purple Mercedes of yours sticks out like a mandrill's butt."

"It doesn't matter now."

"You're wrong. It's all that matters. Why were you there?"

"You're never going to find out now, are you?"

"Was it business or pleasure? And if it was business, whose business were you on?"

"You are an asshole, you know that?" said Masters.

"Look . . . I saw your car, and then I heard a knock on the door. I thought it was going to be you standing there when I opened it, but it wasn't. How long were you sitting out there, asking yourself whether you'd come up or not, working up the courage?"

"The courage to what? And stop trying to make your completely unprofessional evening's intercourse with Ms. Va-va-va-voom out to be my fault."

"That's not my intention. I'm just saying it could have turned out differently, is all."

Masters glared at me. "Oh, lucky me."

"Look, I apologize if I disappointed you, okay?"

"Go to hell. You know what your problem is, Cooper?"

"I have only one?"

"You're dishonest. You think one thing but you say something else entirely."

Busted. "That's a bunch of crap," I said defensively.

Brenda, the ex, had accused me of much the same crime over the years.

"I'm sick of playing games with you, Cooper," said Masters. "We're either on the same team—honest and open—or you're on your own. Why are you so... so...closed down? You've been married, haven't you?" She didn't wait for an answer. "Did she cheat on you? Is that what happened?"

If Masters was expecting me to break down and start sucking my thumb, she was going to be disappointed. "Our relationship counselor convinced me it was never going to work," I said.

Masters nodded smugly. It was clear she now believed she knew what made me tick. "I have one other question for you, Cooper."

My turn to nod.

"What the hell is a mandrill?"

Varvara had three blankets wrapped around her by the time Masters and I had settled on a workable cease-fire. Her teeth had stopped chattering, and she appeared dazed. Masters put an arm around her shoulders.

"Varvara," I said, "you have to leave here."

"I know," she said.

"No, I mean you have to leave here—Germany; Europe. Go where no one will look to find you. Use that passport. We don't even want to know where you're going. And this is important: When you get there, you must *not* use a credit card, for a while at least. Use cash only. It's too dangerous for you here. The fire proves that, if nothing else."

"You're going to arrest that woman, yes?" she asked.

"If you mean Mrs. Scott, no. She hasn't committed a crime, not one I'm aware of."

"You are wrong."

"There are too many questions left unanswered, Varvara. Do you have money?"

"Yes."

"You can stay with me till the morning," said Masters with that protective arm still around her shoulders, glaring at me.

"What?" I mimed.

"Where are *you* going?" Varvara asked, directing the question at me.

"I'm off to the fun capital of the world," I said. "Otherwise known as Baghdad."

NINETEEN

I checked the time on my Seiko. It was just before midnight in D.C., a handful of minutes before 0600 at Ramstein. The sun was coming up on the fog rolling across the apron, and I had a crap that felt like a lump of cold pig iron sitting in my gut. The USAF C-130 parked on the apron, two of its propellers spinning, was my ride to Baghdad. I don't like C-130s. There were a lot of them in Afghanistan and they bring back memories.

The connection cut in again. General Gruyere's throat sounded like she'd been gargling hydrochloric acid, but it could have been the poor line. Of course, Gruyere being who she was, I could easily have been right in the first instance. "Jesus wept, Cooper! Are you fucking trying to tell me Harmony Scott is lying about her own husband's goddamn suicide?" she growled. Yeah, the line had nothing to do with it.

"The truth is, ma'am," I said, "I'm not sure what I believe right at the moment."

"Do you know who or what you're dealing with here, son? If you're even just a little off with this, Jefferson Cutter will peel you like a banana and roll you in rock salt."

I went through my reasons for going to Baghdad, which didn't seem to impress her. But when I added Varvara's conflicting note to the picture, Gruyere reluctantly conceded that perhaps some questions requiring answers were still outstanding. In her way, she was giving me a conditional green light—the condition being that if I fucked up, it would go badly for no one but me. So what else was new?

The line dropped out permanently just as Masters strode through the hangar lugging a bag. "What's that?" I asked when she drew up beside me.

"My grandmother. What does it look like?"

"It looks like you're going someplace."

"I have movement orders for both of us. I'm coming with you. We'll pick up weapons and armor in-country."

"No, you're not."

"Okay then, let me put it another way: Fuck off," she said.

"I need you to stay here and—"

"And what, darn your socks? I don't think so. You don't have a choice, Vin. Now, are we going, or are *you* staying?"

"Excuse me, sir, ma'am. We're good to go," said the captain, a reed-thin man with a head shaved pink.

I picked up my gear. "We need someone to hold the fort here," I told Masters.

"We've got Flight Lieutenant Bishop. I've given him a whole list of stuff to chase through, like getting a line on those Aurora Aviation people. He's also going to be looking into some phone and bank records. Technically, he's still on secondment to us, remember?"

"Yeah. Okay, that's good."

"It gets better," said Masters.

"A dentist's coming with us?"

"Tooth still giving you grief?"

"Yeah," I said. I was about two thirds of the way through my supply of pills and twigs.

Masters pouted in a show of sympathy that lasted

less than a second, and moved on. "Anyway, I called into OSI before coming here. Bishop was going through his computer files and wanted to know if he should delete the copy he made of the general's hard drive."

"You're kidding? He made a copy? That's a break and a half."

"Maybe not. He's still saying the Dungeon program protecting those files is almost impregnable."

"But he's going to keep trying, right?"

Masters nodded.

"Does anyone else know he made a copy?"

"I asked him that. He doesn't think so."

"Good. Can he do something else for us?"

"What?"

"Can he track down the current whereabouts of former members of Peyton's unit? Particularly the noncoms? They've probably had their tour extended along with everyone else still in Iraq. It'd be helpful if we could speak to a few of those guys and find out what really happened."

"What about the U.S. hospital in Baghdad? Did you call?"

"Yeah, the colonel there knows we're coming."

"Good."

"Excuse me, sir, ma'am?" The captain was looking anxious. "We're on a schedule here."

Back to Masters. I wasn't keen on her coming along, for the simple reason that the two of us didn't really need to go and hold each other's hands. That and the fact that the capital of Iraq was still Terror Central. People were losing their lives there every day, and, as far as I knew, none of them were turning up in the lost-and-found.

"Honest and open, Cooper, remember?" said Masters,

attempting to read my thoughts, her ear to the cell. The connection made, she put a finger in her other ear and turned away to talk.

Ten minutes later we were strapped into jump seats in the C-130. I loaded up on painkillers with a sleeping pill chaser, and took off for the Land of Nod.

And then suddenly I was awake as the plane lurched and the pitch of the screaming turboprop changed. The approach to Balad Airport, gateway to sunny Baghdad, had begun.

Masters yelled over the roar of the turbines, "Can you let go of my leg now, Cooper? You're cutting off the circulation."

I glanced down. My hand was locked around her upper thigh and my knuckles were white with the strain. "Sorry," I yelled back, releasing her.

"You need to see someone," she suggested.

I wanted to snap back something witty but my brain was frozen with fear. Not one but two transport aircraft identical to the one we were in had crashed in the last five months—one because of small-arms ground fire closer to the runway, the other because the aircraft was flying a wild approach just to avoid *possible* ground fire. Like us. I remembered reading about it—I've developed a morbid curiosity about air crashes that has increased exponentially as my own fear of flying has grown. Metal fatigue led to the horizontal stabilizer cracking as the plane spiraled downward. The C-130 had cartwheeled into the ground, breaking up and exploding and turning the pilot and copilot into little fireballs squeezed like flaming orange pips from the main body of the tumbling, burning wreckage. Okay, so maybe the bit about the orange pips wasn't included in the news article, but I'm sure it wouldn't have been too far from the truth.

I glanced out the small window. Down on the ground twenty thousand feet below, I could see strings of yellow lights marking the passage of roads across the desert. It looked peaceful enough. The plane dipped sickeningly as we commenced the descending cork-screw. My stomach tried to scramble out of my mouth as the wings flipped seemingly at right angles to level flight. The descent slowed—maybe the pilot over-cooked it—and we went from negative Gs to a fistful of positive ones, my head suddenly weighing three times more than normal. My ears popped as the plane heeled over again, the engines screaming, airframe shudder-ing—the thing about to break up and scatter us all across the sand.

And then the main wheels kissed the runway and squealed reassuringly. I unbuckled, eager to get out and face the car bombers, the suicide bombers, and all the other nut bombers this place had to offer. Anything, in fact, to get the hell away from air travel.

Masters and I stood on the tarmac with our bags at our feet, shivering in the predawn chill, and scoped the sur-roundings. The horizon was so flat it almost curved, and one quarter of it was outlined in orange, green, and purple where the sun was about to make an ap-pearance. On the airfield sat the usual collection of C-130s and C-17s, as well as a couple of F-16 and F-15 fighters. Some frightening-looking Russian aircraft were also parked here and there, seemingly assembled with duct tape, strips of the stuff hanging from various engine panels. Half a dozen Black Hawk helicopters and several Apache gunships were corralled in a separate area, their main rotor blades sagging under their own weight.

A bunch of tents and demountables had been set up as the APOD—aerial port of debarkation, the military equivalent of immigration—and the battery of portable generators servicing them hummed in competition with the air-con units and the distant turboprop growl of approaching aircraft. The Stars and Stripes hung limp from a central flagpole. More Stars and Stripes hung from each of the tents. U.S. Army and Marine Corps combat troops milled about, mixing with aircrews and heavily armored civilians carrying weaponry. Beyond this activity was a large parking lot of Humvees and light armored vehicles bristling with machine guns, grenade launchers, and TOWs—tube-launched, optically tracked, wire-guided missiles. Beyond these was a wall of towering concrete pillars topped with razor wire that said "FUCK OFF" in no uncertain terms to any unauthorized personnel on the other side.

Masters and I walked toward the APOD in silence. "Arrivals over there," said a sergeant, her Kevlar helmet low over her eyes, as we approached the demountable. She pointed with a clipboard toward a cluster of tents where a large number of personnel were waiting in line. We made our way over and joined the line.

Masters passed our movement orders to the army lieutenant and the woman checked us out on her laptop. "Yep, we've got you here," she said, frowning at the screen. "I'll need to scan you in. You want to get around this place, every journey starts with your CAC card. You'll need to flash 'em all over the place. Whatever you do, don't lose 'em. And for God's sake, stay in uniform. Our boys tend to shoot what they don't recognize. *Capisce?"*

We nodded and handed over our CAC cards—the smart cards that contained a chip holding an array of information including, among other things, our blood types. Just in case.

"You're both classed Duty PAX," the lieutenant continued, "so you shouldn't have any trouble getting on a convoy manifest. You been here before?"

Both Masters and I shook our heads. The lieutenant gave us a small evil smile. From it I gathered that we were in for some serious unpleasantness. "We don't move around Eye-rak unless it's in convoy strength. You're heading to the green zone?"

Masters and I nodded.

"You'll love the place," she said, giving us her devil smile again. "All the comforts of home, plus mortar fire. Make your way across to the main demountable and pick up your flaks and Kevlar and M9s. But, if you're in a hurry to start enjoying your time here, better get your names on a transport manifest first. They're filling up fast. Anything else?"

We shook our heads.

"Be safe," she said, this time fixing us with a look of intensity, meaning it. Then it dissolved and she barked, looking at the marine sergeant behind us, "Next!"

We joined another line to get on a transport manifest. That done, we went to the demountable as directed to sign for and collect our flaks, Kevlar helmets, and sidearms.

By the time we left the converted shipping container, the sun had cleared the horizon. The desert night chill had been replaced by a heat that smacked off the tarmac and curled the hair in my nostrils.

* * *

I'd assumed the convoy we'd be joining into Baghdad would be a road-going one, but I was wrong. A duty sergeant pointed us in the direction of six Black Hawks, their turbine engines emitting the familiar flat snarl accompanied by the *swoop-swoop* of the main rotor through the air. One of the Apaches was also winding up to a dull roar. Its nose-mounted Gatling gun swung left and right as the weapons specialist in the front seat went through his checks. Masters smiled and gave my shoulder a pat. Despite the heat, the sweat under my flak jacket was cold.

A loadmaster directed us to the lead Black Hawk, where a crew chief beckoned. He was a little guy whose large helmet gave him the appearance of a green lollipop. It was too noisy to speak, or I was too scared—I'm not sure which. He pointed at my M9 pistol in its shoulder holster. I knew the drill. I removed it and showed him that its magazine had been removed. He gave me the thumbs-up and Masters repeated the action. Satisfied, he slapped his hand on the deck of the forward compartment. Masters propped her gear onto the floor and climbed in after it. The door gunner pointed at the pull-down seat against the bulkhead. I followed and took the seat next to her. The crew chief stepped nimbly up and buckled himself into the seat beside me. It was all very cozy.

We sat there rocking gently with the centrifugal forces driving the helo's revolving parts, the roar of its turbines in our ears. Two riflemen sat in the seats opposite, their heads forward, leaning on the stocks of the inverted M16s as if they were praying. If there was any time to get religion, this was it. The faces I could see looked pretty grim, which wasn't reassuring, particularly when one of them was the pilot's.

The Black Hawk stuck to the uninhabited parts of the desert, which wasn't so hard given that much of it was exactly that. But then we closed on Baghdad and the ride quickly got wilder than anything Disneyland has to offer. We began jinking, climbing, and descending as if the pilot was suffering an epileptic seizure—all while the desert skimmed past barely two hundred and fifty feet below. Both the riflemen opposite barfed into the bags provided. Behind Masters's sunglasses, I could see that her eyes were rigidly fixed on some part of the airframe. The muscles in her jaw were bunching and flexing. The gunners on the doors were oblivious to the motion—this being their office of business—and spent the entire flight tracking dangerous-looking goats and small groups of people down on the sand, nervously swinging their guns here and there waiting for the least excuse to send down a few hundred hot 7.62mm slugs. I was aware of the Apache sitting off our left door about five hundred feet away, looking like some lethal species of prehistoric bug. I was having an out-of-body experience, taking it all in from a disembodied point somewhere high above the scene. I'd experienced something like this before and so I recognized it for what it was—shock.

"You okay, Cooper?"

"Wha—"

"Snap out of it. We're here—BIAP."

"Where?"

"BIAP—Baghdad International Airport."

I suddenly realized that the helo was on the ground and I was the only person in it, aside from the aircrew shutting it down. The soldiers seated opposite were no longer there, and neither were the gunners. Embarrassing. Masters was standing on the tarmac, hands on her hips, looking at me. It was a look of impatience. The air was thick with the smells of hot kerosene and vomit. Not mine, and I decided that was something at least. I released the harness and climbed out.

"You really need to do something about that. How long have you had the problem?" asked Masters as we walked in the heat radiating from the sky above and from the tarmac below toward the Baghdad International Airport APOD.

I countered her question with a question. "How many airplane crashes have you walked away from?"

"None. You?"

"Two."

"Oh. Okay, that makes sense." Masters stopped. "They can help you, you know."

"Who can? Shrinks?"

"Psychologists."

"No, thanks. Their wings are prone to falling off, too."

Masters dropped it, recognizing the conversation was like a goat trail in the desert—it would go nowhere.

The APOD erected in the dirt was reminiscent of the one back at Balad, just a collection of tents and demountables surrounded by rubbish—soda cans, paper, plastic, car tires, and, oddly, a clothes dryer. It was still early morning but the sun's heat was already fierce, hammering down, boring through my Kevlar. We made our way toward the biggest tent, presented our CAC cards to an army corporal, and asked to be put on the manifest for the first convoy heading out for the Baghdad green zone. He told us to hurry. There was room on the next convoy, but it was leaving any second. We kept moving. Half a dozen heavily armed Humvees were idling out back.

A sunburned soldier sitting up behind the roof-mounted M2 machine gun in the last vehicle motioned at us to get in as the lead vehicle began to move off. The door opened and Masters and I jumped in.

"Make yourself at home, folks," said the corporal seated in the front passenger seat, moving a quid of chewing tobacco from one side of his mouth to the other. In his hand was a plastic water bottle still carrying the sticker for some local brand, half filled with a licorice-colored sludge. He turned around, struggling in his flaks, a startlingly wide grin splitting his round face in half. "Where y'all from?"

"Germany," I said.

"Where 'bouts is that?"

"Europe."

"I thought there might be a Germany in South Carolina or somewhere. You know, like how there's a Paris in Texas?"

"No, just Germany—in the land of the Germans," I said, earning a kick from Masters.

"Well, wherever y'all come from, welcome to Eye-rak." He put the bottle to his lips and squeezed out a mouthful of black saliva that coated the bottle's insides. "Can I offer you folks some good ol' American snuff? It's mint-flavored. Keeps the stink of this place out of your nose."

I shook my head. "Thanks for offering."

The gunner's knees occupied the space in front of my face. I spat on the window and smeared a circle of dust away so that I could watch Baghdad flash by.

The convoy slowed when it reached the exit. I saw that the entire airport was ringed with high, reinforced concrete blocks crowned with more razor wire. A collection of Abrams M1 tanks and Bradley fighting vehicles—over five hundred tons of armor-plated steel—stood guard.

"You're new here, aren't you?" the man in front said as we accelerated once more. His grin was vast. I wouldn't have been surprised if his face disappeared and, Cheshire cat–like, this grin remained behind, dis-embodied.

"Yeah. How can you tell?"

" 'Cause I saw y'all hanging around at the APOD and I pegged you as newbies—lookin' around, sorta not knowing what the hell to do next."

"We're investigators," I said. "We're paid to look lost."

"Well, sit back and hang on, folks. It's only four klicks to the green zone and we do it in pretty quick time."

He wasn't kidding. Our vehicles accelerated and held their speed—stopping for nothing and no one. We blasted through a couple of intersections, running red lights. Out on the expressway, we had at least twenty miles per hour on the surrounding traffic, which, for the most part, seemed to be worn-out old European ve-hicles so riddled with bullet holes that they looked like mobile sieves.

Baghdad slid by in the spit- and dirt-encrusted port-hole beside me. Through this looking glass, I could see that the Iraqis largely ignored us, even though we were charging through them at a speed hazardous to their health. Iraqi males stood on the streets, hanging out at shopfronts, talking, or drinking what I assumed was coffee, there being no alcohol hereabouts. They wore a mixture of western and Arabic clothes—jeans and pants or loose, flowing robes. Where they all seemed to agree, however, was on the subject of mustaches. The shaggy caterpillars were everywhere. Every second guy reminded me of Saddam Hussein. The dictator might have been toppled but his barber was still out there, and the guy was making a killing.

I caught a glimpse of the green zone before we came up on it, a vast wall of the same towering concrete blocks and barbed wire out at BIAP, only these were spray-painted here and there with slogans in Arabic that I guessed were probably not warm greetings from the local population. We made our way through lines of ancient, battered European vehicles belching smoke and unburned gas, all caked in fine beige dust. The way ahead was blocked for the locals by Abrams M1 main battle tanks and Iraqi police. These obstructions slowed the traffic to a snarl, and heat boiled off the engines, further cooking the air so that it shimmered against the baked blue sky like running water. No one seemed in a particular hurry to move, unless it was to lean on their horns.

Once inside the walls, the convoy took on a more leisurely pace. I could almost hear the sigh of relief coming from the front seat. The Cheshire cat turned and said, "Well, here we are. Y'all enjoy the ride?" He didn't wait for an answer. "Where can we set y'all down?"

"The HQ, thanks, Corporal," said Masters.

He nodded, turned, and muttered some instructions to the driver. Minutes later we pulled up in front of a building-sized Arabic wedding cake.

TWENTY

The one-star general regarded us silently over the cathedral of his laced fingertips as we stood in front of his desk. He tapped his forefingers together. He was balding and not doing it graciously. A large flap of dyed brown hair originating from a single point above one ear had been artfully coiffed over the roof of his head, thinly disguising the presence of a collection of fat brown freckles. So this was General Harold Lee Edwards, the Judge Advocate General officer for the U.S. Army operating in Iraq, the man widely known as "the hanging judge." His lean face was pinched and drawn toward a sharp, upturned nose that was mostly white gristle. He could play the character of Ichabod Crane in a movie without having to visit the makeup department. His teeth were yellow and appeared to slope backward into his mouth like the barbs on a spear. The word around was that once Edwards got hold of you, he never let go.

"General Gruyere has briefed me already," he said at last, in a voice that reminded me of a piece of wood being worked over by a rasp. I guessed he was a longtime smoker. "She has told me to lend you both every assistance. I won't interfere in your investigation, but you must abide by the rules. You leave this compound, you go in convoy." He leaned back in his chair. "At ease. Do you know who you want to interview?"

"Yes, sir," I said. "We would like to review the

autopsy processes at the Twenty-eighth Combat Support Hospital—"

"You'll need to see Colonel Dwyer. He runs the place."

"Thank you, sir."

"So you will be gone tomorrow."

I wasn't sure if that was a question or an order. I gambled. "There's every likelihood of that, sir."

"Good, I'll get you on a manifest in advance. What about you, Miss ... Miss ..."

"Special Agent Masters."

"Special Agent Masters," he repeated. He checked his briefing notes to make sure he'd got it right. His sight mustn't have been too good. Masters's name was on her shirt not three feet away. "Hot enough here for you?"

"Yes, sir," she said.

"Well, let's hope the *hajis* give you a break and don't throw too many bombs at you and make it even warmer." The general smiled, or at least I thought he smiled—it could have been gas.

Masters gave the only possible answer. "Yes, sir."

"*Hajis*, sir?" I asked.

"Locals—that's what we call 'em." General Edwards coughed and looked down again at his notes. "Room is at a premium here since the Iraqi government decided to reduce our compound. Fortunately, in the past week, some of our people rotated home. I've got you rooms in the Al-Rasheed. My adjutant will see to it. It's a few hundred feet from the wall and prone to rocket fire, but it's not a bad hotel. Also, a few survival tips. When you're outside the wall, stay away from dirt mounds, vehicle wrecks, and piles of rubble. That's where the *hajis* like setting their IEDs—improvised explosive devices. Good hunting. Dismissed." He shuffled his notes like all staff officers do when they want you gone. We took the hint.

The adjutant, a lieutenant colonel, had better things to do than babysit a couple of MPs. I knew this because he said so. He took us across to the Al-Rasheed, a charmless brown lump of concrete pockmarked like an adolescent's face by the aforementioned rocket fire. We walked into the lobby, where a sergeant sat behind the reception desk with her feet up, watching cartoons on a new Sony hooked up to satellite cable. She got to her feet pretty quickly, but the lieutenant colonel ignored her like she didn't exist. He grabbed a key off a board covered in hooks. He tossed it to Masters and said, "Best we can do. Hope you guys enjoy a close working relationship. I know the general said *rooms*..." he emphasized the plural. "Got a problem with it, try finding someone who gives a shit." With that, he stalked out.

"Must be the heat," I said. Actually, the foyer of the Al-Rasheed was cold, air-conditioned down to about Alaska in the fall. I shivered.

"First floor, turn right. Sorry," the sergeant said with a shrug.

We took the elevator to the first floor, wondering about the apology. Was she apologizing to us because we had to share a room? Surely not. We stepped out and were immediately hit with the heat—the air-con was out. Yellow tape was strung across the hallway. Eighty feet beyond the tape was daylight where one of those pesky unguided rockets the general mentioned had scored a hit and caused a minor cave-in.

"Be it ever so humble..." said Masters, keying the

lock. The room wasn't so bad—a time capsule of seventies chic. It was almost the height of modern interior-design fashion, these things happening to come full circle eventually.

I cased the facilities. "Hey, look," I called out. "We've got a Jacuzzi."

TWENTY-ONE

Special Agent Masters didn't respond to my offer of a Jacuzzi ride, but I wasn't expecting her to. I turned on the hot water faucet. A small spider scrambled from the waterspout when the pipes began to thrum. A dribble of brown water followed.

Suddenly an explosion, a big one, rumbled through the Al-Rasheed's foundations. Before I knew it, Masters and I were taking the stairs four at a time. We hit the street and saw a rising column of black smoke half a mile away, beyond the wall. Servicemen and -women spilled out of the hotel and held their hands over their eyes, shielding them from the fierce glare of the sun to get a better look.

"Damn truck bomb," said one marine sergeant, shaking his head slowly.

By the time we arrived at the hospital set up in one of Saddam's palaces in the green zone, the dead and wounded were arriving. Humvees and ambulances were unloading casualties, and so were the helos landing somewhere behind the building. Inside, a parody of a Baghdad traffic jam was in full swing. A gridlock of gurneys was loaded with cut and broken people, exposed skin blackened with burns and soot, dark crimson blood flowing from ragged flaps of skin.

The white marble floor of the main entrance hall was slippery with blood and dirt. Medical staff crawled over each new arrival, their hands flitting over limbs,

torsos, and heads searching for wounds, shouting instructions that were sometimes ignored because everyone in the place was already engaged in a pitched battle
with death. The men and women cut to pieces when
the truck loaded with scrap metal exploded beside their
convoy were mostly quiet, some through force of will,
others because they were in shock, others because it
probably hurt more to scream, their faces melted and
lungs seared. Some whimpered or moaned. Some
called for their mothers. Occasionally, a screamer
would come through making a sound like a wild animal, the veneer of civilization stripped away, the casu-
alty reduced to a primitive state of raw and savage
survival, frontal lobes bypassed and the reptile brain
engaged in the fight for life.

Nurses wheeled around stands containing bags of
fluids and blood, or hooked up IVs, or raced around on
errands. Instructions kept being yelled as, here and
there, patients flat-lined.

The smell of blood, urine, and feces was overwhelming, and so was the noise. I realized that getting sense
from anyone here was going to be, as Brenda would
have said in the lexicon of nineties' positive-speak, a
challenge.

Masters grabbed a passing lieutenant's arm and
shouted, "Do you know where we can find Colonel
Dwyer?"

"There," said the young man, gore caked on his arms
up to the elbows, gesturing at a room off the hall with
a nod of his head. A sign on the wall read "Trauma
Room 2."

Masters and I dodged medical staff rushing from patient to patient, careful not to slip on the slickened
floor. A PFC was spreading sawdust around to soak up
the blood and urine. Trauma Room 2 was similar in size

and shape to the main hall, with a marble floor and a towering vaulted ceiling enclosing an enormous space. Giant mosaics of the former dictator illustrated well-documented moments in his life: firing an AK-47 from a balcony, playing the avuncular leader to his troops, being the kindhearted parent to a child perched on his knee. Smiles all round. Stained-glass windows set with blue, red, and green glass in complicated geometric patterns threw technicolor light onto the upper walls. The intricate interplay of shapes took the eyeballs on a journey to the ceiling, where golden stars twinkled happily in a cobalt blue universe. In all, a nice place to die.

The wounded in this room had been separated from the others. They were the ones with shattered limbs being triaged for surgery. The medical staff wore scrubs over their ABUs, obscuring rank. I asked a passing nurse to point out Colonel Dwyer. He indicated a man close to fifty and as black and shiny as a new tire.

"Colonel Dwyer," I said. "Special Agent Cooper, and this is Special Agent Masters, OSI. I called you this morning?" The colonel looked up from a compound fracture he was assessing. I'd broken with my habit of not calling ahead because it would have been just a tad inconvenient for us if the colonel hadn't been around, given that we'd come all the way from Germany for his assistance.

"Yeah. To be honest, I forgot you were coming," said the surgeon. "Can't it wait?"

I didn't want to be insensitive but we were also pressed for time. "Till when, sir?"

The CO of the hospital sighed deeply, realizing we weren't going to just go away, and then returned to the task at hand. "Just remind me. You're investigating a murder, right?" he said as he probed around a white stick of bone protruding from his patient's quadricep.

"That's right, sir."

"One murder?"

"Yes, sir."

"You've come all the way from Europe to find the killer of just one man?"

"Correct, sir."

The colonel bent down and spoke softly to the unconscious soldier under his fingertips. "You're a lucky woman, Captain. No vascular damage—nothing we can't fix, anyway." He murmured something to an assistant, then pulled off his rubber gloves with a slap. "In the context of what's going on around here, Special Agent, have you any idea how ridiculous that sounds?"

I stayed silent. I didn't think the colonel was really looking for an answer.

"What's so important about this murder victim?" he continued.

"Aside from his rank, sir?"

"Yes, you told me on the phone. A four-star. Wouldn't it be far more beneficial if you and your department could find the individual responsible for all this?" he said with a sweep of his arm, gesturing at the carnage piling up in the room and outside. "You see what I'm getting at, Special Agent?"

"Yes, sir." Actually, I agreed with him. In this hospital alone, where death was being serviced with all the alacrity of a conveyor belt, the preoccupation with one killing among so many did seem puerile. But agreeing with the colonel was one thing and being able to do anything about it was something else entirely. We both had our jobs. I knew that, and so did the colonel.

"Forget it," Dwyer said after a big sigh. "How can I help you guys?"

* * *

"This is Captain Blood," said Colonel Dwyer. "Captain, this is Special Agent Cooper and Special Agent Masters, OSI. Please afford them every assistance. They're investigating a matter of national security. They're interested in knowing how we process the KIAs."

"Yes, sir," said the captain, standing beside his computer monitor.

"Come and see me if there's anything else I can do for you." The colonel gave us both a nod and then departed, diving his hands into a pair of rubber gloves held out by a nurse.

"So, Captain Blood," I said, searching around for something witty to say about the appropriateness of his name.

"Yes, sir?" Blood was tall, with pale red hair and skin the color of a bleached bedsheet. He reminded me of C-3PO. I saw the length of the line forming at the captain's door and decided against being a wiseass. No one in the line seemed impatient to get processed. They had all the time in the world—an eternity, in fact.

"What can you show us?" I asked.

"The best way, I think, is to take you through the procedure. Step by step," the captain said. "Are you squeamish?" He looked first at me, and then Masters. We both shook our heads. He moved to the nearest body with short steps, arms bent at the elbows like a robot, and pulled back an opaque plastic sheet, revealing a black female missing her leg and genitals. Her head sat on her neck in a way that would not have been possible if she were living. The captain moved the head and revealed a gaping wound the size of an English muffin at the base; the spine in that area had been completely and neatly cored out. Her eyelids remained parted slightly as if she'd been photographed in the middle of the act of blinking. This human being had been alive less than an hour ago. I wondered who loved her, who her friends and family were, who she'd left behind. I also wondered about the circumstances of her death. Why these wounds? Why her and not someone else? I felt I should be asking these questions on her behalf, regardless of the fact that she was completely beyond caring one way or the other.

Captain Blood slapped on a pair of gloves and took a scanner from his pocket. He waved it down her arm until the device found the small chip inserted there. "First, we have to ID the body. As you saw, her tags are missing, most probably removed by the shrapnel that took out the back of her neck. An embedded chip helps enormously. Not every soldier has one yet, but it's only a matter of time." The captain connected the scanner to his PC and the two devices exchanged data. A spreadsheet suddenly appeared on screen. The fields for name, rank, serial number, next of kin, and various addresses were all filled in, the scanner having interrogated the chip. There was also a photo. The soldier had the rank of specialist. She was pretty in life, but not anymore. Death doesn't flatter many people.

"Makes things a damn sight easier," said Blood.

The morgue was filling fast. Six other doctors, each with assistants, were in the room processing the victims of the truck bomb. The bodies looked misshapen, like human bladders, their insides virtually liquefied and then poured back into their skins. The room stank of punctured intestines. "With the identification of the soldier confirmed, an autopsy is conducted to determine the cause of death, and then a death certificate is issued. The information goes into the central database at the DoD, and then various government departments and agencies are informed electronically."

"Who performs the autopsy?" asked Masters, aware

that, so far, Blood hadn't told us anything we didn't already know.

"I do, or any one of ten others here certified to do the job," he answered.

Beyond the morgue, chaplains and rabbis were moving among the dead, invoking various rites, the religious equivalent of straightening the tie and slicking down the hair prior to an important interview.

I smoothed a photocopy of Peyton Scott's autopsy out on the tabletop. "Was this performed here?"

Captain Blood cast an eye over it. "Looks like one of ours, and says so right here." He pointed at the box into which had been keyed *U.S. Army 28th Combat Support Hospital.* "That's also our seal on it."

"Do you recognize the name of the person who performed the autopsy?" Masters asked.

"Hmm . . . Captain Homer Veitch. It doesn't ring a bell, but that doesn't mean much. The date on this autopsy is around a year ago. I've only been here ten months."

"Can you tell us whether Veitch has performed other autopsies here or anywhere else?" asked Masters.

"Yes, ma'am. It will be in our records."

Captain Blood's fingers did a one-two, buckle-my-shoe across the keyboard. The cursor cursed, flashing rhythmically. Nothing. I wasn't expecting anything different from the last time we searched Veitch's name, but I was interested in Blood's reactions. And I was rewarded.

"That's odd."

"What is?" I asked.

"Well, this Peyton Scott is the only entry under Veitch's name. It's not likely the doctor would have performed just one autopsy . . ."

I didn't tell Blood it wasn't likely he'd done even one, given that he was three months in the grave by the time Scott died.

"How does the system know who performed the autopsy?" asked Masters.

"The doctor's name comes up automatically when he logs in."

Masters sat, hitching a cheek on the desk's corner. "How do you do that—log in?"

"I use a swipe card and key in a PIC, a personal ident code. The computer then knows who's operating and fills in the necessary blanks."

"Could you show me your card?" I asked.

Blood shrugged and pulled it from a slot in the side of the keyboard. A screen saver showing the crest of the U.S. Army immediately appeared on the monitor, which was, I guessed, the on-line equivalent of a steel door slamming down. No swipe card, no entry. I took the card, examined it quickly, and passed it to Masters. There was nothing special about it—it reminded me of the card I used to gain entry into the OSI offices back at Ramstein. The color of that one was plain white, but this one was red. Both had magnetic strips on one side.

"Ever lost one of these?" Masters inquired.

"Yeah. Had my wallet stolen once, but not here— back in the States."

"How difficult was it to get a new one?" Masters waggled the card between thumb and forefinger.

Blood shrugged. "Filled in a form, waited a couple of days . . ."

"Can this card be used from any terminal?" I asked, glancing at Masters. She gave me an imperceptible nod, obviously on the same wavelength.

"No," said Blood. "It has to be a Department of Defense terminal."

"Does the DoD system know where you're accessing it from?"

"What do you mean, sir?"

"Nothing." Actually, it was something, but not for Blood's ears. I continued, "What happens after an autopsy is completed?"

"The body is then bagged and refrigerated, ready for transportation back home."

"Via Ramstein," I said.

"Yes. Mostly, sir."

"Is there any reason why a planeload of body bags heading for the U.S. would be unloaded at Ramstein?"

"I don't know, sir; I'm not aircrew."

"I mean, are there medical or processing reasons why they'd need to be taken off the flight?"

"Occasionally there are circumstances that prevent us from doing autopsies here, but it's rare. In those instances, we've sent bodies to Ramstein to be processed."

Lamont, the Chief Medical Officer back at Ramstein had said much the same thing.

Captain Blood's work was piling up. Literally. The gurneys were needed elsewhere. On a couple of them, several corpses had been stacked one atop the other. "Is there anything else I can help you with, sir, ma'am?" he asked, looking over our shoulders at his growing workload.

"No," I said and turned to Masters. "Special Agent?"

She shook her head.

"Thanks for your time, Captain," I said. "We'll see ourselves out."

"No problem," he said, returning to his screen and logging back into the system.

We retreated to the main hallway, making our way around the perimeter, trying to stay out of the way. "So why would those body bags that appeared in *The Washington Post* picture have been unloaded for no reason?" Masters said, getting in before me.

"Because there was a very good reason," I said.

"Like what?"

"I think General Scott had them unloaded especially to put them on show."

"For the photographer who took the shot?"

"Yeah. Look at it this way—what if Alan Cobain and *The Washington Post* were just the messengers?"

"You're suggesting Scott might have been sending a warning to someone with the publication of that photo? Why would he do that? He must have known Washington—the White House—would go ballistic."

"Yeah, he must've." Jefferson Cutter's chilly letter to Scott sprang to mind. Something had driven Abraham Scott to do something that went against his training, his loyalty to the air force.

"While we're poking around these unanswered questions," said Masters, troubled, "can we talk through the moment when Scott opened his son's body bag?"

"Yeah, what's up?"

"Well, put yourself in his shoes. If you were a father—I take it you're not, by the way—"

"No, I'm not, but I think I know where you're going. Would I, or wouldn't I?"

"Yeah, would you want to look in that bag, or would you want to remember what your son looked like—"

"Rather than live with the image of your boy ripped up by high explosives and shrapnel?" Masters's point was a good one. People who had died as the result of battlefield trauma didn't usually leave a particularly photogenic corpse, which is why they are usually buried or cremated in closed caskets. Unlike most fathers, Abraham Scott would have had a lot of experience with badly shattered human bodies. All the more reason, perhaps, why he wouldn't want to look inside the bag...unless... "Oh, shit," I said, as the dime dropped. "There's only one possible reason."

"And that would be...?"

"Someone *told* Scott his son had been murdered. And the proof was the discrepancy between the autopsy and the condition of the boy's body. General Scott *had* to look in that bag."

"Wha—"

"What if Peyton Scott had been decapitated as some kind of warning to his father?"

"Hmm...Do you remember the date the 'Death Row' article appeared?"

"Not to the day."

"Me, neither, but it was around six weeks after Peyton Scott's death. That can't have been coincidental."

"What if the message General Scott was sending was intended not so much for the American public, but for his son's murderers?"

Masters chewed the nail on her thumb.

Was it so unlikely? This case was getting stranger and more complex. Either that or we were letting our imaginations get the better of our judgment.

"What was all that about computer terminals?" asked Masters as we approached the exit.

"If you had a swipe card, a PIC, and access to the appropriate terminal, you could get into the DoD system anywhere—not necessarily here at the hospital. But you could make it *appear* that you were working on KIAs here."

Masters nodded, her face grim.

Had Peyton Scott been autopsied legitimately by Captain Blood's department? Or had the report been wiped from a remote location and another autopsy altogether logged in its place? I remembered Lamont saying the DoD database was a closed system and that once the autopsy had been completed and saved it couldn't be altered. But a computer that couldn't be penetrated was about as likely as a twenty-year-old virgin in Las Vegas, wasn't it?

We had reached the exit, and things had quieted down somewhat at the hospital. All the guests invited by fate to this particular shindig had arrived and were being seen to by their hosts. There were well over fifty wounded by the IED. Down this end of the stick, the war was a sad, inglorious business paid for in the flesh and blood of the young. And, although the goods were spoiled permanently, none of it could be returned. As the cliché said, it was the first day of the rest of their lives, but for many of the injured it would be a life without limbs, or an existence spent in a wheelchair, or staring at the ceiling enduring an eternity of immobility, turned on a timer to ease the bedsores, wondering why they'd been chosen for this hell.

"Excuse me, are you Special Agent Masters, ma'am?" It was a nurse in surgical scrubs.

"Yes," Masters answered.

"This just came in for you," she said. "From Germany."

Masters took the paper. The nurse's bloody glove print was smeared across it.

"What's up?" I asked, resisting the urge to read the note over her shoulder.

"It's from Bishop. Peyton Scott's unit is still incountry, but he says there are no original members. About half were KIA—must have been one hell of an unlucky unit—and the rest were rotated home. He says he has located one man, Peyton's senior NCO, Dante Ambrose, but he's left the Corps."

"Let me guess, he's moved to the island of Bali, where he now owns a bar on a beach. And now we're just going to have to go there to interview him."

"No. Actually, he's here in Baghdad."

"Just our luck. Doing what?"

"Works for a private security company. Bishop's sent us the address. Oh, yeah. And there's something else."

"What?"

"Your accommodating friend, Ms. Varvara? It seems she's wanted by the police."

"What for?"

"Arson."

TWENTY-TWO

I called the police in K-town and spoke to a detective who confirmed it. Varvara had lit the fire in her apartment. Kerosene had been splashed around on the carpet and a fire started with a candle used as a timed fuse. The supposed culprit, the kerosene heater, was examined and found to have been faulty. It hadn't been used in weeks. Also, the security camera in the elevator had captured Varvara leaving the apartment with what appeared to be a half-empty bottle of kerosene. Case closed.

I called Bishop next. He said that on the night of the fire she'd called OSI at Ramstein asking for me and had instead spoken to him. He'd let slip that a suicide note penned by the general had been discovered and she'd correctly figured that this would shut down the investigation. In my mind I pictured her setting the whole thing up, putting *Gone with the Wind* in the bookshelf, splashing the kerosene around, pushing over the heater, lighting the candle. Then she'd paid me a visit and made sure I came back with her in time to grab the book before the flames destroyed it. Was I angry about being used? Difficult to say. She'd played me like a stacked deck, and I didn't appreciate that much. But I also admired her for doing what she thought she had to do. And the fact that *doing* me was part of that—well, fair trade. I'd be deeply scarred, but I'd get over it. The simple truth was, if not for Varvara, OSI would not be pursuing the case.

"Do you know where she is?" asked Masters as I ended the call.

I shook my head. "No idea," I said honestly. The fact that Varvara's passport also happened to have been in the same place as the note from the general, and salvaged because of that, should have rung alarm bells, but my bell at the time was suffering from a severe bout of postcoital inoperability.

"How do you feel about all this?" Masters asked.

"I feel used," I said.

"You're full of shit, Cooper."

We stood at the top of the medical center's steps and looked out across the concrete and razor wire wall. The black cone of smoke that marked the spot of the IED still hung in the sky, although it had diminished in size. Helos hovered around it flying overwatch, looking for an excuse to rocket someone.

It was a short walk around the back of the palace to the area where the convoys marshaled. It was an extraordinary building. "The former residents lived well," observed Masters.

"Yeah and if they ever come back, they're going to be mighty pissed off. The sitters are making a hell of a mess in there."

I sensed Masters flinch.

"Answer me something, will you?" she asked. "Does any of this affect you? 'Cause it doesn't seem to."

That stopped me cold. "Listen, I'm not an Oprah kind of guy, and I don't cry in movies. I deal with things my own way." The tone of her question, which implied that I could care less about the destruction of lives, made me angry.

"It's just that it seems like a game to you."

"What do you want me to tell you, Masters? Do you want to hear about the nightmares? The alcoholism? How about the stalled career and the broken marriage? Or maybe the phobias? Will me talking about all the baggage I've collected make you happy? Make working together easier, or get this case solved faster?" I was working myself up. In fact, I'd only ever boiled it down like that for even myself once before, given myself a picture of what my life was, what I'd become.

"Well, I—"

"It's called irony, Special Agent," I said. "It's a great shield—maybe that's why it's called irony, made of iron, y'know? You should try it. If you're going to stay in OSI, you're going to need protection that works for you. Or it'll get under your skin and you'll never get it out."

I started walking again. Within a dozen steps, I felt like apologizing. Being in that hospital had affected me. And Masters was just trying to come to grips with me—my personality. We were going through the process of getting to know each other professionally, while sharing a number of intense life-changing experiences... Jesus. I gave myself a mental shake. I was starting to sound like Brenda.

"Hey, soldier—you want an ice-cold Coca-Cola? Or maybe you want to take the Pepsi Challenge?"

I looked up from my boots and saw a corridor of shops. Apparently, we'd just wandered out of the war zone and into a friendly flea market. Servicemen milled about in the fairground atmosphere. Incongruously, a heavily armed marine walked past with an M249 machine gun in one hand and a bag of groceries in the other, a couple of bread sticks poking up out of the bag. He strolled by, acknowledging our presence with a nod. His face was covered in the fine, beige dust of the street and his fatigues were bleached the color of dried mud. I didn't get to see his eyes. They were behind heavily polarized rose-colored glasses. An interesting choice.

"What gives here, Corporal?" I said.

"New in town, eh?" he replied.

"Yeah."

"Haji shops. The hajis do a little business, earn a few bucks. You can buy anything you want." He leaned in close, putting his armored body between Masters and me, and said, "And I do mean *anything*—know what I'm sayin'?" Although I couldn't see the wink I'm sure he gave me one behind those lenses, there being no misunderstanding about what that "anything" might be.

"Thanks for the heads-up," I said.

A young Iraqi male who was all teeth, wearing a Lakers basketball cap and other branded clothing, was hanging out of the nearest stall, beckoning Masters and me to come on over. He repeated the offer of selling us sodas.

His shop was little more than a trestle table with a large umbrella over the top to provide shade. Others on the strip were more permanent structures with proper roofs and air-conditioning. Portable generators filled the air with a choral buzz. I decided to take him up on his offer. "Two Cokes, thanks."

The boy—he couldn't have been more than fourteen—took the money and handed over the sodas. I gave one to Masters and said, "Peace?"

She accepted the can and clinked mine in agreement. "Peace. Where are we?"

"Beats me," I said.

"You want an iPod? New model out—fifty thousand songs, movies. What's a war without a soundtrack, right? How about CDs, videos? I can get you cable TV," said the vendor. Masters walked on ahead and the young man said, for my ears only, "Are you lonely here? You like to fuck Iraqi virgin—make your nights as hot as your days..."

"No, thanks," I said. I'm no prude, but I was dubious as hell about the wisdom of allowing this kind of activity to go on unchecked in what was supposed to be a secure area. I caught up to Masters and we picked up the pace through the market. There was nothing more either of us wanted or needed here.

TWENTY-THREE

There were seven convoys heading out in the next four hours. Two were supply ops, the others were patrols hunting for the insurgents responsible for that truck bomb. As luck would have it, one was going our way.

"Duty PAX...Duty PAX," mumbled the sergeant checking our CAC cards. "And you want to go where?"

Masters repeated, "Rasafl Street, number seventy-five. You know it?"

The woman fed the information into her laptop. "Yeah, it's in Saddun. A ten-minute ride from here. Sounds familiar; what's there?"

"A company called MaxRisk."

"Yeah, know 'em. We work with those guys—contractors. We can take you there and they can bring you back here when you're done. You okay with that, ma'am?"

"Sounds good, Sarge," said Masters.

We were directed to the lead vehicle, a Humvee with a TOW launcher mounted on its roof. Hanging curtains of Kevlar armor covered the doors and windows. Two riflemen were already seated inside. Masters and I climbed in and received nods from them. It was hot enough to pop corn inside, and it stank of sweat and cigar smoke leaching out of the riflemen's clothing. I guessed the sergeant sitting opposite was the cigar-smoke culprit; his pale skin was reacting to the heat by flushing a cochineal red. A portable CD player thrashed out heavy-metal music, making conversation impossible. Not that I was looking for any.

The convoy moved off, tires crunching over pulverized concrete and other debris, which included a dog that had become roadkill. The shirt beneath my flaks was drenched with sweat and I could feel it trickling down into my pants.

With curtains over the doors there was not much to see, and the grunting and screaming coming through the speakers merely added to the claustrophobia. The soldiers had their heads back, eyes closed, except for the sergeant chomping his cigar, who alternated between glaring at his feet and at me.

Masters leaned forward. Her hair was up, tucked inside her helmet. Strands of it had escaped and some of these were caught in the sweat on her skin. I watched a bead descend slowly, moving from strand to strand. And then I found myself wondering whether the cleavage between her breasts was also perspiring. It was at that moment I finally realized I was attracted to her. Funny how these things work. Maybe it was the grief she'd given me earlier.

Before long, we turned onto a broad freeway. I got tired of the sergeant blowing smoke rings in four-four time so I turned to watch what was happening up front. "Have you worked out what side of the road the people here drive on?" I asked Masters.

She turned to look out the windshield. She pointed to the right, then the left, then shrugged. The road rules seemed to be only suggestions, and vague ones at that. The traffic was involved in a type of slalom, maneuvering around the deep potholes that pockmarked the road. A rumble filled the car, seemingly coming up through the asphalt. Our road merged with another and we found ourselves beside another convoy moving slightly faster. I counted five Humvees and a seventy-ton Abrams bringing up the rear, no doubt the source of the vibration. The half ton of metal in its tracks battered the road surface as it whipped by at around forty miles per hour. The screech of its turbine engine drowned out Metallica as if the music were no more than a squeaking door hinge. The dust came next, blasting through the vents beside my face. The convoy disappeared down a side road and into a cloud raised by its own passage.

The part of town we were heading for was more commercial, with taller, more densely packed-in buildings. The overall hue was light brown and tan, the color of grit. A bridge took us over a dirty gray stretch of water that moved with the speed of a garden slug. The mighty Tigris.

"Rasafl Street—coming up now," announced a voice from the front. "What number you want?"

"Seventy-five," I said.

Children played in the fountain spouting from a burst water main, shooting one another with imaginary guns. Across the road, an old truck had stalled and overheated. Steam boiled out from under the hood. A bunch of Iraqi males rushed around it, yelling at each other as if it was going to explode. Maybe it was.

There was a lot more traffic on the road, but we barely slowed. Motorcycles darted in and out of the flow. There was only one road rule—get the fuck out of our way. Ahead, the lights in a busy intersection turned red. Our driver kept his foot on the gas. An old heap swerved at us, out of a side street. The driver hit the brakes, skidding. We shot around it, avoiding a collision by inches. "Motherfucker!" yelled our driver. "You get your license off the back of a cereal box?

You're fucking lucky I'm a better driver than you, motherfucker!" The Humvee behind us clipped the Iraqi's rear fender, putting it into a spin. We didn't stop to see if the driver was okay.

The street itself was lined mostly with merchants peddling everything from rugs and canned and bottled petrol to Levi's and Nikes. There were westerners, too—civilians. Most were armed to the teeth with submachine pistols or assault rifles. Those little coils connected to earpieces were also the fashion on Baghdad streets, as were blade-style sunglasses with dark orange or burnished red lenses like the ones the corporal back at haji street had worn. I pegged the majority of these people as former Special Forces or ex-infantry with combat experience. They were not interested in the shops. Their heads swung continuously from left to right, assessing threats, calculating lines of fire, planning escape routes, and estimating the collateral damage should they have to use the firepower strapped to their flaks. For the most part, they appeared to be providing security for the unarmed Europeans who were, I assumed, involved in the rebuilding.

I was looking forward to getting out of this mobile oven. The sun was now high overhead, boring down through the blue magnifying-glass sky. The driver counted street numbers on the buildings, when they were provided. "That's seventy-five there," he said, slowing. He pointed at a tan concrete wall with a heavy brown steel gate. Behind it lay a glimpse of dust-covered vehicles in a dun-colored courtyard. Four men, two Caucasian and two massive Polynesian types, stood guard behind dirty concrete blockades.

"Okay. This is it," said the driver. He pulled up. We opened the door and jumped out. The convoy was on the move immediately, wheels spinning up dust clouds. It was gone within seconds, heading down the road, no farewells exchanged.

Masters spanked the grit out of her fatigues as we walked toward the nearest of the men—one of the Europeans. An HK G36 swung from his right hand. "MaxRisk?" I asked.

The man looked me up and down and took his time answering, as if he was thinking of a witty reply that would impress his compatriot, but either he changed his mind or his brain failed him. "It is," he drawled. A fellow countryman. "And who might you be?" He indicated he meant the plural you with a gesture of his head that included Masters.

Masters and I badged him in unison, holding our IDs in front of his face until he got it. This seemed to take a while, which suggested he was in need of either reading glasses or a few extra points of IQ. I gave him the benefit of the doubt and resisted the temptation to speak slow. "You got an American citizen, a Dante Ambrose, working here?" I said.

"Maybe," he replied. "We got a lot of Americans here."

"Sonny, I'd appreciate a straight answer to a straight question. It's either 'Yes, we do,' or 'I don't know.' 'Sir' is optional, but don't give me any of your macho shit. I'm tired and I'm hot and you're keeping me from the hotel pool." I was irritable, but he had an assault rifle. That made us even in my book and maybe in his, too. Maybe a command tone would help get things moving. It did. He swallowed and said, "Okay . . . okay . . . just head up to the office and ask the man at the desk." He aimed a remote at the gate and pressed a button. It slowly swung open.

"Thank you for your cooperation," I said.

He nodded and spat onto the road.

Good comeback, pal.

A sign painted on a large rectangular board sat on the brickwork over the building's main entrance. It said, *"MaxRisk. Let us minimize yours,"* in orange lettering outlined in black against a pale blue background. Unlike many buildings on this street, this one looked recently constructed. It could easily have been some kind of government garage before the invasion, and was the perfect digs for a heavily motorized security outfit. The building itself was a U-shape, a main block with two wings enclosing the large open courtyard. More than half a dozen pickup-style vehicles were parked rear bumper to the wall, and each carried a fearsome inventory of weaponry. Quite a few Europeans and Polynesians were hanging around servicing their weapons or having a smoke. Others were trying to get a game of soccer up and running, and were rolling empty fuel barrels into position for goalposts.

We walked to the main entrance, where a sign that said "Reception" pointed the way up the concrete stairwell. Music blared from somewhere ahead, Eminem at the end of the tunnel. A man was singing along to it like it was karaoke and he was convinced he was about to be discovered. If so, he was deluded. Masters and I rounded the final flight of stairs and walked into what was more an operations room than a reception area. There was no reception desk—just a row of filing cabinets separating the stairwell from the office space. A large black man was the source of the sing-along. He wore combat fatigue pants—same as ours—but with a black T-shirt. On the front was a grinning death's-head skull with the single word *Smile* above it. He was tapping something into a computer keyboard while he sang. Massive gold rings throttled his fingers except for one, his trigger finger. He seemed not to have noticed us, so I took a moment to scope out the room.

A man in his early thirties, dressed similarly to the singer but with a different T-shirt, blue with some sort of surf motif on it, was leaning back in a chair with his dusty boots up on the desk in front of him, talking on the phone. Occupying one entire wall was a laminated street map of Baghdad. It was covered in grease pencil marks. Other items on the wall ranged from wanted posters featuring unhappy-looking bearded locals, to photos of smiling men packing enough heat to quell a major Central American coup, as well as assorted military memorabilia and a motivational poster with a bunch of guys in a long rowing boat, titled "Teamwork." The caption beneath read, *This is where we all follow the guy with the loudest voice to our inevitable doom.*

The room was deliciously cool and two air conditioners punched into the brickwork thrummed away. Plastic streamers waggling like colorful worms on speed writhed and flicked in the stream of refrigerated air gushing from the vents.

There were also numerous posters of pouting naked women suggestively holding various items from shock absorbers to shoulder-launched Stinger missiles. I wasn't sure what the suggestion was—did they want to have sex with the cameraman or the items in their hands? Whatever, this was an office environment the PC weenies back home had not yet invaded, although these men were obviously ready for them if they tried, because two M4 carbines leaned against the wall within easy reach. The weapons were well used—the bluing worn away in places—but immaculately clean with a light sheen of oil on the barrels. It was the sort of office General von Koeppen's twin would have had if he had a twin and that twin was his polar opposite.

This was MaxRisk's operational HQ. I guessed the company probably had business offices somewhere else in town with Muzak, talking elevators, and secretaries, where contracts were negotiated and clients won over, because there was a shitload of money to be made in this game in Iraq and MaxRisk was a company doing just that.

"Can I help you, sir, ma'am?"

The black man with his death's-head T-shirt and gold rings was leaning on the filing cabinet between us. He was powerfully built. The clear, brilliant whites of his eyes and teeth spoke of health, as did the muscle bulk of his shoulders and arms. His voice was deep and smooth as peanut butter.

I got right to the point. "We're looking for a Mr. Dante Ambrose."

"Who's asking?"

I gave him a look at my star and said, "Special Agent Vincent Cooper, OSI."

"And your friend?" he said, motioning at Masters.

"His trusty sidekick. Special Agent Anna Masters, OSI," she said, holding her ID where he could see it.

The man folded his massive arms on his chest and regarded Masters and me for a few seconds. Then he fired the remote unit at the sound system, silencing Eminem mid-abuse. In the sound vacuum, he said, "It's about time you goddamn people showed up."

TWENTY-FOUR

I asked the man if I could see some identification.

He produced a wallet from his back pocket, and showed me the plastic window occupied by a CAC card. The name said Dante P. Ambrose, and the man standing opposite wore the face in the photo.

"Is there someplace we can talk to you, Mr. Ambrose?" asked Masters.

"Yeah," he said, with a hint of the deep South in his voice. "Teddy—you mind holding the fort awhile?"

"You got it," said Teddy with a bored wave.

The room Ambrose showed us into was a storeroom. Locked, khaki-painted steel gun cases were bolted and heavily chained to the wall. There was a desk, two chairs, a few columns of cardboard boxes, and a small fridge. It was hot and stuffy in the room. Ambrose turned on the air-con and I noticed he'd brought his rifle. My eyes followed it.

"Don't let Marlene bug you, Special Agent; I sleep with her. Spend more than a week in this country and you'll be doing likewise. Get you a drink? The heat will kill you. We got Dr Pepper or Diet Sprite. Take your pick."

Masters and I went for a Sprite and a Dr Pepper respectively. I also asked for Tylenols, if there were any to spare. Ambrose called out to Teddy, who thankfully played requests, and I washed three down with the doctor. To break the ice, I said, "So, MaxRisk. What do you people do here?"

Ambrose gave us the sales pitch. "Mostly, we do CP—close protection—get paid to chew on a bullet for the people we watch over so that they can go about their business. We specialize in anti-hostage work. No one under MaxRisk's CP has ever been taken by insurgents. That's a record we're pretty proud of. We've also had no deaths, no accidents recorded among staff or customers. At the moment, we're contracted to the U.S. Army as well as an Australian company—water-treatment specialists."

"You were pretty hard to find," I said.

"Yeah, well, that's a good thing." He allowed himself a smile. "Might keep me alive a bit longer. Before we go any further . . . Reassure me you ain't CIA."

I was offended. CIA people had a certain look about them, like their mothers dressed them before they came to work. "No, we're not CIA, nor are we after you for unpaid parking fines, Mr. Ambrose."

Masters said, "You know why we're here."

"*I* know why you're here, but I guarantee *you* have no idea why you're here."

"What do you mean by that?" Masters again.

"When are you going to start asking me about Peyton Scott?"

"Start at the beginning, Mr. Ambrose," I said. "How well did you know him?"

Ambrose swallowed a mouthful of soda and said, "Scotty was my sergeant. I was his senior NCO. I met him before we left the States. We did a little house-to-house and room-to-room stuff—trained together with a bunch of Israelis before we landed here. You know what I'm sayin'?"

"Yeah. You get along?"

"Yeah, we got along. He was the son of a general and could have been an officer, but he wanted to soldier from the front line—get his white-boy hands dirty. He was good at it—a good soldier. The men liked him, respected him. I liked him. He knew what he was doing and none of our guys got a scratch while he was alive."

"And after he was gone?" I knew the answer before I asked the question.

"Our unit got shredded. Within three months we'd lost seven guys to insurgents, booby traps, IEDs, and drive-bys. We went from the luckiest squad in Iraq to the unluckiest outfit in the whole fucking corps. Some guys left—got out—others went to new units, but the killing didn't stop."

"What do you mean?"

"I'm saying that my men—all of us—were targeted. And it all started with Peyton. Even after the men left—went home—they kept on dying."

Bishop had already confirmed as much about Peyton's old squad when it was in-country, but what Ambrose was talking about smacked of something more sinister. "How do you know that?" I asked.

"Because everyone I've contacted has turned up dead. Three guys were snuffed out in fires; four in car crashes; there've been accidental electrocutions, drownings, boating accidents; one guy's car fell on him—he was working under it in his garage. Some pretty weird shit has been going on, that's for damn sure."

The word "fire" rang alarm bells.

Masters asked, "And you think they've been murdered?"

"Not according to any police report I've seen. Every single damn one has been an accident."

"How many accidents are we talking about?" I asked.

"Twenty-four," said Ambrose.

I swallowed. Hard. I thought back to the other people who'd inadvertently come into the Scotts' circle and ended up whacked—Alan Cobain, François Philippe...I hoped my insurance was up-to-date. I thought of the Whiteboard back at Ramstein with those names on it, and about adding twenty-four new ones. This picture mingled with another one—the gurneys lined up patiently for Captain Blood's attention, loaded with human beings the shape of football bladders, and, despite the heat, a shiver began in my boots and rolled up my body. "You left the Marines. What brought you back here?"

"Two thousand George Washingtons a day, plus benefits."

"Besides the money."

"I looked up a couple of the guys who lived in Mississippi. I arrived the day one of them was pulled out from under his daddy's tractor. I stayed for the funeral and then went to check on the other. The man's house was just a burned-out husk. You want the truth? I got scared. Here I can carry a gun out in the open. I hang out with badass warrior types. At MaxRisk, we got ex-Delta, ex-SAS; we've got the cream of the cream, as well as some real nasty motherfuckers from the island of Fiji. Basically, while I'm protecting people, my guys are also protecting me. But I know my day will come. Maybe today. So even with all the lunatics and crazies running around in this country, I still feel a damn sight safer here than I do back in my own."

I took a long drink of soda and tried to get my thoughts in order. I had not expected to hear what Ambrose was telling me. I suddenly realized he was right: I had absolutely no idea why I was here—or, at least, what I expected to find here. The death of General Abraham Scott suddenly seemed almost trivial against the background of what was obviously murder on a mass scale. And yet, I had a feeling that finding out what happened to the old man, and why, were the keys to the slaughter.

Masters said, "Do you want to tell us what happened to Peyton Scott, Mr. Ambrose?"

"Call me Dante, Special Agent. And no, not really—not if I can avoid it. Can I avoid it?"

I shook my head. "No, I don't think so."

"I knew it," he said, and those massive shoulders of his slumped. "We need to go for a drive—back to the spot."

I thought it would be a good idea, but I checked it with Masters before agreeing. Accord was clearly part of our détente. She nodded. Permission granted.

TWENTY-FIVE

The temperature soared the farther we got from the influence of those air-con units. Heat radiated up the stairwell from the open door below. It was just after 1400 hours—the hottest part of the day. The heat had a sadistic quality about it. I wondered whether it was antihuman or just anti-American. I recalled how unaffected the locals seemed to be by it and decided it was probably the latter.

Teddy, up in the main office, must have relayed the news that we were headed out because the courtyard was a markedly different place from the one we'd seen on our arrival. For one thing, the soccer game had been abandoned. For another, one of the pickup trucks had pulled away from the wall and four men were readying it for service, loading it up with ammunition for the door-mounted machine gun, the roof-mounted MK19 40mm grenade machine gun, and the Browning M2 machine gun sitting on top of a post rising out of the rear tray.

Parked in front was a modified Toyota 4X4 with its doors removed. M249 machine guns—one on each side—were mounted where the rear passenger doors used to be. They looked like postapocalyptic RVs, because I guess that's exactly what they were.

"Teddy is going to try to get us logged in to the army's patrol schedule—line us up with infantry and gunship support if things get rough," said Ambrose. He frowned and put a finger to an ear. "Okay, we're cleared in." There was no need to relay this to the men, as they'd already received the same information over their tactical radios.

Ambrose drove and Masters took the front passenger seat. I sat in the back between two mountainous Fijians, our waist gunners. The islanders ignored me, turning their snarls to the outside world once they'd checked out the white boy sitting between them. I returned their hospitality. Ambrose fired up the Toyota and set the air-con to stun. We rolled out, past the guys with HKs looking left and right, either checking for threats, or, in the case of the man I'd first met, looking for that lost chromosome.

"What do you think of Baghdad so far?" Ambrose asked Masters.

"Three words: dangerous, dusty, hot," I heard her say.

Those gorilla shoulders shrugged. "Yeah, that's all true, but this place grows on you. They's not all Loony Tunes, you know—the Iraqis. The crazies here are like them vocal minority people we get back home. They's the only ones you hear about 'cause they got the loudest voice."

Yeah, only here the vocal minority does all its talking with rocket-propelled grenades and Semtex, I thought.

Ambrose continued. "Iraqis are not so different from us. They love their country. Seeing invaders strutting around the place gets them pissed. How do you reckon we'd like it if one day the Canadians invaded us?"

"Don't get me started," I said from the back stalls.

"Don't get him started," Masters echoed.

Masters and Ambrose talked. I tuned out and tried to focus on the implications of what Ambrose had told us so far. The killings seemed to be mounting up faster than I could sprout fingers and toes to count them on. I wondered whether, buried somewhere in General Scott's files, there was a copy of that original autopsy, the one done when Peyton Scott's remains were delivered to the 28th Combat Support Hospital on the day he died.

I glanced out the window. We were on a main road with plenty of other traffic, heading in a northerly direction. The housing on either side of the road was not Baghdad's finest. "When we first came in," I heard Ambrose say, "the Iraqi resistance would warn the local people about IEDs by the roadside or packed into the Armco fencing. They'd write a warning in the local lingo on the road nearby. So the Iraqis would give these IEDs a wide berth, but we'd just blunder straight on into them. We've wised up now—and the result? More Iraqis get killed because warnings are no longer given. Fun and games."

Well, games at least.

Masters and Ambrose continued their friendly chat. I wondered when they'd move on to discuss their favorite restaurants. Ambrose turned hard left and dove into a narrow lane between close-packed homes. Sensibly, the Iraqis were in the shadows, out of the direct heat of the sun. There were still plenty of kids around, playing soccer or chasing each other. It reminded me a little of home. Kids are kids all over the world. Ambrose slowed and used plenty of horn to clear the road. The Toyota was mostly ignored but a few fists were raised in our direction, accompanied by a shout or two. Clearly there weren't many Iraqis who owned nice new Toyotas, with or without doors.

The streets got narrower and darker and we slowed

some more. Fewer people were out on these streets. I caught the unmistakable stench of long-dead human, and then I saw the movement down a narrow alley darkened by deep shadows. Rats the size of rabbits squabbled with dogs over the remains. After Afghanistan, I was intimately familiar with this most acrid of smells. There the cold often hid death's presence. Here, it was different. The heat stripped away any restraint. But cold weather or hot, the olfactory palate of a long-dead human being was as complex in its way as a fine French perfume, although, unlike the latter, definitely not to be worn behind the ears. I wished I'd taken the sergeant up on his offer and accepted some of that mint chewing tobacco.

Lying in these shadows was the corpse of someone's father or son, wife or daughter. The stench and the loneliness brought back the memory of the airless cold and the image of slashing steel in Afghanistan.

I noticed that the dogs were hanging around in groups of three. These animals had long since ceased to be man's best friends. Instead, they'd taken up employment in the Baghdad city sanitation department for the uncomplicated promise of all they could eat, free.

Despite the heat, a shudder went through me. I forced my attention back to the conversation Ambrose and Masters were engaged in. The former marine said, "We came to this part of town to search for weapons. Nothing out of the ordinary." As he spoke, we burst out of the shadows and into bright sunshine with the Tigris beside the driver's window. "We'd pretty much finished the patrol and weren't expecting trouble," he added over his shoulder. I leaned forward between the seats. "We were retracing our steps through the streets I've just taken you through, but found our way blocked by vehicle wrecks. I thought we'd just made a wrong turn but I was wrong."

The river's floodplain was below us on the left, on the other side of a low retaining wall. On our right were the brick and concrete walls of the local residents, built high to keep prying eyes away from the women.

Ambrose slowed the Toyota to a crawl. "We found ourselves here." He pulled to the side and stopped. He picked up the microphone from the radio set mounted under the dash and called in our position. I glanced behind us. A couple of the men had jumped out of the pickup. They were moving to form a perimeter defense, checking the angles, their personal weapons pointing toward the sky. Ambrose grabbed Marlene and a backpack from the passenger floor and got out. Masters followed. One of the Fijians swung his legs to one side so that I could pass.

The heat bouncing off the concrete surfaces was intense, and the air was laced with the scent of a mound of raw sewage piled beside the road, upwind.

"We came down here in a convoy of four Humvees. Our minds weren't on the job. We were hot, tired, and looking forward to getting back to the compound and then something hit us, and hard."

"A land mine?" I asked.

"No, man, it weren't no land mine," Ambrose snorted. "You saying a land mine means you've seen Peyton Scott's autopsy report."

"Yeah, have *you*?" I asked.

He nodded. "Peyton's old man showed me. The general. After Peyton's body was shipped home, he came to see me, flew down from Germany . . ."

Bingo, I thought. The general's missing days—more of them accounted for.

". . . the autopsy report said Peyton had been killed

by a land mine explosion—shrapnel wounds to the body, right?" Ambrose snorted again. "You ever been spritzed by a man's brains, Special Agent?"

"No," I said.

"I was standing beside him. We were talking. And then suddenly Scotty's head was gone and my skin was cool. It was Peyton—atomized. All over my arms, my face. Y'know, his hands reached out to me. Can you believe that? Like he could see, but there was nothing to see with 'cause his brains were all over me. An image like that—it burns itself onto your mind." He shook his head as he looked at the ground, no doubt seeing the image he couldn't erase.

I nodded. I had my own memories keeping me company.

Ambrose dug into his backpack and produced a clear plastic bag. He held it up and said, "Anyway, it wasn't no land mine. This is what killed him."

I took the bag from his fingers and examined it. Inside were bullet fragments, something big and unusual.

Masters asked, "Where'd you get this?"

"We came back here the day after to check the place out—make some sense of what'd happened. There was a hole punched in the wall—you can see where it's patched." Ambrose ran his hand over a rough, unpainted section. "The round that killed Scotty did that. And then it smashed through a forty-four-gallon drum filled with stored drinking water on the other side. We found the remains of it—what you're holding in the bag—in the bottom of the drum."

"Jesus," Masters murmured.

Masters was right to be impressed. It would have taken a hell of a lot of force to punch through into a steel drum after bashing through concrete.

"I think the round that took down our Humvee was different, maybe an armor-piercing incendiary round. It went through the radiator, shattered the crankcase. We didn't look for that round—there wouldn't have been anything left of it."

"What would fire something like this?" Masters examined the bag.

"An AMR, an anti-material rifle," I said. "Possibly a Barrett gun." I'd seen Barrett guns in action in Afghanistan. From across the valley, I'd watched a team of Australian snipers clear a hilltop of giant scorpions from a mile away. It was a formidable weapon.

Ambrose agreed. "For what it's worth, that's what I reckon, too."

The fragment Ambrose had removed from the drum sure looked like the remains of an AP round—the tungsten penetrator. Also bagged were a few fragments of the copper jacket that would have peeled away when the round hit the wall. Whoever killed Peyton Scott wanted no mistake, but also wanted the body left relatively intact. It felt like we were getting lucky—having the forty-four-gallon drum in place to catch the projectile that killed him—but I didn't want to say as much for the very reason that the bullet had gone through Ambrose's buddy to get there. But, all the same, we *were* fortunate. We now had evidence literally in the bag, and Peyton's DNA—specifically, his gray matter—could still be on the copper casing fragments. Of course, I didn't mention that, either. With Ambrose's eyewitness account to go with the fragments, we could call into question the authenticity of the Veitch autopsy report.

"You wouldn't still have Peyton's Kevlar, by any chance?" I asked. His helmet might still contain hairs, skin, and possibly blood fragments, all of which would contain his DNA. We'd need that reference to prove any DNA still present on the copper casing fragments was Peyton Scott's.

Ambrose smiled. "Indeed, I do." He opened the backpack. Inside was another clear plastic bag. This one contained a helmet.

I was officially excited. This was another genuine break. I accepted the backpack. "Can you tell me what happened next, after Peyton went down?"

"We started shooting up shit. We were as jumpy as hell. But there weren't nothin' to shoot at. Look around. It's just the same now as it was that day. We called it in and a Black Hawk flew overwatch for a while, but, well, nothing..."

I looked around. The walls of the houses backing onto the street curved away with the floodplain. The sniper's hide could only have been on the other side of the river, a good mile and a half away in the heat haze, but well within the range of a Barrett gun. "Any other shots fired?"

"None came back at us. One shot took out our vehicle. The next whacked Peyton. And no one even heard those shots."

Most likely the shooter had buried himself in an abandoned building with a clear line of sight to this bend. The rifle was probably also equipped with a baffle—no muzzle flash and no sound to give away the shooter's position.

"Was Peyton's body medevaced out?" asked Masters, beating me to it.

"Yeah. We also had one walking wounded—leg wounds. Shrapnel from the hit on the Humvee."

"You said you were retracing your steps through the

streets, but you found the way blocked. You want to tell us more about that?" Masters asked.

Ambrose took a small map from his back pocket and spread it on the Toyota's hood. "This was our route in and out." He traced it with his finger. "By the time we pulled out, barricades had been set up here and here. When we came to a barricade, we tried to find another way around it—we didn't want to break through them in case they were stacked with IEDs."

"So you believe you were herded through this point here?" Masters said.

"Yes, ma'am."

"That means you're saying you think the whole thing was planned and executed—"

Ambrose didn't like Masters's disbelieving tone. He cut her off. "Yeah, that's what I believe. Of all the men who were with Peyton on that day, I'm the last man standing. And now Scotty's father—the general. He's dead, ain't he? That's the real reason you people are here, ain't it?"

I didn't look at Masters, although I felt her eyes flick to me. "Yeah, that's why we're here," I said.

The road was quiet. There weren't even any dogs or cats slinking about. Ambrose's men had formed a perimeter. They were watchful and patient, good soldiers whether wearing their country's uniform or not. There was the faint hum of traffic floating across the river from the far bank, as well as the ever-present noise of helicopters, but nothing else. No bomb blasts, no *tat-tat-tat* of distant gun battles. Under the sun's naked flame it was unbelievably hot and still. So why were chills crawling around under my skin? "You said General Scott came to visit you. What about?"

Ambrose walked toward the retaining wall and

looked out across the Tigris. "It was a week after Peyton's death. He wanted to know what had happened to his son. Like I said, he showed me Scotty's autopsy. Cause of death was trauma from a land mine. I knew that was a lie, and because the general had seen his son's body, he knew it was a lie, too. I think he just wanted Scotty's murder confirmed by an eyewitness."

"Do you think someone told him his son had been murdered?" I asked.

"I don't know for sure—he didn't say—but why else would he not have believed the autopsy report?"

I nodded. *Yeah, why else?*

"How long did he stay in Baghdad?" Masters asked.

"Just one day, I think. And he was wearing the uniform of a lieutenant colonel."

"Didn't you think that was odd?" Masters said.

"No."

"Why not?"

"Well, ma'am, because a four-star tends to attract attention. Lieutenant colonels? Not so much. He wanted to be here incognito."

"Did Peyton have any enemies?" I asked. There was that question again, the one that always gets an airing in murder investigations. I was expecting Ambrose to give the usual answer, but he surprised me.

"Yeah, I think he did have enemies—maybe the same ones his father had. Scotty began to talk about how he was in danger, how people might try to get to his father through him. We all laughed about that—we were in Iraq, for Christ's sake, and every motherfucking one of us was in danger. So we thought he was just full of shit—mucking around, y'know? But now, with Scotty dead and all my men dead and his dad dead—and probably a lot more folks dead that I don't know about, right?—well, I don't think he was so full of shit, after all. Now I'm a believer."

"A believer in what?" I asked.

"You ever heard of a group...a group that calls itself 'The Establishment'?"

TWENTY-SIX

The establishment. No, amend that. Not the airy one we all refer to, a euphemism for the status quo. He was talking about The Establishment, a different animal entirely—one with a capital T and a capital E and, apparently, an appetite for blood. I stood there not knowing what to say for a couple of seconds while Varvara's words ran through my brain. *The Establishment killed him—the same people also killed his son, Peyton.* She knew. Had Varvara mentioned the name of this shadowy organization just to see if I'd react? To see if I was in the loop? What had Abraham Scott told her? Was it possible there really was a group called The Establishment out there punching people's tickets? And, if so, why? At the time, Varvara had been correct in assuming that, had she just laid it all out for me, I wouldn't have believed her. But now...? "Did Peyton tell you what or who The Establishment was?" I asked Ambrose.

Something rang. It was Ambrose's Iridium phone. He held up a hand to put me on hold for a moment and pulled the unit off the clip on his belt. He answered it, saying a few quiet words I didn't catch. The call finished, he hooked it back on his belt, placed a finger in his ear, and then repositioned the thin tube that contained the tiny microphone in front of his mouth. He muttered something into it; again, nothing I caught. Then he told us, "Sorry. Just got the word. Been told by

The Man to clear this sector." Ambrose hopped up on the Toyota's doorsill and slid behind the wheel. The men assumed their positions in the two vehicles behind. "Getting back to Peyton, Special Agent, I can't tell you too much more. Scotty wasn't long on detail. Maybe he didn't know what he was dealing with. It had something to do with his father—that's all he said. I wish I knew more. Then maybe I could use the information to get a little leverage, get whoever or whatever to lay off; you know what I'm saying?"

I knew. Ambrose was scared and he had every right to be. I wasn't feeling too comfortable myself, and neither was Masters if the frown on her face was anything to go by. I stood there on the road, my mind a black hole of confusion. I had questions but I didn't know which to ask first. One pushed its way to the front. "You said the general came here for a day."

"That's right, but I don't know exactly how long he hung around. He only spent the morning with me. He said he was leaving but I didn't see him get on the plane or nothing."

"Okay," I said, taking this in. Sergeant Audrey Fischer, the PA in von Koeppen's office, said Scott had taken three weeks off. We now knew that he'd spent one, possibly two days in Iraq with Ambrose sorting the facts from the lies surrounding the death of his son. Varvara had said he'd gone to Riga for a week. At the end of that time, he'd returned to Germany, taking her back with him. That left us with a number of days still unaccounted for.

"Earth to Cooper . . . ?" Ambrose said.

I was holding up the show.

"Huh? Oh . . . sorry," I said. Everyone was loaded up and ready to roll. I climbed in—this time in the front seat beside Masters—and pulled the door shut. Ambrose stood on the gas, turned hard right, and we plunged into the darkened streets. The narrow houses flashed by but I didn't see them. I was trying to organize what we now knew, and what the implications of that knowledge might be. My instincts told me Peyton Scott had been murdered as some kind of warning to his father—just as Peyton had told the men in his squad. But, for whatever reason, the general didn't heed that warning and so *they* killed him. From what Ambrose was saying, the mysterious *they* were The Establishment. If so, what was the motive? *They* also had to be a connected and powerful organization with serious reach and resources to erase a four-star general from the roster.

A movement out of the corner of my eye distracted me. It was a truck coming down a side street. Fast. I turned to watch it pass behind us. Shit! It was going to hit the—

I heard Ambrose say, "What the fuck—"

And then my neck snapped around as my head whipped to the right, hitting the door frame. My helmet strap tore at my chin and I bounced into Masters. We'd been rammed in the side by a truck—not the one I'd seen crash into the pickup behind us, but another that had launched into us from out of shadows. Ambrose fought with the wheel. We were being shouldered into a row of houses by the truck. The Toyota's tires screamed in protest and then we slammed into a stone staircase. The front of our vehicle buckled. The air bags deployed across the dashboard, pinning me against the seat. The vehicle rolled. Everything became a tumble of grinding metal and breaking glass. We clipped something, smashed into another wall, the front windshield shattering, splintering the light. It happened so damn quick. We hit something solid and the Toyota bucked high and came down again hard. The world fell silent.

Ambrose and Masters were below me. No one moved. I smelled gas. Either the tank had ruptured or the fuel lines had ripped out. I reached down, twisting the ignition key to the off position. The engine died. Steam sprayed from the buckled hood. Someone groaned—Masters, I thought. The bags deflated. I checked the backseats. I counted the Fijians. At first there were two. But then, as my head cleared, the two became one. And the one that remained was clearly now consorting with his ancestors, or whatever it was that Fijians did when they left this life. The odd kink in his neck and the blank stare were dead giveaways.

"The windshield—kick it out," Ambrose stammered. He was hurt, and the fact that he was straining beneath the weight of both Masters and me pressing down on him wasn't helping any. I got a boot to the glass and it separated from its seal on the third kick.

I climbed out and fell onto broken masonry. I turned and helped Masters out. She fell and rolled on her side with a grunt. I reached inside the cabin. Ambrose gripped my hand and pulled himself up. His arm shook with the strain. He winced and I saw that his teeth and gums were red with the blood streaming down his face from an ugly gash above the bridge of his nose. "You okay?" I asked.

"My arm," he said.

He didn't need to elaborate. I could see it for myself. The wrist of his free arm had a depression in it like it had gone through a metal press that stamped out frying pans from sheet steel. The truck had hit our Toyota just behind Ambrose's shoulder. His body had absorbed the full impact. I helped him out as flames leaped from under the hood. They seared my face. The pool of fuel under the vehicle erupted into a wall of flame with a *whoomp* sound. Masters came forward and helped me lift Ambrose. I noticed that my boots were on fire. We made it across the floor of what appeared to be a bedroom in someone's home. There were sheets and blankets and I used the fabric to extinguish the flames, beating them out, just as my feet were beginning to feel the heat.

Masters and I led Ambrose through the doorway, into a hall, away from the burning vehicle. I noticed that a man with his wife and three children were on the other side of the room, huddled in the doorway. He had an AK-47 in a one-handed grip, his other arm around his sobbing family, holding them close. The weapon's muzzle made small circles in the general direction of my testicles. Ambrose said something in Arabic that I assumed was along the lines of "We come in peace," but I didn't think the man would buy it, given that we'd just demolished the front of his house with two tons of Japanese steel and were now burning the remainder of it to the ground.

After a momentary standoff, our host decided it would be best to retreat. He backed his wife and kids beyond the doorway, not taking his eyes off us, and was gone. A small explosion erupted from the front room. I felt the heat of it on my back and the concussion in my eardrums. I wrapped an arm around Ambrose's torso to help him walk and he sagged against me. I knew why instantly. Several of his ribs were broken. He could also have internal injuries, I realized. Ambrose was a big man; Masters and I struggled to get him to the door.

We made it, finding ourselves in a high-walled courtyard with a wood-paneled gate through which the man of the house had presumably left with his family. A load of washing was left half finished in a stone sink. There was a knee-high garden bed bordered with brickwork where various herbs and vegetables drooped in the heat. A small amount of some kind of animal droppings—goat or donkey, I guessed—had been shoveled into a corner of the courtyard. The animal itself was nowhere to be seen. Perhaps it had departed with the occupants. Here and there were toys, reminders that this was a family home. Through no fault of our own, we had brought the war into this house.

Ambrose was close to collapse. We laid him on the ground and tried to make him as comfortable as possible, which amounted to making sure we didn't step on him. There wasn't a hell of a lot else we could do, except maybe get him to a hospital, and quickly. "You okay?" I said to Masters.

"Yep."

"Did you see what happened to the pickup behind us?"

Masters shook her head.

"Don't expect any help from them," I said.

Suddenly, a mushroom of flame bloomed in the wall that surrounded the courtyard. The sheer violence of it confused me for a moment. How had it happened, what caused it, and why? The Toyota was behind us and we were on the other side of the house. What was going on? The flame rolled into a black ball that boiled up into the sky. A hole the size of a man's fist was left in the wall. As I watched, another ball of orange-and-black-streaked flame erupted on the wall, close to the first explosion. Something whizzed by my face. I glanced down and saw blood dripping onto my singed boots. I put a dirty hand to my face and pulled it away, bright red with blood.

Yet another ball of flame burst through the wall. I felt the pressure wave wash over me and then an entire section of the wall fell inward.

A projectile slammed the wall at the back of the house, inside the courtyard this time. I felt the power of the hit vibrate through the soles of my feet. Concrete dust and masonry fragments blew outward. A fragment of something fizzed past my ear at supersonic speed and buried itself in the wall by my shoulder, sending out a cone of chips that nicked the skin on the back of my neck. I rubbed it and my hand again came away bloody. I threw myself on the ground, pulling Masters down beside me. I knew what was going on. The wall retaining the garden bed exploded into dust and earth and plants slid out of the breach.

The wood-paneled door was next to go, bursting into a hail of splinters. I buried my head under my arms as they rained down on us and stuck into the exposed skin on my hands and arms like porcupine quills. I gagged in the dust.

"It's an AMR," I shouted. Barrett guns were used to take out bad guys hiding behind walls. Apparently, a Barrett worked equally well against good guys doing the same.

"What?" said Masters as more rounds slammed into the wall, causing a large section of it to collapse into the street.

"Never mind!" I'd explain later, if there was a later. It occurred to me that, as far as I knew, the Barrett gun was not a weapon used by the insurgents, which either meant they'd figured out its advantages, or we were being attacked by . . . who? Our own people? Peyton Scott had been executed with a round from a Barrett. I grabbed Ambrose under an armpit and began to drag him back to more secure cover. Masters realized what

I was doing and did what she could to help, lifting one of Ambrose's huge legs, staggering a little under his weight. We were retreating back inside. In my view, we had a better chance of surviving snuggling up to the burning Toyota than behind a single barrier made of Third World–strength concrete.

Ambrose was drifting in and out of consciousness. We propped him against a wall. Now we were trapped between the burning vehicle behind and the steady destruction of the building in front. Ammunition in the vehicle began cooking off, copper jackets whining as they ricocheted off the brickwork in the sunroom by the front door. Whoever was operating the AMR wasn't satisfied with the job done on the external courtyard wall and had begun shooting out the back of the house. I pulled the M9 from the shoulder holster and popped the clip, making sure. Fifteen rounds. No spare magazines. I pulled back the slide and thumbed the safety. Even though we were completely outgunned, I at least had something I could fire in anger. I reholstered the weapon. AMR rounds began finding their way into the back of the house, carving out enormous holes in the wall and showering us with stone chips. Fragments of concrete and metal peppered my helmet. Masters and Ambrose were bleached white with dust except where blood oozed or trickled from numerous cuts and gashes. We had to get out.

I patted down my pockets, looking for something—anything—that might help. I had a CAC card, a couple of Tylenols. I also had a . . . hang on, the CAC card, a *get-around* card! Christ! Of course. We were spliced into the army's patrol system. If we could get word to central command, they'd send the cavalry. I bent over Ambrose and unhooked his Iridium phone. All I had to do was punch the redial button and I'd get through to

Teddy back at MaxRisk and...Shit! The damn thing was crushed, its plastic case cracked, the screen smashed. It was as dead as the Fijian. The brickwork behind my head exploded, showering me with rubble. The force of the pressure wave knocked the wind out of me. A fragment from the round pinged off my helmet: The impact felt like someone had slammed my head with a baseball bat. I fought for breath. It came eventually, along with a cloud of dust that penetrated deep into my lungs and gave me a coughing fit. I dug into Ambrose's other pockets to see what else he had: a big, fat nothing.

I had to get back to the Toyota. There was a radio there. I hadn't noticed whether it had survived the crash. And, if it had, what were the chances that it wasn't burning or shattered by stray rounds? Another AMR round drilled into the wall, forcing Masters to curl into the fetal position.

Much of the external wall had collapsed now, providing whoever was shooting at us with an increasingly clear shot. It was now or never. I crawled on my belly back through the house. The ammunition in the Toyota was still exploding, although at a much reduced rate. A round of something cracked off the ceramic plate on the back of my flaks. The gas fire had died a little, the source of the leak either pinched off or the fuel consumed. I made my way through flames to the steering wheel. I pulled myself into the vehicle. The power light on the radio's face was not lit. I took another chance, reached down and turned on the ignition. Shit! The light came on. I grabbed the receiver, hit the send button, and told whoever was out there that we had crashed and were under fire.

I hoped the friendly radio stations in the vicinity

were manned by diligent, able persons itching to play their part in our rescue, like they are in the movies, not the overworked, underpaid, and underlaid people who seemed mostly, at least in my experience, to occupy the real world. I had no idea whether anyone received the broadcast. Nothing came back through the speakers.

Then, the light on the radio winked off. It had died. Shit. I tapped the set with the microphone: nothing. I had a quick look around the vehicle to see if there was anything we could use, in particular Ambrose's rifle, Marlene. I couldn't see it. It had probably been flung from the Toyota along with one of the Fijians.

Snaking on my belly, I made my way back to Masters, where the world had miraculously stopped collapsing. The boiling dust clouds began to settle. Masters and I both coughed to clear our lungs of the grit. Ambrose was oblivious to it, lying as still as a fallen onyx statue. "Help me move him into a corner," I yelled to Masters. If the shooting started again, I wanted Ambrose sheltered by as much of the remaining walls as possible. We wrestled him into a more protected position.

In the back of my mind, I wondered why the shooting had stopped, but I didn't want to tempt fate by thinking about it too hard. I crouched and tried to peer through the settling dust to the road beyond. It appeared that the house we were in backed onto a large intersection with some kind of well in the middle of it. The area was deserted. If Ambrose had been on his feet, I'd have considered making a run for it—but he wasn't, so that plan was out. And, besides, where would we run to? Okay, dumb idea. I was considering the options when I saw it. Movement. Four figures dressed in light clothing and black ski masks. They were maneuvering for a better position. Jesus. They were about to fucking assault our position! "Can you see them?" I yelled to Masters.

"Yeah, I see them," she said calmly, like she'd asked me to please pass her the cream and sugar. Her M9 was in her hand. She thumbed off the safety. I removed my weapon and ran to a corner of crumbling brickwork. It was odd, but I was relieved that we could now see who we were fighting. At last, we had some targets of our own.

The enemy moved forward in pairs, covering each other. Whoever they were, they'd done this before. They carried Kalashnikovs—AK-47s. Our M9s were outgunned, like taking on swords with plastic airline cutlery. We didn't even have hollow-points, bullets that might have mounted a persuasive argument on our behalf to fuck the hell off. Instead, we had regulation U.S. Army 9mm ball—nice hard rounds that went in clean and tidied up after themselves on the way through.

As I looked, the enemy took cover around two hundred and fifty feet away. I placed a few ranging shots in the vicinity of one of the insurgents and was rewarded with two puffs of dust against the side of the well he was crouching behind. But any satisfaction I might have had was short-lived. Another man stood up behind the well and raised a weapon to his shoulder. Oh, Jesus . . . "Incoming!" I yelled. I buried my head between my arms, pulling it down into my chest. If I could have, I would've brought it down farther and kissed my ass good-bye.

I heard the characteristic sound of an old sheet being torn, the sound of a rocket-propelled grenade through the air, ripping it apart as it accelerated on its vapor trail. I had a fraction of a second to consider this before the warhead covered the short distance across the square. I felt an enormous pressure on my chest and then everything went out and a solid black nothingness filled the gaps.

TWENTY-SEVEN

I opened my eyes. My surroundings were unfamiliar. I had no idea where I was or how I'd come to be there. The world was blissfully silent. I lay on the ground and looked up at the ceiling. The air was filled with swirling golden dust. I watched it writhe like floating snakes and realized that it was afternoon sunlight catching billions of particles hitching rides on the currents. It was beautiful. I lifted my hand through the cloud, but something was wrong. It sure as hell didn't look like my hand; this one was black and red and streaked with white plaster and covered in small bleeding lacerations. Blood rimmed each fingernail. I wondered whose hand it was, poor bastard.

Then I realized the ground beneath my back was also not particularly comfortable. I'd awakened believing I was on a bed, but no bed I'd ever slept on had a mattress stuffed with what felt like broken bricks. I began to cough, but it was odd because I couldn't hear the sound. And then it all rushed back—the crash, the Fijian, my burning boots, the man with his terrified family, the walls being shot away, the weight of Ambrose, Masters's two-handed grip on the M9 and how it jumped with the recoil as she fired at . . . Shit!

I rolled over. My pistol was on the ground. I picked it up with the hand I now realized was mine. Then I stuck a finger in an ear and wiggled. It came out dripping blood. Ambrose lay across the room, spread-eagled on the ground. Was he dead, or just unconscious? Masters was covered in shattered bricks, but she was stirring. How long had I been out?

A slight movement caught my attention. Close by, two of the men in ski masks picked their way across the rubble like they were crossing oyster-covered rocks barefoot. The sun caught them as they hobbled over the rubble. One of them carried a shaft of pure gold. What the hell was that? They were headed for Ambrose. They lifted his head and the gold flashed in my eyes. Jesus H. Christ! No! I realized what that shaft was and what they intended to do with it. Slashing steel! What is it with these people and decapitation? Stupid fucking question. It was in the Qur'an, of course. I'd researched it after Afghanistan in an attempt to try to understand the enemy, and now the words swam in my consciousness:

> *Remember thy Lord inspired the angels: "I am with you: give firmness to the Believers. I will instil terror into the hearts of the Unbelievers, smite ye above their necks and smite all their fingertips off them." This because they contended against Allah and His Messenger. If any contend against Allah and His Messenger, Allah is strict in punishment.*

Basically, if you can't convert the infidel, it's off with his head, *Alice in Wonderland*–fashion. I raised the M9, aimed at the guy closest to Ambrose, and began pumping the trigger. The pistol jumped. I heard no sound. Small puffs of masonry dust marked the strikes of the 9mm ball. My aim was off. I missed with the remaining eleven rounds. Shit. The man with the knife leapt up, no doubt seriously pissed—at least I think he was; I couldn't see his face beneath the ski mask.

He came at me, knife raised high for a death strike. As he brought it down, I thrust up with half a brick clutched in each hand. I deflected the blade with one of them and continued with the other into his face. I felt something crunch beneath it, the gratifying vibration of skin, bone, and teeth giving way running through the brick and into my fingers. The hit stopped him for a moment, gave him something to think about. I followed this ancient karate brick-in-the-kisser maneuver with an elbow strike to the side of his jaw. He wobbled on his feet, but I held his wrist, the one connected to the blade, and twisted it around. Searing heat suddenly ripped through my arm, forcing me to break the grip. His buddy had shot me. The guy with the knife backed away from me, but he tripped and sprawled on the ground. His friend, the one who'd shot me, went to his aid, helping him to his feet. Then he leveled his rifle with his free hand and took a couple of halfhearted potshots in my direction as they backed out the way they came in. All but one of the rounds went wide. The one that didn't slammed into the ceramic plate on the front of my flaks, knocking me over. I saw the insurgents turn and run. I rolled onto my side and kept them in sight through what was left of the back of the house. An old bullet-riddled sedan with two masked men in the front seat rolled into the square and skidded to a halt. Our assailants ran to it and dove in the back. The vehicle took off, the door still open. Something had spooked them.

I stumbled back to check on Ambrose. I said something, but I couldn't hear my own words. Masters's ears and nose were bleeding. She said something back, but I had no idea what. The air around us suddenly filled with choking, blinding dust, as if a hurricane had swept in. I looked up and saw the flickering edge of

a silver-and-orange disc in the sky. It slid overhead
and I recognized the shape of a Hughes Little Bird
chopper, a wicked six-barrel minigun mounted off an
outboard pod.

Masters was kneeling over the prostrate Ambrose
and gave the thumbs-up sign. He looked dead; the only
giveaway that he wasn't was the trickle of fresh blood
running from the coagulated mess on his forehead. I
felt a hand on my shoulder. I wheeled, expecting the
worst and ready for it. I looked into the clean-shaven
face of a U.S. marine sergeant. His mouth moved. I
heard nothing. He repeated it, the cords and blood ves-
sels standing out in his neck. I just looked at him. He
gave up yelling and saluted.

The squad's medic ran to Ambrose and began checking him over. At the same time, a glint in the rubble
caught my attention. I went over and picked up the object. It sure wasn't mine. I checked Ambrose's wrist. It
wasn't his, and I'd have noticed if Masters had been
wearing one. It also couldn't have belonged to the Iraqi
householders. There was only one other possible answer. But how likely was it that a Muslim extremist
would be wearing a Rolex Submariner wristwatch?
And wouldn't he be pissed when he discovered he'd
left it behind? These things cost a fortune!

An hour later I was lying on a cot back at the 28th
Combat Support Hospital. I wiggled my fingers and
toes. All present and accounted for. Miraculous. The
doctor, a captain, had finished sewing up the ripped
skin under my arm where the round had nicked me,
and was continuing his examination. More worrying to
me was my hearing. It was coming back, but was still
fuzzy. The doctor continued talking as he peered into

my ear hole through some kind of device. "You could have been playing beer drums in a band called Damage." At least, that's what I thought he said.

"I beg your pardon?" I said.

"Paying for eardrum damage," he said, more loudly the second time.

"Oh," I said, nodding.

He swabbed the blood from my ears with some kind of solvent that felt cool on my skin. Alcohol? I wondered how the locals would feel about the consumption of a little medicinal booze. Fuck that, make it a lot of medicinal booze. The thought of throwing back half a bottle of single malt was pretty appealing, but I didn't like my chances in this place.

"Headache?"

In fact, I did have a headache, a mild one, but I ignored it because I suddenly saw a bigger opportunity. I shook my head and said, "Toothache."

"You've got a toothache?"

I nodded.

"Open wide."

I did as I was asked. He bent over me, shone a pencil light in there, and had a look around. He took an instrument and lightly tapped the offending molar. I flinched like I'd been poked with a few thousand volts.

He shook his head and said loudly, "Looks bad. Impacted. Can't do anything about that. You're looking at a general." I assumed he meant general anesthetic. "Too busy at the moment. We had a big truck bomb earlier."

Yeah, I remembered.

"I can give you something for it to tide you over." He reached into a drawer and pulled out a blister pack of ibuprofen tablets. "Keep the pack," he said. "We get free samples."

Wonderful. I took four out immediately and dry-chewed them.

"Careful," said the doctor. "Taking that many at once isn't good for you."

"Gee, I'd better be careful, then," I said.

He gave me a look of strained patience and said, "Keep your sutures dry, and have that wound checked daily. It was a clean hole, but there's still a chance of infection."

"Thanks, Doc," I said, doing up my shirt buttons. I ached all over. The local in my arm was wearing off and I was starting to feel like I'd been shot. My chest felt sore and tender thanks to the slug fired point-blank from the AK-47. But there was nothing broken and the cuts from the stone chips and wood splinters were superficial. Masters was in the room next door getting pretty much the identical once-over. She hadn't been shot but she, too, was covered in cuts and bruises. No doubt about it, we'd been damn lucky. It turned out that the radio hadn't worked. My message had been lost somewhere in the ionosphere. The Little Bird pilot had spotted the black smoke from the burning Toyota and had directed a nearby patrol to the location to investigate. Another couple of minutes alone with our attackers and Masters and I would have been meat on Captain Blood's slab.

The captain said something I didn't catch. He gave up trying and instead just indicated that I should get dressed. I sat up, feeling a lot older than my years, and swung my legs off the cot. I'd had time to think about our incident, or, should I say, ambush. There was nothing accidental about it. The MaxRisk pickup behind us had been scuttled, and everyone in it killed. We'd been center-punched moments later and shouldered off the road by a second truck. Split-second timing would have been required. Maybe we'd managed to get farther than our attackers had expected. We'd deprived the shooter behind the Barrett gun of a clear line of sight on our position, so enter the masked men. They'd been dressed to look like insurgents, but I didn't believe they were. The question was, who were they? Again, the mysterious *they*. The Establishment?

The doctor gave me a nod to send me on my way. I loitered outside, waiting for Masters. She came out from behind one of several examination rooms partitioned by yellow plastic curtains. The small cuts on her face and arms had been swabbed with some kind of orange disinfectant. Only two nicks required stitches—one on her forehead, the other on her chin. There was still white dust and grit in her hair and small deposits in the fine laugh lines that curled from the corners of her eyes. She gave me a smile that said she was happy to see me. It was easy to return it.

Masters said, "How's your hearing?"

"What?"

"I said, how's your . . . Never mind."

"I'm joking. I'm fine."

Masters shook her head at me in a way that suggested I should grow the hell up.

"Let's go check on Ambrose," I said.

We eventually found him in a ward with twenty other soldiers classed as lightly wounded. We found him because he was making a hell of a noise, even loud enough for us hearing-impaired.

His chest was heavily bandaged and his broken arm had been placed in a temporary cast. A nurse was attempting to give him a shot, but Ambrose wasn't keen on the idea.

"You know this man?" asked the large white woman with a round face and a little piggy snout. She was wearing plastic coveralls big enough to throw over an SUV.

"Yeah. Having trouble?" I asked.

"Yes. And I don't have time for it. If he won't take his medicine, he won't get better. I'll be back in five minutes, Mr. Ambrose. And then you *will* have your injection."

"What is it?" I asked Ambrose when she was half-way out the door.

"I don't know. She says it's antibiotics. Could be anything. That's the point." He sat up in bed and threw his legs over the side. "I've got to get away from here."

"Why? Don't you feel safe?" asked Masters.

"Look around, ma'am. Where's the security?" Ambrose was angry. He tried to stand. "You were there with me today. You tell me that wasn't planned. Maybe I was right about today being the day. Hell, maybe they wanted to kill three birds with one stone. Did you think of that?"

Actually, I had thought of that.

Ambrose didn't get halfway up before he had to sit down. "Can you pass my clothes?" he said when his head stopped spinning.

I took the bundle off the end of the bed and handed it over. Grit and sand rained onto the sheets.

"What are you going to do?" said Masters. "Just walk out of here?"

"Yeah, you got it. They've got no recovery facilities here. They'll just pack me off to Germany or some-place, unless I die of causes unknown administered in the dead of night by that Goodyear blimp armed with her mystery hypodermic. No way, José. I'd rather take my chances out on the streets."

I was dubious.

He saw my face and added, "There's nothing the U.S. Army can do for me here that MaxRisk can't, unless you count keeping me alive. In short—I'm out of here."

Ambrose pulled up his pants with some difficulty. Masters gave him a hand with his shirt and boots. He stood, this time making it all the way up, sweating with the pain. Masters steadied him. "You sure about this?" she asked him.

He nodded, teeth gritted.

The nurse returned but busied herself with another patient. She didn't notice us walk out behind her vast fast-food ass. "How do you plan to make it back to MaxRisk?" Masters asked Ambrose.

"Same way you did, ma'am. Get on a manifest. I've got a CAC card and I know a lot of the people here besides. No problem."

We stood at the top of the stairs and looked out across the grounds to the concrete blocks bleached middle-aged gray by the sun. Ambrose had quickly regained his equilibrium—at least, he could walk. He was in a lot of pain, though, if the grimace etched on his face was any indication. After a moment, he said, "Look, thanks for saving my butt back there. I heard the fuckers were about to make a doorstop out of my head."

"I keep thinking there are a whole lot of questions we should be asking you," Masters said.

"I think you've got it all, ma'am." Ambrose held out his left hand for Masters and me to shake, which we both did. Gently. "Give my regards to the folks back home. Oh, that's right—they's all dead."

I knew why Ambrose said that. He wanted us to remember that no one was safe until whatever was going on had been busted wide open. For some reason, I pictured telling Harmony Scott that I'd spoken with the last man to see her son alive. Harmony. I'd forgotten about her completely. "There is one last thing," I said.

"Shoot."

"Did Peyton ever talk about his mother?"

Ambrose shook his head slowly. "No, never. Never talked about her."

I found that extraordinary, having met the woman. "He never mentioned Harmony? Not even in passing?"

Ambrose looked at me as if he'd misjudged me. "Harmony? She wasn't Scotty's mother, man. She was his *step*mother."

"His stepmother?"

"Yeah. And he always talked about her enough to know he thought she was his *evil* stepmother; you know what I'm saying?"

Yeah, I knew what he was saying.

TWENTY-EIGHT

I had to be slipping, or maybe going soft. Peyton's death certificate said he was twenty-eight. Harmony herself had told me how long she'd been married to Abraham Scott. I even remembered the conversation. *I knew my husband. That's what happens after twenty-four years of marriage.* Of course she was Peyton's stepmom.

I was starting to get a picture of the Scott family, and, despite Harmony's assertions that they were close, that wasn't what I was seeing. Abraham and Peyton were tight. And maybe, at some stage at least, Abraham and Harmony had been an item. But Peyton and Harmony had been estranged from the beginning, if the photos collected in the garage and in Scott's study were any indication. And I believed they were.

Masters and I batted this back and forth while we made our way to the Al-Rasheed.

"I wonder what happened to Scott's first wife, Peyton's mother?" asked Masters as we reached the row of haji shops.

Yeah, I wondered about that, too, and I now felt I knew enough to make an educated guess.

We both bought cheeseburgers and fries, and ate while we walked. The ibuprofen might have worked on the toothache, but not on anything else. My body ached so much I felt as if I'd been beaten like an egg. The walk to the Al-Rasheed was five hundred very long yards. But I was glad to count my blessings, even if some of them were pains and bone weariness. There were people in this place who'd no doubt woken up in the morning fully expecting that they'd see out the day. The woman with the missing spine awaiting Blood's attention came to mind.

"What happened to your marriage?" asked Masters.

"What?"

"Your marriage. You've said something about a counselor. You asked me whether I wanted you to tell me about your marriage."

"That was rhetorical."

"I'm still asking."

"I'm not married."

Exasperated, she said, "Okay, so I deduce that you're divorced. When you *were* married, what happened?"

I sighed. Masters was learning. Perhaps a little too quickly for my taste. My usual evasion tactics were becoming ineffectual. Common wisdom says you should talk things out. I don't buy that. Some things are best buried in the damp earth and left to the worms. "Okay, I married for all the wrong reasons."

"Such as?"

"Musical chairs."

"What?"

"Musical chairs—my theory about marriage. Want to hear it?"

"Wouldn't miss it for the world."

"Okay. People get married at a certain age because they think the music's about to stop and they don't want to be left without a chair to sit on, so they marry the nearest person before the switch is flicked."

"Are you kidding me?"

"Think about it."

"What's to think about? No one's that cynical."

"I didn't want to be left standing. Brenda was nice,

the sex was great, and I didn't think I was going to find any better. I don't think Brenda's motivations were too much loftier or deeper than my own. Like I said, people get to a certain age, and that's the age when they think they should be hitched. Maybe that's why there are so many divorces. The music stops, you get hitched, and then one day you realize the people who didn't find a chair were the real winners after all."

"You're damaged goods, aren't you?"

"Why do *you* think people get married?"

"Because they meet someone they love and they decide they can't go on without them."

"Quaint."

"Maybe I haven't been kicked in the guts enough."

"Yet."

"So what happened? You haven't told me anything."

I sighed, the resigned sigh of someone who knows he can't escape. "Brenda and I were having problems. She'd decided that she needed to find herself. Before I knew it, I was drinking green slime for breakfast and eating roots for dinner. I needed to grow a second stomach to digest it all. She stopped shaving her legs, took up yoga, and spent the household budget on kinesiology seminars and bulk purchases of aromatherapy oils."

"What were *you* doing all that time?"

"The usual. Jumping out of planes, killing people who disagreed with Uncle Sam."

"You grew apart."

"No. We didn't grow apart. We just stopped liking each other. Nevertheless, we followed advice and went to a counselor to find out why. After a while, I refused to go, when I felt the advice from the counselor was maybe a little one-sided in my wife's favor. I was told these feelings were just a manifestation of my resentment toward her spiritual growth. And I was even starting to believe it until I came home early one day and found her on her knees in the shower, blowing him."

"The marriage counselor? Oh, shit."

"Yeah. Actually I think they were precisely the words he used when my wife stopped trying to suck his tonsils out through his cock and he opened his eyes and saw me standing in the doorway."

"What did you do?"

"I dragged him naked onto the lawn. Then I bitch-slapped him in front of the neighbors until he begged me to stop."

"And did you?"

"Stop? No. I got blindsided by the MPs. My wife called them. Maybe it was just as well. I don't think I'd have been able to stop."

"Why not?"

"It was that moment when I ceased to believe in the dream. You know, the one you have when you're growing up and you imagine what you're going to be and do, and how you're going to be different. That was the moment I realized I wasn't any different from anyone else. I was just an ordinary, everyday fuckup. I beat the colonel up for it."

"Jesus! The shrink was a colonel?"

"Right. Didn't I mention that?"

Masters half laughed, half snorted.

We walked in silence. Part of me hoped Brenda was happy now that the divorce was through and we really were going our separate ways, free to pursue the life we each wanted. The other part of me hoped she'd choke on the colonel's genitalia.

"My turn to ask a question."

Masters replied, "Depends what it is."

"When you were parked outside the pensione the other night, were you about to pay me a visit? Or did you have my apartment under surveillance? And if you were watching me, why?"

Masters didn't answer immediately. Then she said, "If I was staking out your apartment, do you think I'd do it in a mandrill's butt, as you call it, and park it right across the road from you?"

"No."

Silence.

"Well...?" I prodded.

"If you must know, I had a bottle of wine and a couple of packets of peanuts with me. I remembered you had a toothache and decided the nuts were a bad idea, so I went home."

"Come on, you can do better than that."

Masters considered the challenge. "Okay, the truth? The case was closed. You were going back to the States. I felt bad about the way we'd started off. I decided that was mostly my fault. So I bought some wine. I figured we could just talk about the case and perhaps part on better terms. Also, I didn't buy the suicide thing, and I wanted to see how you felt about it. But then I had second thoughts about coming up. I thought maybe you'd misunderstand my intentions—it was nighttime, the wine, your hotel room, you know...I was wrestling with this when a cab pulled up and Ms. Viagra stepped out ready to party, and hustled into your building. I decided three would be a crowd."

"I would have."

"Would have what?"

"Misread your intentions."

We arrived at the Al-Rasheed. It had been a hell of a day at the office. I felt like I'd been awake for a week straight. I wanted to spend some time thinking through the case but my brain was wandering around the place like a drunk in the dark. Several servicemen and -women were sitting out front in the cool dark night air having cigarettes, the tips glowing and illuminating their faces momentarily. Here and there, faces appeared in the blackness and then vanished. The effect was eerie.

Being so near the perimeter and well within range of RPGs and sniper fire, the hotel was blacked out. We dragged our carcasses up the short flight of stairs outlined in low-light red and made it to the reception area. The same sergeant was still on duty, and still watching television. Masters gave the room number, obtained the key, and we shuffled toward the elevator.

"The first day's always the worst," the sergeant offered behind us.

"What's day two like?" I asked.

"Fucking awful, I'm afraid. Oh, and you'll have to take the stairs. The elevator's out." She added a shrug by way of apology. It was only two flights to the first floor, but I felt every step.

The night was getting cooler by the minute. With the sun gone, the heat leached rapidly from the dry desert air. Masters opened the door to our room. A night-light was on, throwing a thin yellow veil across the shadows. The windows were blacked out by heavy plastic taped to the frames. "You know what would really improve this place?" said Masters.

"A truck bomb?" I suggested.

"No, lava lamps."

I grunted and collapsed on the double bed, which instantly took on the shape of a hammock. It's beds like this that keep chiropractors in Porsches. But I was way past caring.

There was a thunderous pounding on the door. I

wasn't sure what it was at first. I thought maybe it was mortar fire coming in real close, or maybe an RPG round or two had decided to join us. How long had I been asleep? Where was my M9? I hate being awakened.

"Can't you answer the door, Cooper?" said Masters as she stormed out of the bathroom, toweling her wet hair, dressed in light blue men's pajamas. She went to the holster lying on the night table, extracted her weapon, pulled back the slider, and thumbed off the safety.

I glanced at my watch and realized I'd been asleep all of twelve minutes. I felt like I'd been arc-welded to the bed.

"Who is it?" Masters demanded.

The door was thick and I couldn't hear the reply, but Masters seemed satisfied. She opened it. General Harold Lee Edwards's adjutant strode in. I managed to peel myself off the bed and give him the courtesy of standing up. The man looked like he'd swallowed something that didn't agree with him; either that or his sphincter had been sewn closed and his personality had gone septic. He was the type that collected clipboards.

"Can we help you, sir?" said Masters, replacing her weapon in its holster.

"Get your bags packed. There's been a change of schedule. Your plane leaves in..." he checked his wrist, "...fifty-two minutes. I hope you've enjoyed your stay with us and that you tell the folks back home only good things. Transport downstairs will take you to the marshaling area. Your names are already on the BIAP manifest."

His eyes shifted behind his dirty glasses from Masters to me and then back. I knew just what was going on in his mind. I half expected him to lick his lips, and I thought of a lizard digesting a fly. I decided not to disappoint him. I took a step toward Masters and put my arm across her shoulders. To tell the truth, I think I was just looking for an excuse. The perfume from her freshly washed hair filled the air around her. Her skin felt soft and smooth and clean and warm beneath the cool cotton fabric.

TWENTY-NINE

I stretched the sleep out of my body when I stepped off the back of the C-17's ramp and onto the Ramstein tarmac, careful not to rip the sutures out of my arm, and then shambled toward the building indicated by the loadmaster. Winter wasn't retreating from Germany without a fight. A cold, hard rain was slanting in, driven by a blustering wind that also picked up the water pooled on the ground and blew it forward in sheets. After the heat of Baghdad, the cold was a shock. It went straight to my tooth, which, despite the bullet wound, reigned supreme in the land of pain and discomfort that my body had become. Masters and I were both drenched by the time we made it to shelter.

I'd only a vague recollection of the last five hours. I'd snoozed in the Humvee to BIAP, dozed while waiting for the Black Hawk to Balad, and sat frozen with terror as we jinked and swooped through the full range of the aircraft's performance envelope in the sightless void of a moonless night over the desert, with only the fluid sloshing around in my inner ears for reference. Sleep hit with the force of a left hook as the C-17 taxied to the Balad threshold markers. And, mercifully, that's all I remembered till we bounced down the runway at Ramstein.

Beneath the nerve-jangling effect of an ambient temperature just a handful of degrees above freezing, I was still bone tired, and so was Masters. The local time was 2345 hours, and I had a date with my mattress back at the Pensione Freedom. We hitched a ride with one of the flight crew to the parking lot at the main gatehouse. Masters and I both looked at her Mercedes and came to the same conclusion without speaking a word.

"Cab it?" she said.

"Yeah."

We'd both caught a little paranoia from Ambrose. I wasn't keen on getting in her car until it had been checked over. We could have done that ourselves, but the thought of doing it in the rain didn't appeal. A couple of taxis were leaving the base, having dropped off fares. We shared one back to K-town. The cab smelled of garlic sweated out of the driver's pores.

Masters said, "You've got a dentist appointment first thing in the morning, remember? I arranged that on your first day here."

"You do care," I replied.

Masters closed her eyes. We sat in silence for the remainder of the journey.

"Pick you up at oh-eight-hundred," she said as the cab pulled in front of my pensione.

"Okay." I opened the door and the wind nearly ripped it out of my hand. I noticed that the weather had swept the normally busy street clear of foot traffic. I stood on the sidewalk and motioned for her to wind down the window. "You did good over there," I said.

She smiled and replied, "Thanks. You were average."

The cab drove off before I could snap out a reply. Yeah, Masters was learning all right. I watched the taxi's taillights disappear and felt the rain hammer into me. It was freezing but it felt good on my skin, which was still impregnated with the dust and the heat and the death of Iraq. I picked up my bag and turned toward the pensione. A man walking the other way bumped into me. I was about to apologize because maybe the collision was my fault, but then I realized it wasn't.

Perhaps it was the ski mask he was wearing, or the way he swung the length of pipe in his hand—like a baseball bat. He was athletically built, lean but muscled, and under six feet. The pit bull type. The rain and the darkness made it impossible to see his face. The ski mask didn't help, either. I thought I was about to get mugged, but the way he moved—carefully, keeping his balance with his center of gravity low and at a point between his feet, aware of each step—told me the pipe was a disguise. He was no street thug. Two other men, also wearing masks, detached themselves from the shadows and cut me off from the Pensione Freedom. They spread out, moving to encircle me. The rain came down harder and the pellets pounding onto the road made a roaring sound. A veil of shattered water and mist swirled above the ground. Waterfalls ran off my nose and chin. I rubbed my hand over my face to clear my eyes. The movement made me remember the bullet wound in the back of my arm.

There was nowhere to go but backward. Three against one. Not good odds. One of the men produced a knife with a long thin black blade—a dagger, a thrusting knife rather than a slasher, the sort Special Forces use for quick, silent killing, pushing the point up into the base of the skull from under the chin or at the back of the head where the brain stem meets the spinal cord, or sliding it between the fourth and fifth ribs into the heart muscle. I'd used one myself a couple of times. You had to know what you were doing to use it well. The dagger was intended for extremely close-quarter use, like when you were sneaking up behind an adversary who was thinking about Ms. July in the magazine tucked under his cot.

Number three had no weapon, which meant either he was confident without one or he'd dashed out of the house and forgotten that his knuckle-dusters were in his other pants.

My mind raced through the options, assessing the situation. I knew, for instance, that there would be some indecision between the assailants about who would strike first. Basically, they risked getting in each other's way. They were maneuvering me back into the darkness of the alley. I turned slowly, keeping myself in the middle of the circle, waiting for the first strike.

The muscles of the guy with the pipe twitched. He was reacting to something behind me. My feet moved before I thought about it. I stepped to the side, split the angle. The knife jerked past the space occupied by my head an instant earlier. Light caught the length of the pipe as it swung through the air. I ducked and heard it bat a path through the rain, a low thrumming sound. They were feeling me out.

The plumber got cocky. He stepped forward, pipe raised high to bring down on my skull—a kendo strike. I went forward, down on one knee, prepared to wear the blow, raising the bag I was carrying above my head. The pipe whacked into the soft, rain-drenched leather, and hit Peyton's Kevlar helmet inside. I struck back, burying my fist deep into his testicles, slamming them into the corner pockets. He collapsed as I rolled to the left and came up beside him, facing his two buddies.

The guy armed only with his fists came next. Suddenly the heel of his boot swung through the air. It thudded into my bandaged arm and it fucking hurt. I dropped the bag, which instantly disappeared in the rain bouncing off the pavement. He drove a punch into my extremely tender sternum. Fortunately, I caught the edge of the blow on an elbow, deflecting it slightly. My stomach muscles weren't quite what they used to be and the wind was driven out of me. I staggered backward and tripped over my bag. I rolled over several times on the pavement, half gasping, half drowning. I came up on a knee, still sucking in air. The two remaining assailants were looking around like I'd just vanished, Merlin the Magician–style. The darkness and the mist rising from the asphalt had hidden my withdrawal. I was congratulating myself on this when a man materialized out of the water in front of me. The guy with the pipe. I dove at him and knocked him into the pavement. Something cracked beneath my shoulder—a bone. It wasn't one of mine, which was all that mattered. I scuttled away as the other two raced across toward their fallen pal. A vehicle turned into the narrow road five hundred feet away, its headlights illuminating all three of us. The man with the dagger lunged forward. I reacted, catching his wrist, deflecting the thrust. The speed of the move must have caught him unaware, because it unbalanced him. I helped him along by twisting his arm the wrong way, threatening to break it off at the shoulder ball joint. The headlights bounced nearer. For some reason, I looked at the man's wrist. Was it possible? I hesitated. Bad mistake. From the edge of my peripheral vision I saw the pipe swinging toward me. I tried to bury my head in my shoulder. Too little too late. The pipe smashed into the side of my—

"Vin . . . Vin . . ."

It was Masters's voice, gentle, soothing. I wasn't ready to open my eyes. Her sympathetic tone told me that I was probably in a hospital. The hospital smell confirmed it, as did sheets with so much starch that they felt like photocopy paper against my skin. I remembered the fight. I remembered getting hit, and I remembered something else. I kept my eyes closed for another handful of seconds, just to see whether this kindly tone in Masters's voice would condense into—if there really was a God—mouth-to-mouth resuscitation.

"Could you call my pager when he wakes?" said Masters to some unidentified other person in the room.

"Sure," a male voice said with an accent I couldn't recognize.

"My number's on the card."

I received no kiss. My commitment to atheism would have to continue. I opened my eyes.

The white ceiling was framed by a stainless-steel curtain railing. Yep, no doubt about it, I was in a hospital.

"Special Agent? The patient is awake," said the stranger's voice. This time I pegged the accent as Italian. A young man appeared in front of my face, a stethoscope around his neck. Am I imagining it or are doctors getting younger? This guy had a bad case of acne and his nose was red and shiny. His hair was black, oily, and unwashed. He looked like he should still be in school, or maybe in a grunge rock band.

He flashed a pencil light in my left eye and then my right. He told me to look up, then down, left and right, and asked me how many fingers he was holding up. I must have guessed right because he moved on to check my ears and throat. Masters appeared beside him while he continued the examination. She was wearing her best smile. Everyone was smiling at me. I must be in a bad way, I thought.

"What happened?" I asked.

"You took a hit," Masters said.

"How bad?"

The doctor, having concluded his cursory examination, said, "You're lucky, Major."

"Lucky" was a word I'd been hearing quite a bit, lately. It was the sort of word I grouped with winning the lottery, not with being mugged. "How lucky, exactly?"

"Severe concussion, heavy contusions, you've lost a tooth, but—"

"Lost a tooth?" I scanned my mouth with my tongue and, lo, the offending molar was gone. In its place was a space big enough to park a Winnebago.

"The root was infected and the tooth probably needed to come out anyway. I wouldn't worry too much. It's amazing what they can do with replacements these days."

I could barely contain my excitement. The doctor was right. This was luck. I tried to sit up, but couldn't. My arm was heavily bandaged and strapped against my chest and every muscle and joint protested loudly.

"You've suffered pretty extensive bruising, but nothing's broken. As I said, you're lucky."

"You're damn right, Doc," I agreed. "Have you any idea how hard I've been trying to get that damn tooth taken out?"

All things considered, I actually felt terrific. And I was almost giddy with relief at the thought of being free of toothache. "What about the guys who attacked me? I'd like to buy them a drink," I said. I remembered the fight, the rain, and that something else.

Masters said, "There were a couple of backpackers staying at your hotel, Vin. You owe them big-time.

They were in a taxi, saw the fight, got the driver to flash his lights, honk the horn. Your attackers ran off."

"A couple of Canadian backpackers? Two males? Drunk?"

"Yes to all three, as a matter of fact. How did you know?"

"Just a guess. How long have I been out?"

"Thirty-six hours, thereabouts."

"What?"

Masters nodded.

"You were hit pretty hard," said the doctor. "We had you sedated for a while, but, for the last fifteen hours or so, you've been sleeping. Your body must have needed it."

"Jesus," I said. "What have I missed?"

"Plenty," said Masters.

"Could you help me sit up?"

The doctor touched a button and the bed changed shape, bending in the middle, lifting my shoulders and head higher. The change in altitude made my brain throb.

A nurse popped her head in, requiring the doctor's assistance elsewhere. He told Masters he'd look in later and departed.

I looked past the nurse and recognized an NCMP armed with an HK in the hallway—the bearded French refrigerator guy.

"What's with the guard?"

"Guards—two men, round the clock." Masters pulled a plastic bag from her briefcase and put it on the sheet over me. "Recognize this?"

"Yeah."

"We found it at the scene. As the man said, you are lucky, Cooper. That's a Special Forces dagger. It wasn't a random attack, and they weren't after your wallet."

"I know. I also know who they were."

Masters raised her eyebrows. I had her attention.

"They were the same men who attacked us in Iraq."

"What?"

"One of them had a large white watch mark on his wrist. He'd lost his Rolex. Maybe someone told him I'd sold it on the black market in Baghdad and he was out for revenge."

"Did you?"

"Sell it? No, of course not. But it did cross my mind."

Masters lit up the room with another smile, and then a thought occurred to her. "Could you identify them?"

I tried to picture what they looked like—even just one of them—but couldn't. I shook my head. "Be on the lookout for guys wearing ski masks."

"Is there any other way we could trace them? To get back here so quick—there are only so many flights in and out of Iraq . . ."

"Yeah, but there are a lot of them and they're full of soldiers, DoD contractors, private security personnel, diplomats." That road led to nowhere. "It's a dead end. What have you been up to?"

"Lots," she said. "Mrs. Scott's back from the funeral. I've been trying to get her permission to have another look at the general's records, but she's not cooperating. She's packing the house up for a permanent move back to the States. Also, I've been tracking down the people in Peyton's squad. Ambrose was right. So far, they've all turned up dead."

We would catch up with the widow Scott later. "Tell me about Peyton's men."

"You've never seen so many accidents. And because they're scattered around the country, no connection has been made between them all. And Ambrose hadn't made any noise about it."

"Who could blame him?"

"Oh, and another thing. Abraham Scott's first wife. Her name was Helen Wakeley. Died in a car crash."

"I was guessing house fire."

"Peyton was three years old at the time. He survived the crash."

"What? He was in the car?"

"A bystander pulled him out as it caught fire."

"Jesus," I said. "Any investigation into the crash?"

"No, but an eyewitness account suggested brake failure. The car went through an intersection, hit a truck, and caught on fire."

"This isn't looking very good, is it?" I said.

"For whom?"

"Well, it could look as though Harmony Scott is involved in some kind of conspiracy involving the U.S. military that has been bubbling along for a very long time."

"And General Scott?"

"I don't know. Maybe he was about to let the cat out of the bag." I pulled the covers off my legs with my good arm.

"Where are you going?" asked Masters.

"Back to work. Do you know where my clothes are?"

"Yeah." She opened up a cupboard and placed a clean, pressed ABU on the bed.

"Anything gone from the minibar? What's the checking-out procedure?"

"Already signed you out, Special Agent."

"Am I that predictable?"

"Yes."

The door swung open and the doctor came in. "Where are you going?"

"I have a game of tennis."

He looked at me for a moment and decided against a protest. "Then I'd better get a nurse to cut away some of those bandages."

"I'd appreciate it, Doc."

The phone rang.

Masters picked up. From the intensity of her expression, I gathered someone was telling her something exciting. She put the phone down.

"What?" I demanded.

"That was Bishop. He's cracked into General Scott's hard drive."

THIRTY

The extended sleep had done me a world of good. I was sore in places I never knew I had places, but the exhaustion was gone. My brain was sharp and I was keen to kick some investigative butt. Whoever these assholes were, they'd had two cracks at us—me, in particular. It was clear that someone out there wanted me removed from the picture. In a way, that was reassuring. If Masters and I were heading down a blind alley on this investigation, no one would bother with us. But now we were on the clock, and it was ticking. Maybe next time there'd be no drunken Canadian backpackers wandering past to save my ass.

I pulled the visor down and took a look at the face in the mirror. I barely recognized the person staring back at me. There was a deep purple-and-black shiner around my left eye, fading to sickly yellow around the other eye and cheek. The whites of both eyes, the left in particular, were flecked with blood. I peeled the dressing off the left side of my face. The skin was bruised, swollen, and split—mashed—but the injury was already beginning to scab over nicely. My face was also covered in small cuts and a suture or two. Anyone could see I'd been playing hard. I decided to leave the bandage off and let the wound breathe.

I flipped up the visor. It was a gorgeous day. The fluffy clouds were back, pasted onto that baby blue sky. Ramstein looked as if it'd been washed and scrubbed clean. This being Germany, I wouldn't have been at all surprised if it had been. The sun was out and behaving nice, saving its worst for Iraq, no doubt. I was real pleased to be back here, in this place, even if it wasn't home, and that made me feel guilty. *I* could leave Iraq, but over a hundred thousand Americans there didn't have that kind of freedom, unless they were zippered into a bag.

A phalanx of U.S. Marines—a couple of platoons— jogged by in the opposite direction, their white T-shirts gray with sweat, a large black man chanting out a rap-style cadence. According to the man, they were basically off to "teach those Eye-rakis a motherfuckin' lesson, 'cause it be the You-Ess Marines gonna do the messin'." We drove past slowly. I couldn't help feeling that young warriors have been going off to war like that since the Battle of Troy, convinced of their own bravery, invincibility, sense of purpose, and righteousness. I also couldn't help feeling that Iraq would beat that piss and wind out of them pretty hard. They might have been some of the best-trained fighting men the world had ever seen, as their sergeant proclaimed, but Iraq was probably not what they were expecting. I wondered which of these men the Reaper had marked as his cut. Even the men who did manage to walk out would be changed in some deep and permanent way. Kosovo and Afghanistan had taught me that war rarely brings out a man's best. Mostly, it brings out the worst, and, no matter how good you are, you find out that you have the bad in you. If you're lucky, you discover that the balance between the two is about equal. But, whatever the ratio, the memories and the self-knowledge stay with you, poisoning your sleep with memories you wish you'd never had. I suddenly realized that Masters had been talking. "Sorry," I said. "What did you say?"

"I said, I'm a bit insulted that no one has tried to whack me."

"What . . . ?"

"As I said, I'm working this case, too. Why *you* while I'm apparently ignored?"

"You're joking, right?"

"Well . . . yes and no."

"Have you had a good look at me lately, Anna? Happy to swap if you like."

"Look, I am half serious about this, Cooper. All I ever wanted to be was an investigator in the military. That's an offbeat ambition, I know, but that was always my dream. So now I'm here. What do I have to do to be taken seriously?"

"You sure as hell don't have to be shot or mugged," I said. I turned to face her against my body's better judgment, every muscle, sinew, and joint screaming at me to give them a break. "Okay, all bullshit aside, you *are* doing a great job. You ask good questions. You cut through the crap and you get to the heart of the problem damn quick. You did your job in Iraq when we were under fire. And you've made some fearless decisions when plenty of others would have turned chickenshit. You marched into Harmony Scott's house and secured those records. I wouldn't have done that. You've got balls, lady. You got this case off the ground."

We drove in silence for a minute or two. And then Masters said, "Thanks, Cooper."

"Now can we go find that Jacuzzi?" I said. I realized how far Masters and I had come when her smile didn't fade.

"So, have you spoken with General Gruyere while I've been sleeping in?" That was a call I was dreading having to make, but the boss was due an update.

"Yes, as a matter of fact," Masters said. "Is she as tough as she sounds?"

"How did she sound?"

"Like, like—"

"Like she smokes cigars in bed?"

"Yeah, like that."

"She's a tough old buzzard, but I like her. More important, I respect her."

"Well, she said, basically, that you were a fuckup and that the minute you got back home she was going to pack you off to Eielson AFB, Alaska, to change traffic-light bulbs."

"We have a special relationship. Did she say *when* she wanted me home? Are there orders on the way?"

"No, I updated her on the case. But she wants you to call when you've recovered sufficiently."

I nodded. That gave me plenty of room for interpretation. I could probably stretch it out to twenty-four, maybe even thirty-six hours.

"Your cell's in the console, by the way, if you want to check your messages." Masters tapped the box between our seats.

I hesitated. Who'd be calling? I ran my tongue in and out of the expanse left by my dearly departed molar. I'd handed out a few business cards. Could be a whole range of people, two in particular. What the hell. I took it out and fired it up. A few seconds after the thing made a connection, it began to chime. Once, twice, three times—four, five, six . . . I had half a dozen text messages and twice as many recorded messages. Several minutes later, I had ascertained that Brenda, my former wife, wanted to talk. Urgently. She didn't want to say about what in a recorded message. No one else had called. I was secretly hoping one of the messages would be Varvara dropping me a line for old times' sake, even though I'd told her to disappear but good. Number two on that list of fantasy calls was Fischer, von Koeppen's PA. But no, every single one was Brenda. Twelve times. There was nothing I wanted to say to her that I hadn't already said, and I couldn't think of anything she could say to me that I'd want to hear. We were done. Finished. Over. *Kaput,* as I think they say in this country. At the very least, she could wait. I turned the phone off and dropped it back into the console as we pulled into the OSI block's car spaces.

"Everything okay?" inquired Masters as we came to a stop.

"Yeah. The messages are from my ex."

"All of them?"

"Uh-huh."

"You want some privacy to call her back?"

"No."

"No, you don't want privacy, or no, you're not going to call her back?"

Was it my imagination here or was Masters giving me a hard time? "No to both."

"A bit childish, don't you think?"

"Actually, I think it's adolescent, which is a rung above childish."

Masters fixed me with a look, the one that says *I'm placing you on the scales, buddy, and I'm thinking that you're not measuring up right at this moment.*

"Special Agent, it's all too close and the memories are fresh. And please, don't tell me I have to let go of my anger, or any such New Age mumbo jumbo. I want to stay good and angry for a while longer."

"Okay, I won't," Masters said cheerfully.

I got out of the vehicle, ending the conversation, moving with the athleticism of a tin man left out in the rain. The NCMPs standing guard on the front door

saluted as we approached. Others, I noted, were pa-
trolling the building's exterior. I thought maybe the security was a bit over the top given that we were in the
middle of Ramstein Air Base, but that was Masters's
call. I saluted back, trying not to wince with the discomfort the action induced.

We walked into the room Masters had set aside for
the investigation. It was more ordered than I remembered. The names I'd written up on the Whiteboard
were untouched, but Masters had added substantially
to the list, as well as setting out in bullet points the facts
as we knew them. It felt like years since I'd been here,
but it'd been days. Several people I didn't recognize
were hunkered over keyboards or speaking down
phone lines. I recognized only one of them, Flight
Lieutenant Peter Bishop, and his cheeks still reminded
me of hamburger buns. He glanced up, snapped to attention in his seat—if that's possible—hastily ended his
phone call, and came over.

"Special Agent Cooper, welcome back," he said, his
eyes shifting to the various cuts, bruises, and abrasions
on my face. "You're looking a bit fragile. Can I get you
a seat?"

I wavered momentarily between the resentments of
being treated like an old man, and feeling like an old
man. In fact, I did want to sit, on account of I was a bit
light-headed, and I consoled myself with the knowledge that having your brain pretty much batted out of
your skull would do that to just about anyone.
"Thanks," I said.

"Sit here," he said, pulling a chair across, "and I'll
take you through what I've found."

I sat, making a supreme effort not to grunt like an
old man as the weight came off my bones.

"I've debriefed the team on what we uncovered in

Iraq." Masters motioned at the Whiteboard. Headlining the list was *The Establishment*.

"Okay, as the computer program's name suggests," Bishop began, "Dungeon is a prison, but, in this instance, it's a prison for information—the stuff you want to lock up and then throw away the key. Imagine concentric circles, a circle within a circle, each circle made up of fire walls."

I nodded.

"As you get further in toward the center, the fire walls get thicker, more impregnable. It's hard enough breaking into the first wall, let alone the subsequent walls of encryption. And, of course, to get into the center you need to break through all of the walls. These defenses take up a lot of hard-disk space. Dungeon is roughly five megs in size but the cells in this virtual prison are small—"

Masters interrupted, perhaps for my benefit. "Which means...?"

"Not a lot of room inside for information, ma'am. Also, the advantage of Dungeon, aside from each of its cells being almost impossible to break into, is that it can't be wiped out or erased. The hard disk actually has to be physically removed from the hardware and destroyed. The information is kept safe, locked away from prying eyes and secured against all but the most determined attempts to see it or destroy it."

"No offense, Flight Lieutenant. If Dungeon's so impregnable, how come you managed to break in?" I said.

"None taken. I went to school with one of the chaps who wrote part of the program. He was most helpful."

I nodded. "Oh."

"The old-boy network, you know," he said.

"Yeah, I know." Actually I didn't know. Most of the kids I went to school with were making license plates at the Mid-State Correctional Facility in New Jersey, or assembling auto parts at the one factory outside the small town I grew up in. Unless I needed to start an expensive, imported sports car in a hurry without a key, or fence a bunch of used household items out of someone's garage, my old-boy network wasn't a hell of a lot of use.

"Unfortunately," Bishop continued, "he could only help me get inside the first circle. He had a key, I guess you'd call it. But it doesn't fit the inner cells. He believes other programmers might have created their own keys for their cells. Of course, I've asked him to contact these former coworkers and enlist their assistance. He thinks they may consent to help."

"Good," I said. "So what've you got?"

"Well, it's interesting, but I can't tell you what it means. From the looks of things, General Scott was conducting a research program, part of which involved U.S. trading partners over the past eighty years, with particular interest in the balance of trade with Imperial Japan."

"What?" The word snuck out before I could pull it back. I'm not sure what I was expecting, but what the flight lieutenant had just told me wasn't on the list.

But it did jog my memory. "Masters, have you got your camera? The one you used to take photos of the general's study?" I was thinking about that section of shelves crammed with reference books on Japan, its brutal war in China, Pearl Harbor, the war in the Pacific, and other related topics.

"Yeah, I haven't downloaded the shots yet." She went to her desk and retrieved a little Sony digital. Moments later, the images of Scott's library were up on the screen.

I remembered thinking it made some sense that a

general might be interested in WWII and the events that led up to it. But how was it connected—if at all—to his death?

Bishop clicked on an item. The photos disappeared. In their place was a document displaying columns of figures. "Hey, I recognize this. In my bag—the one I took with me to Iraq. Is it here?"

Masters nodded. She leaned back behind her and pulled it out from under a desk. I noted that the leather was still slightly damp. This bag had saved my head from being split like a coconut. I opened it. Inside was a folder containing the photocopy of the Veitch autopsy and the laser-printed sheets of figures. The way the columns were laid out seemed to match those on the screen. I said, "Could you search for five hundred and seventy-four thousand, three hundred and seventy-six?"

Bishop tapped the number into the "Find and Replace" box and hit enter. The six-digit number came up instantly, highlighted in a red box on page seventeen of fifty-six. "Well, I guess we know where this printout came from," I said. "But do we know what it's about?"

"I believe so, sir," said Bishop.

"Let's hear it."

"Scott's Web log indicates that he spent a fair bit of time digging around in the archives of the U.S. Office of Trade and Economic Analysis, among other places. I think what you're looking at is the numbers of that trade activity."

"With Japan?" I said.

"Yes, sir," Bishop replied.

"Before the Second World War?"

He nodded.

"Any idea why?"

"The general compiled a brief historical summary, the events of the day, the background to those figures. That might tell us something."

"Let's have a look at it."

The flight lieutenant tapped a few keystrokes. Another window appeared.

"Can you print out a couple copies of that?" I asked.

"Done, sir," said Bishop, manipulating the mouse and clicking.

I glanced at the screen and checked the date this folder had been created: two months before Peyton's death.

I examined the printout. There was no headline or title, just a bunch of bullet points.

- 2/32. Japan conquers Manchuria, sends two divisions to Shanghai
- 12/34. Japan buys shells from Fort Stevens. Exporter assures that the steel will not be used for war materials
- 12/34. Japan renounces treaty restricting the size of its navy. U.S. continues sale of oil and steel
- 34–36. Political unrest in Japan. Imperial Army factions move against those they consider "weak." Parliament and War Office seized
- 11/36. Japan joins Germany and Italy in Anti-Comintern Pact
- 7/37. Japan invades China
- 12/37. Imperial Japanese troops occupy Nanking, the Chinese capital. 50,000 killed in city
- 12/12/37. Japanese bombers sink U.S. Gunboat *Panay* along with three American tankers on the Yangtze River, China
- U.S. exports to Japan are *increased* 500%

- 3/38. Hitler seizes Austria
- 21 railcars of scrap steel sent to Japan. Despite pickets, exports continue
- 7/20/39. Bill introduced to embargo the sale of steel to Japan. President Roosevelt *opposes* the bill—it is defeated
- 9/39. Nazis invade Poland. WWII begins. Washington ports send 70,900 tons of scrap steel to Japan
- Japan has an army of 51 divisions, 133 air squadrons—one million men at arms and three million reservists
- 9/26/40. Japan invades Indochina. Roosevelt declares embargo on scrap steel, effective 10/15/40
- 9/27/40. Japan signs Tripartite Pact with Nazi Germany and Italy
- 10/11/40. Seattle's streetcar lines, many tons of steel, are loaded onto Japanese freighter. It sails despite union protests
- 12/40. Japanese ships load railcars of steel ingots at U.S. ports. Roosevelt's embargo does not include *melted* scrap
- 8/4/41. Export of crude oil and gasoline sharply curtailed
- 12/7/41. Japan strikes Pearl Harbor. Pacific War starts
- Two years into the war, U.S. standard of living increases 12%

"So we were selling oil and steel to Japan almost right up until Pearl Harbor!" Masters sounded shocked.

"Looks like it," I said. "But what's it got to do with General Scott—alive or dead?"

We had no idea, bright or otherwise.

"Why'd he include that last point about the standard of living?" Masters wondered. "Did he think that was the intention of America's trade policies back then? To start a war so that the country could enjoy the good life?"

No one jumped in to answer that one, either.

"Flight Lieutenant, you said this Japan stuff was part of Scott's research. What else was he digging around in?" Maybe, I thought, we'd find the answer there.

"There are a few files. I haven't really looked at them yet. Should I print them all out?"

"Yeah, and make a copy for Special Agent Masters."

Bishop highlighted a number of PDF icons and dragged them into the print tray. Five minutes later, Masters and I were examining an extraordinary range of material that covered a detailed report on the $2.3 trillion the U.S. was expecting to spend on the development of military hardware over the following half-decade. Over the title page was scrawled in heavy black ink, "First Convention!" There were also documents covering the Russian crisis with Chechnya, as well as the smuggling of sex slaves from the old Soviet Union states to western Europe.

"What the hell is all this?" asked Masters.

"Beats me," I said. "First Convention ring any bells?"

Blank stares. Apparently not.

Masters said, "Two point three trillion. Are we spending that much?"

"I don't know," I said honestly. And, even more honestly, I didn't care. All I wanted to know was what it had to do with Abraham Scott and, in particular, his murder. "Got anything else there to show us?" I asked Bishop. "Anything on something called 'The Establishment'?"

"No, sir. This came for you, though."

He handed me a postcard of the Eiffel Tower. I

turned it over. In small, careful handwriting was written an address: *Alu Radakov, 231 Dzimavu-iela, Riga.* The card was unsigned, but I knew immediately who'd sent it.

"Anything?" Masters asked.

"Junk mail," I said, but I gave her a surreptitious look that said "later." "Are you running tests on the penetrator and casing that killed Peyton?"

She nodded. "I've sent it to a civilian forensics laboratory in Frankfurt. I've also sent Scott's helmet for DNA comparison tests."

"Frankfurt?"

"Yeah. We don't have the resources to conduct that sort of testing here. I could have sent it to D.C., but I thought it would be best to keep it local."

It was my turn to nod. I knew what Masters was saying. Her circle of trust had shrunk to more or less encompass the people in this room. I understood. And I concurred. "When'll we get the results?"

"Five working days. And that's with a rush on it."

"Okay. Have all the men in Peyton Scott's squad been accounted for?"

"They have," said Masters.

"And?"

"All dead, with the exception of Ambrose."

My eyes were drawn to the Whiteboard. "The Establishment" had been written large on it, like it was the headline and the various deaths and other clues were the details. I had the feeling the facts of our oil and steel exports to Japan in the thirties should be added to the list, along with Scott's other research insights, and perhaps even the words "First Convention." I took a deep breath. "What else are we doing?" I asked.

"We're checking with local police forces to see if any of the deaths of Scott's men have been investigated.

We're also looking into Aurora Aviation, the company that sold Scott the instruments for his plane. Turns out it's quite a large company that also supplies avionics to the U.S. Army and Marines, as well as several large civilian carriers. But they're taking their time processing our inquiry—better things to do, it seems."

"In the meantime, something interesting has turned up in Captain Aleveldt's phone records," said Bishop, pulling out some sheets of paper. He handed them across. There were several highlighted phone numbers. "These are calls he made to the command HQ here at Ramstein over the six-month period that preceded the crash of General Scott's glider."

"Aleveldt was Scott's buddy," I said. "So what's the significance?"

"But they weren't calls made to General Scott. This is General von Koeppen's direct line—bypasses the secretarial staff."

"Really?" I said. Interesting. What was Aleveldt calling Himmler for? "We might have to go chat with him about that. What about his bank accounts?"

"Nothing unusual that we can find—brings home what a captain in the Netherlands air force earns. Most of it goes to his mother back in Utrecht. What's left gets spent on food, housing, gliding. Doesn't save much, unless his mother's putting it away for him."

If inability to save was a crime, then I was also guilty. "Anything turned up on Varvara Kadyrov?" I avoided the inevitable look of disapproval from Masters by addressing the question to Bishop.

"No," he replied. "The local police arson squad has an all-points out on her. The belief is that she's left the country."

"Does local law enforcement want to speak to me?"

"No, sir. They've accepted the statement you gave at the scene."

"Hmmm," I said, rubbing my chin but giving nothing away. I knew exactly where Varvara was because it was she who'd sent me the postcard.

"Nice watch, by the way," said Bishop, nodding at the Rolex. "I've always coveted one of them."

"Me, too. Picked it up cheap in Baghdad," I said, admiring the watch that had replaced my old Seiko. "Well," I said, clearing my throat, moving right along. "I guess we should go and pay our number-one fan a visit."

"That would be Mrs. Abraham Scott?" said Masters.

"Who else?" I replied.

THIRTY-ONE

Alu Radakov." I dropped the name as we drove down the highway to K-town in a borrowed OSI vehicle. "Ever heard of him?" I pulled the postcard of the Eiffel Tower from my breast pocket and handed it to Masters. She turned it over a couple of times.

"Radakov. No. Should I have?"

"He's a Latvian who deals in sex slaves."

"Nice. Friend of yours?"

"He's the man who owned the girly bar Varvara worked in called The Bump. She mentioned it when we first interviewed her. I think he sold Varvara to General Scott. The postcard's from her, by the way."

"Hang on, Varvara was *sold*? As a sex slave to Abraham Scott?"

"She didn't say as much, but she insisted she and the general weren't lovers."

"With what?"

"Some things she said, and the fact that Scott was investigating the smuggling of sex slaves into Europe."

"Because of one Internet download? Bit of a stretch, don't you think?"

"Maybe. It's my gut speaking."

Masters gave the postcard a closer inspection. "Back at OSI, you didn't want to mention this postcard was from her. Why not? Don't you trust Bishop?"

"Yeah, I trust him, but, as far as the world is

concerned, Varvara has disappeared. She kept her end of the bargain. I think we should keep ours."

"So what's your gut saying about this people-smuggler, Alu Radakov?"

"That we need to go see him." I'd been trying to re-call the details of the après-sex confessional Varvara and I had shared. If my memory served me correctly, Radakov had another business aside from running a lap-dance bar in Riga, Varvara's hometown. In his downtime, he slipped into the role of Chechen rebel.

"Uh-huh." I caught Masters's tone. She was less than impressed. "Anything else you'd care to tell me? Any other details you've failed to mention?"

"No, not that I'm aware of."

"What about the watch?"

"What about it?"

"Why aren't you putting it into evidence? There'd be skin, hair fibers we could—"

"Look, the guys that jumped us are military or ex-military. Either way, I'd bet you this watch that there's no record of those guys ever being born, let alone hav-ing a nice, handy DNA signature we could compare that's lying around in some cyber filing cabinet. Fuck it. Call it a spoil of war." I was working myself up. Those assholes had tried to kill us. But Masters was right. I should have entered the watch into evidence and run DNA tests, even if for future reference. I had a feeling, though, that the original owner and I would run into each other again some day, and I wanted the pleasure of bringing him down with it on my wrist.

We'd turned off the highway and down the exit ramp to K-town. Masters said, "Those highlighted flights to Riga in the Ramstein ATC logs. *My* gut's telling me they're connected to this."

I nodded. Masters was pointing out the obvious.

They undoubtedly were connected, but we still had no idea why or how. Whatever the answers, the questions were big enough to get Scott, a four-star general, concerned enough to get up and go to Riga personally. A four-star general investigating? That in itself was highly irregular. I made a mental note to ask Bishop to look into the aircrews on those flights. Some of them might still be flying out of Ramstein. The investigation was reaching the point where the same names and places were beginning to turn up, but through new and different connections. A pattern was emerging.

The beginnings of K-town slid past. It was getting close to 1930 hours. We began to pass joggers, military personnel for the most part, identified by their youth and hair buzzed down to the scalp. The Black Forest lay ahead, like a big welcome mat to the blue-gray granite hills beyond. Masters appeared to be deep in thought. She was thinking, most probably, like I was—about how to handle Harmony Scott. We were getting close to the widow's lair. So far, neither of us had managed to extract anything from her that she didn't want us to know. "I'll follow your lead," Masters said suddenly.

"Sorry?" I said.

"Your lead. You direct the questioning. I'll look for holes."

"Just don't go too hard on the widow, when you see one of them big ol' holes opening up," I warned.

Anna Masters replied by giving my leg a friendly punch. I glanced at her to make sure that's exactly what it was—friendly—and I was rewarded by a smile, and something else I couldn't quite put my finger on.

I turned into Harmony Scott's street. It looked the same as the last time I was here—unwelcoming.

"Shit," said Masters.

"What?"

"That BMW parked out front of her house."

"What about it?" I said. One Beemer looked like every other Beemer in my book, and they were everywhere in Germany—almost as ubiquitous as Mercedes-Benzes.

"I know who owns it."

I gave the eagle-and-deer knocker a workout. The front door eased open and a waft of chill air rushed out. I had the image of an old tomb with a curse on it being opened. The air held a complex array of odors, a mix of Harmony Scott: the tang of cigarettes, French perfume, blended whiskey, cosmetics, and something that was familiar in a distant kind of way, like a face you see once in a crowd and then again a month later but in a different, unrelated gathering. The smell was vanilla and pine. I'd noted it before when I'd been here, but I hadn't nailed it at the time. Now I knew what it was. It was the smell of General von Koeppen. I remembered it from being in his office, a cross between aftershave and trough drops—those things they throw in the bottom of urinals in public toilets.

I wasn't sure but I think I detected the very slightest surprise in the widow when she opened the door, like maybe she was seeing a ghost. "Yes, can I help you?" she said. The loose skin under her chin quivered as she spoke. She looked up at me with those gray ice-pick eyes of hers; the color of snow clouds and battleships. She was wearing beige slacks and a white cotton shirt. On her feet were sandals; her exposed toenails were painted red. This was a different Harmony Scott from the one I'd previously met. She was almost feminine. The slacks were tight and the shirt was also body-hugging, the top buttons undone, revealing the hint of a white lace push-up bra doing what it could to plump up her small breasts into the rumor of cleavage. Her hair was loose this time. It fell to her shoulders, was newly dyed blond, and tousled rather than pulled tight and wound on top of her head. I noticed that her small figure was well proportioned and, in the right light, her forty-eight years could pass for thirty-eight. But this wasn't that light. Her face was still expressionless. There was, no doubt, enough toxin injected beneath the skin to tip the hunting arrows of half the tribes of the Amazon Basin.

"Special Agent Cooper and Special Agent Masters," I said, holding up the badge where she could see it. "We have a few further questions we'd like to ask you about your husband's death."

"I know who you are," she said. "Will it take long?"

"That depends on the answers, ma'am," I replied.

"But the investigation is closed, Special Agent," said a man's voice as a shadow stepped out from a doorway off the hall.

"General von Koeppen," I said, feigning surprise. "Special Agent Masters and I are just cleaning up a few loose ends, sir. Do you mind if we come in, ma'am?"

Harmony Scott hesitated.

"We could continue this out on your front porch, if you'd rather," I said. In other words, lady, we can do this in private or we can put on a show for your neighbors. Harmony might not have been prepared to let us know she had company, but Himmler's presence there required some explanation. I couldn't wait to hear it.

"Come in," she said, holding the door open for us. We stepped into the hall and then followed her when she walked past. Von Koeppen brought up the rear.

Harmony led us down the cockroach hallway and then into what I guessed was a sitting room. It held a collection of antique chairs—gold frames with green velour upholstery—and a couple of heavy black leather Chesterfields.

"Are you okay? You both appear to have been in a fight," she said, glancing at me and then Masters, whose face was also still carrying cuts with stitches.

"Yeah," I said, "the Special Agent and I have been playing full-contact debating."

More old farts looked out in judgment from the walls. I wondered whether these were General Scott and Harmony's paintings or whether they'd just walked in to this furnished museum and plugged their electric toothbrushes into the bathroom's wall socket. Empty boxes were stacked against one wall. Harmony didn't appear in any hurry to get them packed. Perhaps she had a good reason to hang around. And I now believed I knew what, or rather who, that reason was.

"Can I offer either of you a drink?" she asked. "You both look like you could use one."

The offer threw me. A drink? I noticed a quart of Maker's Mark in her collection of bottles—a worthy stand-in for my usual brands of choice. I believe I actually licked my lips. I'd made a pact with myself after my last hangover that I'd give the booze a miss for a while. It annoyed me that Harmony was the person tempting me to break that agreement. Masters said no, snapping me out of the trance, and I likewise declined. Harmony shrugged and fixed herself a Scotch on the rocks, extracting the ice from a bucket with gold tongs, and then poured von Koeppen a Pernod. Next, she tapped out a cigarette from a packet of Salems lying on the cabinet and lit it with a gold-and-pearl lighter, blowing a mushroom of blue haze toward the ceiling. She took one of the chairs and directed Masters and me to the Chesterfield opposite. Von Koeppen chose to remain standing. "I'll repeat the question," said the widow. "How can I help you?"

Beneath the attempt at civility was still the fuck-you superiority that seemed to be her normal disposition. I said, "Mrs. Scott, why didn't you inform us that Peyton was not your son, but your stepson?"

Without missing a beat she replied, "Because you didn't ask the question, Special Agent Cooper. If I'm not mistaken, as an investigator the questions are *your* job. And besides, what difference does it make? Peyton was my son. I've known him and loved him since he was three years old. He wasn't my son genetically speaking, but in every other sense he most certainly was."

Her answer was perfectly reasonable, and yet I couldn't help but feel that there was about as much emotion in it as there was in her facial expression. And, of course, there was Ambrose's assertion that Peyton thought his stepmother was, well, "evil."

And then Masters pitched in with her own question, the one we'd mulled over when she'd seen von Koeppen's car parked out front. "General, how long have you and Mrs. Scott been having an affair?" If nothing else, as an attention-getter it was a much better opening than mine. So much for Masters filling in the holes.

"I beg your pardon?" said von Koeppen, his face instantly flushing streetlight red and his carotid artery throbbing. His mouth opened and closed like a fish that suddenly found itself outside the bowl.

"Please answer the question," I said, backing Masters's lead. There were any number of other reasons why General Wolfgang von Koeppen might have called in on Harmony Scott, and not one had them banging each other's lights out. Still, we had nothing to lose by asking, excepting our commissions, of course. I said, "We believe General Scott was murdered—there's some question about the authenticity of the suicide note. We also believe Peyton was murdered rather than killed in action and that somehow the two killings are connected. Love, lust, call it what you like, is a statistically common motive in homicide.

"Therefore, we need to know how long you two have been seeing each other because, whether you like it or not, your relationship is relevant to the investigation." I kept my eye on Harmony Scott during this flurry of body punches. I'd just told her that I believed her to be involved in the deaths of her husband *and* son. Yet Harmony managed to stay utterly calm. She put down her drink and cigarette, and clasped those small, white, bony hands that reminded me of chicken's feet on her crossed leg. She didn't swallow, lick her lips, or even blink more than was necessary to keep her icy eyes moistened. I couldn't help but admire her control. But in that moment I knew for sure she was involved in this case in a deeply disturbing way, for in my experience even a totally innocent person will get jumpy and anxious when wrongly accused. And, of course, there was that suicide note. Where did it come from? How did it miraculously come to appear days after the general's death?

"That is an outrageous accusation!" Von Koeppen's face was now the color of a bruised plum. "I will see that you are court-martialed, do you hear me?"

I heard him, as had anyone a block away. He'd reacted exactly as I'd thought he would. No doubt I would be getting an abusive call from Gruyere any moment. But I also knew that Harmony Scott was the only person we had who was anything like a suspect, even though we had not a single shred of evidence to connect her with any crime. Masters and I needed to jerk the cord to see if anything fell out.

Harmony reasserted her control with a squeeze of her lover's hand and replied with infinite calm, "Who could have forged the note, Special Agent?"

Odd—she'd completely skipped over Peyton. "We're working on that," I answered, holding her gaze. There was only one person who had the access, and I was looking at her.

She sipped her drink and the ice cubes shifted noisily. She said, "Wolfgang and I have been seeing each other for six months." She ran her hand along the top of her leg, and smoothed over the crease pressed into her pants. "Abraham had been involved with his mistress for some time by then. Everyone was doing what he or she wanted to do. The arrangement suited all parties. And now General von Koeppen and I would appreciate your discretion. Just as my husband's extra-marital partnership was kept in the background, so we've attempted—and will continue—to do the same."

Jesus. Without a doubt, she was one cool bitch. She had completely ignored my accusation and had instead weighed up the odds and given Masters and me a little honesty, just enough perhaps to prick the bubble of suspicion. *Of course we've been fucking each other purple, Major, as were my husband and his squeeze. Everyone knew what was going on. We're all adults here.* "Why didn't you tell us all this last week, Mrs. Scott?"

"As I said, you're the investigator." She shrugged. "Besides, an affair is not the sort of thing one willingly talks about, is it?"

I said, "I don't seem to recall you having any difficulties informing me of your husband's infidelity."

Harmony answered with a tilt of her head and a

shrug that together implied her husband was dead and so nothing would hurt him.

Despite von Koeppen's outrage, I think he was relieved. He'd been let off the hook. His lover had taken on the responsibility of confessing the affair for both of them, so he didn't have to. It was easy to see who wore the pants in their relationship. The general moved behind Harmony and put his hand on her shoulder. Harmony patted it. I wondered if he knew how much danger he was in.

He said, "So, are you accusing us of murder, Cooper?"

"Special Agent."

"I beg your pardon?"

"You can call me Special Agent," I said.

The artery began pulsing in his neck again. Satisfied that I had won the tussle, I said, "No. But I will get a search warrant and have your phone and bank records reviewed." This was a dangerous game Masters and I were playing. You can ask general officers to address you correctly, but you can't go around accusing them of killing people. Fuck it, I decided. "And while I'm on the subject, sir, why would Captain Aleveldt, Scott's gliding pal, be calling you on your direct line at HQ?"

"I talk to many people. I run the base, remember?" he said. The plumbing above his shirt collar was now working overtime. I hoped he wasn't going to spring a leak.

My partner was quiet. She was thinking, and I knew what about. At first, Masters had found it hard to believe that von Koeppen was having his sausage sauced by Harmony Scott. And that wasn't necessarily just the resentment of the man's former girlfriend talking. I remembered his PA, Sergeant Fischer, saying von Koeppen's interests lay primarily in young skirt.

Harmony Scott was a couple of years older than he was. So was there something else in it for Heinrich Himmler? Advancement? Money? Position? I certainly believed him capable of being the gigolo type.

Harmony stood. She walked to the liquor cabinet to freshen her Scotch. "So who do you think killed my husband, Special Agent? And why do you think Peyton was murdered?"

Harmony had changed tack again and the shift was seamless. I wouldn't have been at all surprised if she shifted once more, became the distraught mother and wife, produced a white hanky, and began dabbing the corners of her eyes. There was just enough concern about the fate of her husband and son to make it believable. Almost. I didn't believe the show. I considered, again, how different this Harmony Scott was from the woman I'd met on my two previous visits. It wasn't just that she seemed more relaxed; she'd also sloughed off the ferocity, the aggression. My attitude had changed toward her, too. I realized I was also no longer concerned for her safety.

"We are currently chasing down a number of leads," I said. "We'd also like to have another look at your husband's records and his computer."

Harmony replied, "Certainly. More than happy to help."

"Good, we'll secure them first thing in the morning."

I removed my notebook from a thigh pocket, flipped it open to a blank page, and made out like I had a bunch of questions written down there. "Mrs. Scott," I said, "do you have any idea why General Scott was so interested in traveling to Riga?"

Harmony began to shake her head and then von Koeppen said, "Latvia is a relatively new member of

NATO. I believe he took a personal interest in bringing them into the fold."

"Yeah, that could be it," I said, but I doubted it. Why Latvia? Why not Lithuania or Estonia? Or all three? They were all relatively new to the NATO club. What was so special about Latvia that Scott had to get on a plane and go there not once but several times? Was it just because that's where Varvara lived? No, his interest in her had come along later. "Mrs. Scott? Any ideas?"

"No, none at all."

I scribbled a bit of nonsense on the page, then said, "Has either of you heard of a man named Alu Radakov?"

"Sounds like a tennis player," Harmony said.

"He's a people-smuggler."

"Oh. And why would we have heard of him?"

Harmony knew all about General Scott's girlfriend. She even knew he'd put her up in an apartment. Was it possible she didn't know where Varvara had come from, and under what circumstances? Not likely. "Did General Scott ever talk about people smuggling?" I asked.

Harmony returned a blank stare, but I couldn't determine how much of it was truly due to the Botox and how much was acting. Von Koeppen was a different matter, however. He was as open as an Amsterdam brothel. He rubbed his chin and said that he didn't. He was lying.

"Did you know that General Scott's girlfriend was brought into Germany from Riga, probably on a military aircraft, and with a false passport?"

"No, I most certainly did not!" he said indignantly.

"Mrs. Scott," I said, "did you ever meet Helen Wakeley, Abraham's first wife?" I knew the answer I'd get before I asked the question, but I wanted her to know that we were looking way back and maybe digging around in things she would prefer were left alone.

"No. Helen had died long before Abraham and I met." If I didn't know better, I'd have sworn I'd caught the widow frowning.

"For the record, where did you meet?"

"At one of those endless D.C. functions."

"Was it while Abraham was working as military attaché at the Kremlin?"

"Yes. What's all this got to do with your investigation, Special Agent?"

"Probably nothing," I said, meaning it. I consulted my notebook again. "Mrs. Scott, after Peyton died, the general took some time off. He went to Iraq for a couple of days to look into the circumstances of his son's death. We also know he went to Riga for about a week. There is still some time unaccounted for. Do you know where he might have gone?"

Harmony appeared to be giving my question some serious consideration. Finally, she shook her head. "No, no idea. Abraham and I hadn't talked much for some time. He rarely provided me with an itinerary."

If she knew, would she tell me? I only had one question remaining. I took a breath and asked it. "Has either of you heard of a group called The Establishment?"

"The establishment..." von Koeppen echoed, scratching his head with two fingers. "No..."

"The establishment? As in established society? The status quo? Of course I have," said Harmony.

"No, I mean a specific 'The Establishment,' Mrs. Scott—a secret quasi-government black-ops organization that kills people, among them possibly your husband and stepson."

"Absurd," said von Koeppen.

"Is that where you've been going with all this? You're on the trail of some kind of international plot?" There was derision in Harmony Scott's voice.

I wanted to tell her that, yes, that's exactly what I believed. I believed Abraham was killed to protect some secret, and that Peyton was murdered as a warning to his father to keep it. I also believed that this mystery group, The Establishment, was cleaning house, cutting back the numbers on the need-to-know list, killing people father and son might have talked to—desperate to keep its existence secret. I wanted to tell her that I believed she was part of The Establishment, this organization, this club. Whatever, a member. My phone began to vibrate against my leg. I pulled it out and recognized the number on the screen. I excused myself and walked to a corner of the room. "What's up?" I said. It was Bishop.

"Sir, we've managed to crack into the second Dungeon level. One of the programmers contacted us and gave us the key."

"Great. What've you got for us?"

"Sir, you're not going to believe this if I simply tell you about it. You have to see it."

It was also, apparently, something we needed to see in a hurry. We concluded the interview without complaint from either Harmony Scott or von Koeppen, though I was certain the general would make one to Gruyere about us at the earliest opportunity. Masters and I made it back to Ramstein in record time.

THIRTY-TWO

Bishop said, "I'll pull it up for you." On the screen between us was a ring of interlocking blue bars warbling with electricity generated by the computer's graphics card. Bishop reached between us and his fingers tripped over the keyboard. Suddenly, a number of the interlocking bars circling on screen slowly detached themselves, revolved ninety degrees, and then broke away. The entire graphic was then gobbled up by the animated electricity. The door of the Dungeon had apparently been opened, revealing three folders on the otherwise clean desktop of the laptop. "Click the one on the left, sir."

I did as the flight lieutenant suggested. The folder opened; inside it were half a dozen JPEGs. I double-clicked on one of them. A digital photo filled the screen.

"Shit," Masters said quietly.

Yeah, I thought, make that a double shit. Bishop was right: I wouldn't have believed it.

I clicked on the other JPEGs and different views of the same scene were revealed. I was familiar with the image, but I'd only seen it in black and white—or, more accurately, in the black and yellow of old newspaper print.

"Does this mean what I think it means?" said Masters.

"Yeah, I'd say it does," I said. General Scott's reflection was caught in the window of a nearby vehicle, a camera to his face and those body bags lined up on the tarmac. He'd snapped a photo of himself snapping a particularly sensitive photo.

I studied the photos. An unidentified U.S. Army soldier—a PFC—kneeled over one of the bags while two others were doing a head count, or a zipper count, or whatever is done to make sure the same number of corpses loaded on to the transport plane in Baghdad had been carried off at the other end.

"So now we've got General Scott taking photos and passing them along to a journalist, knowing full well he's going to send the White House into a spin," said Masters.

"And the journalist subsequently ends up dead," I added. "What else have we got here?" I double-clicked on the second folder. Inside was one unnamed PDF file. "Any idea what this is all about?" I asked Bishop.

"No, sir." He shook his head. "I've been trying to get into the next level."

I double-clicked it. Another surprise. It was a report on OSI letterhead made some sixteen months ago. I scanned the cover sheet and summary. The investigating special agent was a Captain Toby Sumner, also stationed at Andrews. The case involved the theft of a batch of three hundred CAC cards. There were no charges brought, no arrests. "Can you print copies?"

"Sure," Bishop said.

I skimmed the report again. What the fuck did all this have to do with anything? I'd been wrong about the case having reached its extremities—this was one goddamn universe that kept expanding. I clicked on the third file and found two Word files. I skimmed them. One appeared to be an overview of the various military development programs presently being funded. The other was information obtained under the

Freedom of Information Act, documenting the legitimate payments made by various armaments companies to practically every senator and congressman from New England to New Mexico.

"I'll get you copies of these, too, sir," said Bishop. I barely heard him. I hobbled to the Whiteboard, touched the print button, and ran off a copy of what had been written up. Then I wiped the board clean and said, "Okay, this is what we've got. Fourteen months ago, General Scott notices that there are several unauthorized flights shuttling to and from Riga, Latvia, and goes there to check them out. A couple of months later, Peyton Scott is murdered in Baghdad by a sniper. The autopsy is performed by someone who couldn't possibly have done the job, and the reason given for the cause of death is a lie. The body arrives here at Ramstein. It's reasonable to assume the general has been tipped off that something is wrong with it because he insists upon looking inside the body bag. He orders another autopsy to be performed in secret on Peyton's body. The guy who does it dies soon after.

"Meanwhile, Scott heads to Baghdad to find out what really happened to his son. After that, he disappears for a couple of days. Then he surfaces in Riga.

"When the general arrives back at Ramstein, he's a changed man by all accounts. He also has a new girlfriend with him, a Latvian, most probably traveling on false documents—a German passport. In the meantime, his wife, Harmony, is having an affair with his second-in-command, General von Koeppen.

"Things are falling apart for General Scott. He spends all his time gliding, mourning the death of his boy, Peyton, and he embarks on an Internet research program across a range of seemingly unrelated topics. He takes a highly sensitive photo of a row of body bags and gets it published in *The Washington Post*, which earns him a stern reprimand from his daddy-in-law, Vice President Cutter. Within a couple of months, he's turned into a hearty stew when his glider forgets how to fly. I arrive, a murder investigation begins, and then his widow turns up with a 'good-bye, cruel world' note from the general that we all think is a fake. All the while we're being ambushed, shot at, rocketed, and mugged, while too many people are dropping like flies in all kinds of convenient accidents." I looked at the Whiteboard. It looked as if a four-year-old with ADD and a handful of pens had gone to work on it. But that was okay. Going through what we knew, piece by piece, had a crystallizing effect. At least, I hoped it would. "Have I missed anything?"

"Alu Radakov," said Masters. "The Chechen people-smuggler. The man who sold Varvara to General Scott as a sex slave. Where does Radakov fit into all of this?"

I caught Flight Lieutenant Bishop raising an eyebrow. Four-star generals didn't normally purchase people for sex—or any other reason, for that matter.

"Yeah, you're right. I must be going soft. There's the whole World War Two thing as well," I said. Where the hell did that connect? There were also the payments made by the military-industrial complex to U.S. politicians—campaign donations, most likely—along with the list of new weapons currently under development. And now there was the business of this CAC card theft. Was any of this relevant to the general's death?

My mind was a little like the Whiteboard—a mess. I glanced at the Rolex on my wrist and it reminded me of the ambushes in Baghdad and K-town. Whoever these people were, they'd made a mistake. Masters and I had survived. If we'd been killed in Baghdad, our deaths would've been written off as unfortunate strokes of fate. The attack on me outside the pensione could also have been seen as a mugging, just a random attack. I was still certain the people involved in these attacks on us were former Special Forces. If not for a little good fortune, we'd have joined Alan Cobain, François Philippe, and all the rest. Was this hit squad part of The Establishment?

"It's time to call it a day, folks. I'm not thinking straight," I said, realizing my thoughts were jumping all over the place. Any minute now, I was going to get flippant. Concussion always has that effect on me. It was getting late, and the mere thought of getting horizontal was making me giddy with happiness, but the egg on the side of my head left by the assailant with the pipe might also have had something to do with it.

Another random thought struck me. "Given that von Koeppen and Harmony aren't U.S. military personnel, we're going to need to bring the German police in on this if we're going to get a look at their phone records."

"We've worked with a couple of the local cops before," said Masters. "They'll be happy to play ball."

I said, "Yeah, but will they cooperate?"

Special Agent Masters gave me The Look.

I cleared my throat and said, "Great. And Peter—if you get some time tomorrow, go have a talk with Captain Aleveldt. Ask him about those calls to von Koeppen. And take a peek into General Scott's financials. In particular, dig around and see if he used a credit card to book any flights in the weeks after Peyton was killed. We've also got the widow's permission to pick up General Scott's computer and his files. Let's get onto it first thing."

"Yes, sir," said the flight lieutenant, taking notes. "Anything else?"

"Yeah, there is. Go back through the air-traffic-control records. Look at all the flights to Riga in the six months before Peyton Scott's death. See where the crews that flew those missions are now. If they're not on the base, find out where they are and give them a call."

"What do you want to know?" Bishop asked.

"Whether they're still alive."

An hour later, as the sun went down, Masters parked her purple Mercedes across the road from the Pensione Freedom. Life had returned to the street with the sudden burst of warmer weather. The skirts were seriously short. I could get used to Germany.

"How're you feeling?" Masters asked.

"Fabulous," I lied.

"Well, see you tomorrow." She gave me a smile tinged with concern. "Sure you're okay?"

"Yeah, thanks. Tomorrow . . ." I said as I slid out. I stood on the sidewalk and waited for her to drive off. She motioned at me to go inside. We were concerned about each other's safety. I told myself the danger had passed like an afternoon thunderstorm and that from here on things would be fine and sunny. The alternative would be to have a close-protection squad around us 24/7. But that would make investigating the case difficult, to say the least. Danger came with the territory, for both of us. I gestured at Masters to go, and watched her taillights join the line cruising the strip.

The aromas of various cooked meats drifted on the light breeze from the restaurants sprinkled along the road. My stomach growled, fought a minor skirmish with my head, and lost. What I needed more than food was sleep. I walked zombielike up the steps of the pensione. The frau was signing in a couple of customers at the front desk and didn't look up from the paperwork as I shuffled by. I walked straight into the open elevator and listened to the whine of electric motors as it took me to my floor. It jerked to a stop and the doors wheezed open.

I made it to my room and lay down on the bed in my clothes, careful of the wound in my arm, breathing a loud sigh. The bed seemed to absorb me like water into a sponge. I thought about kicking off my shoes but I didn't have the energy. In the room next to mine, the Canadian backpackers were playing music that sounded like a bunch of instruments being thrown down a stairwell. It pounded into my room laced with a whiff of marijuana. I didn't mind the smell, although I wondered why the smoke detectors hadn't picked it up and sounded the alarm. The music wasn't so bad— it wouldn't keep me awake. But there was an insistent banging at my door, and that would stop me from sleeping. "Okay, okay," I said as I stood up. "Who is it?"

"It's Anna."

I opened the door. "I thought you might want this," Masters said as she walked inside.

"What?" I said.

She handed me a folder. "I forgot to give it to you. Copies of all the general's files—just in case you wake up and want something to read. Oh, yeah, and I also thought you might like a drink." In her other hand was a bottle of Jack Daniel's and two tumblers. "I never trust the glasses you get in these places. People spit into them. Got any ice?"

I was too tired to protest. And a drink would be good. I felt I'd earned it. I absolved myself of keeping the pact. "Yeah, I think so." There was a small bar fridge tucked under a bench with one tray of ice cubes some thoughtful prior guest had organized. I took the Jack and the glasses and set them on the bench.

"Just rocks, thanks," said Masters, settling against the windowsill as I cracked the bottle's seal. "So what did Varvara tempt you with when she came to your room?"

"Scrabble," I said. "Is that why you're here? To tempt me?" I handed her a drink.

"We started off on the wrong foot, and I thought it would be good to have a drink and just talk, you know?"

I lifted the glass. The bourbon was cold but it went down warm. It invaded my stomach and the warmth spread, chasing a shiver into my arms. I liked that sensation, the feeling of the first drink. The only trouble was, for the last year or so, I hadn't been able to say no to the next drink and the one after that and the one after that, until I forgot that saying no would be a good idea and I woke up not knowing what I'd said or done or who I'd fought and whether or not there'd be charges. My last drink had been with Arlen; a lifetime ago, it seemed.

"Feel good?" Masters said, holding up the glass.

"I'll let you know in an hour," I replied.

Masters put her drink down on the bedside table, took mine out of my hand, then set it down beside hers. "Fuck the talking," she said in a whisper.

She took a step toward me. I smelled her perfume and felt her breath against my cheek. Yeah, I liked this woman, possibly all the more because we'd been through so much in such a short time. We'd compressed a year's worth of living into a handful of days, faced down death together, and I, at least, had rediscovered what it meant to live. In some ways, I realized, I'd been in a state of waking sleep for a year. Her eyelids closed like butterfly wings as her lips brushed mine. She pulled herself close, running her hands gently up my back. Her lips touched mine again, this time welcoming my tongue, and I tasted cool Jack Daniel's and the chill of the ice on it. My breathing shortened as we tried to climb into each other through our mouths. The kiss got more desperate, and I became like a drowning man gasping for breath. I wondered if she could feel me harden against her stomach. I think the answer was yes, because Masters lifted her shirt from out of her pants, and began undoing the buttons. I got the hint and took over.

The cell in my pocket began ringing.

Masters released the bra clasp and my hands cupped her breasts. They were warm, larger than I'd thought. My fingers bounced across the firmness of her nipples, the flesh crimped and bunched around them with excitement.

The cell kept ringing.

"Jesus," I hissed.

"Don't answer it," Masters whispered.

I had no problem with that.

The ringing stopped.

And then it started up again. Whoever was on the other end was one persistent motherfucker.

"Shit," said Masters. "It's not going to stop, is it?"

We both knew the answer to that. "Have I told you how much I hate these damn things?" I said. I took the cell out and hit the green button.

"What?" I snapped.

"Cooper! Is that you? Damn it to hell. What in the name of dry fucking are you doing?"

"General Gruyere!" I said. For an instant I believed the big cheese might have had a camera secreted in the room.

"I just got a call from General von Koeppen and I can tell you it wasn't a social call. He said you accused him and Harmony Scott of murdering her husband. You'd better be damned sure of yourself, Special Agent."

I wasn't.

"Well? I'm waiting."

"Ma'am. Mrs. Scott and General von Koeppen are involved in an intimate relationship with each other. I also believe it's possible that they are involved in, at the very least, the murder of General Scott."

"How? You got anything in the way of evidence to back your assertion?"

After a pause, I said, "No, ma'am." It was hard to say, but there was no other answer.

"Cooper, you know damn well your intu-fucking-ition won't cut it in a court-martial. And further-more...Furthermore, I don't know where to fucking furthermore..."

I pictured General Gruyere leaning over her desk, clutching the handset away from her face and yelling straight at it, the veins in her forehead pumping like fire hoses. She was not happy. I couldn't give her an executive summary of the case as we knew it—there were too many extraneous appendages. "I'm going to need another week," I said.

"You *are* crazy, Cooper. Asking me for another week proves it. You are *so* out of time; it's yesterday for you—do you understand me?"

I'd kind of picked that up already. "Yes, ma'am."

"You are done and fucking gone on this case. The DoD investigators are on their way with the FBI. You are hereby officially replaced."

The DoD investigative service was rumored to be made up of no more than two hundred agents. They worked exclusively and directly for the Secretary of

Defense and handled, so rumor had it, only the biggest, most secret cases. I'd never met any of these DoD guys. They had reached almost mythical status.

There was not much I could say, so I said nothing. I knew Gruyere was aware of what had happened to me both in Iraq and in the attack in Kaiserslautern. I also knew she wouldn't give a lab rat's pink puckering anus.

"You were a good investigator, Cooper, and the past tense is no accident. But for reasons beyond me—and against my better judgment—the Vice President himself personally picked *you* to look into the death of his son-in-law."

I believe my mouth opened at that news, and the change in pressure over the mouthpiece gave rise to an electrical roar in the speaker against my ear. What had she said back at Andrews that first morning? *Someone up there likes you* . . . Yeah, that's right. That had vaguely puzzled me at the time. So that someone was Jeff the Cutter, Vice President of the United States of America!

"I have been asked by von Koeppen to have you escorted out of Germany. If I were you, I'd get my bags packed."

"Yes, ma'am," I said. A blue light flickered dimly against the wall. I made my way to the window and pulled back the edge of the lace curtain with a couple of fingers. Half a mile up the road, an NCMP vehicle was driving too fast down the wrong side of the street, playing chicken with the oncoming traffic. The urgency couldn't be a coincidence. Von Koeppen, Harmony, and now General Gruyere wanted me out of Germany, and fast.

"I want you standing in front of my desk, with all your notes on this case, tomorrow morning D.C. time," said Gruyere. "Are you clear on that?"

Crystal. "Yes, General," I said. Gruyere terminated

the call. I didn't need to tell Masters that our moment of intimacy was gone. She was fully dressed, and the dreamy look in those astonishing blue-green eyes of hers that I now decided reminded me of a tropical sea was replaced with concern and uncertainty.

Masters said, "Was that as bad as it sounded?"

"We have to leave right now," I replied.

"That would be a yes, then," she said.

I grabbed my bag off the floor and began stuffing things into it, starting with the folder Masters had brought over. I could go quietly, or I could decide to take leave—starting immediately and without telling anyone or filling in the required forms and waiting for Gruyere to grant it whenever she damn well felt like it—and it'd be the end of my career in the OSI. Either way, I was fucked. But maybe I'd be less fucked, I reasoned, if I could make a few more connections in this case to make sense of it. Or maybe my reasoning powers had been addled by concussion coupled with a nasty bout of coitus interruptus. I was convinced I, or rather we—Masters and I—were close to something. I thought I could feel the knowledge, the certainty, coalescing, taking shape. And that shape was ugly. I grabbed the postcard of the Eiffel Tower off the counter and flicked it into the open bag. I hesitated, took it out, and read the name on the flip side.

Masters and I didn't have a lot of time. I stuffed the postcard in a back pocket and headed down the hall to the room next door. I thumped on the thin door panel, loud enough for the noise I made not to sound like part of the racket being played on the other side. The volume went down and someone called out, "Who is it?"

"Your neighbor."

Something bumped against the door and then a voice said, "Oh, sorry, dude—we'll turn it down."

"No, it's okay. I just wanted to thank you."

The door opened. I recognized one of the young men I'd seen, what seemed an eternity ago, staggering drunk and laughing hysterically under the weight of his pack. "Hey, you're the army dude, right?" he said.

"Air Force," I said.

"Sweet. We just wanted to help, you know?"

"Yeah, thanks a lot. I'm glad you came along when you did. It was a close call. Hey, is that weed you're smoking in there?" I said, cutting to the chase.

"Um, no, it's um . . ."

"It's okay, man. Me and my lady friend wondered if we could buy some, you know."

The Canadian was young, tall, and thin, and was suffering from an acute case of pillow hair. Fragments of chips had gathered at either corner of his wide mouth. He was in the grip of the munchies, obviously. "Surely, dude. It's totally wicked pot. We've got plenty—came down from Holland, man. It's like so cool there, you know? You can just walk in off the street, have a cup of coffee, buy some ganja . . ." He patted the front pocket of his shirt slowly, his motor reflexes inhibited by the cannabis, and produced a packet of Marlboros. He flipped the top, extracted a large pre-rolled joint, and handed it to me.

I said, "Sweet, dude. Totally awesome." I couldn't believe what I was saying, let alone what I was doing. "What do we owe you?"

"You can have it, dude. Consider it like a present to a fellow traveler in the cosmos."

"Thanks. Got a light?" I asked.

"Sure, man."

The Canadian sparked it up with a disposable butane lighter. "Thanks," I said again, turning away in a hurry.

"Dude, careful with the fire alarm," I heard him say

to my back as Masters closed the door behind me. The volume next door returned to the permanent-brain-damage range.

"What are you doing?" demanded Masters.

"With any luck, giving the frau downstairs a head-ache." I glanced out the window. The NCMPs were stopping across from the pensione's front steps to give a big "fuck you"—or whatever they say in German—to the traffic jam that would build up behind them. The Humvee's doors swung open while the vehicle was still in motion and I watched a man hit the pavement at a run. The rear door followed and another man jumped out and bolted after the first. These boys were a little too keen to follow orders for my liking.

I took a massive drag on the joint and blew it at the ceiling. Nothing. I took a second drag and repeated the action. The smoke detector suddenly began to war-ble. The device was wired to a central alarm and the air was filled with an electronic scream, an earsplitting noise similar to the one I heard in Varvara's apartment building.

I snatched my bag along with Masters's hand and pulled her out the door and into the hall, the adrena-line charging through my system, overwhelming my fatigue and the injuries, and headed for the fire escape, a narrow chasm of a stairwell beside the elevator. As we passed the elevator, I saw that it had stopped mid-floor. The power to it had been automatically cut, tem-porarily imprisoning the occupants. With any luck, both MPs would be inside it, encased in darkness. I was thinking this as a middle-aged man came puffing around the corner of the stairwell, dressed in the uni-form of an NCMP, a sergeant. No time to think. I dropped my right shoulder into his solar plexus. I hit him so hard the air hissed out of him like a slashed tire.

He was not a big man and the encounter caught him by surprise. He sank to the floor, winded, his eyes wide with shock and his mouth open, gasping, hoping to find air but failing.

His partner coming around the corner had a little more time to react and was in the process of raising his pistol when I drove my elbow down into his chin. The shock wave generated by the blow rolled through his jawbone and exploded in the part of his brain that controls consciousness. His eyes rolled back in their sockets to look at stars and tweetie birds and he collapsed where he stood, his tongue lolling. I caught him by the front of the shirt as he went down so that he wouldn't smack the back of his head on the concrete. I wanted him out cold, not dead.

I heard other doors opening into the fire escape as people began to make their way out of the building. The NCMPs would be found within half a minute. Three flights of stairs later, Masters and I opened the exit door out onto the narrow side lane where I'd been jumped the night before. "Where's your car?" I asked.

"Blocked in."

"What do you mean, blocked in?"

"The NCMPs. They've blocked me in." Masters pointed at her Mercedes and the NCMP vehicle stopped beside it, the revolving electric blue light washing over its roof.

We started to walk quickly in the opposite direction, away from the pensione, as dazed and bewildered guests began spilling onto the street. A few hundred yards down the road, a pair of fire trucks peeled out of a side street, their sirens wailing. All the flashing and revolving lights danced over the vehicles and buildings and gave the impression that an emergency-services outdoor nightclub was in full swing. Meanwhile, the traffic situation was turning ugly as drivers stopped to gawk, no doubt expecting that the show might be improved upon at any moment by the appearance of naked flames suddenly leaping from upper-story windows or, better yet, people.

We kept walking, but not fast enough to attract attention. There must have been four MPs. The two I had seen jump from the Humvee before it stopped had taken the elevator; their pals had followed a beat later up the stairs. I didn't feel good about putting two of our own people away, but it was necessary.

"What now?" said Masters.

"Where's the nearest international airport?"

"Why? Where are we going?"

"Not *we*. Anna, this time you're staying here. You've got to bring the German police up to speed and get those phone records. And we need surveillance on Harmony and Himmler . . ."

"Who?"

"Von Koeppen."

"Okay, let's assume for just a moment that I am staying here. Where exactly are you going, Cooper?"

"To check on the going rate for sex slaves."

THIRTY-THREE

Masters and I argued for a couple of minutes about whether she should come with me, and then, once she agreed to stay behind, whether or not she should stay in close company with a protection squad. She insisted she didn't want to give the impression that she'd been intimidated. And, as the violence seemed to have been centered on me, it was a no to close protection. But she could see why we needed to split the team. Begrudgingly. There was plenty to get on with back at the ranch.

I was pleased I wasn't operating a vehicle, rental or otherwise. Not driving around in something with my name all over it made me feel like a smaller target. Cabs would do just fine. Part of me felt I was being overly paranoid; the other half—the half that had been shot at and mugged by the Rolex gang—thought the half that wasn't paranoid needed to have its head examined. It also occurred to me that I might possibly have the same mind-set General Scott had had after his son was murdered. Was I not on exactly the same road to the same destination, and going possibly to ask the same questions?

Masters interrupted my thoughts. "You'll need cash. And you'd better take this."

"What is it?"

"A charger for the cell. You'll need it."

I opened my bag and she dropped it in. Then I

cupped my hands and she filled them with assorted small-denomination notes and coins.

"That cleans me out, I'm afraid. A little over a hundred euros, plus change. Don't spend it all at once," she said playfully. I hailed a cab. As it pulled up beside us, I squeezed her arm and promised I'd be back in a couple of days. I climbed in and closed the door. I wanted to kiss her, bury my nose in the soft chocolate folds of her hair, but I was way too tough for that. Actually, more truthfully, I was afraid of rejection, afraid that we'd had our moment and that it had passed, never to return. I looked back as the cab pulled away and saw her wave at me, the image filtering through a film of dirt across the rear window. I knew damn well I should have kissed her, taken the risk.

"Stuttgart Airport, thanks," I told the driver.

"Stuttgart Airport?"

"Yeah, Stuttgart Airport, Stuttgart. It's a little town about ten klicks south of Heidelberg." I knew that because Anna had told me where to go, and how far.

"I know vere it is," he said. "A long vay. At least sewenty kilometers."

"Can we stop at an ATM somewhere? I'll need to get some money."

"You don' need cash. I take credit."

"I hate credit," I said.

The driver shrugged. I opened the window to get some air.

He drove a block and a half and stopped in front of a building made from huge black granite blocks, no doubt intended as a metaphor for the bank's permanence. The street in front of the bank was empty except for a tall, skinny kid with a grimy face and elaborate tattoos up his forearms, who I doubted was one of its customers. He wore a fluorescent T-shirt and pushed a broom with a small roll of grit and paper in front of it. He didn't look up as I crossed his path. I accessed the hole in the wall and cleaned out my savings account, which amounted to the sum total of twelve hundred euros. I had thirteen hundred euros altogether—a little over sixteen hundred U.S. dollars. It wasn't a lot, but it would have to do.

The NCMP guys I thumped in the stairwell would be making a report right about now. A soldier gone AWOL wasn't exactly a fugitive, but this case was weirding me out some. How energetically would I be pursued? I didn't want anyone except Masters knowing where I was going, and credit cards would leave a trail. Masters was sure no one had seen her come up to my room— the frau had apparently not been in attendance in the lobby—and I was sure no one had seen her leave with me. She was in the clear, although, being my partner, some mud would undoubtedly stick. Her Mercedes was outside, but she could always claim I'd borrowed it.

I climbed back into the cab. A short while later we were on the autobahn heading east. Signs flashed by announcing the distances to Ramstein AB, Worms, Mannheim, Heidelberg, Stuttgart. I reached into my bag and dug around for the cell phone. I found it and turned it off. I didn't want another call from Gruyere. And there was also the risk that Brenda would start phoning again—and that I could definitely do without.

The adrenaline was leaching out of my muscles, leaving them and me even more exhausted than we'd all been before. But I didn't want to go to sleep, not yet. I wanted to store up the fatigue till I got on the plane. I wondered what I'd managed to pack before the hasty exit. Placing the phone on the seat beside me, I turned on the ceiling light and dug around in the bag. I found a toothbrush, two pairs of underpants—both of them dirty—a clean ABU and one pair of dirty socks. I'd have to buy some clothes. There was also the folder of printed material. I sorted through the contents. There was the printout detailing U.S. exports to Imperial Japan prior to WWII; a similar set of figures yet to be identified; a fat file on the new range of weapons our government was currently developing; a breakdown on U.S. military spending and the overview of defense-industry payments to senators and congressmen; a report on the sex-slave trade; a one-hundred-page brief on the history of the recent wars Moscow had waged with secessionist Chechnya; the OSI report on the theft of three hundred CAC cards; and a black-and-white laser print of the body bags lined up behind a C-130. At the bottom of the pile was a photo of the OSI Whiteboard at Ramstein on which we'd written thirty-two names, most of them united by an untimely death. I stared at the list headed by the title The Establishment. The question running through my head pretty much said it all: What the fuck was going on here?

It suddenly occurred to me that Abraham Scott, being a four-star, pretty much had the highest security clearance possible, yet most of his information had been downloaded from the Internet. From that, I drew three conclusions. One: Scott didn't believe he was getting the whole truth in the official assessments he received. Two: he didn't want anyone to know he had an interest in the topics he was researching. Three: a combination of points one and two.

I picked up the print of Scott's photo of the body bags and examined it again under the ceiling light as we sped down the autobahn. "This must have really pissed you off," I said quietly. By you, I was referring not to Abraham Scott but to his father-in-law, the VP, Jefferson Cutter, who'd written to the general about the photo's appearance in *The Washington Post*. Cutter knew enough about me to recommend me to Gruyere as the lead investigator into the death of his daughter's husband. So . . . how *much* did Cutter really know about me? He must have known that I'd been shooting myself in the foot so much over the past year that I was practically walking on stumps. Was it possible that I'd been chosen because he thought I'd fail? I looked up and blinked a couple of times. Was that possible? Did Jeff the Cutter pick me because he wanted what the record suggested I was: a broken-down fuckup who would pretty much guarantee the murder of his son-in-law would end up in the freezer with all the other cold cases? For some reason, that line of logic seemed to make a hell of a lot more sense than the other possibility—that the Vice President thought I was a fine, outstanding special agent whose impeccable record showed him to be a loyal, dedicated, and tenacious investigator who wouldn't give up till the truth was uncovered. Actually, I knew guys like that. With the occasional exception, they were poor investigators. My theory here was that they were unable to see the flaws in themselves and so were unable to recognize them in others. They investigated cases by the book and took too much of what they found at face value. But then again, having flaws, I *would* think that.

It made sense, on the surface at least, that a wife would want to see her husband's killers brought to justice. Yet that picture didn't fit my image of Harmony Scott. Was she her father's daughter? Were father and daughter two peas in a pod? It's not often a major gets to feel sorry for a four-star general but, surrounded by laser printouts and dirty underwear, that's exactly how I felt as I tore down the autobahn at a hundred and fifty kilometers an hour.

* * *

I am one of the world's rare human beings who can read
without getting carsick, which was just as well because I
had a lot of it to do. Seventy kilometers later I knew
pretty much everything there was to know about those
super-smart weapons systems Scott had been checking
out, the ones making a big hole in that $2.3 trillion ex-
penditure on the military. I knew about the new Boeing
AH-64D Apache Longbow helo and how it can detect
and classify one hundred and twenty-eight more targets
and hit four hundred percent more of them than the
AH-64A. I also knew about the new Boeing-Sikorsky
RAH-66, the first helo to employ stealth technology;
about the F-22 Raptor, the new aircraft that makes ob-
solete every other fighter jet deployed by every other air
force in the world; I knew about the new day/night version of the Harrier Jump Jet, the II Plus (AV-8B). I was
brought up to speed on the new Joint Strike Fighter, as
well as on the new A-10 Thunderbolt II, the new
Tomahawk missile, and the new ABL YAL-1A Attack
Laser mounted on the nose of a modified Boeing 747-
400. I read up on the new Predator unmanned aerial vehicle that can stay aloft over a battlefield for sixteen
hours before having to land and refuel, and I caught up
on the new C-17 Globemaster III cargo plane, the troubled Tiltrotor V-22 Osprey, the new Sea Shadow Stealth
destroyer, the new Javelin shoulder-launched missile,
the new M1A2 Abrams Main Battle Tank, the new M6
Bradley Linebacker fighting vehicle, and the new non-
lethal Vehicle-Mounted Active Denial System that fires
a beam of electromagnetic energy at people, causing
them extreme pain. I also boned up on the new Line-of-
Sight Anti-Tank missile, a radical kinetic energy missile
with no warhead, that does the job simply because it

slams into its target at five thousand feet per second. New. New. New. New. All of it cutting-edge, high-tech stuff. And, of course, all of it hugely expensive.

The thrust of the material Scott had downloaded was that the funding of these programs was the result of pressure on Congress applied by the giant defense conglomerates—Lockheed Martin, Boeing, Raytheon, and others—combined with the willingness of individual senators and congressmen to keep the weapons' production lines in their own states humming along with new products coming down the pipe. So, military technology is big business—tell me something I don't know, I said to myself. Still, the facts and figures made fascinating reading. I dug around for the paragraph that had stuck in my mind:

> *The U.S. accounts for more than 34% of the world's military spending. The next biggest spender is NATO, one of the biggest customers of U.S. military technology and getting bigger as it absorbs new members, all of whom must then make their military contribution to the whole.*

And from whom did they buy the military hardware with which to make this contribution? Uncle Sam, of course.

Interesting as the report was, I still had no idea why General Scott found it so. I watched the passing lights whip past, the illumination from the glowing white and orange balls diffused by water vapor condensed on the taxi's window. I wondered what Masters was doing. If she had any sense, she'd be tucked up in bed. If I had any sense, I'd be tucked up beside her. Or on top of her. The cab's headlights lit up the overhead sign and the suggestion that the left lane should be taken for Stuttgart Airport. The driver flicked the turn signal.

Twenty minutes later I was standing in a largely vacant airport. I went to the Lufthansa counter, it being the only one still staffed at this hour. I asked about the next flight for Riga and was told it departed at 0700 the following day. I must have looked beat because the next bit of helpful information volunteered was that I could get a room at the nearby F1 Hotel. Rolex time said 2300 hours. Sleep was the best suggestion I'd heard in a while. I said thanks and went off to find another cab to take me to the hotel. A short while later, I rented a small box on the ground floor. I brushed my teeth and then stripped. The bump on my head had gone down but the dressing on the wound in my arm was crusty and black with coagulated blood. I removed it and found that I'd pulled a couple of stitches out, but the others had held and the bleeding had stopped. It looked ugly, but I'd live. I climbed between the sheets and closed my eyes.

There was a lot on my mind and so I dreamed. I dreamed of crashing in a glider, of spinning to the earth and of ending as a splash of flesh and blood and hair. I dreamed of kissing Harmony Scott and of tasting the poison in her soul. I dreamed I saw Varvara sitting on a bench in a Roman slave galley, dragging an oar while she blew the sweaty Roman colonel standing in front of her. I dreamed of Anna Masters's breasts and the firmness of her erect nipples. I dreamed of von Koeppen dressed as a Nazi SS general standing up in a new open-topped Mercedes convertible and smiling while a boxcar full of human beings smelling of excrement and fear pulled out of the siding. I dreamed that four assassins came into my room, under the door and through the keyhole, and offered to sell me their timepieces. But I knew that to be a dream while I dreamed it because the door didn't have a keyhole; it had a swipe card and you couldn't get in without one. And then I woke to a burst of static through the clock radio just as I dreamed I was about to grasp something important in this case. The memory of the images of my sleep hung around like the last shreds of a fog.

I'd set the clock two hours earlier than necessary, 0430, and it was still dark. I wanted to be exhausted for the flight so that maybe I'd sleep. Already the thought of getting airborne made me want to go to the toilet. So I did, and I took some more of Scott's files to read.

I checked out at 0545, wearing yesterday's underwear. I paid cash, which raised the interest of the gothic teenager on night shift behind bulletproof glass only slightly less than zero. She took my notes from the slot under the glass without once making eye contact.

Stuttgart Airport was considerably busier at 0615 than it had been when I was last here. The place was full of businessmen hurrying to get somewhere or other. I bought a return flight to Riga with the homeward leg open-ended. I paid cash and received a wary look from the man behind the counter, although I had no idea why. Wearing an ABU and with all the required paperwork in order, I was hardly a risk. But let's face it, no one pays cash these days unless they have something to hide.

It was too early to ring Masters, although I was tempted, if only to hear her voice. My dream, along with the memory of her skin under my fingertips and the way she smiled, was still strong. The gate lounge wasn't too crowded on the Riga flight. The plane began to board as I arrived. The beads of sweat were starting to muster on my forehead, my top lip, and in the small of my back. The attendant smiled at me and motioned to come through. I made the universal sign of "I must use my mobile phone" and took a seat away from the passengers lining up for the flight. I pulled it out of my bag and looked at it. Maybe it wasn't too early to call Masters, after all. Did I really want to turn the thing on? What shit would come down the line? I took Masters's card out of my wallet, punched the power-on button, and waited for a connection. As soon as I had a signal, I keyed her number.

"Special Agent Masters," said a sleepy voice.

"Anna," I said.

"Is that you, Vin?" she said, suddenly awake.

"Yeah."

"Where are you? Never mind that." Masters was suddenly wary. Digital-cell-to-digital-cell calls were supposed to be impossible to tap, but neither of us believed that. She changed the subject. "How'd you sleep?"

"Okay," I said. For some reason that had mostly to do with a complete lack of backbone, I was unable to say anything of an even remotely personal nature. "Any news?"

"Yeah, as a matter of fact. Got a call from Bishop last night."

"Does that guy never sleep? Let's have it."

"We found out who owns Aurora Aviation, the company that provided the instruments for Abraham Scott's plane."

"Yeah? Who?"

"Another company owned by another company whose major shareholder just happens to be the Vice President of the United States, Jefferson Cutter."

THIRTY-FOUR

"Excuse me, please. If you're taking this flight, we're about to close the gate," said the attendant in heavily accented English. She leaned over me with a look of concern cracking her makeup.

Jefferson Cutter, the father of the widow, my so-called influential friend, and the owner of the company that provided the instruments for Abraham Scott's doomed glider. His name was starting to pop up a little too often, wasn't it? Coincidence? My definition of co-incidence: events whose connections have yet to be uncovered.

"Sir?" said the woman again. She had a kind face but it had spent too many hours in the air, and her skin looked about ready to shed.

"Okay," I said. I picked up my bag and fed my boarding pass through the machine. I walked down the square hallway until I intersected the tube with a door and another flight attendant. There were no windows to tell me that I was about to catch a plane. It could have been a train, or a narrow cinema. I tried to tell myself this as I followed another flight attendant's directions to my seat. It was on the aisle, and the two seats to my right were empty. I shoved my bag in the overhead locker, reached across and closed the plastic blind, and sat tight. The woman sitting across the aisle glared at me. I smiled at her, probably more of a grimace, then I closed my eyes and tried my damnedest not to urinate.

* * *

It was raining heavily in Riga, a murky sheet over the town that made the medieval center seem even more of a time capsule. Ancient spires pierced the low cloud cover and disappeared into it. Behind the old rose the new, a twentieth-century city. The old city reminded me of the towns I'd seen in stories as a child, the sort where trolls lived under the bridges. My cab driver was Russian. I knew this because he told me. He also told me he was a communist and that he loved vodka and cigarettes. He didn't need to tell me about the cigarettes because he was smoking and the interior of the taxi smelled like a spittoon, butts piled in the ashtray so that every time he braked, the load shifted and a couple toppled out and dropped onto the floor. I hoped the vodka thing was just a bit of lighthearted banter, but, from the way he meandered back and forth across the road's center line, I doubted it.

"Riga, jewel of the Baltic," he announced as we crossed the rat-gray river behind which the city was built. "Where you going?"

I flipped open the folded postcard and said, "Two hundred and thirty-one Dzimavu-iela. Did I say it right?"

He shrugged and said, "Drink half a bottle of Russian vodka and try again. You'll get it."

"Your English is good. Where'd you learn it?"

"I was translator for Red Army. Your English is good, too."

The driver was around fifty, with wiry gray hair, the putty nose of the heavy drinker, and deep laugh lines emanating from the corners of his eyes. He had a broad, gray-bearded face and few teeth. The ones he had stood like old marble tombstones among the weeds.

An old, dull green car blowing more smoke than a forties movie star pulled out in front of us, filling the cab with the fumes of baking grease and unburned fuel. My driver wrestled with the wheel and swore at the vehicle, swerving around it and losing the inch of ash curling off the end of his cigarette, which fell between his legs. I hoped for the sake of his unborn children that there were no embers in it.

We skirted the old town, swerved right down a wide boulevard lined with art nouveau buildings, one of which I noted housed a department store, and pulled up across from a building with a stone gargoyle with large curled toenails perched on a shield over the arched doorway. Beside it was a neon sign in blue and pink of a naked woman. She was leaning over to spank her butt and each time she did, a different bunch of neon tubes filled with color, animating the figure so that she simultaneously winked. How lucky was that gargoyle? The name of the place was a roadkill of consonants, all the vowels having hit and run.

"The Bump?" I asked the driver.

"*Da,*" he said with a nod.

"Is it open now?"

"*Da.* Open twenty-four hours. I know better place than this," he said, dismissing it with a wave of his hand, as if casing a titty bar at eleven in the morning was an everyday occurrence. "More girls, prettier— virgins. I take you."

Of course they are. I said, "Do you know of a hotel nearby? Walking distance? Not too expensive."

"You pay a hundred dollars U.S.?"

"If I must," I replied. The driver pulled back into the traffic, did a U-turn, and lurched to a stop outside The Bump.

"There is a hotel on top," he said. "A hundred a night."

How convenient. I thanked the driver, who gave me his cell number and told me I should call him if I found the girls at The Bump too old and ugly and unvirgin-like.

I was eager to check in, but more eager still to get fresh underwear. I took a walk to the department store half a block away, struggled through the language barrier, and bought a few pairs of boxer shorts and a change of clothes. Then I went back to the hotel and got a room for one night.

It was nearly noon and I was dragging my feet. I took a shower and lay down on the bed. For whatever reason, sleep wouldn't come, so I took out the folder containing Scott's downloads and started reading about Chechnya. I woke up ten hours later, not knowing where I was.

The sleep had done me good. I took another shower, put on the white T-shirt and loose brown corduroy pants I'd bought, and rode the elevator down to the ground floor. It was 2300 hours before I made it to The Bump. A Beyoncé track played as I handed over the entry fee to an old matron done up like a madam from a French bordello, perched behind a cash register reading—from the looks of the cover—a romance novel.

I walked through a cave, pushed aside a heavy red velvet curtain, and entered a vast, crowded space. A woman, tanned and tall and dressed in no more than a tiny skirt made from transparent red mesh, strode past on heels high enough to induce a nosebleed. Her hair was long, wavy, and yellow and she prowled rather than walked, as if maneuvering to play with an injured mouse she'd spotted. She smiled at me in a way that communicated she wanted to have sex with me right here, right now.

I made my way to the bar, which ran the full length of one very long wall. Bottles of liquor of every color lined the shelving backed by a mirror, lit by alternating pink and white spotlights. The bar itself was a combination of stainless steel and zebra skin and was three or four deep in male customers. Liberally scattered among them were young women who laughed and chatted with the men as if they were good friends, seemingly oblivious to the fact that they were, mostly, next to naked.

The theme of the place reminded me of a set for a sixties *Playboy* shoot. Large mobiles with orange, red, and pink circles within circles hung from the ceiling. The motif was continued in various wall hangings and on the thick carpet.

At each table, skewered by a brass pole that ran from floor to ceiling, a naked woman performed various feats of advanced leg opening. Around the walls, red leather booths held intimate gatherings. The place was humming. Everywhere, young women were either taking off their clothes or were already entirely naked, their ankles in the air. No one seemed to be complaining about this. Indeed, the men mostly watched these performances silently, glassy-eyed and tense, their endocrine systems dumping quarts of testosterone into their systems while their elbows bent subconsciously, pouring alcohol down their throats as if to extinguish a roaring fire within.

Over the PA system a male voice announced something in what I assumed was Latvian and a number of men surged to a large glass tank filled with water. Two blondes appeared out on stage from behind a glass bead curtain, wearing gold bikini tops and ultrashort gold miniskirts. They couldn't have been more than eighteen, yet they had huge breasts and impossibly small waists, just like Varvara. They strutted to the platform in front of the tank and undressed each other. The men licked their lips. The two women climbed into the tank, kissed passionately, and began soaping each other up with hands that were far from shy.

If, as Varvara had suggested, this was a front for the Chechen separatists, it was a movement I could happily consider joining.

I ordered a Coke. The drink came as I was enveloped by a woman's scent—the very same one Anna Masters used, if I was not mistaken—and I felt a cool hand slip under my arm. I flinched slightly, acutely aware of the gunshot wound above her fingers. I turned and looked into the face of an angel wearing spectacles. I know it's trite, but my first thought was *beauty* and *brains.* Her hair was straw-colored, wavy, and tumbled around her shoulders. She wore pink lipstick and a tight white sheath of Lycra so that I had to use my imagination, but not too much. Her voice was light and clear, like a bird chirping in a cage, and she was speaking to me in what I decided must be more Latvian. I shrugged to let her know I didn't understand a word she was saying. She immediately switched to English and said, "Hey, stranger, don't be shy. Where you from?"

"A little town—you wouldn't know it."

"Oh, you are American. I love Americans," she said. She'd picked my accent, but I couldn't return the compliment. She could have come from one of the Baltic states, Russia, Georgia, the planet Venus. She ran a fingernail lightly from my ear across my cheek and down my neck and chest, stopping at my belt buckle. "You have nice body. My name is Katarinya. I would love to dance for you."

"I'd love that too, Katarinya, but first I have to meet someone. Maybe you know him?"

"Oh, you know someone in Riga?" One perfectly plucked eyebrow arched higher.

"We've never met. His name is Alu Radakov," I said.

Katarinya almost jumped at the mention of the name. She didn't know how to react, whether to be extra friendly—if that were possible—or suddenly cautious. After a moment of internal turmoil, visible on her face, she decided on the latter.

"Yes, Alu. That is him. Over there, the man partying with the redheaded woman." She gestured at a booth where a considerable number of women were entertaining a cluster of men. The word "cavorting" came to mind. I wasn't sure which man Katarinya was referring to, there being two attentive redheads in the group, clearly earning their pay.

When I looked back to clarify this, Katarinya had vanished, but then I spotted her with her arm around the neck of a fat, middle-aged businessman while she rocked on his lap, her back arched in apparent ecstasy. Maybe she was moving on his wallet.

I strolled over to the booth. "Alu Radakov?" I said. There were six men and eight women. All but one of the men were bearded. The mood of the party went from bawdy lust to leery in a heartbeat. I toasted them with my Coke and said, "Varvara Kadyrov and I are good friends. She said if I ever came to Riga I should look you up."

A clean-shaven man, in a white body shirt opened to the breastbone so that more hair than on a barbershop floor was revealed, leaned back. His body language told me he was the man I'd come to see. I

knew when I was being evaluated, so I did likewise.
Radakov's head was round like a bowling ball and his
hair was black and waxed into short, unruly quills. His
eyes were cold and gray and the lids drooped, giving
the impression that he'd been awake for a week.
Maybe he had been. It wasn't a kind face, nor was it especially brutal. He appeared to be fit, if the thick mus-
cular neck was any clue, and his forearms were
bunched with well-defined muscles that reminded me
of cable. After a moment's consideration, he smacked
the rump of the stunning redhead perched on his
knees. She yelped playfully, got the message, and skit-
tered away rubbing her ass, high heels clicking on the
polished marble floor.

"Yes, and you must be Special Agent Vin Cooper," he
said. His accent reminded me of Varvara's and Flight
Lieutenant Peter Bishop's rolled into one. Educated in
England, perhaps? "I've been expecting you. Can I get
you a drink?"

Expecting me? I glanced at my glass, which now held
mostly ice. "Thanks," I said.

He said something to the men at the table. All had
peasant faces with broad Slavic features—high cheekbones with eyes set wide enough apart to make me
question their origin in the gene pool. One was
painfully thin with sallow skin, sunken cheeks, and a
nose that reminded me of an eagle's beak. His eyes
were black pits beneath a solid, single brow. All the
men except Radakov wore black vinyl jackets. When
Radakov had finished having his chat, the men smiled
warmly and toasted me as if they'd just been told I had
five daughters of childbearing age, all of whom were
virgins. I raised my glass in a return salute as Radakov
came out from behind the table and herded me toward
the bar.

"You've come a long way," he commented.

I shrugged. "It's a shrinking planet. How did you know I was coming here?"

The woman behind the bar ignored the men waiting their turn and served Radakov. "There's not much I don't know about my friends and enemies. What are you drinking?" he asked.

"Coca-Cola. Which one am I—Friend? Or enemy?"

"That stuff will kill you—too much sugar. I myself drink lime and soda. And I haven't yet decided."

"If you know who I am, then you know why I'm here."

"You are investigating the death of Abraham Scott," he replied.

"More accurately, his murder."

"Yes," Radakov agreed. "Unfortunate business." He made a gesture in the air and was attended immediately by a tall, dark waitress who wouldn't have been out of place in Italian *Vogue* or on a Brazilian beach. He said a few words to her, and she raced on ahead and cleared one of the booths occupied by women taking a break from taking their clothes off.

When we were settled in the booth, I said, "Why was it an unfortunate business?"

"Can I call you Vin?"

"That's my name," I said.

"There is much you don't know, Vin."

"Fix the problem and fill me in."

"How long are you staying in Riga?" He watched a woman with white wavy hair down to her buttocks strut past. She winked at him and rolled her tongue around her upper lip.

"As long as it takes." I didn't want to tell him that, more truthfully, my stay would expire when I ran out of cash, which, at current levels of expenditure, gave me until the day after tomorrow.

"You are staying here? In the hotel?"

"Yes," I said.

"Excellent. Then you shall stay as my guest—I own it."

I was immediately uncomfortable, my Protestant work ethic compromised by the knowledge that I was living off the proceeds of a known people-smuggler, and who knew what else. "I'm happy to pay," I told him.

"Nonsense. Do you see anything here you like?" he said.

I figured he wasn't talking about the décor. "No," I said.

"You Americans—you are all so . . . repressed," he concluded, shaking his head.

"Let's talk about General Scott."

"General Scott started out repressed, but I brought him around. He came to have a fine appreciation of the female form, even if he didn't partake."

"I know. I met his girlfriend."

"Yes, Varvara. Exquisite, but troublesome. She was one of my star attractions here. The general fell in love with her."

"Really," I said.

"So I gave her to him as a present."

"Or a bribe?" I said.

Katarinya, the young woman who'd approached me at the bar, distracted Radakov. Actually, we were both distracted. She strolled past on her way to somewhere, leading a young man by the hand who was practically panting. My eyes followed her, unconsciously. Her glasses intrigued me. I didn't usually associate eye-glasses with women who oozed sex. It was like lusting after the school librarian. Her perfume eddied around our table.

"So, you like Katarinya?" said Radakov.

I didn't answer.

"Yes, she is beautiful. From the Ukraine, from an extremely poor family. What you see is genuine. She has not visited my surgeon, one of the few women here who hasn't."

I sipped my drink.

"You want to fuck her, I know," he said. "I can arrange it."

"Why did you have Abraham Scott killed?" I said, ignoring his offer.

Radakov sighed. He shrugged. "It was not me. I was against it. There were others who insisted on it."

"Will you tell me who these others are? Are you referring to The Establishment?"

Radakov turned to face me. "You have no idea what you are dealing with."

"Like I said, enlighten me."

"Perhaps. But not tonight."

"After General Scott's son was killed in Iraq, he went to Baghdad for a couple of days. Shortly after that, he came here to Riga. In between, he went somewhere else. Do you know where he went?"

"Yes, I do."

The woman who had shown us to the booth came over and whispered in Radakov's ear. "Excuse me, Vin," he said, "I have a business to run. Tonight, as I said, enjoy my hospitality. We will talk more tomorrow." He spoke to the waitress and motioned at me. She nodded a couple of times and then Radakov walked away.

The woman flashed her professional smile at me. "Anything you want, let me know." Like Radakov, she turned and melted into the crowd. It was past midnight now and the place was jammed. The growing number of customers had been matched by an influx of Radakov's women. The two blondes who'd bathed in the tank earlier were now onstage, doing a double act. I felt as if I was watching reruns. Time to leave.

I walked out of The Bump, past a line that snaked down the road. Riga might have had a massive gender imbalance in its population, but that didn't seem to have affected Radakov's business. The place was a gold mine.

I was in a busy part of town, the street lined with restaurants and bars. Riga was a lively place. I found a joint that served steak, and took a table outside. Women of all ages cruised the street, apparently on the hunt for available men. I knew this because several times I had to inform complete strangers that, no, I wasn't dining alone—my wife had just gone off to powder her nose. I bought a glass of wine and an entrée and had them placed beside me to cement the ruse. I didn't want company. In fact, I was starting to wonder about the wisdom of being in Riga at all. What the hell was I thinking? I didn't owe Abraham Scott or his wife anything. And now I'd pretty much ended my OSI career by thumbing my nose at the big cheese, ignoring the order to return to Washington. Was it just my resentment at being shot at and mugged? What drove me? I wanted to believe that it was a heightened sense of judgment, or was it justice? Was I trying to prove something to myself—that I could still do this gig? Showing off to Anna? "Jesus, what the fuck were you thinking?" I said quietly to myself.

The steak arrived and it was good, but, despite the growl in my stomach, I had no appetite. I forced it down and left. The night was chilly but I didn't feel it—

I was too busy thinking about all the information in this case, all the facts that led nowhere, all the deaths, and the cold reality that I had no solid leads to a suspect. In fact, I was grasping so hard for something to hold on to, I'd even considered adding Jefferson Cutter to the list of people of interest. I had absolutely no doubt that Radakov was mixed up in this mess—he'd admitted as much. In a way, he'd also confirmed the existence of The Establishment, but I had no authority here to extract anything from him that he wasn't willing to divulge.

Radakov, the Chechen separatist and peddler in sex slaves; General Scott, four-star general of a huge NATO airbase; Harmony Cutter Scott, his wife—the chief players in this drama. Perhaps General Scott was trying to find out what made Radakov tick, hence all the information that he'd downloaded on the Chechen separatist movement. And what about The Establishment? Was it a government think tank of some kind? Or something else entirely? Several times during this investigation I'd felt a sense of the whole coalescing, or, given the amount of blood that had been spilled, coagulating, but then something new would pop up and the feeling would dissolve. As Anna had observed, someone out there obviously thought of me as a danger or potential threat; otherwise, why the attempts on my life?

I glanced up. My feet had found their way back to The Bump. The line outside had lengthened and the music was still pumping. Somewhere within, a door opened and a hot ball of stale beer fumes, body heat, and perfume rolled over me. It was getting on to 0130 hours and, although I wasn't feeling tired, I'd had enough, and I wanted to get up early so that I could get on Radakov's case. I walked through the entrance to the hotel, lost in speculation.

My room was quiet and dark. I turned on the bedside lamp and stripped. I needed a shower, if only to get the airborne testosterone from The Bump off my skin. I climbed under the hot water, careful to keep the gunshot wound high and dry. Ten minutes later I got out, toweled off, and went back into the bedroom.

I stood in the doorway, towel around my waist, frozen. When I was last there, like, just before I got in the shower, I didn't remember seeing a woman kneeling on the bed. But that's exactly what was there now. I recognized her. It was Katarinya, only she wasn't wearing her glasses anymore. In fact, she wasn't wearing anything.

She said, "I know you want to fuck me. I felt your longing for me. I have thought about you inside me." She put her head down on the covers and stretched forward with her hands, keeping her ass high. Her fingers slid between her thighs. They began to gently stroke and rub her vulva. "Please fuck me," she begged. There was suddenly a look of intense pleasure and pain on her face, as if someone had flicked a switch. She'd turned on a sexual hunger that could only be sated—if what I was hearing and seeing was any indication—by a good ol' Yankee boy in the saddle. But I didn't buy it. Aside from the fact that if I had this effect on women I was sure I'd have experienced it already before now, I'd seen this very act performed by several women earlier tonight for men who had responded by inserting dollars under their G-strings with their teeth. Yeah, I was aroused, but that was offset by the pity I felt for her for being manipulated, used as someone else's instrument, and by my anger at Radakov for doing the using.

"Katarinya, please get dressed," I said, squatting down on my haunches beside her.

"What's wrong?" she asked.

"Nothing's wrong," I replied. I put my hand on her shoulder. She responded by rubbing her cheek against my fingers, and then softly biting one of them.

"I am not sexy for you?" she asked at full pout, coming up on all fours and advancing toward me, her full breasts swaying between her arms.

"You're not here because you find *me* attractive." My throat was annoyingly dry. "Radakov told you to come."

"Yes, he did. But I like you, especially because you're resisting me." She sucked in her bottom lip and held it under her teeth suggestively. Her eyes went to my towel. "Oh, and it is all an act, see?" There was mock surprise in her voice as she reached in and fondled me. I was hard but, while my body might have been a boiling sea of willing hormones, my head and heart said, emphatically, no.

I stepped back from the bed, beyond reach. "You have to leave now." When I met with Radakov in the morning, I didn't want him to think I owed him anything. And there was another reason for this reluctance and her name was Anna Masters.

Katarinya sighed, got up from the bed, and put on her clothes, or rather cloth—the white Lycra sheath. In a matter of a second or two, her attitude swung from crawling-the-walls-horny to utter indifference. She slipped her feet into her high heels and left without a backward glance. If she were a cat, she'd have flicked her tail with disdain.

I cleared my throat. The door closed. Four men charged at me from the shadows. No time to move. I watched them come, mouth open in surprise, blind-sided. They hit me like a stampede. Katarinya, a decoy. I went down on the carpet. I recognized them. Radakov's men, his companions from The Bump. I elbowed one across the bridge of the nose. The bone collapsed like a crushed aluminum can but the injury didn't slow him any. They pinned my arms behind me, and locked my head in a wrestling hold. Two of them sat on my legs as the door opened again. Black boots, black pants walked in. The assailants wrenched back my head to face the newcomer. The black shoes belonged to the man with the monobrow, the beak, and the black eyes. He lifted something in his hands. What was he holding? Shit, was it a hypodermic? A small jet of clear fluid shot from the sharp end. *Jesus, fuck!* He drove his knee into my ribs and slammed the needle into the side of my neck.

"You fuckers," I yelled. "I will personally farrmm bleeeeeo..."

THIRTY-FIVE

My senses came back online slowly. "Euphoric" was the word that best described how I felt, a warm glow concentrated way down in my groin, spreading its fingers up through my chest and down into my legs. I felt like I had just had the best sex of my life. I was conscious that wherever I was, or whatever I was in, it was on the move. I tried to open my eyes but couldn't. Fingers ripped the surgical tape off my lids, giving my remaining eyebrow a Brazilian. The feelings of love pretty much evaporated at that point.

"Ah, Sleeping Beauty awakes," said Alu Radakov, seated opposite, an AK-47 across his lap. "You have been out for hours, Vin. If I didn't know better, I'd have put your exhaustion down to Katarinya's athleticism."

It took a few moments for my brain to catch up with the information it was receiving. The sensation of movement was because I was in the back of a truck, and it was moving. Of course. Radakov sat opposite with three of his men. One of them, I was pleased to see, had a bandage across his nose and two black eyes. He smiled at me. I smiled back—no hard feelings, pal. Like Radakov, they were armed with Kalashnikovs. The guy with the beak and the sallow complexion was seated beside me and I decided he had a face like an angry weasel.

Ropes around my chest and legs held me on the seat,

my shoulders and chest tied back so that I wouldn't pitch forward. My wrists were cuff-locked together, and a cannula had been inserted in the back of one of my hands.

"Midazolam," said Radakov. "Commonly used in anesthesia. It induces amnesia, and makes the patient compliant—in your case, for hours. Did you have any erotic dreams, Vin? It's a side effect of the Midazolam."

That explained a number of things: the hardware in the back of my hand, why the heavens had suddenly shifted from night to daylight, how I came to be in my present predicament, and why, until now, I was so relaxed about it all.

I noted that I was wearing an older style U.S. Army–issue battle dress uniform with European camouflage pattern. The air stank of manure, rotting hay, and something light and sweet I couldn't quite identify.

"Where are we?" I said, the words croaking in my throat.

"Within an hour's drive of Grozny," said Radakov.

Grozny. Grozny? Where was that? It rang a bell.

Maybe Radakov could see the gears turning. He said, "Grozny, capital of Chechnya."

Chechnya? "What?" I said, the single word encapsulating my complete bewilderment. Chechnya was over a thousand miles from Riga.

The truck bounced and came to an abrupt stop so that we all lurched sideways in our seats. Radakov and his men made their way to the back of the vehicle, skating on the ooze. The weasel guy slipped the knots on the rope tying me to the chassis and sliced away the cuff-locks with a pair of scissors. He smiled at me—not a pleasant sight. I decided the drug's aftereffect had nothing to do with his likeness to the animal.

The canvas flap at the back of the truck was flung

open by a heavyset guy, his face covered in red blotches—some kind of birthmark. He looked fifty but was probably closer to thirty. My copassengers jumped down, and Radakov turned and beckoned me to follow.

"Come," he said.

I stood uncertainly, my legs still rickety from the drug.

We were on the outskirts of a village sitting at the base of a set of sparsely wooded hills. The village itself was poor, the buildings low and mean. Thin blue smoke coughed from chimneys. Women dressed in loose-fitting print dresses and gum boots, with scarves tying up their hair, wandered about on their daily business. There were a few mangy dogs sniffing around and children hung out in twos and threes or sat listless by the road. We were in the countryside, only the place stank of rotten-egg gas and burnt grease. I spotted a rusted, blackened armored vehicle with Russian markings still visible. Weeds sprang up inside it. I estimated the wreck to be no more than a month old.

Our truck had pulled up beside a paddock housing two tan cows whose ribs and hips showed clearly through their hides. They tottered on their hooves as if they were about to topple over. In the center of the field lay a tangle of old pipes, rusting oil drums, and, if I wasn't mistaken, drilling gear. And then it clicked—the stench of the place. They were drilling for crude here, "they" being the villagers. The earth squelched under my feet and I looked down. Black crude was breaking through the crust. This place was an environmental nightmare. No wonder everyone, everything, looked so sick.

A cluster of people appeared from around one of the buildings in the village, coming up the road toward us. We met them on a wooden bridge across a stream.

Radakov had chosen not to keep me restrained and I knew why. Where was I going to go? Still dazed by the anesthetic, I glanced over the side of the bridge and saw a couple of children sitting by the creek. A large globule of oil broke from the bank and swung slowly out into the center of the flow before being carried away downstream.

I looked back at the approaching villagers: a couple of young men, an old woman, and two teenage girls. Radakov said something to them in the local language—Chechen, I supposed. The teenage women were pushed forward and Radakov conducted an inspection of them as if they were horses. He checked their teeth, their ears, lifted their hems and groped them, and then put his hand inside their dresses and fondled their breasts. Apparently satisfied with what he found, he motioned at the weasel guy, who produced some paperwork, which one of the young men—perhaps the only literate one among them—perused. The young man seemed satisfied and there was suddenly much laughter shared by everyone except the two young women, who stood with their sullen heads bent, staring at the ground. A pen was produced and the older man scratched his autograph onto the document, followed by the old woman. Radakov then produced two rolls of what looked like U.S. dollars and handed them to the signatories.

The group walked off back to the village, herding the girls in front of them. One of the young men was left behind, and he went into a huddle with Radakov. Radakov's cronies joined in and an intense, animated discussion ensued. There was a fair bit of pointing over the hills. Eventually some agreement was reached and the young man hurried off down the road toward the village, hands buried deep in his pockets. Something, as they say, was up.

"What gives?" I asked Radakov as he turned to walk back to the truck.

"We walk," was all he said.

A few words were exchanged with the driver, who rubbed the red splotch on his forehead, and then Radakov led the way to the oil-polluted stream. We went down into the gully and followed it back up toward the hills. I didn't need to be told that we were taking this route to avoid Russian patrols. What I didn't know was where we were going, or why.

The crude oil clogging the stream made the going tough, possibly more because of the gagging, solid stench of it than the fact that keeping a secure footing was nearly impossible and we all slipped numerous times.

Eventually, we reached the hills and the smell of sulphur receded. We climbed through the trees for at least an hour. The sun was setting when Radakov called a halt. Two of his men lifted some stones and began to dig beneath them. A couple of feet into the loam, they struck a metal box. Five minutes later, Radakov cracked open the box and handed around the contents: black ski masks, packs of C4, timers, RPGs, and armor-piercing rounds to go with them. There was also a set of U.S.-made night-vision goggles—NVGs—the latest and greatest.

"You going to tell me what this is all about, aside from people-smuggling and prostitution?" I asked as we set off along the ridgeline.

"Not yet—first I want you to see what's going on here with your own eyes before you judge The Establishment."

"Okay," I agreed cheerfully, "The Establishment. That's a good place to start."

"No. First you must see."

Radakov took the lead of our little column, scouting with the NVGs. We walked for maybe another hour, down into the next valley, where there was a village pretty similar to the one we'd visited earlier, except for one reasonably crucial detail: It was swarming with Russians. Russians, Chechens, high explosives, and AP rounds. I'm no clairvoyant but I could see that noise, death, and trouble were just around the corner. Confirming as much, Radakov handed me a ski mask.

We took the long route, skirting the village, avoiding contact with Radakov's enemy. Eventually, we arrived at a farmhouse, outside of which were a couple of Russian vehicles—LAVs. It was a moonless night, ideal for NVGs. Two Russian soldiers stood outside, on sentry duty. They were smoking. Two of Radakov's men snuck up behind them and silently slit their throats, holding their hands over the wounds to muffle the sound of the sucking, bubbling noise. Another Russian sitting in one of the vehicles met the same fate. A short while later, two Russians walking out of the farmhouse were clubbed to death soundlessly with fence posts conveniently lying about. Radakov walked into the small building and I heard two muffled shots. He exited seconds later and motioned for me to join him. When I hesitated, the weasel tapped me on the shoulder with his rifle, indicating that I should get a hustle on.

The stench of vomit and feces reached me before I stepped inside. But nothing could have forewarned me of the scene I was confronted with. Two Russian soldiers were sprawled against a wall, each with a gunshot wound to the eye, their brains sliding down the rough walls. One of Radakov's men hawked up some mucus from the back of his throat and spat it on the nearest of the dead Russians.

The reason for the Russian presence in this farm-house, and now ours, was a man in his early twenties duct-taped into a chair, sitting unconscious in his own filth. His face was battered raw, and fresh purple bruises and welts stood out on his body. But that was not the worst of it, not by a long shot. His mouth was smeared with blood, which I assumed was the result of the numerous beatings he'd sustained. Then I realized it was caused by something else. Radakov lifted the man's right hand, revealing the bloody stumps of his index and middle fingers. Mounted on a small table nearby was a meat grinder of the type used to turn bovine muscle and bone into sausage. The realization of what had been happening here hit me: They had ground off the man's fingers and forced them into his own mouth. Suddenly I found myself kneeling on the floor, the contents of my stomach burning the back of my throat as they passed through on their way out. One of Radakov's men was beside me on the floor do-ing the same.

The weasel, who by now I assumed was the band's medic, was checking over the man strapped to the chair. When my stomach finally stopped convulsing, I stood. One of the Chechens pulled the jacket off a Russian while another untied the dead victim. Then they wrapped him in the jacket and the two of them carried the corpse out of the farmhouse.

A night breeze was creeping down off the hills, bringing with it a chill mixed with damp moss and de-cay, the smell of the grave. A shiver like scuttling bee-tles ran under my skin. Radakov said something quietly. The group separated. The weasel and one other man made their way to the Russian vehicles. The rest of us, including the body wrapped in the jacket, went off in the other direction. Soon after, a deafening explosion split the air. I looked back. The LAVs were burning brightly, lighting up the night sky.

"We don't have much time. There is only one way in," Radakov explained as he motioned at the road. We double-timed across the steepening fields and out of the immediate vicinity. When he muttered something to the men carrying the body, we stopped. The bigger of the two Chechens hoisted the corpse over his shoulder and then continued toward the hills. Radakov and the rest—me included—doubled back and took a course that paralleled the road, and scouted for cover. Radakov found it behind a weed-choked mound of earth overlooking the road, two hundred yards back from it. He made a hand signal. We dropped behind the mound and waited.

I heard the vehicles before I saw them. They were moving slowly along the road. There was a foot patrol reconnoitering the way ahead. The approaching Russians were cautious. Experience probably gave them a fair idea of what they were dealing with. I counted four vehicles: three armored track vehicles and some kind of truck. It looked like the entire Russian presence in the village had come to investigate.

A prodigious explosion suddenly engulfed the lead vehicle; the mighty percussion wave filled with shrapnel hacked into the foot patrol. We ducked behind the earth as the pressure wave rolled over us. I heard the nearby crash and thump of a large piece of metal hitting the upper branches of a tree and then falling to the ground. As the sound boomed and reverberated through the hills, I heard some of the Russians whimpering. The sound they made reminded me of the U.S. hospital back in Baghdad. Radakov and his men were merciless. They stood up from behind the berm and, using the light provided by the burning armored track vehicle, fired off rocket-propelled grenades at the last two vehicles. The RPG rounds found their marks with earsplitting crashes. Halfhearted small-arms shots were fired blind by the pathetic survivors. These were countered by the men Radakov had sent to bury the deadly IED in the roadside. Within minutes, the rifle fire was silenced and everyone in the Russian patrol lay dead. I stood and saw the torn, ripped bodies in the light of the flames roaring among the vehicles. Secondary explosions sent showers of dancing orange sparkles toward the stars.

THIRTY-SIX

The ambush was a long way behind us now. The glow from burning tires and fuel oil was no longer visible from our position high in the hills. No one had spoken a word, saving our breath for the climb. Radakov called a halt and some bread and cheese was passed around. A couple of the men joked privately. No fire was lit. "How does it feel to be a Chechen rebel, eh?" asked Radakov in a whisper as he carved off a chunk of cheese with a knife that glinted in the starlight and fed it into his mouth.

"You going to answer my questions now?"

"Why don't you ask them and we'll see how far we get?"

This was not quite the response I had hoped for. I said, "Did General Scott come on one of your little field trips, too?"

"Yes."

"Why did you bring him?"

"I wanted him to witness the important work being done."

"Being done by the separatists?"

"No, by The Establishment."

"This is an Establishment operation?"

"What isn't?" he replied.

"These answers aren't going to make much sense until I know who or what The Establishment is," I said.

"I can't tell you that."

"You can't because you don't know the answer? Or can't because you've been told not to?"

He gave an ambiguous shrug.

I took a different tack. "So the mission you brought the general on was what? An attempt at recruitment?"

"You could say that."

"You wanted Scott to join The Establishment?"

"Yes."

So the general wasn't a member of this . . . this ultra-covert organization. "Did you tell General Scott what The Establishment was?"

"No."

"Why not?"

"I didn't have to."

"Why not?"

"Because he'd been told."

"By whom?"

"By his wife."

"Harmony?"

Radakov nodded.

I don't know why I was surprised to hear this. "Did Harmony Scott conspire to kill her husband?"

Another shrug.

We heard the distant thump of helicopter rotor blades way down in the valley. The Russians would have a Hind out searching for the insurgents who whacked their patrol, so the men were keen to vacate the area.

"Is that why you've brought me here, too? Part of your recruiting drive?"

"No."

"Then why?" I could only think of one other possible answer to that question: to make me disappear. I'd had two attempts on my life in the past week. Was The Establishment going to go for third time lucky? I felt a presence over my right shoulder. I knew who it was before I looked—the weasel. Radakov got to his feet and I followed. The three of us stood there for what seemed like half a lifetime, the cold starlight sheening off our perspiration. Radakov appeared uncertain, maybe putting the question of whether to kill me or not on the scales. I turned my back on the pair of them and walked off to sit on a rock. Nothing I could do would influence the situation in my favor. Up here, with no one around for miles, I was completely at the mercy of these men.

I watched Radakov speak briefly to his lieutenant, who then slipped something sharp and metallic into his belt. Both men came toward me, Radakov's man smiling, which, even in the poor light, was not a pleasant sight. Radakov stopped beside me but the weasel kept walking. "I should kill you," he said.

"Why don't you?" I said while the voice in my head screamed, *What are you doing? Don't fucking taunt him!*

"If you are killed, someone else will take your place." He said this as if it was a matter of fact. Maybe it was, but I had my doubts. I was now pretty certain I'd been chosen for this gig because no one expected or wanted a result. Not great for my self-esteem. Lucky for me, I have a thick skin. And it made me all the more determined to shove it all back in their faces. I was suddenly deeply committed to peeling the scab off this little sore, because I was now certain that a voracious and malignant cancer was hiding below it.

The wind shifted slightly. It brought with it the *thump-thump* of helicopter blades, closer this time. "We must go now," Radakov said, looking down the valley. We resumed the climb and reached the ridgeline a short while later, where the going became easier. There were a lot of questions in my head. I took potluck and asked one: "Were General Scott and Varvara lovers?"

Radakov actually laughed at that. "Lovers? No. He was full of American sexual repression. Just like you."

"So, if they weren't lovers, then why would Scott go to all the trouble of taking Varvara back to Ramstein?"

"He did not like my business. After his son died in Iraq, he wanted to save someone. It was as simple and as complex as that."

The image of the two women back in the village came to mind. They were beautiful and young, born into a life of grinding poverty, war, and zero choices. Thanks to Radakov, they would spend that youth and beauty being screwed by loveless men for money, none of which they'd ever see. They were purchased human beings: slaves. Could I imagine General Scott, grieving over the loss of his son, risking everything to save just one person from this life?

That got me thinking about Abraham Scott. He'd been a mystery man when I began this investigation, but I was getting to know him. He was a man with morals, admired and respected by the people in his command. Something had disillusioned him and so utterly compromised his belief system that he risked his only child to bring it down. It was a gamble he had lost, and the guilt of it had crushed his spirit.

"Why do you trade in women?" I asked Radakov.

"Because it is easy money. There is a ready market and a willing supply. We Chechens are fighting a war, Cooper. Guns and bullets don't fly into our hands."

"You mean, grow on trees."

"What?"

"Never mind."

And I finally saw it. Perhaps it was the fucked-up metaphor, not mine but his—the one about guns and bullets not flying into their hands—that peeled back the clouds over this case and let me see those confused markings on the ground with clarity for the first time. "When did General Scott realize that you were using NATO planes to fly sex slaves into Germany?"

Radakov didn't answer right away. At that moment, he was probably reconsidering his decision not to kill me. "You are a clever man, Cooper. He is right to fear you." The men walking up ahead paused to listen. I wondered exactly who "he" was. I was about to ask when Radakov raised his hand to stop me. The night was filled with the noise of crickets and frogs, but no more sounds from helicopter blades, distant or otherwise. Satisfied, the men ahead trudged on, climbing steadily into the frost, picking their way through the trees. "Over a year ago, Scott came to Riga looking into some unauthorized NATO flights," said Radakov softly.

Yeah, the flight-progress strips, the highlighted RIX entries on the ATC log . . . I also remembered glimpsing Varvara's passport. "What about identities for the people you smuggled in?"

"German passports are not all biometric yet. They are relatively easy to forge. Moving outsiders around Ramstein was the only difficulty, but we found a way."

"That wouldn't have been by giving each of them a CAC card, would it?"

He glared at me, perhaps thinking he'd given up too much information. "You know about these?"

I nodded. There were those three hundred missing CAC cards the general had been checking into. Scott must have put two and two together and come up with a big fat rat. Radakov's human cargo had been smuggled into Ramstein on NATO C-130s, posing as returning U.S. servicewomen. I almost laughed—a breakthrough at last. "So you must have a contact inside Ramstein. You going to tell me who it is?"

"No."

"Is this still happening? Using Ramstein as a slave port?"

"No. There were six flights over a year ago—none since."

The flights Scott was looking into. I let all this sink in. Who was Radakov's inside man? I knew it couldn't have been Harmony Scott, and not because she was the wrong gender. It had to be someone who had complete access to the base, someone who could authorize flights, someone with top-level security access. Then it hit me. *Jesus H. Christ!* I knew exactly who it was. And this time, I did laugh. And, yeah, he had every damn right to fear me.

"You will be quiet now, Cooper," said Radakov, tense.

Not in a million years would I have guessed the identity of Radakov's Ramstein connection. I sucked in a breath to get the mirth under control. There was nothing remotely funny about killing or slavery. I'd been looking forward to getting back to Ramstein to see Anna. And now I had something else to look forward to—the pleasure of stomping very hard on a murderous asshole.

THIRTY-SEVEN

I got nothing more from Radakov. If there was anything else for him to give, he'd decided to keep it to himself. We trekked in fatigued silence for four more hours as the terrain steepened. The body we'd taken from the farmhouse was making the trip on a litter made from saplings roped together with bootlaces. I got the impression that none of the men felt particularly heroic or inspired about the enterprise earlier in the evening. Either they'd killed too many Russians over the years to give it any thought, or they would rather have been at home with their wives and children—if they had any—than walking cold, wet, and hungry toward the dawn. Perhaps they knew that the Russians would exact their revenge from people who were innocent of any crime, except for the one of being Chechen. Or maybe these men were just the walking dead, the light of their souls extinguished by a lifetime of hatred and bloodshed. In the end, did either the Russians or the Chechens gain anything except for a bunch of fresh holes dug in the ground?

Scott's fascination with Russia's spats with Chechnya still puzzled me. I couldn't see how it fit in anywhere, unless it was to get an insight into Radakov. But I doubted that. There was something I'd missed, or something I didn't know yet. According to Scott's notes, the Russians had been fighting these people off and on for centuries. Apparently, even Leo Tolstoy had fought here, back in 1851, and the fighting was just as brutal then. Now, however, there was a new factor in the mix: oil. Moscow wanted it. Was that what this was all about? Oil? Or was the fighting here about something else entirely? There was nothing that stood out from Scott's research, nothing that struck me as being related or significant.

The moon rose at some time during the night. It just appeared, a sliver of dull tin beaten over a cold, black stone. It emitted a ghastly light that fell exhausted through the trees. After this, if there was an after, I was taking a goddamn vacation.

We eventually came through the trees onto a muddy, rock-strewn road and picked our way along it for a time. Up ahead, a truck was parked, nuzzled into the bushes. One of the men whistled softly and the notes were echoed back by someone hiding in the deep shadows. It was the man with the red face, his rhubarb-colored splotches showing black in the ghost light. Another man jumped down off the back of the truck. I recognized him as being the man who'd read through Radakov's purchasing agreement for the two teenagers, the same man who also—I assumed—provided the intelligence on the activities and whereabouts of the Russian interrogators. There was some quiet conversation between him and Radakov's men, and then he knelt beside the body on its litter, wiped its face with a rag, and then gently kissed its dead lips. I heard him cry.

"It was his brother. He will be buried here," said Radakov beside me, as the corpse was carried back into the trees.

"Where to now?" I said to Radakov.

He answered with a gesture indicating that I should get into the truck with the rest of his men. I didn't have much choice. I pulled myself up, stepped under the tarp, and entered the familiar cocoon of smells that included shit, animal hide, and the rotten-egg stench of crude oil. I took a seat on one of the benches and found myself looking at the bent heads of the two young women from the village. They were sitting opposite. Wherever we were going, the girls were coming with us. One of the men stuck his hand up the skirt of the girl beside him. What he found there appeared to amuse him because he gave a hearty laugh like he was some pseudo Mexican bandit in a B-movie. Radakov stepped into the truck and whispered hoarsely at him to pull his finger out, or words to that effect. There was a brief, angry exchange of whispers between the two men, which, I suspect, had nothing to do with protecting the girl's morals and more to do with not spoiling the merchandise.

I felt something brush my hand. It was the weasel. He'd managed to dock a syringe into the cannula on the back of my hand. He smiled. I shuddered. And then the lights went ou—

THIRTY-EIGHT

I was dreaming one of those dreams, the kind you never want to wake up from because this sort of thing never happens in reality. I dreamed I was lying in a warm bed in a dark room with sheets that were cool and crisp and smelled vaguely of soap. Masters was also in the bed, naked. I smelled her perfume and felt the warmth of her skin on mine. She stroked the sensitive spot behind my scrotum lightly with her fingertips, as her mouth moved rhythmically on me. I reached down and ran my hand through the softness of her hair, and tried not to come. This was our first time together and I wanted to hold on—I didn't want to blow it, as they say.

I was aware that it was the Midazolam—had to be. Hadn't Radakov said erotic dreams were a side effect of the drug? Yeah, he had said something like that. This was the kind of side effect I could get into. I remembered the cannula, the hideous smile, and, in drug-induced euphoria, I didn't even cringe at the memory. That was all a bad dream. This was a good dream. I pushed the bad thoughts away. Anna was being very determined about bringing the situation between my legs to a conclusion. It was getting to the point where I wouldn't be able to hold back. I started to get concerned about coming in her mouth and was about to say as much when . . . damn, too late. I opened my eyes.

Reality.

The last thing I remembered was the smell in the back of the truck and looking at—

"Hmm, so you like Katarinya now?" said a voice under the sheets.

I froze.

A head popped up from under the covers and a warm body climbed on top of me. She straddled me and I entered her involuntarily as her legs wrapped around me and she began to move her hips. "My turn," she said.

Katarinya? The girl from The Bump! *Jesus!*

I pulled her off me and turned her so that she landed heavily on the bed beside me. After a moment's hesitation, she said, "So you like it rough, yes? I can—"

"Shhh!" I said, putting my hand over her mouth. This was not what I wanted or, rather, *who* I wanted. I was completely disoriented. Had everything been a dream? The raid on the farmhouse, those bloody stumps where fingers used to be, the climb through the hills, the young girls bought and sold? I raced through my memory. How much time had passed? "What day is it?" I demanded. I looked at the face under my hand. Katarinya's eyes were wide. I was scaring her. I didn't care. This woman was part of Radakov's bullshit. I hadn't dreamed any of it, except maybe the part about Anna . . .

The last time this stripper had been in my room, Radakov's thugs had come through the door, shot crap into my veins, and abducted me. That was not going to happen again.

The body in the bed beside me was getting nervous. She kicked me in the groin. My knee deflected most of the force of the blow, but enough of it connected to make me go fetal. I released her, dimly aware of her backing out of the bed and grabbing her clothes off the floor. Her ass flashed white in the darkness as she went through the door, slamming it behind her.

"Bye," I groaned.

I waited for Radakov's men to make an encore appearance, charging through the other room, but it remained dark and quiet. I snatched a glance at the clock radio. 0500 hours. I had no idea what day it was. How much time had I lost? The pain in my balls subsided to a dull ache and I could see straight again. In my mind, I apologized to Katarinya and Anna for the mix-up. I was innocent. If there was a guilty party here it was Radakov, or maybe it was inequality that was the real villain. Katarinya was probably no different from the two girls who had made the trip out of Grozny in the stinking truck. She'd probably left nothing behind in a small, dirt-poor rural town, only to have an empty life elsewhere—here.

The glow of the city beyond the window formed a thin blue halo around the drapes. It was the same room I'd checked into. I rolled out of bed and found my bag. Everything had been pulled out, but I couldn't spot anything missing. I still had the general's downloads, but that was all printouts, anyway—there were no originals, nothing worth stealing. I reached for my cell. I was tempted to turn it on. Anna would have left a message for sure, along with Brenda, Gruyere, and the fuck knew who else. I tossed it back in my bag. I'd connect when I returned to Germany.

I crawled across the carpet, cupping my testicles, and made it to the bathroom. I turned on the hot water and five minutes later slipped into a steaming bath. I lay there until the sunlight deposed the infiltrating neon of the street, mentally retracing my steps over the past week and a half.

* * *

I still had the Russian cab driver's phone number, so I called it from a public phone in the hotel foyer. Fifteen minutes later, I opened the car door and climbed into a miasma of cigarette smoke. "You were right about The Bump," I said, fastening the seat belt. "It sucked."

"You Americans never listen. Where are we going?" he asked as we pulled into the traffic.

"The airport," I said.

"Here," he said, passing me a pink plastic drink bottle. "You look like you need this. Real Russian vodka. Better than the shit we export to the West. You can still taste the soil on the potatoes." We swerved around a horse and cart and the former Red Army translator said something loud and no doubt unpleasant out his window at the ensemble.

"No, thanks," I said, declining the offer of a drink. Aside from the fact that it was barely 0800 hours, I hadn't eaten anything, and the nozzle on the bottle was chewed and unappealing. Ordinarily, though, none of this would've bothered me. I'd have taken a mouthful or two, and big ones, the reason being I had a plane flight ahead. But this time, I'd made the decision to face it without a crutch. I'd been flying a lot lately, and I'd noticed that not one of those aircraft had fallen out of the sky. The episode in the C-47 in Afghanistan, the flashing knives on the mountaintop, and the scorpions in my dreams were not so much receding as being replaced by more recent events. The reality of the suffering of the Chechen villager, his fingers ground into pulp and fed to him, was proving a powerful purge.

"Next time you come to Riga, you call. I show you

real nightlife—even in the daytime," promised my driver.

"Deal," I said, although I knew I'd never be coming back to this place. I looked out the window and watched the city flash past in the rain. The weather was still cold and gray. It suited my mood. I wondered why Radakov had given me so much information. I was sure his original plan had been to kill me, but, for whatever reason, he'd decided not to go through with it. Instead, I'd been given facts enough to put some heavy people in front of a jury and seriously embarrass NATO. Was that why—because he had something against NATO? Or was it simply that Radakov admired and liked General Scott and was angry about what had happened to him? I knew his decision to let me go was connected to something else—this mysterious organization that kept cropping up: The Establishment.

Was it real, or the figment of a collective imagination, like the bogeyman or UFOs? At least I now knew who to question about it: my favorite widow. I'd asked Harmony Scott before about The Establishment, and gotten nowhere. Now, however, thanks to Radakov, I had new insight and my questions would have more bite.

The Russian slammed the brakes on at the drop-off zone at Riga International. "You sure?" he said, holding up the drink bottle and giving it a waggle. "You look like you need it."

"Thanks," I said, shaking my head. "Next time. What do I owe you?" We settled on an amount in euros, as I didn't have any local cash. I retrieved a few notes, including a generous tip, from the crinkled ball in my pocket. I was getting low on funds, but it didn't matter— I had enough to complete the job. I said good-bye and watched the Russian narrowly avoid an accident as he accelerated into the traffic flow, careless of anyone's safety, including his own.

I didn't have to wait long for a flight. The takeoff was tense, but when we didn't stall and plunge into the ground, I managed to loosen up a little—enough to skim through the general's notes again and go over what I did know. When I got back to Ramstein, I'd be dropping a bombshell on the place and I wanted to make sure it hit the bull's-eye.

I slept dreamlessly for an hour of the three-and-a-half-hour flight and woke up when the screws under my seat whined, signaling that the flaps were being deployed. I tried not to think about crash statistics that say the takeoff and landing phases of flight are the most dangerous, that altitude is a plane's best friend and that we were fast losing ours. But we landed without incident and, twenty minutes later, I was walking through customs and into the terminal at Frankfurt International.

I passed a newsstand and stopped. From a poster for *Der Standard*, Germany's equivalent of *The Washington Post*, a familiar face smiled out at me. It was Heinrich Himmler—my good buddy Lieutenant General Wolfgang von Koeppen. I picked up a paper and his face was all over it, and I recognized some of the photos from the wall of the Melting Pot. Damn, I thought, I was too late. The media had somehow run down the story. I couldn't read German, so I picked up a copy of the *International Herald Tribune* to see if they also carried the scandal.

I found it on page three. The headline read: "NATO General Dies in Car Accident."

What?

The photo from the *Der Standard* poster ran alongside the article in the *Trib*. It was von Koeppen's official head-and-shoulders shot; the general wore a comfortable, easy smile. It reminded me of the photo of General Scott. Both smiling, both very dead, neither smiling now. I read the brief accompanying paragraphs.

German Lieutenant General Wolfgang von Koeppen, acting commander of Ramstein Air Base, the vast NATO facility in southwest Germany, was killed two days ago when the car he was in slammed into a wall.

Witnesses to the crash said the vehicle failed to make a sharp turn and hit a roadside retaining wall head-on.

Police crash investigators have attributed the accident to brake failure.

The commander of Ramstein Air Base, USAF General Abraham Scott, died in a glider accident one month ago.

Also killed in the accident was the driver of the vehicle, USAF Special Agent Anna Masters.

THIRTY-NINE

I don't know how long I stood there at the newsstand reading that article, but it was long enough for the guy who owned the store to tap me on the shoulder and give me the "buy it or move along" eyeball. I bought it.

Also killed in the accident was the driver of the vehicle, USAF Special Agent Anna Masters. Anna, dead? A car accident? Brake failure? Where this case was concerned, there were no such things as accidents. They were planned and executed. General Scott's first wife, Helen Wakely, died in a car accident caused by brake failure. I felt a pain in my heart and a lump in my throat that I couldn't swallow.

I hired a cab and headed for Ramstein. I had just over three hundred bucks remaining of the original sixteen-hundred-dollar float. I thought about what I was going to do next as the autobahn flashed past. Anna, dead? No, it wasn't possible. I saw her face, the freckles sprinkled across her nose, those blue-green eyes and her luscious hair. In the picture in my mind, she was smiling that smile of hers that lit up the room. Somehow, the motivation for pursuing this investigation had evaporated and all that was left of it were overwhelming feelings of exhaustion, loss, and helplessness. The tears streamed down my face. I hadn't done that for a very long time—cry. Contrary to what I'd heard, it didn't make me feel better. Anna had finally received the attention she believed she deserved. Someone had taken her seriously enough to kill her. What a fucking waste. The cab driver passed back a box of tissues.

In my life, I have seen a lot of death, but I'd never lost anyone I'd been in love with. Yeah, I was in love with Anna, and it was only at this moment that I realized it.

I asked the driver if he knew any good hotels in Kaiserslautern. I didn't want to go back to the Pensione Freedom in case it was being watched. In broken English, the driver told me he had a brother-in-law whose father had a share in a tourist hotel in K-town. I had him drive me there, paid the fare in cash, and then went to a hotel a block down the road from the one he'd recommended. No, I wasn't being paranoid; I was being careful—careful is paranoia with cause. On the way, I bought two bottles of my old buddy, Glenkeith, for company. I had a hundred and twenty dollars left—a hotel room for three nights, or two nights with food. I didn't intend to do much eating.

I got to the room, pulled the curtains, stood in the shower an eternity, and then sat on the bed, naked, with the two bottles of booze clinking together beside me on the mattress. The Establishment had killed Masters. Why? Was it a warning to me? Was this the price of the knowledge Radakov had given me? If so, why kill von Koeppen, too? I hadn't a shred of evidence. There was so much in this case I couldn't fathom and yet, at the same time, I knew the answers were staring me in the face. Maybe, if I'd been a little more attuned to them, Masters would still be alive. And while I was beating myself up about this, it occurred to me that she'd also probably still be alive if I could've convinced her to accept close protection.

I cracked open the seal on the first bottle and didn't bother with a glass. I drank a third of it in one hit. It didn't taste as good as I remembered, most probably Glen's way of punishing me for ignoring him. Well, never mind, I intended to reacquaint myself over the next day or so. The heat hit my empty stomach like the angry bulls that chase those idiots down the streets of Pamplona, goring them, and went to my brain with the same nasty intent. Just what I needed.

I don't remember too much from there on. When I woke, I had no idea whether it was day or night. Nor did I care. I took another shower, drank another third to take away the headache, and lay back on the bed and gazed unseeing at a spider that had made its web in a corner of the ceiling. I felt nothing, which is a good thing to feel sometimes, even though I was aware that I had no career left, nowhere to go, and no one to go there with. I was so drunk I didn't care. I drank the remainder of the second bottle and said good-bye to another day. Or was it night?

I was snarled in the sheets with the two empty bottles. There was a sourness in my gut and vomit on the pillow. I had enough sense to know there was nothing left to drink and almost nothing left to buy it with, unless I used a credit card. That was always an option—a solution in itself: "Hey, you fuckers, here I am. Come get me."

I raised my head and took in the room. It was a small box with a window that opened onto a brick wall and a nest of pipes evacuating sewage from the upper floors. Beside the bed was my overnight bag, open, the contents spilled onto the linoleum. I focused on the cell phone. There'd be messages on it. I couldn't hide from them forever. I sat up and felt the hammers in my head go to work on the back of my skull. I reached for the cell with my foot and toed it toward the bed. I picked it up and hit the power-up button. The screen illuminated briefly, then turned black. The battery was dead. I caught sight of the charger and recovered it, again with my foot. Anna had been right about it coming in handy. I plugged one end into the wall socket beside the bed and the other into the phone and tried turning it on again. Second time lucky. The thing started ringing almost immediately. I pressed the receive button and the automated voice informed me that I had seven messages. I hit the button to begin receiving them.

The first two were from General Gruyere. She sounded as if she had something red hot probing an unfortunate place.

Next, surprisingly, was a message from Arlen Wayne, my last remaining bud, back at Andrews. He wanted to know what was up. "Heard a bunch of bullcrap that you gone AWOL, boy," he said. He went on to reaffirm that he didn't believe it but recommended that I get my ass back to where it goddamn belonged. Yeah, I thought, in a sling. Thanks, Arlen. I knew he meant well and it was nice to know someone cared.

Brenda followed with a couple of urgent requests to call her back. She had news and didn't want to leave it in a message, she said. Nothing new there. She'd already told me that in the last score of rants deposited.

The next message got me sitting up, which gave the hammers in my skull something to get seriously angry about. "Vin," Anna said. "Something has turned up here. We've got a lead on Scott's expenditure. We found a receipt in his files. It concerns that missing week. It seems he booked himself a flight to the U.S.— Washington, D.C. This is the weird part: He could have taken a C-5 any day of the week, but he chose to pay cash, maybe for the same reasons you did—to keep the fact that he was moving around hidden." There was a smile in her voice. "I guess this solves one of our little mysteries. Call back in when you can. I . . . I miss you—who'd have thought? Bye."

I'd bitten my bottom lip hard and tasted copper flooding into my mouth. I missed her, too. And now I'd be missing her for good. Hearing her voice . . . it was like the photo thing, seeing someone you knew was no longer among the living, smiling out at you as if they were sharing some private joke with a punch line you didn't understand. Hearing her speak was a voice from beyond.

The messages kept coming and didn't allow me time to stop and think, or get any more maudlin than I already was. Next I heard Bishop's BBC voice, as formal as ever: "Special Agent Cooper, I believe Special Agent Masters has informed you of the movements of General Scott in the period after the death of his son, Peyton. We have the forensics report back on the bullet fragments recovered from the water barrels in Baghdad, and the helmet. We can confirm that the blood on the helmet and the hair and blood on the bullet fragments are from the same person. The blood type matches Peyton's, but his was O positive, the most common blood type.

"From this evidence, sir, we can say with authority that the bullet went through the helmet and that the person wearing it received, in all likelihood, a fatal head shot. We just can't be a hundred percent sure that the person in question was, in fact, Peyton, because we have nothing to compare the DNA sample with."

"Hmm," I said to Bishop's voice. "Fair enough." Given Dante Ambrose's assertion that the helmet was

Peyton's, and that he'd seen the event in question, I was satisfied on that score—that Peyton had been shot in the head by the bullet whose fragments we had in our possession. Before DNA, this would have been enough to convince even the most cynical board. Bishop was just being careful and thorough, looking for loopholes, looking at the way an inquiry would consider the evidence.

"And something else has just now turned up, sir. We have a lead on one of General Scott's downloads—those figures he'd been examining. We took a section of the numbers and got a few hours on a Cray computer to run a search on them. It seems they relate to the U.S. balance of trade with the Russian Federation over the last few years. Special Agent Masters believes he might have been looking for similarities with your—I mean, the U.S.'s—trading relationship with Japan in the thirties. As for the Dungeon, still no luck there, I'm afraid. The programmer concerned has not yet been located. That's it for now, sir."

Bishop must have called before Anna was—The computer voice informed me that I had one last message in the bank. "Cooper, I don't know where you are or what you think you're doing, but this is important. No doubt you've heard about General von Koeppen and Special Agent Masters. Things are happening that I can help you with. But only if you come in. Call now."

Gruyere again, but, instead of ranting at me, she'd chosen a tone I'd never heard before in her voice. For starters, it contained not one swear word. Also, if I was not mistaken, Gruyere sounded scared. But was she scared *for* me, or *of* me? Interesting.

The voice informed me that there were no more messages and asked whether I wanted to hear them again, delete them, or save them. I deleted the messages from Arlen and Brenda, but saved the ones from Anna and Bishop, and that last troubled message from General Gruyere. Then I stared at the cell, and tried to get my hungover brain to think straight. After Peyton Scott was killed in Iraq, General Scott flew there to investigate his son's death. He then went to Washington—obviously to see someone. The question now was, who? Then he went to Riga and made a deal with Radakov, the payment for which was the release of Varvara Kadyrov into his care. The blanks were filling in and I was starting to harden up a few theories of my own. The news about those figures representing recent U.S.-Russian trade was interesting, and scary. Was Anna's hypothesis about them right? Were we setting up the Russians for something, manipulating them just like we did Japan nearly seventy years ago?

I replayed the messages in case there was anything I missed, or in case hearing them again might spark fresh thoughts, but I was incapable of either. All I got was the lump back in my throat when I heard Anna's voice.

And then suddenly the cell jumped in my hand, vibrating and ringing and scaring the shit out of me. A phone number I wasn't familiar with appeared on the screen. I considered not answering the call and screening instead through voice mail. For an instant, I even believed that it might be Anna. Maybe that's why I thumbed the green button. "Hello?"

"Vince, is that you?" said a familiar voice.

My heart nearly blew a gasket. For an instant, I believed it really was Anna.

"Brenda," I said, with far more enthusiasm than I intended—but I was still getting over the notion that the voice had been Anna's. "What's up?"

"Are you all right, Vince? I've had OSI all over me

these last couple of days. All I could get from anyone was that you'd vanished."

"Vanished? Nope, still here. Just out of curiosity, who gave you this number?"

"Arlen," she said.

Arlen Wayne. I told myself to give him a big thank-you when I got home. If I got home.

"Where are you exactly?" Brenda persisted.

"Bren, you know better than that. Where are *you* calling from?"

"From home," she said.

That would mean a landline. There was no doubt in my mind that it would be tapped by some particularly unpleasant people who were going to get a huge dose of bad karma coming back at them if there was any justice in the universe—shit, a couple of moments talking to the ex and I was thinking like a Deepak Chopra self-help tape again.

And then it occurred to me. They—whoever *they* were—wouldn't need to tap the call; they could simply trace the cell on the network by triangulating the signal it emitted. In the U.S. that process took anywhere between eight and twenty minutes, depending on the size and strength of the network. What was the deal in Europe? How much time did I have? Did *they* also reach into the phone companies here? I'd been hit several times out of the blue while conducting this investigation. How had I been found, unless, of course, the mysterious *they* knew where to look? During those incidents, the cell I'd been given by Anna had been turned on only for brief periods—not long enough for the networks to get a fix. Had a GPS marker been placed in the cell to give an instantaneous fix when the unit was powered up? That could explain the rapid ability the bad guys had for picking up my scent. Or should I seriously think about changing my brand of deodorant? Anna had given me the charger along with the cell. The question I was now asking myself was whether that had been an innocent decision on her part. Or had she wanted me to keep the cell charged up so that it and the person holding it—me—could be located immediately?

And while I was thinking around in paranoid circles, I thought about Anna. She'd been killed in an accident with von Koeppen. I knew they'd been lovers. Had it really been over between them? Jesus, too many questions, not enough answers.

"Vince! Did you hear me?"

"I'm sorry, Brenda. What did you say? It's a bad connection." I had to end this call and get as far away from the cell as possible. And fast.

"No, Vincent. There's nothing wrong with the connection, not the phone line's connection, at least. You've always had a problem being in the here and now—with me."

Here we go, I thought. "Brenda, you've caught me at a bad time. I have to go. What's your news?"

"I just told you. You are unbelievable! You weren't even listening!" A big all-suffering sigh followed. "I said, Lucas and I are getting married."

Silence.

"So?" she said.

"So what? What do you want me to say?"

"So what do you think?"

"What do you think I'd think?" Both of us could see where this was leading. And now I could sense Brenda wanted out of the phone call as much as I did. Like I said, what did she think I'd think? She was marrying Colonel Lucas Blow Job, relationship counselor—the amoral fuck who was telling me I was a bad husband while he was boning her. The memory of that moment, walking in on them, brought back the anger.

"Vince, be happy for us. Be happy for me."

"I'm ecstatic for you."

She didn't miss the sarcasm. "Vincent, you and I— we were over long before Lucas came on the scene. You know that. I just want to be happy. I loved you, Vince, when we met. Remember? And it's because I remember how I felt about you that I want you to be happy, too."

I closed my eyes. Yeah, I could remember those days, and she was right: We had been happy. But somewhere along the road the understanding between us had just...dissolved. And that was no one's fault, was it? It just happened. The silence and the tension between us now had a life of their own, self-perpetuating. I realized that I was angry at her simply because I was angry at her and for no other reason that I could think of. Everyone had a right to happiness. Even Brenda.

"I love Lucas. He loves me. And we're getting married. I just wanted to be the one to tell you rather than one of your jerk-off air force buddies."

I didn't know what to say to fill the silence that followed, so I didn't say anything.

"You'll meet someone, Vince. One day, you'll meet that special someone and know we did the right thing."

The right thing. The right thing? Once, not too long ago, a comment like that would have lit my short fuse. But now, all I was thinking about was Anna, because I'd met someone special, too, and now she was gone and I might never clear up the questions in my head. "Brenda, I have to go."

"Okay, but can you do one thing for me?"

"What?"

"Wish me happiness."

It was a good wish. As far as wishes went, happiness was the star at the top of the tree. Brenda had managed to catch me in a moment of susceptibility. So she wanted me to wish her happiness. It was a small thing, but I could also see that it was everything. Personally, I didn't think she had—what was that unlucky guy's name? Buckley? Yeah, I didn't think she had Buckley's chance of finding happiness with the colonel, but to each their own. And, all of a sudden, my anger was gone. "Yeah, I wish you happiness, Bren."

"You mean that?"

"Yeah."

"Thanks. Bye, Vin. And Vin?"

"Yeah?"

"Be safe."

"Thanks."

Be safe—what the troops in Iraq said to each other before going out on a mission to get themselves ripped apart by IEDs. Kind of appropriate given what I had ahead of me. "You, too." I hit the red button first, killing the call, then turned the cell off. I walked unsteadily to the toilet, vomited into the bowl, and then dropped the cell in after it. I didn't know how much time I had, but valuable seconds were slipping away.

Civvies, or battle dress uniform? I threw on the ABU, the one Anna had found for me, before we went into Iraq. Minutes later I walked out of the hotel with my overnight bag, taking the emergency exit out the back. I walked around the block, across the street, and staked out the front of the hotel.

I didn't have long to wait. An NCMP SUV wove through the traffic with its siren off but its blue light flashing and screeched to a dramatic stop opposite, outside the hotel. The doors flew open and four men jumped out. They sprinted into the hotel with their hands on the butts of the pistols on their hips.

I gave myself a small pat on the back for trusting my own instincts and walked down the street and around the block until I found what I was looking for—a bank of pay phones. I checked the number in my notebook, fed some loose change into the slot until the light went green, and dialed the number.

It picked up after a few rings and a familiar voice said, "Flight Lieutenant Bishop."

"Peter. Vin Cooper," I replied.

"Jesus, sir!" The Brit instantly switched to a whisper. "Everyone's been worried. You've heard about... about—"

I cut him off. "Give me your cell number."

"Sir?"

I repeated the request and got what I asked for. I wrote it down. "Can you get to a pay phone?"

"Yes, sir."

"How long will it take you?"

"Five minutes, max," he said.

"Go there now. Take your cell. I'll call you again in six." I ended the connection and glanced at my watch.

While I waited, I bought a pastry from a street vendor to feed the animal gnawing at my stomach wall and watched the mothers with strollers as they wheeled their newborns and toddlers about in the bright midday sunshine. These people breathed the same air, occupied the same sidewalks, but our worlds were a universe apart. Summer had arrived early, banishing the indecision of spring. Even the smog from the passing traffic had a fresh tang to it. It was a beautiful day, but there were black clouds boiling up on the horizon—at least, there were in my world.

The alcohol fog had lifted and Bishop's earlier recorded message invaded my thoughts. Those figures, column after column of them, page after page. I still had a copy of them in my bag. So, they represented our balance of trade with Russia? What the hell was going on there? Was Scott really expecting to find a parallel between our relationship with Moscow in this new century and our behavior toward Imperial Japan in the last? From his notes, I gathered that Scott believed the U.S. deliberately got Japan hooked on oil and steel, the raw materials of war, allowing it to pursue its aims on the Chinese mainland. And then pulling the trade rug out from under the Rising Sun, forcing it to head down through Southeast Asia and seek raw materials there.

And why would we do that when it would cost so many American lives to put the genie back in its bottle? To raise the standard of living back home a couple of points?

Hmm . . .

Six minutes were up. I went back to the pay phone and dialed Bishop's cell.

"Sir," said Bishop. "I'm here."

I was taking a risk with the Brit. Could I trust him? Could I trust anyone? What choice did I have? And, if Bishop was what he appeared to be, was I risking *his* life by contacting him? Again, I had no choice. He was probably a marked man, anyway. The only chance we both had lay in my ability to break open this case, and as fast as damn well possible, before anyone else got themselves murdered.

"Call back on this number," I said, reading out the digits on the pay phone. I ended the call. A handful of seconds later, the phone under my hand bleated.

"What can you tell me about the crash? About

Anna?" Somehow I succeeded in keeping my voice even.

"Special Agent, what's going on? The word is you've deserted."

In my best command tone, I said, "I have not deserted. As for what's going on, I don't exactly know." Here, I faltered. I needed Bishop's cooperation and I'd get more of it, and with more conviction and urgency, if he knew what I knew. So I told him. Not all of it. I withheld any mention of The Establishment—what did I really know about the organization, or even if there was an organization of this name? I still had no concrete evidence of its existence. I also avoided giving him the name of Radakov's contact at Ramstein. But I gave him enough. When I'd finished, the line was silent. "You still with me?" I said.

"Sir, that's..."

"Flight Lieutenant, I'll say it again. You still with me?" My meaning was different the second time around, but Bishop got it.

"Yes, a hundred percent."

"Okay. What can you tell me about Anna?"

"All I know is that she was killed in a car crash with General von Koeppen. The local civilian police force here in K-town is handling the investigation—it happened on their turf. I haven't seen the report. It has been classified."

Why was I not surprised? "Do you know why Anna was with von Koeppen at the time?" I asked.

"No, sir."

"Can you give me a name of someone in the police I can talk to, and an address?"

He gave me the details and I scribbled them in my notebook.

"What about Scott's hard drive? Any developments there?"

"No. The programmer of the final level's proving difficult to track down. But I'm working on it."

"Have you talked to Captain Aleveldt?"

"Yes. It's as you suspected. He said von Koeppen asked him, as General Scott's friend, to keep an eye on him after his son died, and to let him know how he was getting on. I believe Aleveldt. I don't think there was any sinister intent there. Also, we tracked down the aircrews on those Riga flights, sir."

"And?"

"Over the six-month period before Peyton's death, there were sixty-three flights to Riga. All crews have been accounted for except for three who flew those six suspect flights. I don't know how they did it, but the crews identified as having flown those flights never existed, sir."

I wasn't surprised—I'd expected as much. "Good work, Peter. So has a replacement stepped into von Koeppen's shoes yet?" Small though they are, I neglected to add.

"We've got an RAF air vice marshal in temporary command of the base."

"What about at OSI?"

"Oh, right. You wouldn't have heard."

"Heard what?"

"Your boss is here. I've heard you refer to her as 'the big cheese'—"

"Gruyere?"

"Yes."

"What's she doing?"

"I'm not sure, but I think she's preparing the handover."

"The handover? To whom?"

"To another group of investigators."

"From?"

"Rumor has it your DoD."

Shit. Those fuckers. So much for the myth. I had seriously run out of time.

FORTY

The local police station was reasonably big. I don't know what I expected, but I think it had something to do with gingerbread and lederhosen. But, like any town with a sizeable chunk of population, Kaiserslautern had all the human sludge police have to deal with—perpetrators of rape, robbery, fraud, and, of course, murder.

The building reminded me of a giant greenhouse, complete with stained, streaked panels etched by acid rain. I stopped at the front desk. They directed me to a security desk where I was put through the ubiquitous metal scanner. After I put my boots back on, I rode the elevator to the third floor. At the front desk I badged a fat, bald uniform with busted facial veins who reminded me of half a dozen guys I'd met doing the same job back home and who were also fat, bald uniforms with busted veins. Maybe they pop them out of molds at birth for this job, one of those molds that don't get broken.

Without looking up, the man used his chins to point me in the direction of Sergeant Fritz Bohme. Bohme. Bishop had given me the officer's name. The detective was about forty, thin except for the basketball-shaped paunch pushing against the edge of his desk, with a badly chipped front tooth and a mouth that frowned so much it had lines at each corner giving gravity a helping hand like they were pulling it down. He was hunched over a laptop, the keys stained brown with use, stabbing at them with his "fuck you" fingers.

"Sergeant Bohme?" I asked.

He looked up from the keyboard, lifting an eyebrow. My ABU had the Stars and Stripes stitched to the shoulders and this told him not to bother speaking German. "*Ja?* Unt you are?"

"United States Air Force Office of Special Investigations." I badged him and moved right along, avoiding specifics such as my name and star sign. I wasn't keen to give details, just in case they set off some kind of alarm. "I believe you're heading up the investigation into the crash that killed one of our people, Special Agent Anna Masters, as well as the acting commander of Ramstein, Lieutenant General Wolfgang von Koeppen."

Bohme looked up at me and stroked his chin as if he had a beard, which he didn't. "Correct," he said, breaking the word into three syllables. *Corr-ek-t.* "You haff seen my report?"

"Yeah," I said. Like hell.

"Unt how can I help you?" His manner suggested he'd rather I turn around and keep walking till I found the elevator and the front door shortly thereafter.

The phone rang. He answered it. I looked around the floor while he chatted to someone in German. There was the usual collection of wanted posters pinned to the low gray cubical walls, mixed with portraits of wives and children. Pins for the bad guys, frames for the loved ones. Nests of used coffee cups were gathered on most desks along with paper, folders, the usual detritus of police work. *Nothing to see here, people; move along.* The sergeant hung up the handset as he chortled to himself. The call had changed his mood for the better. "My daughter," he explained. "Getting married. To an accountant."

I felt like telling him that marriage was no laughing matter, but I let it go. The framed portrait photo of the woman on his desk told me he was married himself and therefore probably already aware of that. So instead, by way of polite preamble, I said, "Good choice. Those guys run the world."

"You vould like to haff a look at the wehicle?" he asked, standing up, now full of cooperation. Bohme wasn't especially tall but he was thin, which gave the impression of height. In this job, some guys eat, some guys drink. He looked like he took all his meals in a tumbler with ice.

"You read my mind," I said. I hadn't known exactly what I wanted to see when I came here. I was flying blind now, without support, checking my six for bogeys, as I've heard fighter jocks say. Maybe I just needed to see Masters's purple Mercedes squashed into half its previous size before I believed that she had really gone. Yeah. It would be difficult, but I felt I had to do it, see it—just like Scott had to look inside the bag.

"Follow me," he said, weaving a path for me to follow through the open-plan wasteland. The elevator was busy so we took the stairs.

"How did you know I wanted to look at the vehicle?" I asked as we passed a couple of overweight detectives—eaters—wheezing up the stairs, carrying cartons of takeout coffee and pastries.

"I haff had many of you people here already vanting to see the wehicle. You'd sink your special agent and our general vere royalty, even Hollywood stars."

"He was," I said.

"Voz wot?"

"Royalty. Von Koeppen was royalty. He was a count

or something." I couldn't remember the details, except that Fischer, his secretary, had called him "a vain, supercilious cocksucker." At least that had stuck. Fischer was a fine judge of character; although, in von Koeppen's case, she was perhaps a little too reserved in her judgment.

We walked out the building, down to the end of the street, and threaded our way through the traffic to the other side, heading toward a compound secured by cyclone mesh and razor wire. Inside were a large number of vehicles—cars, trucks, motorcycles, and even a yacht. Not all of these were smashed up, though most were.

"Ve haff had an American general here, amongst others," said Bohme as he signed us in. "Vot did you say your name vass?" he asked, pen poised over a space on the form.

I knew this moment would come around sooner or later. I hadn't given him my name. The question was, would I risk doing so now? If it came to it, I was confident of putting Fritz here away, but I'd be trapped inside this compound. There was only one way in and out. "Special Agent Vincent Cooper," I said, risking it. He didn't seem to react as I watched him scratch down my details with the ballpoint tethered to the clipboard by a length of dirty string.

"That general who came here. Was it a woman?" I asked.

"*Ja*. You know her?"

"My boss." So Gruyere was snooping around. What was she looking for? And on whose behalf? "Who else has come to see you about the vehicle?"

He handed me the clipboard. I flicked through the entries made over the past couple of days, looking for names I recognized. Bohme's had been entered on four separate occasions, and he'd been accompanied on each of those by officers whose names meant nothing to me. I smelled the DoD. I handed the log back to Bohme, who passed it on to the security officer sitting behind the window.

The sergeant stepped onto the asphalt of the compound. I followed him as he walked around a badly mangled truck. Behind it was a vehicle I recognized. But it wasn't the one I thought I'd be seeing. It wasn't Masters's purple Merc, but von Koeppen's BMW sitting there squashed like a bug on a windscreen, the front end buckled under, the engine punched through the firewall into the space previously occupied by the front seats. The Beemer was unrecognizable scrap. No one could have survived such an impact. The lump in my throat returned. I hoped Anna had died quickly.

"And you believe brake failure was the cause?" This was a new BMW. New BMWs did not have brake failure.

Bohme caught my drift into skepticism and shrugged. "Yes. Zere vere no skid marks, no uzzer traffic inwolved. The car failed to take a corner at speed. It crashed srough a vall, ran down a hill and hit a tree. No skid marks from either the BMW or other vehicles to indicate a collision or near collision."

"Were the brakes tampered with?" I asked.

"Vee haff sent ze brake fluid avay to be analyzed, and ze brake master cylinder to BMW for tests. Ve vill know for sure in a veek. But I sink ze tests vill come back negatiff. As a policeman—one policeman to another—you get a nose for zese sings. My nose tells me zey vere lovers. I sink maybe she was giving him some love vith her mouth at ze time. It happens. Especially on ze autobahns here." He added a knowing wink to this insight into Anna Masters's last moments on earth.

Bohme was telling me that Anna was no different from my ex. Was it that hard to swallow? Anna and von Koeppen had been lovers once. Maybe they'd decided to stoke up the fires. Had they gone for a little drive, for old times' sake? The detective must have read something in my face, perhaps a reluctance to accept his hypothesis, because he added, "Accidents are accidents, vhere ze improbable meets ze probable."

The philosophy sounded like the sort you get from a fortune cookie. "When did it happen?"

"Some time after four P.M."

"Witnesses?"

"None."

Given the time of day, that was a bit odd, but who comes forward to help the cops these days? A sign of the times. "Have autopsies been performed on the occupants?" I said, keeping my voice devoid of emotion.

"Yes, I belief so. Ze general who came to see me had ze bodies removed to Ramstein for zis."

I nodded as I fought the X-rated show playing out in my head. There could have been reasons why Masters was in von Koeppen's vehicle other than Bohme's theory.

And then something occurred to me. "The newspaper article I read said that Special Agent Masters was the driver of the vehicle." This meant, of course, that her head couldn't possibly have been below the dashboard making von Koeppen's day.

"Don't beliff everysing you read, Special Agent."

Good advice. It also reminded me not to believe everything I was told.

My mind fast-forwarded to Masters, laid out on a stainless-steel tray down in the bowels of the Landstuhl Medical Center, her fluids draining away, like the guy who'd been squashed by a tank, impervious now to

Major Pierre Lamont's good cheer. I was tempted to try to see her, and for the same reason that brought me here to view the wreck. Balanced against that, though, was the desire to remember Anna Masters as she was— the arguments for and against were familiar territory. The decisive factor was that I knew I wouldn't get closer to the morgue than the front gate. The word was out that I was back in town. The van's arrival at my hotel earlier in the day proved that. No doubt the security posts had a photo of me next to bin Laden's under a laser-printed headline that went something like, *If you see these men, shoot first.* And, of course, said photo would be pinned, not framed. No, going anywhere near Ramstein would be bad for my health-care provider.

"Anything else, Special Agent?" asked Bohme, breaking into my thoughts.

"Not for the moment, Sarge," I said.

"Vhere do I reach you iff somesing turns up?"

I gave him my number so that he could contact my cell, which by now was bobbing around in the bowels of the local sewage works. Anything he could tell me later was too late. I didn't have much time left before I began looking at life through a bunch of vertical bars. A day if I was lucky. An hour or two if I wasn't.

I signed myself out at the front gate and said goodbye to the sergeant and wished him luck with his daughter's wedding, neglecting to add that I hoped she would beat the divorce statistics. I heard a gunned motor and scream of tires nearby. Suddenly a blue NCMP SUV slid to a stop in a spray of loose gravel just beyond the gate, its rooftop blue emergency lights spinning. Time to go. I turned to run, but I knew it was hopeless. I was cut off from escape, unless I wanted to try my luck on the razor wire.

The passenger door opened and a familiar officer

jumped down. It was Flight Lieutenant Bishop, a satchel tucked under his arm. His feet hit the ground running. The security guard in his hut stuck his head out the door to see what all the noise was about.

"Sir," said Bishop before he reached me, puffing. "Cracked it."

"Cracked what?"

"The Dungeon, sir. Level four. I figured you'd want to see what I found ASAP, if not sooner."

FORTY-ONE

Damn right, Flight Lieutenant," I said, walking toward him, my heart pounding now for a different reason. "Let's take it back to the vehicle. You trust the driver?"

"Yes, sir."

Whatever Bishop had uncovered on General Scott's hard drive I had no intention of sharing with Bohme, who was nosing around.

I recognized the man behind the wheel of the NCMP SUV. It was the French guy, the refrigerator with the five o'clock shadow. He gave me a nod. Yeah, I could trust him.

Bishop climbed in the back. I followed. "Drive," I said. We merged into the traffic.

"What you got?" I said as Bishop booted up the Toshiba.

"I haven't looked. I wanted to get to you as quickly as possible. Keep in mind this last Dungeon level is the smallest cell of the lot. There's not much in it."

I nodded: "Bishop?"

"Sir?"

"Win, lose, or draw, I just want to say that you've redeemed your countrymen."

"Thank you. I think..."

The screen came to life. Bishop double-clicked on the small castle icon and the screen fluttered, revealing the familiar pulsing bars alive with electric light. He mentioned something about algorithms with a fuzzy logic base while he tapped away at a succession of keys. Suddenly, the animated electrical pulse vanished and the bars fell away, revealing two small icons marked "File A" and "File B."

I clicked on File A, which caused Acrobat Reader to load, and then the file itself. It was a JPEG of a passport, a Russian passport. I read the name. It was unfamiliar: Petrov Andreiovic. I recognized the face, though, and the recognition was like a slap across my own. "Jesus," I said. Then I clicked on File B, which loaded another JPEG. The type was small, so I enlarged it. It was a paragraph in what appeared to be the minutes of a meeting. The paragraph was labeled "The First Convention." I read the text, and, by the time I finished, I knew I was feeling the same dismay Scott felt when he read it. This was a betrayal of everything I believed in. No, worse than that. It was a betrayal of the *only* thing I believed in.

"Sir. You okay?" asked Bishop.

I must have looked like I was in shock. I sure as hell felt as if I was in it.

"Yeah," I said. The experiences of the past month were beginning to make a crazy kind of sense. I now knew why there'd been so much killing, and why I had to keep myself alive long enough to pass this shit on to someone I could trust. The trouble was, right at that moment and with the exception of the people in the SUV, I couldn't think of anyone.

"Bishop, you have to drop me somewhere," I said.

I was now familiar with the street, the way it curved languidly through manicured gardens and fountains. For more than sixty years, since the end of WWII,

American officers and our NATO brethren had rented these homes embedded within expansive, genteel gardens. It was an affluent neighborhood. A power neighborhood. I wished I had a tank-mounted flamethrower so that I could burn it all to the ground. At the very least, I was going to bring one household crashing down. If not for myself, then for Anna. And for General Scott and his son, Peyton, and for all the others . . .

The SUV pulled up at the head of the cinder footpath that led up to the familiar fountain. I noticed that it was dry today, like my throat. I cleared it—my throat—and got out. I gave Bishop some instructions, what to do with himself and the laptop and so on, then shook his hand. This was good-bye. He had to get a long way away from me—that is, if he wanted to keep on breathing.

I strolled up the path toward the fountain. The bronze dolphins and the warrior figures were wearing crowns of bird shit. I noticed that the once immaculate grounds were untended, a weed or two among the flowers. Decay had begun to move in here, happy to share the place with its other resident. I glanced across at the garage. The doors were open. If my theory was right, I expected to find something in there that I'd overlooked.

I slid between the doors, into the darkness beyond, and waited a moment for my eyes to adjust. It was cold in here, and dry. I smelled Scott's Mustang: grease, leather, and age.

I knew what I was looking for, but I wasn't at all sure where I'd find them, or even *if* I'd find them. I made my way across to the workbench to where I'd seen the photos that charted Peyton's relationship with his father. Abraham Scott and his son, Peyton. One growing old, the other growing up. The pictures told their own story, but not necessarily the one I'd originally thought. When I'd first seen these pictures, something about them had bothered me. Eventually I'd worked out what that something was. I'd been satisfied with the revelation at the time, but only because I hadn't then known what to look for. But now I did.

I went on a hunt for a trash can and eventually found several of them in the shadows, tucked under the far end of the workbench. I pulled out the first one and dragged it across into a shaft of pale afternoon light falling through a side window. I dug through the papers, sawdust, and various empty plastic bottles until I reached the bottom. Nothing. The same result with the second trash can. What I was hoping to find lay in the bottom of the third. I felt around with my fingers until they brushed it, and then I pulled it out. I wiped away the sawdust and saw a photo of a young Harmony Scott with a four-year-old Peyton, lying together on a carpeted floor with a model car between their smiling faces. I recovered seven more framed photos from the trash, moments in the life of a once happy family—Abraham, Harmony, and Peyton—that had at one time sat up on the workbench. Abraham Scott had, for some reason, purged them from the lineup of the other Kodak moments. I believed I knew what that reason was. In fact, finding these pictures, as I thought I would, confirmed a lot, and none of it was pleasant. I scoped the house across the lawn and saw Harmony Scott looking down on me from a second-story window, talking into a portable phone.

FORTY-TWO

I banged the eagle-and-deer knocker several times and heard the resounding boom roll through the hallway behind the solid wood door. I waited impatiently for the sound of Harmony's footsteps to follow. She knew I was waiting out here on her front step. I also knew she could care less. I tried the doorknob on the off chance that it was unlocked and was rewarded by the heavy door swinging inward on its hinges. I smelled Harmony's perfume mixed with her brand of cigarettes and followed them to their source.

The surroundings were familiar, the seventeenth-century gloom with its dark paneled walls and the stuffed shirts looking down from their heavy gilt frames. I found Harmony where I thought she'd be: close to the liquor cabinet. Indeed, she was seated on one of the Chesterfields, several glass tumblers on the low table in front of her along with a couple of bottles of Glenkeith, my brand, and a pile of used tissues. Dressed again in black and without makeup, she looked like an extra from a zombie movie. Her eyes were red from tears, alcohol, or cigarettes—I wasn't sure which, although three packets of Salems were scattered on the table in front of her. Two of them were empty. A glass ashtray piled high with butts sat between the packets. She peeled the wrapping off the third pack, pinched out a cigarette, and lit it using the dying embers clinging to the filter smoldering between her lips. "I hate drinking out of dirty glasses. Don't you?" she said, slurring her words, turning the *d* in drinking to a *j*. She dropped the butt in the ashtray and sucked on the fresh cigarette, pulling the smoke down into her toes, and blowing a blue cloud at the ceiling. Then she picked up her drink and polished it off.

"Depends on whose dirt it is," I answered.

Frowning, she seemed to consider that for a second or two before giving up. "Well," she said, "you want a drink or not?"

I was way past playing the puritan. "Single malt over ice," I said.

She studied me for a moment, then said, "Well, what do I look like? Your servant? Glasses are over there." She gestured at the liquor cabinet with a tilt of her head. "You can get me a fresh glass and ice while you're at it. I hate drinking from a dirty glass."

Yeah, I know.

I went to the cabinet and organized a glass for myself and for Harmony, adding rocks to both. "When did you tell your husband?"

"Tell him what?" she asked.

"About Helen. That her death wasn't an accident."

"You think you're so goddamn clever."

That's something I've always hated about rich people, though maybe hate is too strong a word. It's the assumed superiority that seems to accompany a hefty bank balance. More money, more brains. No money? Well, you must be a half-wit. With Harmony Scott, this feeling had been refined. She oozed with the presumption that those without wealth and position were less than human—Neanderthal, maybe.

"When did Abraham find out that, for most of his life, he'd been played?"

Harmony's reaction was to pour herself a couple of

additional fingers and toss them down, and from a dirty glass. And then she began to cry. "They killed him," she blubbered.

"Who? Your husband?" I asked.

"Wolfgang," she said. "They killed my Wolfy." She ripped out a tissue from the box and held it to her nose.

That caught me by surprise. Had the target been von Koeppen and not Anna? Was Anna just collateral in the hit on the general? It had been his car. Somehow that made her death worse, like it was just bad fucking timing.

"I loved him. I loved him and the bastard had him killed," she sobbed.

I wondered whether that love was genuinely reciprocated by von Koeppen. He supposedly had a preference for young women and, given his extracurricular interests, plenty of opportunity to have that particular thirst slaked. Perhaps he really did love her. He might have had the dream of uniting his vaguely royal German blood with that of a patrician American family. The man certainly had the ego for such a plan.

Tears streaked Harmony Scott's face. I've seen some bad shit in my life but, for some reason I'll never understand, I'm not immune to a woman turning on the waterworks. I didn't want to feel sorry for Harmony Scott, but that's what I felt. I let her cry and poured myself a drink, supersizing it. Throughout this investigation, a mysterious "they" had often been referred to—the so-called Establishment. Harmony's mention of "the bastard"—an individual—was a first. I pretty much knew who she was referring to although I thought I'd ask, if only to get her to say his name.

"Who are you talking about, Mrs. Scott? Who had General von Koeppen killed?"

That seemed to sober her up a little. Harmony Scott

blew her nose, took another sip of her drink, put it down, and then wrung a wad of tissues between her fingers. In the ashtray, three cigarettes burned. This was someone under intense pressure. "Do you intend to charge me with anything?" she asked, dodging my questions. "Do I need a lawyer?"

She was a civilian and, as such, outside the jurisdiction of the Uniform Code of Military Justice. Under civilian statutes, she could be charged with being an accessory to murder, or perhaps conspiracy to murder, but those were nuggets a civilian investigator would have to consider. And, besides, I was after a much bigger fish. "Whether you call a lawyer or not is up to you, Mrs. Scott, but, you being a civilian, there's nothing I can charge you with. I'm just here to ask you some questions, clear up a few things—that's all."

She nodded, her red, swollen eyes a long way off.

I repeated my earlier question. "When did your husband realize that his first wife had been murdered?" I knew it was within the past sixteen months: That's when those photographs had been removed from the workbench, and from Scott's study.

"Cooper, I'm going to give you some history. I'm only going to give it to you once. I'm also going to deny I told you anything. The only reason I'm speaking to you at all is that I want my own revenge, and not just for Wolfy's death. I've been used my whole life. When I was in my twenties, I went to the White House to meet the Soviets, before their house of cards came down. There I met a handsome major, a widower with a young son. His wife had been killed in a car accident and I guess he was just about getting over the loss. Back then, I was considered beautiful. I was also promiscuous, and single. I seduced him. You know, we fucked in

the Rose Garden. Can you believe that? Back then, surveillance wasn't quite what it is today.

"It was only years later I realized I'd been sent there
to meet the man I would marry. I'd been precondi-
tioned to be attracted to him. My father had told me
about this young air force officer who would be at the
party and how he was being groomed for great things,
that I needed to be careful with him—protective—
because of the tragic loss of his wife. I knew he was a
fighter pilot. And, let's face it, when you're a twenty-
something party animal, who would you rather meet,
a war hero who could fuck all night, or a bunch of old
Soviet drunks who spent their time in Washington
bouncing between hookers and vodka?"

I didn't answer. Harmony lit another cigarette to join
the others still smoldering in the ashtray, and stood,
teetering like a building in a violent earthquake. She
steadied herself against the armrest on the couch, then
set off on a wobbly circuit of the room, bleeding cigarette smoke.

"You might not believe it, but Abe and I got married
because we were in love. And I loved his son, Peyton.
We moved to Moscow, where Abe continued his tour
at the U.S. Embassy there. Just as my father had said,
my husband was being groomed for the top. Promotion
followed promotion, Abe's star hitched to his father-in-
law's wagon. When Peyton turned eighteen, he joined
the marines. He went in at the bottom, against his father's wishes. That he even wanted a military life went
against my wishes.

"As for Abraham and me, I don't know when things
began to fall apart, but it happened fast. We went from
post to post and maybe the soda just went flat."

Yeah, I knew what she meant.

"Some of the fault was mine. I got bored. By the

time Abe received his fourth star and took command here, we were distant acquaintances living in the same house. And then things started to go seriously wrong between us. He said he'd come to the conclusion that his first wife had been killed to make way for me. He also said he was going to launch an investigation, that Ramstein was being used in a people-smuggling racket, and that he was going to find out who was responsible."

"And then Peyton was KIA," I said.

"Don't interrupt," she snapped. "Yes. Peyton was killed."

"Were you seeing von Koeppen by then?" I asked, ignoring the demand.

She answered with her silent stare.

I'd had about enough of Harmony's fairy tale. She needed to know the facts.

"Wolfgang von Koeppen was smuggling women from the East—countries like Russia, the Ukraine, and the Baltic states—into western Europe," I said. "He dealt in human misery, Mrs. Scott. Either your husband figured it out, or someone tried to enlist him in the scheme, possibly even von Koeppen himself."

"No."

"Your boyfriend dreamed up bogus missions in Riga, Latvia, and sent NATO C-130s there. On the return flights, these aircraft brought back women. Many of them were subsequently sold into the European sex trade as slaves."

Harmony was shaking her head, as if she was trying to keep my voice from reaching her ears.

I continued. "They were given ABUs and CAC cards on arrival at Ramstein and hustled off the base. Somehow, your husband found out about that. He threatened to have it stopped and was told to lay off, or else. He wouldn't. And then Peyton was KIA in Iraq. Only it was murder and your husband knew it was murder. He knew it because you told him."

"No."

"You were the messenger."

"Enough!"

"How did you break the news to your husband that his son had been murdered, Mrs. Scott?"

It suddenly dawned on me that she might have had some tangible proof.

"You showed him the original autopsy report, didn't you?" I said. The shame written on Harmony's face told me I was right. An autopsy in accordance with U.S. Army practices in Iraq had indeed been performed on Peyton Scott's remains. It had then been subsequently erased on the DoD's system, despite Captain Blood's assurance that such an action was impossible. But a hard copy of the report was in existence, and this woman had it.

"Your husband had to be certain. There was no other way. He had to look into Peyton's body bag."

She shook her head.

"Was it worth it, Mrs. Scott? Was the love you shared with von Koeppen worth losing your humanity for?"

"Peyton was dead. Nothing I could do would bring him back."

I could feel my own heart rate rising with anger, indignation, and a little fear. I was in the presence of someone who'd traded her soul to the devil for a relationship that was doomed.

"General Scott went to Iraq, to the hospital there," I said, "to talk to the men your stepson fought alongside, and to question the medical officer whose name appeared on the autopsy report that stated Peyton had been killed by a mine. And then he went to Washington, to see your father."

Harmony Scott pinned her trembling hands between her knees to get control of them. "I'm not saying anything more," she insisted.

"Fine. Happy to continue uninterrupted," I said.

"Suit yourself," Harmony replied, her eyes sliding in and out of focus, her fury ebbing and flowing.

"Are you going to show it to me?" I asked.

She replied, "Show you what?"

"The autopsy report, the original one performed by someone who wasn't already dead. The one documenting that Peyton Scott, sergeant, USMC, had been decapitated."

"No," she said.

"Why not?" I asked.

"Because you're leaving now."

"I am?"

Her eyes slid from me to the door behind me. I heard the slightest noise, or maybe it was the faint change in air pressure across the hairs on the back of my neck. *She'd been on the phone. Who had she called?* I turned and saw a man I recognized kneeling on the floor. He was wearing army ABUs, the European pattern. Against the brown walls, his camouflage made him stick out like a pork chop in a vegan's soup bowl. The silenced M4 carbine he had aimed at my head made me decide to keep my mouth shut about the pork-chop thing. Four other men also armed with silenced M4s swarmed past him into the room. They checked it out quietly and efficiently and then came straight for me, and it was not to shake my hand. One of them gestured with a flick of his rifle that I should put my hands up. I obeyed and he cuff-locked them together, tight. The soldier who did this had a face that reminded me of a road still under construction. That's what happens when you get hit with the ancient karate brick-in-the-kisser move, one of my personal favorites. I remembered the moment in Baghdad and savored it. Whenever I met these guys, they put me in the hospital. I knew that was a professional disappointment to them, on account of their intention having always been to put me in the morgue. I felt the rifle butt, then watched an explosion of white and orange fireballs inside my skull. Good night.

FORTY-THREE

No erotic dreams accompanied my return to consciousness this time, though I had a pain in the back of my head equal to the worst hangover of my life.

I kept my eyes closed, none too eager to see what was on the other side of my eyelids until it was absolutely necessary. Whatever was going on, I had a feeling I wouldn't like it. The quality of the air, the occasional thump, the engine drone. I was in an airplane. The Pavlovian association of getting a rifle butt to the back of the head wasn't going to help my flying phobia any, and just when I was getting used to flying again.

There was a shift in engine noise and various gear whines somewhere under my feet. The plane lurched. I opened my eyes and mouth. Two men in suits were seated opposite, both staring at me. The one who cuffed me before the lights went out smiled. He held up his wrist and gave it a waggle. I recognized my watch. Or more accurately his watch, now definitely his again.

"Nice fake," I said, groggily. His smile faded. *Fuck you, buddy. And thanks for giving me a look at the time.* The man's face was badly bruised where I'd smacked him with the brick, and a large bandage covered his nose.

The little hand was past the eleven and the big hand was coming up to forty minutes past the hour. My mind was working slow, like a ten-year-old's, so only slightly slower than usual, the unkind would have said.

The sky was black beyond the porthole. That made it 2340 hours. Genius. First mystery of the day or, rather, night, solved.

It hurt my brain to use it. I took in my situation in the hope of getting it kick-started.

It was difficult to move. I glanced down and found out why. My hands were still cuff-locked together and I was strapped down tight into a comfortable, expensive leather chair, or it would have been a comfortable chair if I'd been sitting in it attended to by a pretty flight attendant with a beverage cart. The plane was small and expensive, an executive jet. I wondered whose.

Apes dressed in Armani sat around me: two opposite, two in swivel chairs in what normally would've been the aisle, and one beside me. Another leaned against a bulkhead, looking at me with about as much expression on his face as a store dummy's. So these were the asswipes who had jumped Masters and me in Baghdad, and then performed a little dentistry on me a day later outside the Pensione Freedom. I knew I'd meet up with them again. Someone break out a deck of cards; I felt like we were old friends.

I wondered which of them knew their way around a Barrett 50 cal. I wanted to tell them that they were dud shots, but they would have known the bravado was hollow, given that it was me and not them who was the prisoner here, wearing a bump on the back of his head the size of a dodo's egg. I was plainly at their mercy, theirs and the person funding their fashion sense.

Where the fuck was I? Where was I being taken? How long had I been out? I decided to try to break the ice. "Have any of you guys got a mint?" I asked. "It's either my breath or someone here needs a shower real bad. I'll give you the benefit of the doubt and say it's me," I said, keeping it light. I got more response from the overhead locker. "So, where we headed?" One of the men reamed the inside of a nostril with his index finger and then flicked the harvest at me. He missed.

Aside from that, I got no other reaction. Ten minutes later I was getting so bored I almost cracked and gave up everything I knew. But then the plane jumped as it hit a thick layer of cloud and I remembered that I was flying rather than competing in some world championship silence competition.

I looked out the porthole, expecting to see the earth rushing up at some crazy, life-threatening angle, but all I got was more cloud, the wingtip strobe blinking metronomically as it sliced through the silver tufts. And then, just as I was about to look away, I saw the briefest flash of a city beneath. A big city. Again I wondered how long I'd been in the air. I also wondered why I was so threatening to these guys that they had to sit almost on top of me. I mean, it wasn't likely that I was going anywhere or capable of doing anything very much, trussed as I was. I could maybe breathe at them aggressively, but that was about it in the retaliation stakes. It took me a while to realize the reason: I made them nervous, simple as that. I was a threat to these people and to whoever was pulling their strings. I was unpredictable. They'd tried to remove my piece from the board several times and failed. It was they who were scared of me. "Boo," I said to test the theory. No reply. One of the men was asleep. Another yawned. On the other hand, maybe I was just blowing smoke up my own ass.

I closed my eyes and tried to get my thoughts in order. My last memory, and a hazy one at that, was of Harmony Scott's liquor. I should have realized that she would call someone when she saw me in the garage snooping around. Even now, I still wasn't completely sure where exactly Harmony fit into things. She'd given me the picture of a woman who'd lost the man she loved, felt him drift away, hating the way their marriage had turned out. I also saw her as playing a starring role in the manipulation of her husband—either willingly or unwillingly—over many years. And, of course, when it came to Peyton, she had ultimately shown herself to be self-absorbed and utterly heartless.

That brought me back to Abraham Scott. There'd been a lot of time between Peyton's death, the taking of the body bag photograph, and his own "accidental" death in the glider. All up, a year. Why so long? Had the general discovered that the people-smuggling racket operating between Riga and Ramstein was not just about money used to finance Radakov's separatists? I figured he'd discovered a bigger game, and he'd needed time to put it all together. So he kept a low profile, kept his nose clean. I was sure he'd uncovered the same cancer I had—the research into our trade with Japan and Russia were at least circumstantial proof of that.

The descent became rocky. The clouds played a vigorous game of shuttlecock with the plane, batting it up and down and sideways. Windshear. Rain droplets smeared the porthole. It was a shitty night in wherever. I heard the flaps fully extend as the motion played havoc with my Eustachian tubes. I was vomiting before I knew it, too fast for my friend fond of flicking boogers about the place to avoid the projectile bile heading toward his lap. Oops. Better out than in, pal.

An instant later, my face was stinging from a backhanded strike. I was tempted to explain that I didn't mean it but I knew I wouldn't be believed: Lies need conviction to stick.

I turned away. We were coming in low over the city. Air traffic control took us on a sightseeing tour. I could see a bunch of lights through the cloud, but the effect was like a sock on a bank robber's face and I still couldn't recognize the place through it. Suddenly a patch of clear night sky opened up below the wingtip. I looked down and saw clearly where I was. Familiar monuments lit up stark and white instantly nailed this city of empire. Christ, Washington, D.C.

Mystery number two cracked.

My heart began to pound. I felt it muscle up against my ribs, wrestling for space. D.C. That meant I had a very good chance of cleaning up this mess. Though, of course, shortly thereafter I would be dead.

FORTY-FOUR

The aircraft touched down without incident, which surprised me as it always does, and taxied up to and then inside a hangar. No immigration, no homeland security checks. That meant whoever was in control could pull powerful strings, but I already knew that.

The Rolex guy lifted the latch on my seat belt and motioned at me to stand. I did as I was told without causing trouble. I'd antagonized them enough and baiting them would only get me beaten up some more. Who said I can't learn?

The pilots shut down the engines and an ape cracked the hatch. I was shuffled down the stairs, across the hangar floor, and into the back of a black Suburban, accompanied by my simian buddies. The air was warm and humid. With all the rain, I expected it to be cold, like Germany. I was sandwiched in the backseat of the vehicle between a couple of thousand dollars of Italian suit. The windows fogged up almost instantly, but I could still see through the windshield. There wasn't much traffic on the streets. We came to a fork in the freeway: right to Andrews AFB, left to the city. We turned left.

The pickings were still slim in the conversation department. We drove in silence toward the halo projected by the city's lights onto the low cloud above it. The place was pretty much deserted at this after-midnight hour and seemed lit up for a party where the invitations hadn't been sent. I passed some time again trying to work out who these people were who had, at various times over the past few weeks, done their best to kill Anna and me. In their suits and earpieces, they looked like Secret Service types, but the suits made them look uncomfortable, like kids dressed by their grandmothers for church. I pegged them as mercenaries or, in the lexicon of current PC military job speak, "contract security."

The Suburban took it slow, just another government car. No need to hurry. The Potomac was a river of black glass throwing up rippling colors of reflected light. We paralleled it for a couple of miles before crossing the bridge to the city's heart. Here the monuments were easy to pick out: the Jefferson Monument and then, as we crossed the river, the Lincoln Memorial and the Washington Monument beyond it.

This case had given my feelings about national pride, embodied by these grand architectural displays, a bad shake. I was sorry to say I now viewed these symbols as props in a show. They represented an ideal, but not a lot more.

The driver followed the signs to Pennsylvania Avenue and then to Massachusetts Avenue. A couple of ancient Chevys full of rust and young partygoers rolled past, the rap music so loud it made the droplets on the Suburban's windows fizz. Two black guys, naked to the waist, hung out the windows and shouted at us. One of the apes gave them the bird. The White House appeared for an instant as we turned in an intersection. It stood white and clean, bathed by innumerable spotlights. How anyone inside got any sleep was beyond me.

We turned onto Massachusetts and stayed on it for a while, heading for higher ground. The buildings we passed were imposing and impersonal: lots of columns, celebrations of power, a conveyor belt of concrete wedding cakes. I knew where we were headed: The U.S. Naval Observatory. It occupied the hill filling the windshield, its illuminated telescope dome looking like a giant's lost golf ball among the trees. The driver pulled in to the driveway of Number One Observatory Circle, home of the Vice President of the United States, Harmony Scott's daddy, Jefferson Cutter.

FORTY-FIVE

I couldn't help but notice, as I was hauled out of the truck, that at least compared with every other building in the vicinity, Cutter's residence was dark. Maybe his spotlights weren't working this evening. I was escorted up onto the veranda and past the front door to another around the side. I guessed this must be the captives' entrance, just like the servants' entrance, only lower on the social ladder. A pair of snips was produced and the cuff-locks clipped off. I rubbed my wrists. I could run, but I knew I wouldn't get far. Besides, I had a score to settle with the Toe Cutter, although I knew the game inside would be heavily rigged in his favor. We all stood there in the darkness for a handful of seconds. Then the door snicked open, the slatted blinds rattling softly against their windowpanes, revealing two men. My escort handed them my badge, which they checked with a penlight and then returned to me. I hadn't realized that it had been removed from my pocket. The men standing in the doorway were dressed in suit pants, white shirts, and loosened ties. Secret Service, no mistake. They wore cologne, a dead giveaway. They waved a metal detector over me to satisfy themselves I wasn't packing. No words were said at any time during my transfer so I gathered I must have been expected. When I turned around, my escort had melted into the night without making a sound.

The house was more than darkened; it was blackout

darkened. Not so much as a candle flickered, although I noted many diodes glowing from various unidentified electrical gear in almost every room I was led through.

The place smelled cool and clean with a mixture of sandalwood, beeswax, and linseed oil. It was the smell of old money, and lots of it. I guessed the place was full of art and antique furniture, not the stuff most people buy, but things inherited or bought at auctions, won with the crack of a gavel. The floor, however, was relatively new. This was an old building, built in the middle of the nineteenth century, and the original boards would have been creaking like an old man's bones by now. I gave myself a mental kick. I was about to meet the man considered by many to be the most powerful force in American politics. And I was pondering the history of the floorboards? The bump on the head was obviously affecting me worse than I'd thought.

The men took me down the back of the building, up a flight of stairs, and through several doors. My eyes were used to the darkness now. This was a big house. I tried to remember the route in case I needed to leave in a hurry. I wished I had some string I could let out, or bread crumbs like in that fairy tale. Maybe I'd stayed too long in Germany and the place had rubbed off.

Eventually, one of the men produced a key and unlocked a heavy wooden door. I was pushed inside and shoved into a chair, an expensive leather chair that sighed as I sat. A light was turned on and I found myself in what I assumed was a study, or library. The place reminded me of Abraham Scott's: There was lots of wood paneling, oil portraits of various men—many from earlier centuries who, with their powdered wigs, bore an uncanny resemblance to the Queen of England—and books. Lots of books.

"So, Special Agent Cooper . . . good to meet you at

last," said the man standing in a corner behind me. I turned. I recognized him from innumerable press photos and television interviews. Jefferson Cutter reminded me of his daughter, only he was much thicker-set, as if his genes had been spliced with those of a wild boar. He had very little neck that I could see, his shoulders seeming to merge with his jowls. For an old guy, Cutter was still physically powerful—fitness being the current Washington fashion. It was the eyes that were most disconcerting—cold and battleship gray, identical to Harmony's. He snapped shut the book he had open, replaced it on the shelf, and took a seat behind a broad antique desk, the kind topped with burgundy leather. Within easy reach was a large, full bottle of XO cognac, the top removed, and a glass half full of the vile stuff beside it. "Now, Special Agent Cooper, what exactly is it that you think you're doing?" He picked up the glass and drank a couple of mouthfuls as if it were water, rolling it around like mouthwash.

"As I believe I was assigned this case at your request, Mr. Vice President, I think you already know." Fuck this guy. Veep rhymed with creep and I told myself not to be intimidated.

"Yes, indeed. I'd conveniently forgotten that," he said, *tsk-tsk*ing, shaking his head, scolding himself. "And have you found what I set you out on the path to uncover, the identity of General Abraham Scott's killer?"

"Yes."

"Then your job's done, is it not?"

"It's not that simple, sir," I said.

"Why not?"

"Knowing who did the killing and being able to prove it are not the same thing."

"Ah, yes. The burden of proof."

"There's also another pesky little detail called motive."

"The reason or reasons why."

"Yes, sir."

Cutter sat behind his big fuck-off desk, those gray eyes locked unblinking onto mine, his fingers making a steeple that touched his thin lips. I sat opposite, enveloped by leather, far from comfortable. We sat like that, in an extended period of silence, both sizing up the situation or, more likely, each other. I moved my eyes to the framed oil paintings on the wall behind him, a silent implacable jury. The identities of these men looking down their noses at me suddenly became clear, perhaps because I recognized Dan Quayle's goofy mug. They were all Veeps, the more recent ones mixed in with others going back to George Washington's day.

Cutter unlocked one of the desk drawers. He pulled it out, wood squeaking on wood, and produced a triangle of old cheesecloth, which he placed on the table in front of him. He unwrapped it and then took his hand away. It was a pistol, something small and easy to conceal, a Beretta 21 by the look of it. A peashooter, but at this range—half a dozen feet—deadly enough.

"What do you need that for, sir?" I asked, managing to keep the quaver out of my voice, but my Adam's apple was going up and down like a department-store elevator.

"This? It needs a clean. Tonight's chore."

Yeah, right. The thing was polished to within an inch of its life—bad analogy. It was spotless, nickel plating gleaming. Would he use it on me? I'd been wrong in the past about who would and wouldn't fire a gun at an unarmed person, and I had the scars to prove it.

He picked up the gun and gave it a rub with the cheesecloth. "I'm an insomniac. I used to think sleeplessness was a burden, but I've come to think of it as a blessing. While the world switches off for the night, I don't. Have you ever considered how much you could get done if you didn't sleep?"

I shook my head. Aside from not being particularly interested in small talk, the thought of working twenty hours or more a day—and in my line it would be without pay—didn't hold a whole heap of joy.

"No? So . . . are you going to tell me who killed my son-in-law and why?"

I'd been in better positions in my life. I was locked in a room with a man holding a gun and I was about to tell him some things he wouldn't enjoy hearing. I wondered whether he wouldn't enjoy them enough to fire that Beretta at me, after all. "Sir, you know and I know who killed Abraham Scott, and a lot of other people besides."

"No name? I get it. You're nervous about telling me. You needn't worry; this room is completely soundproof. We'll just keep it all off the record then, shall we? You look like a man who needs to unburden himself."

"You killed him, Mr. Cutter. You and your business partner, the late Lieutenant General von Koeppen."

Cutter seemed unperturbed by the accusation, perhaps because he knew it was only that—an accusation, with not a molecule of evidence to back it up.

"And, because I've been here in Washington all this time, we're talking conspiracy to murder, then?" he asked, mock seriously. "Would you care to elaborate on the hows, whys, and wherefores, Special Agent Cooper?"

I was getting happier by the moment to oblige, if just to wipe the sneer off his face. "General Scott was a gliding enthusiast. He spent a lot of time in the sky with a

Royal Dutch Air Force captain by the name of Reinoud
Aleveldt, an unwitting snitch on the general's movements. Aleveldt informed von Koeppen that Scott intended having new instrumentation fitted in his glider.
Aurora Aviation, *your* avionics company, performed the
upgrade and installation. Some technicians from Aurora
arrived at Ramstein with all the right credentials—
they're there all the time anyway, servicing military aircraft—and installed the new gear under the noses of
NATO personnel, along with another modification the
general didn't ask for, one that would eventually fail
and cause his glider to crash."

"You should think about writing fiction, Special
Agent. You're very good at weaving a story."

"Mr. Cutter, I've just given you the *who*. The *why* is
a far more interesting story—and be surprised, sir;
you're the main protagonist in it." *I haven't even begun
to tell you what an asshole you are, asshole.* I'd had a shaky
start, but I was firming fast. "You conspired with
Lieutenant General Wolfgang von Koeppen to murder
Abraham Scott because he discovered your plans.
Worse than that, he disappointed you."

"Disappointed? How so?"

"You had him picked out from the start, earmarked
for something. He was a young officer—a war hero, no
less, who had an impeccable record—working inside
the Kremlin. He fit perfectly into your plans. The first
step was getting a man on the inside—or better yet, a
woman. You had just the person in mind, but there was
a problem. He was already married. So you had his
wife, Helen, killed. It was easy. I don't know whether
it was the first time you had someone murdered, but
the car 'accident' worked so well you made it the
model for many killings in the years that followed.
Then, after a respectable period of mourning, you set

up an opportunity for your daughter—the unwitting informant—to meet the promising young widowed officer. You knew your daughter, and you knew what would happen. They eventually got married and then your plans really took off.

"Just interrupt me if you think I've left anything out," I said. I could see I had Cutter's full attention. He was frowning, not a happy camper. Good. Fuck you. Sir.

"A father steering his daughter in the direction of a suitable union is hardly a crime, Cooper," Cutter said.

"No, it isn't. But your motives had nothing whatsoever to do with Harmony's happy-ever-afterness," I replied.

"Then what were my motives, since you seem to know what was on my mind all those years ago?"

"Let's just zip forward in time. Abraham Scott fulfilled his early promise. He rose steadily through the ranks. Having a powerful politician in Congress working hard on appropriating funds for various weapons programs didn't hurt his career any. Only there was an unforeseen glitch, something much more difficult to fix than the pesky presence of a preexisting spouse. Abraham Scott was a genuinely honorable man. He was incorruptible."

Cutter gulped back his drink and then poured himself another belt. "Go on, I'm enjoying myself immensely," he said.

"All your backroom work paid off. Your boy landed the plum: the command of Ramstein, the biggest U.S. base outside continental America. You already had a guy on the ground there—von Koeppen. He was doing very well for himself, smuggling sex slaves from the old Soviet states to western Europe. Abraham Scott uncovered the operation and launched his own small-scale investigation before you could stop him. He went to Riga, where he met with a so-called Chechen separatist by the name of Alu Radakov, the contact supplying von Koeppen with human cargo for shipment back to Germany in NATO C-130s. Only, when he met up with Radakov, he got a big surprise."

FORTY-SIX

I flashed back to the moment when Bishop cracked open the final Dungeon level, and then back further to my own experiences with Radakov at The Bump, in Riga. I remembered the way Radakov treated those frightened young girls he bought like cattle. I also remembered the way he killed Russians.

"The general befriended one of the dancers at Radakov's sideline business, a strip club. I think you might be familiar with her name, at least: Varvara. She managed to get a photocopy of Radakov's passport and passed it to Abraham Scott. Now it was your son-in-law's turn to make a mistake. He told you about it, didn't he? He said he was writing a report on the smuggling operation and sending it to Congress. In terms of a scandal, it would have made Watergate seem like an honest mistake." While I'd taken a number of leaps in my Perry Mason monologue, they were nothing compared with the one I was about to take. But I had nothing to lose. If I was wrong, I'd get laughed at. If I was right, well, maybe that's why Cutter had that gun on the desk. So much for nothing to lose. I took a breath and plowed on. "That's when you tried to recruit him. It's also why you've brought me here. To see if I can be recruited." I was going to say corrupted, as in this instance they were one and the same thing.

Cutter sat hunched over his brandy, his gray eyes increasingly bloodshot with booze and, I hoped, stress.

He was deliberating, silently running through the options. I wondered if I'd be able to dive the seven feet across his desk and get to that gun before he could move his hands the six inches required to grab it, lift it, and exert the two pounds of pressure needed to fire a bullet into my head. This case had left my thirty-four-year-old body feeling sixty-four. I probably wouldn't even get to spill his cognac.

"You might find this hard to believe, Special Agent Cooper, but I'm pleased that you proved to be every bit as agile an investigator as your record suggests. We need men like you." He cleared his throat and stood without swaying. He might have been drinking for America, but he apparently had the constitution to handle it. For a second I almost admired him, but the second passed.

"Vincent, the First World War ended the old European empires and began a new one: the empire of the United States. We found ourselves the one superpower in a world exhausted by war. And so the roaring Twenties roared for us like no other nation on earth. Our industrial base, already vast, expanded exponentially. Then the Great Depression struck and brought us to our knees, along with every other industrialized country."

Cutter pocketed the Beretta and began to pace as he talked, not at me but at the floor and the ceiling, like he was giving an oration to Congress. I kept my eyes on that pocket while he droned on. "Why did it happen, the Great Depression? More specifically, how did it get a hold of our economy so quickly and strangle it so completely? There are many theories, of course, but there's a widely held but little discussed belief that a significant cause was simply this: The United States, along with most of the rest of the world, had eschewed the manufacture of armaments after the carnage of

World War One. In so doing, a sizeable portion of the international community's *stabilizing* economic activity was wiped out. Since then, a number of private-sector as well as government studies have put the very nature of war and the military complex under the microscope. And do you know what these studies have consistently revealed about war, Special Agent?"

"That it's a great way to kill a bunch of folks?" I said. I wanted to tell him that I didn't give a rat's ass about either the question or the answer, but the truth was that I was *very* interested in hearing what Cutter had to say. He was giving me The Speech, the same one he'd no doubt given to Abraham Scott shortly before the general told his father-in-law he didn't give a rat's ass either and, as a result, unwittingly sealed the fate of his son, Cutter's own step-grandson, with a Barrett gun's bullet.

Jefferson Cutter dismissed my comment by not acknowledging it. He continued with his spiel. "They found war essential to a nation's economic well-being and even, perversely, to its political stability. They also found that if a war itself is not available, then the threat of war will do if the threat is big enough. Either one will stimulate investment in new technologies, manufacturing and, through it, employment. Why was this type of investment so vital?"

I shrugged.

"Because the investment in war is made *independently* of any other economic activity. In short, Vincent, the economic stimulus that results from war is not a windfall bonus; it's the very foundation of any strong economy. And governments know all about these findings. They simply choose not to say anything about them."

And it was not hard to imagine why, I thought. No

government in its right mind would come out and say, *Hey, everyone, war is good fer yew!*

Cutter picked out a book from the shelf, inspected the cover, and waggled it at me. "In 1967, during the height of the Cold War and the blossoming conflict in Indochina, a book purporting to be the leaked findings of a secret Washington think-tank examination of the social and political implications of an outbreak of peace was published. It was called *Report from Iron Mountain*. Among the conclusions reached by this think tank was that human sacrifice, organized population culling, and other substitutes for war will need to be found if armed conflict between nations is abandoned. At the time, before the so-called leak was revealed to be a hoax, there was intense media pressure on Washington to reveal whether the book was genuine and whether such a think tank actually existed. President Lyndon Johnson refused to either confirm or deny that existence, because, in fact, a top-secret committee *had* been formed decades before to examine this very question. Like the fictitious group in *Report from Iron Mountain*, the real one had a similar makeup: academics, industrialists, scientists, politicians, historians, sociologists. Its mandate, though, was radically different. It was charged to examine, isolate, and even *engineer* triggers for potential wars. This group called itself The Establishment. Its greatest achievement was Pearl Harbor."

There it was. The Establishment. It existed. *And its greatest achievement was Pearl Harbor!* I let it sink in and tried not to let the rush of emotions boiling through me show. A group such as The Establishment would be by far the most powerful single body in the world.

"So, what...? You...this Establishment. You start wars for us, for the U.S.?" All the research Scott had been doing on our oil and steel sent to Imperial Japan...the sudden ban on these exports. Abraham Scott had simply been trying to verify what I'd just been told: that the organization calling itself The Establishment had willfully planned America's entry into WWII, actually setting us on that particular collision course years before it happened.

"No, you weren't listening, Vincent. The Establishment doesn't *start* wars. Occasionally, however, if the need arises, we might manipulate some factors to set the whole thing in motion. It's rare, but it happens."

"So America's exports to Japan during the 1930s... That was your idea?"

"Not mine, Vincent. May I call you Vince? I wasn't even born at the time."

I let the misunderstanding go. I needed a few minutes to get my head around this notion, reminding myself that I'd just heard about it from the man who was just one step away from being the commander in chief of the most powerful armed force on the planet. "So, The Establishment...you're what? Like some kind of death trust, looking for opportunities to keep our military-industrial complex chugging along?"

"The death trust," he said, nodding. "Catchy, Vincent. You definitely should be a writer, when you're through with the air force, that is. Right now, though, your country needs you. These are trying times."

"So I join or you shoot me? Is that what's happening here?"

"The gun. Does it make you nervous?" He opened a desk drawer, removed the weapon from his pocket, and dropped it in. "There. Better?"

I was right about the recruiting thing as, I had no doubt, I'd been right about what happened to Abraham

Scott, and why. "Are you the chairman of the board of this little group?" I asked.

Cutter almost chuckled. "No. I'm just one of many contributors, although I have particular roles, responsibilities, and . . . projects."

I nodded, still somewhat dazed by the implications of what I'd just learned.

"You must understand that what I'm talking about here is national interest. It's one of the great scams that war and the military-industrial complex that supplies it are merely tools of diplomacy. In fact, the reverse is true. Drink?" he asked as he sat and reached for the XO.

I indicated no with my hand. If Cutter was prepared to tell me everything, I needed a clear head with which to remember it.

"Suit yourself. This is exquisite brandy, by the way. Over a hundred years old. These grapes were picked before the outbreak of World War One. Imagine that. Horrendously expensive stuff. Evaporates when it hits your tongue." He waggled his fingers in front of his mouth and nose to demonstrate the effect. "Well," he said, clearing his throat, "like most people, you probably think that there is some kind of grand conspiracy operating at the highest level. The belief is actually nothing new. At the end of the nineteenth century, another book with an international conspiracy theme was written. This one was titled *The Protocols of the Elders of Zion*. It was an anti-Semitic tome written to frighten us gentiles into believing that there was a Jewish conspiracy in place to enslave Europe. The Nazis used it as one of the justifications for their Final Solution. Of course, *The Protocols* was another hoax, but the underlying notion of an unidentified someone or something out there pulling the strings has persisted. The true nature of this identity has yet to be fully grasped by the wider community, but our own research tells us that most people generally think they're not being told the whole truth about how our society—and the economy that keeps it fed, clothed, and housed—is really structured. The truth of it is as simple as this: Society is a parasite on the military-industrial complex. Civilian society exists purely to support the military—a symbiotic relationship, if you like. Put another way, and quoting the author of *Report from Iron Mountain*, 'War is the principal organizational basis of the nation state.'"

I stared at him. My personal reality is that I've never given any thought whatsoever to the whole conspiracy thing. At least, not until I took this case. Actually, that's not a hundred percent accurate. I do subscribe to the belief that the alcohol companies are trying to get us all permanently drunk and that, with me, they'd largely succeeded, at least over the past year. Looking at Jefferson Cutter, whose face was now rapidly becoming the color of a distance runner's at the end of a long race, they had him by the scrotum, too. As if reading my mind, the Vice President poured himself another tumbler before continuing.

"The evidence of this relationship is all around us," he said, unable to keep the smugness out of his voice. "In this country—in fact, in most countries—the military has its own infrastructure operating with very little assistance, if any, from civilian organizations. It is completely autonomous, with its own cities and towns where civilians are forbidden entry. It has its own legal system and law-enforcement agencies—your OSI is a prime example. The military has its own health system, educational institutions, administration and government. A world within a world. Look at any list of jobs for which the military recruits and you will see cleaners, bakers, electricians, mechanics, plumbers—"

"So, the First Convention. That's another triumph of The Establishment, isn't it?" I said, cutting him off.

He seemed surprised. "You know about that?"

The JPEG contained in the last level of Scott's Dungeon was burned into my brain. It was the record of a secret meeting I now believed included elements of the government, the military, and key industrialists. Without a doubt, something so sensitive would have been top-secret and therefore headed for the shredder, pronto. I knew the words by heart, and quoted: " 'Insofar as no arm of the U.S. military shall purchase by government tender any part, artifact, or system, or parts thereof, utilizing new technology or new combinations of existing technology untested in combat . . .' and so on, et cetera." The First Convention, the so-called "quality clause." It meant that only items tested in war could be bought for wholesale use by the U.S. military. It was a bombshell, a cynical ploy that kept billions of dollars flushing through the military-industrial complex so that our armed forces could be equipped with new hardware. God only knew how Scott had come into possession of the information, given its ultrasensitivity. And then I realized there was only one possible source. Cutter was shaking his head.

I said, "General Scott secretly photographed the minutes you showed him, didn't he?"

"I believed Abraham was on our side, that he could see the convention's necessity."

"And why is it necessary?" I asked, enthralled and horrified at the same time.

"As I've explained, both the military and civilian societies require conflict to remain healthy. The military-industrial complex is the point of crossover. It's where the civilian and military realms connect and feed off each other. The First Convention is merely a tool to facilitate that interaction."

Cutter drained his glass and poured another before continuing. "Like any technology, military hardware has a life span. Roughly fifteen years. It's no mistake that our conflicts—at least since the Korean War, when we were caught napping—have enjoyed roughly the same interval."

"So today's war is the proving ground for technology to be used in tomorrow's? And we need it proved every fifteen years?"

"Yes," said Cutter bluntly. "In recent years, however, because of the exponential rise in technological breakthroughs, and the concomitant redundancy attendant with the race to maintain our military edge, we can expect that generational life span to be reduced to ten years."

He paused to collect his thoughts. I had nothing to say. I was struck dumb.

"Moreover," he continued, "the First Convention guarantees that the military-industrial complex will supply many test items to the armed forces free of charge if a conflict arises. It ensures that our military is constantly being supplied with new and—please excuse the pun—groundbreaking technology, which it is, of course, tempted to put to practical test. The Patriot Missile is a prime example. An unknown quantity prior to Gulf War One, prime export item after it. The postwar international sales of that missile, let alone the contracts to our own forces, more than made up for the millions of dollars spent on free samples to the U.S. Army."

"A war every ten years. Parents of potential robocannon fodder can rejoice in their usefulness," I said.

"As I said, Vince, we are not monsters. New ways are being developed all the time to wage war at a distance, reducing American and allied casualties. I personally have had a hand in promoting many of these in my capacity as leader of the Senate."

I shook my head to clear out the crap Cutter was depositing in it. I'd read about those ultratech weapons and the billions spent in their development. All the clues to this nightmare were there, in Abraham Scott's Dungeon. Had I been half the investigator I thought I was, I'd have been able to put them together sooner and, just maybe, Anna would still be breathing. And, as for that bit about not being a monster, if Cutter had hollow fangs, lived in a coffin during the day, and sucked the juices from the veins of virgins during the night, he wouldn't have been half the monster he was in reality.

The disappointment in my professional abilities notwithstanding, I was fed up listening to the history of the world according to Jefferson Cutter. I said, "You had Peyton shot dead as a warning to Abraham to back off and not interfere with von Koeppen's people-smuggling activities."

"My son-in-law was a great disappointment. He—"

"Yeah, we've already talked about that," I interrupted. "And you brought your own daughter into the loop when you discovered that she and von Koeppen were banging each other's doors."

"It was time," said Cutter with an almost imperceptible shrug.

It was fucking *time*? Cutter had been manipulating his own daughter from the day she was born. "Through your contacts in the Department of Defense, you had Peyton's autopsy and death certificate deleted. You had new information logged in the system but sent the original certificate to General von Koeppen. He passed it to Harmony when the time was right. Through von Koeppen, you had her show it to Abraham so that he'd know the truth about his son's murder. The only way Scott could verify the truth was to compare his son's corpse with the paperwork. You made sure he opened Peyton's body bag. But you miscalculated."

It dawned on me that Jefferson Cutter appeared to be mighty relaxed—almost jaunty—about admitting to being a killer, a conspirator, and a traitor to the American people, my people, the people I had sworn to protect against people like him. Cutter had to be certain I wouldn't be passing on the details of this conversation to anyone.

"We are not going to make the mistake of underestimating you," he said. "There's far too much at stake."

On the basis that a best defense is a good offense, I said, "It's all over for you, Jefferson. You're heading for a lethal injection. Von Koeppen is dead—another killing I suspect you ordered, along with the men Peyton served with, the medical officer who performed the first autopsy on Peyton's headless corpse, the journalist from *The Washington Post*..."

Cutter shrugged. I took that as a yes, which meant he was also personally responsible for the death of Anna Masters.

"Vince," he said, shaking his head in mock disappointment. "A few insignificant and inconsequential deaths is not what this is all about."

The complete absence of any remorse for his actions, specifically what was obviously Anna's collateral killing, held the sting of a slap. I felt my eyes go hot and moist, but the pain helped me complete the picture. Cutter was right. It wasn't just about the murders. This organization, The Establishment, had been set up by some unnamed government department to isolate and exploit potential threats to our national security for the benefit of our bottom line. When it all came out into the open, I had the feeling that no one would be putting their hand up to claim this nasty little child. Sometimes, it—The Establishment—went further. Cutter said it himself: *"Occasionally, however, if the need arises, we might manipulate some factors...It's rare, but it happens."* In the last century, we had the Nazis and then the communists. Now we have the evil genius who controls the world from a dirt-floor cave in the mountains of Pakistan. Thanks to him—and Cutter no doubt believed the master terrorist deserved a big pat on the back for it—we were spending billions more on war than we ever had during the Cold War.

If I was reading Cutter right, The Establishment was now looking beyond Muslim extremism, the current dominant threat to our national security, to find the necessary grist for the military-industrial complex's mill. And, at our current rate of expenditure of more than two trillion dollars over the next five years, it had to be a hell of a lot of grist.

And I knew what it was.

"Abraham Scott nailed Alu Radakov's true identity," I said. "If his merry band of killers had known it, too, they would've turned Radakov into a worm farm."

"Yes, I do believe you're onto it, but would you mind explaining the details, just so I can be sure you've got it right?"

It didn't look like I had much of a choice. Cutter was holding all the cards, but I'd have told him anyway, shoved it down his chickenshit throat, even if just to watch him choke on it. I took a deep breath. "Abraham Scott recognized Radakov from his time serving at the U.S. Embassy in Moscow. Maybe Scott had been unsure at first because that was a long time ago and people look different with an extra twenty years hanging off their faces. But then he got a look at Radakov's passport, his *Russian* passport. Petrov Andreiovic, alias Alu Radakov. Back when Scott first met Radakov, the Russian was KGB. So Scott knew Radakov's secret: He wasn't Chechen at all. He was Moscow's man. And the fact that he knew made everyone nervous, especially the Kremlin.

"Scott figured that with Radakov, and probably others like him, Moscow had infiltrated the Chechen leadership. So what about the massacre in Beslan's School Number One a few years back, the one where all those children were killed. Was that really a Chechen operation? Or was it a Russian job just made to *look* like the separatists' work?"

Cutter sat behind his enormous desk, the seal of the Vice President of the United States of America on the wall behind his head. He was nodding. The Beretta, I noticed, had made a reappearance. I'd hit a nerve. It was motionless, aimed at the middle of my chest.

"As you've deduced," said Cutter, "we are helping the Kremlin and the Kremlin is helping us. As I said, a grave threat to a state's security is actually a politically stabilizing factor. The ongoing fight with the Chechens allows the Russian president to be strong, to centralize power and hold the Federation together. That's in our interest. We don't want a collection of autonomous independent states in that part of the world, running amok with their own agendas and foreign policies. And then there's the important factor of economic stability. As I've explained, the military-industrial complex requires a threat equal to its output, and Russia's needs in this vital area are the same as ours. Properly directed, the Chechen separatist movement is the one stone that kills both birds."

I didn't care who he was or what organizations he belonged to. Jefferson Cutter was operating way outside the law—civilian and/or military. At least, the laws of my country.

I thought about the players. Radakov needed to show his rebel buddies that the cash for their fight was coming from somewhere other than Moscow. That's where von Koeppen came in. The people-smuggling was the perfect front, until Scott came along and threatened to put an end to it. So they—they being Cutter and von Koeppen—murdered Scott's son as a warning. And, when they discovered that he'd refused to heed it, they killed him.

Radakov wasn't in on it. Scott had come to some kind of arrangement with him. Radakov wanted out of the deal with Cutter and von Koeppen, and Scott wanted Varvara. It was a fair trade, quid pro quo. This deal forced cracks between Cutter, von Koeppen, and Radakov that killing Scott couldn't smooth over, and each realized his vulnerability. The sick bond holding them together was broken. Von Koeppen thought he could protect himself from Cutter by getting close to the VP's daughter. Wrong. Cutter thought he could remove the threat to himself by having a washed-up investigator put on the case of his son-in-law's death. Wrong. What about Radakov? He had to believe that Cutter would get to him sooner rather than later, especially after von Koeppen was removed from the picture. Now I knew why the Russian had allowed me to leave Chechnya when he could so easily have wasted me. I was his attack dog. Radakov couldn't get to Cutter, but he knew I could. Wrong again. I looked down the black eye of Cutter's Beretta. Something told me my attack-dog days were over.

Other things fell into place. I thought about the men who'd brought me here from Germany, the same bunch who'd hit Masters and me in Baghdad and subsequently mugged me outside my hotel. I'd pegged them as Special Forces and they were. Only they weren't ours. They had to be Spetsnatz, or maybe FSB, the Russian Federal Security Service, the current incarnation of the KGB. That also explained why they'd said not one word to me on the plane trip across the Atlantic, ignoring all my attempts to while away the flight with witty conversation. They couldn't understand a word I was saying.

I continued. "So your son-in-law threatened to bring everything down on your head. Then he demonstrated his determination to do just that by photographing the lineup of body bags from Iraq and leaking the photo to the media."

"Yes, right again, Vincent. Congratulations." Cutter's aim wavered slightly as his thumb searched for the handgun's safety. "I should never have enlightened Scott about the First Convention. Up till that moment, he believed our troops in Iraq were there for reasons that had nothing to do with the reality—the *necessity*—of testing new weapons systems so that they could be sold to our armed forces and hence to other nations and, of course, NATO. He threatened to do whatever it took to get our people back home. As you said, we miscalculated with Abraham. Have you any idea what damage a man in his position, a serving four-star general, could do to America's notion of itself if he revealed the truth?"

"The miscalculation was yours," I said. "You killed

his son, the only thing in this world he truly loved. *You sent General Scott to war.*"

I had one question outstanding, but it wasn't one that Cutter could or would answer. Our time was up. I brightened and said, "So, where do I sign?"

"Sign what?" Cutter stood and took half a step back to steady himself.

"You know, the membership papers? The Establishment? You've sold me. I'd love to join. With all that money, you guys must have great resort facilities, member housing loans, that sort of thing."

Cutter informed me that I wouldn't be joining. "There'll be two gunshot wounds. One here," he said, grabbing a handful of fat on the side of his belly. "The second shot will be fatal. For you. You threatened me, I pulled my gun to defend myself, there was a struggle. You had the upper hand at first and shot me, but you lost your balance and I got lucky."

Cutter had worked it all out. He could so easily concoct a believable story about why he had granted me this late-night interview. *Special Agent Cooper had been investigating the death of my beloved son-in-law before mysteriously going AWOL. Then he suddenly turned up here in D.C. and claimed to have news . . . At the very least, I owed it to my daughter to hear him out and, of course, to keep a weapon handy just in case things turned sour . . .* After all, I was, as everyone knew, "unpredictable."

"You had me brought here to kill me." I tried to appear relaxed about stating the obvious and put my feet up on the edge of his desk to demonstrate it.

"Well, you know, if you want something done right . . ." He displayed his expensive bridgework. Or was it a smile? I wasn't sure.

"I have a copy of Scott's hard drive. If you kill me,

I've left instructions for it to be forwarded to the media." It was an oldie but a goodie.

"I didn't give you enough time to make those arrangements. I expected more from you, Vincent. You really think I'd fall for that old ploy?"

Shit! "Believe what you want."

Cutter raised the Beretta. I'd already assessed the distances, the angles, and the potential force required. I was waiting for the opening, but it was clear Cutter wasn't going to give me one. I had half a second left. I shoved the desk toward him with my legs as hard as I could. The damn thing was heavier than I expected. My chair shot backward, but not before his precious hundred-year-old bottle of XO teetered.

Cutter wavered as he watched the bottle fall, his concentration on me breaking for the briefest instant while he considered catching it. I launched myself at him, flying over his laptop as the bottle smashed on the marble floor. I drove into his gut with the point of my shoulder and he slammed into the wall with an animal grunt. We both dropped to the deck, rolling into the puddle of XO and smashed glass. He had the gun, but I had his wrist pinned to the floor. Blood was everywhere. The Beretta went off. Whatever the slug hit, it wasn't me. The gun fired a second time. Plaster dust drifted down from the small hole in the ceiling. Cutter was a strong fuck, despite his age. Our hands were interlocked and we both shook with effort as we battled each other's grip. He was attempting to turn the weapon on me. I was trying to prevent that from happening.

I drove my head down into his face. I missed his nose and instead heard his cheekbone crack like a Styrofoam coffee cup underfoot. Cutter released the Beretta as his bloody hands flew to his face.

I stood over him, swaying, blood pumping from deep cuts to my lower legs and arms, but I had the gun, which meant I'd won. Then the door burst open. The Secret Service guys rushed in, Glocks raised. It all happened in slow motion. It was like an out-of-body experience, and I knew how it was going to end: badly—for me. Here I was, standing over the Vice President of the United States, a man these two Secret Service types had sworn to protect with their lives if need be. Their boss was down, there was blood spattered on the floor, the walls, his desk. The weapon in my hand had discharged—I noticed the neat bullet hole in the door for the first time. That first shot. It must have been what had brought them in. Their training took over. They had no choice but to do what they had sworn to do. I swung away, bringing my hands up in front of my face as I turned. "No!" I yelled as they fired into me at point-blank range.

FORTY-SEVEN

I'm not sure exactly when I realized I wasn't dead. It might have been when I tried to play my harp and found I couldn't move my arm. Either that or I didn't have an arm. Nevertheless, I felt no panic. Morphine is like that. It's like a heavy, warm blanket thrown over the senses, similar to that period of sleep just before awakening, when the bed is the most supremely comfortable place in the universe. I could get used to morphine, except for the vomiting.

I floated for I don't know how long. Could have been hours or minutes. The previous month came back to me in bits and pieces and not, I suspected, in chronological order. I remembered Anna, for instance, but not that she'd been killed. That came later. Being shot myself was also a late arrival, but I eventually remembered Cutter and those scorpions with their knives on top of the mountain in Afghanistan. Was that part of this investigation? My memory was a bunch of jumbled fragments. Gradually, though, I sifted out the salient points and strung them together into some kind of order.

The reality wasn't great.

The beeping sound was familiar and so was the smell. I sensed a presence hovering over me. I opened my eyes and waited for the recognition. It was male, pushing fifty, with pattern baldness. A stranger.

"Take it easy, soldier," he said. "You're in the hospital. Let's have a listen to your lungs."

"Which hospital?" I managed to say.

"Andrews AFB. Base hospital," he said, maneuvering the stethoscope inside my hospital gown.

"Breathe," he said.

I breathed.

"Again."

I breathed again. We went on like that for several breaths until I got seriously light-headed.

"Pretty good," he said. "Considering."

Considering what?

"How do you feel, Special Agent?" he asked.

"Light-headed and thirsty," I said. "Aside from that, I haven't a clue."

"Good. Means the morphine's working."

"What's the damage, Doc?" I asked. By now I knew I'd been shot. I just wasn't exactly sure where because, like he said, the morphine was working.

"We believe a gun you were holding in your hand deflected the first bullet. That explains the broken fingers. You were lucky. The second bullet entered your arm here," he said, pointing to the muscle under his upper arm, "entered your bloodstream, and traveled to your heart. We had to remove it."

"My heart or the bullet?"

"What? Oh, right. Funny." He wasn't smiling.

A joke popped into my mind. I had the feeling the doctor wouldn't be amused, but I launched into it anyway, slurring because of the morphine. I said, "A patient says to his doctor, 'Doc, if I give up drinking, smoking, loose women, and fast cars, will I live to be a hundred?'"

The doctor, looking down on me, said, "No, but it'll seem like it."

"Oh, you've heard it," I said.

"I'm a doctor, I've heard every doctor-patient joke in the book." He tapped an IV line. "You've lost quite a lot of blood. We removed several large slivers of glass from your legs. They severed a few veins, but no arteries. Good luck there, too."

All this good luck. Too much more of it would kill me.

He poured me a cup of water from a jug beside the bed and held it to my lips while I drank. I'd never tasted anything as good and as sweet as that water.

"I've reduced the morphine dose a little, but if the pain gets uncomfortable, just squeeze this ball and you'll get a small release of morphine." He placed the ball in my hand.

"What day is it?" I muttered. I closed my eyes and let my head sink into the pillow.

"You've been here fifteen hours. It's Monday afternoon, just after five P.M."

"Thanks," I said, eyes still closed. Along with the blood, I'd lost a lot of time.

"Do you feel up to visitors, Special Agent?" he asked.

"Who is it?" I replied.

"Only me," came a familiar voice from behind the curtain separating my bed from the others in the room.

It was Gruyere.

The doctor had a brief whispered chat with the general, none of which I could hear. I guessed he was probably telling her not to stress me out. If that's what he was saying, he was too late. I glanced at the monitor wired up to my heart. It was registering a hundred and fifteen beats per minute and climbing. For the first time I noticed I was connected up to a spaghetti of tubes and wires. If I didn't know better, I'd say I was sick. When I looked back at Gruyere, the doctor had gone. The general was holding up a copy of a newspaper so that I could read the front page. At first I had no idea why. Then the headline in large black letters beneath the masthead swam into focus. It read, "CONSPIRACY." A smaller headline said, "Military's 'Quality Guarantee' Delivers War Every 15 Years."

"Was this fucking necessary, Special Agent Cooper?" said Gruyere, giving me her angry grandmother routine.

"Yes, ma'am," I said, not feeling up for games.

Bishop. I'd given him instructions to pass the details of the First Convention to *The Washington Post.* If the press pulled that thread, the whole mess would unravel. I'd called Bishop just before I went to interview Harmony. He was to contact the paper if I failed to call him within eight hours. It was supposed to be my insurance policy. And it might have worked had Cutter believed in "that old ploy." Cutter and I both had a lesson to learn: he for being too clever, me for being too unimaginative.

Gruyere seemed to accept my answer, and I was surprised by that. She folded the paper and let it fall on the end of my bed. "Been putting your body on the line again, I see."

"I thought you were at Ramstein, ma'am," I said.

"I was, but now I'm here."

"Because I'm here?"

"Among other reasons," she said. She stood beside the bed, arms folded, scowling. "You gave us a few scares, Cooper. You're a most unorthodox investigator."

"Is that good or bad?"

The big cheese shrugged and said ambiguously, "It is what it is."

"When do you want my report, ma'am?"

Plenty of time for that. Besides, Anna Masters gave me a full update before the crash. And I've already read Flight Lieutenant Bishop's report. Forensics have cleared you of manslaughter, by the way."

"Manslaughter?" As far as I was aware, I hadn't killed anyone. Not recently, anyway.

"Jefferson Cutter."

"Ma'am?"

"You shot the Vice President in the temple, Cooper. A ricochet."

"I what?"

She nodded. "Officially, it is being called an accident— cleaning his gun when it went off, apparently. Happens all the time."

Yeah, but not to vice presidents.

"Secret Service have been debriefed. Harmony Scott has been arrested and charged with conspiracy relating to the murder of her husband. We searched her house and found this." Gruyere pulled an evidence bag from her briefcase and put it on my stomach. Inside was an official form. I had a good idea what it was even before I saw "U.S. Army Autopsy Report" in large black letters at the top of the page. It was the very first autopsy performed on Peyton Scott's remains, the one subsequently wiped from the DoD's computer in Washington. I caught the words "massive trauma" and "decapitation" in the "cause of death" section.

"There is some consideration being given to charging her with various acts of treason. I say consideration because we believe any good lawyer would get her off those charges, and we know she'll be hiring the best."

"What about the suicide note?" I asked.

"Forensics came back clean. We suspect von Koeppen had it forged and hid it in the book. Harmony went along for the ride. Who else would you like an up-date on?"

"Radakov," I said.

"You'll find a small piece on him on page five." Gruyere nodded at the newspaper. "There wasn't much left of him to bury. Seems someone told his Chechen friends that he was former KGB."

I wondered who that someone was. I didn't believe it was Cutter—at the end, he was more concerned about me than about Radakov.

Gruyere continued. "Now, as for the case, I think you know already that the DoD and the FBI have taken over. This is out of our hands now. Smuggling humans is a serious crime. You've done a fucking great job here, Cooper."

I might have been doped to the gills but I wasn't in la-la land. This whole speech was carefully worded for my benefit. I doubted there'd be much of an investigation. And, with Radakov dead, there was no one left who knew the whole story. Except maybe me, but, as my file suggested, I was easily discredited. "My cell was bugged with a homing device, ma'am. You knew where I was most of the time."

"Yes, I did. It was important for us to know where this case was taking you."

"Was Anna in on it?" I asked. *Anna Masters gave me a full update before the crash.*

"Anna knew more than you about certain things."

"Such as?"

"She knew von Koeppen was up to something illegal—as it turns out we just had no idea what. Masters was working the case. Von Koeppen probably thought he was pretty clever, dating someone from OSI. I can tell you it wasn't something she enjoyed."

I took my mind back to the moment in Anna's Mercedes when I'd asked her about von Koeppen. I wished she'd confided in me then. The German might not have passed under my radar for as long as he did if she had. Things might have turned out differently if I'd known what he was capable of from the beginning. Maybe she'd still be alive. "Why didn't you brief me on von Koeppen?" I asked.

"The situation was delicate. We didn't want him to know he was under suspicion until we had something solid. It would have been too easy for him to just lie low."

"And then General Scott died," I said.

General Gruyere nodded. "Yes. The Vice President's interest in the case was immediate. I shouldn't have been surprised—Scott was his son-in-law. But, I have to admit, his insistence on *you* taking the case did intrigue me. As you know, you weren't my first choice. Or my second or fifth, for that matter. On the strength of your current performance review, you weren't up to something like this. Cutter gambled on you fucking up, and lost." Gruyere had her back to me as she gazed out the window, her arthritic hands clasped behind her.

"Why did you take me off the case when it looked like I was getting somewhere?"

"You and I both know you work best under pressure. I simply applied some."

Okay, there was some truth in that.

"It's safe to say a little redemption is due to come your way as the result of all this, Vin."

Oh, oh, first names. Run for cover.

"That bullet you picked up in Iraq. There's another Purple Heart in it for you. You're assembling quite a collection."

I felt like giving the morphine ball a squeeze.

"The business about the First Convention finding its way into the public domain isn't so great, but that storm will pass. The convention works for the military—it has to be that way. We can't afford the latest and greatest unless private enterprise is prepared to take the investment risk. And no one wants our men and women at arms to have to use second-rate equipment—stuff that doesn't work when and where it's supposed to. Call it a warranty."

That was another way to look at it. I changed the subject. I wanted to talk about her membership in a certain club. "You're part of The Establishment."

Gruyere turned. "What, as in the status quo?"

"You know what I'm talking about." I noticed my BPM had come way down. I was calm.

The general regarded me over those half-moon spectacles of hers for several moments before speaking. Then she said, "By The Establishment, I take it you mean a secret society that conspires to manipulate world events for the benefit of America's coffers."

Close enough. I nodded.

"No such entity exists, Vin. You and I need to be straight on that point."

"And, if I'm not?" I heard myself saying.

"You sound like someone fending off a threat."

"Am I?" I asked.

"No, Vin. I'm not going to threaten you. Hypothetically speaking, if there was such a group, my guess is that it'd have to be governed by a pretty strict set of rules. One of those rules would surely have to be that its members didn't embark on individual, unsanctioned projects. If that were to happen, I believe such a group would act to protect the very institutions it was brought into existence to serve."

The effects of the morphine were wearing off. My mind was sharper. So was the pain. My arm felt like it had been chewed on, and my other arm, the one that'd received the bullet hole in Baghdad, didn't feel much better. Jesus—I saw it. I suddenly realized what Gruyere's—The Establishment's—end game had been all along. "Which is why I was manipulated into killing the Vice President for you."

Gruyere gave me a thin, sympathetic smile. "Whatever anyone wanted is now, thankfully, immaterial. The fact is that the fates took a hand and tidied some loose ends—hypothetically speaking, of course."

Radakov. I was right: Cutter wasn't the one who fingered him.

I looked at Gruyere and she at me. Neither of us spoke for several minutes. I had not one shred of evidence that The Establishment existed, let alone that she or anyone else was a member. Cutter and von Koeppen were dead. No one else would come forward, certainly not Alu Radakov. Not anymore. And Harmony Scott knew what she knew, but like me, I doubted she had evidence to back up any claims. There was Scott's Dungeon, of course, but there was nothing on it about The Establishment, and, if there had been any evidence in Scott's files, I doubted it would still be there.

"It's over, Vin. You did your job and now it's time to stand down," she said.

I found my mind wandering back to Cutter's study. What had really happened there? I remembered the two Secret Service types coming through the door, their pistols raised and in the shooting position. Those guys do not miss, especially not at the range they were shooting from. If they thought I'd shot Cutter, or was about to, they'd have whacked me but good, no question. Except I was still alive and the Toe Cutter was down in hell standing on his hands in a room full of excrement. That meant the pair who came through the door were not Secret Service. It also meant I doubted the Vice President had been killed by an accidental ricochet.

"I know what you're thinking, Vin, and you need to move on. Also, you should know that I have retired. It has already been announced. Effective from today, actually. I have grandchildren I want to spend more time with."

I nodded. "Sorry to hear that, ma'am," I said perfunctorily. In fact, the only people I felt sorry for were those grandkids.

"Something you may not be aware of, Vin," she said. "Abraham Scott and I were friends. When we were younger, we were more than friends. We stayed in touch over the years. He came to see me after Peyton was killed, after he'd been to Baghdad. He told me he believed his son had been murdered and that the autopsy report had been altered. For reasons of his own, he chose not to tell me what the motive for that murder was. I believe that, at the time, he didn't know, or wasn't sure. I checked into the autopsy issue quietly, but couldn't see how the records had been tampered with. Now, thanks to your investigation, we know what Cutter was up to."

That explained why Gruyere had treated Scott's fatal glider crash as a homicide from the first. She already had suspicions planted by the victim himself. It also resolved for me where Abraham Scott had gone after his trip to Iraq and before he went to Riga. He'd looked up an old flame, to see if she could apply some heat to get some answers. "Was Cutter a member of The Establishment?" I asked.

"I won't comment on whether the Vice President was or wasn't a member of any hypothetical group or organization of that name. I will say, though, that Jefferson Cutter had spent a lot of time in the former Soviet Union. He believed a strong and stable Russia was in America's best interests. Let's just say he was out of step."

Exhaustion was beginning to creep over me. I wanted to retreat to the warmth of a morphine-induced slumber. I also wanted to get out of bed and give the general officer a good shake. She'd been manipulating me from the get-go. My eyelids had become as heavy as sheet lead. After a few minutes of lucidity, it was getting difficult to concentrate. Had I dreamed all this? No, there was one inescapable fact: Anna Masters was dead. That reminded me. I said, "Why was Anna in von Koeppen's vehicle?"

Gruyere almost smiled, damn her. "From her notes, I gather she intended to question the general about the missing CAC cards. Perhaps Anna caught him leaving to go somewhere—her Mercedes was parked outside the Ramstein administration block—and so, to save time, she chose to go with him."

I closed my eyes. So Anna had figured it out, tied the CAC cards to von Koeppen. "Has she been buried yet, ma'am? If not, I'd like to go to the funeral."

"No, you can't, I'm afraid."

Of course. Anna had been dead almost a week. She'd have been laid to rest by now and—

"Anna's not dead, Vin."

It took several heartbeats for my brain to register what Gruyere had just told me. Not dead? The room was silent except for the *beep, beep, beep* of the machine, which was suddenly racing. "But th—"

"Special Agent Masters was pretty banged up after the crash. When I heard what had happened, I flew straight to Ramstein to get her out of there safely. Her death was announced to remove her from the attention of people who may have wanted to do her an injury. I had her repatriated immediately to the safety of this facility."

"She's . . . here?"

General Gruyere pulled back the curtain separating my bed from the one beside it. "It looks worse than it is. Anna's out of immediate danger now. The doctors had her in an induced coma for several days. She's sleeping. Her injuries are extensive: punctured lung, fractured skull, broken ribs, and she has lost a toe. But Masters is fit and strong. The doctors expect her to make a full recovery."

That shake I wanted to give Gruyere? I could now happily exchange it for a hug. Like me, the person in the next bed was full of tubes. I couldn't recognize her—her head was heavily bandaged and what I could see of her face was badly bruised. Anna? A wave of relief crashed over me. No, not relief. Joy. Anna? Alive?

"I'll be leaving now, Vin. I doubt that our paths will cross again. I have to say that it has been interesting working with you. There's a handpicked security detail on this room. I don't think you'll need them but their presence might make you feel more . . . comfortable. Get some rest and get well—both of you."

Gruyere turned to leave and then stopped. "Oh, and this came for you today." She removed a card from her breast pocket and put it in my fingers. It was a postcard. It showed a picture of the Sydney Opera House. A couple of giant-sized, tanned, naked girls rode on the building's sails. A speech bubble coming from one of the women announced suggestively, *We love it down under!*

There had to be a mistake here. I didn't know anyone in Sydney, Australia. I turned the card over and read the scrawl. It said, *"Please take care of my cat"* and was signed *"V."*

Acknowledgments

I'd like to recognize and thank a few people without whose help and/or expertise this story would have died.

Lieutenant Colonel Keith, not his real name, is currently serving with the U.S. Army somewhere in Asia. He has also served in the army's CID, its criminal investigation division. I pestered LTC Keith for clarification on a range of issues and details on a daily basis for over a year.

Second on the list is Major Woody, also not his real name, USAF (retired). The major flew F-16s out of Ramstein, one of the key settings in the novel, and made sure the narrative pertaining to the base wasn't wildly off-course.

Allan has a couple of important contracts with the U.S. Department of Defense, which is why you're not getting his full name. Allan read drafts and pointed me in a few interesting directions.

About the Author

DAVID ROLLINS is a former advertising creative director who lives in Sydney, Australia. He is the author of *The Death Trust* and *A Knife Edge*, both international bestsellers. Bantam Books will publish *A Knife Edge* in April 2009. Visit his website at www.davidarollins.net.